Matt Hilton worked for
security and the police f
in Ju-Jitsu. He lives in C

www.matth...............

Praise for Matt Hilton's JOE HUNTER thrillers

"Matt Hilton delivers a thrill a minute. Awesome!"
Chris Ryan

"Vicious, witty and noir...a sparkling new talent."
Peter James

*"Check the edge of your seat – it's where you are going
to spend most of the time when in the company of Joe
Hunter."*
www.thrillers4u.com

"Roars along at a ferocious pace."
Observer

"Action-packed from start to finish."
Heat

"Electrifying."
Daily Mail

MATT HILTON
Joe Hunter thrillers
Dead Men's Dust
Judgement and Wrath
Slash and Burn
Cut and Run
Blood and Ashes
Dead Men's Harvest
No Going Back
Rules of Honour
The Lawless Kind
The Devil's Anvil
No Safe Place
Marked For Death
—eBook only short stories—
Six of the Best
Dead Fall
Red Stripes
Hot Property
Instant Justice

Tess Grey and Po Villere thrillers
Blood Tracks
Painted Skins
Raw Wounds
Worst Fear

Novels
Preternatural
The Shadows Call
Dominion
Darkest Hour
Darke

DARKE

MATT HILTON

MATT HILTON

DARKE

MATT HILTON

First published In Great Britain by Sempre Vigile Press
2018

1

ISBN Paperback: **978-0-9935788-4-7**
Also available in eBook

BEFORE...

Brandreth House was rotten at its core, a place of mould and decay and crumbling masonry, of dusty cobwebs and creeping shadows. Its walls were buckled, its roof missing slates, and barely any window retained glass, and those that did were cracked or discoloured with a patina of grime. Deformed woodland surrounded the house, a barrier of trees and shrubs at odds with the hills that loomed overhead. A pond excavated from the earth by its Victorian owners had brought ruination to the house and their fortune. Seepage from the naked slopes had flooded in, turned the surrounding land to a bog that crept to the house's foundations. If the rot didn't claim the building, the morass would sooner or later suck it into the bowels of the earth. It was a fitting home for the last surviving heir of the Brandreth family, because through to his core he was rotten too.

He was a young man driven by unhealthy tastes, an alcoholic, with an unsavoury sexual appetite. He was a shambling brute, surly, unkempt and stinking, whom his neighbours avoided. On the rare occasions he'd met trespassers, he'd shown his displeasure, exerting his right to eject them from his property with threats of extreme violence. He was a danger to all, and in particular to the most vulnerable members of society. He wouldn't entertain uninvited visitors, though it was rare in the past few years that a particular room had gone unoccupied. The basement was at most risk from the rising water, but until now its thick walls and stone floor retained its integrity, and it was the most soundproofed. There his unwilling guests were held, and there he fed his sick appetite, all under the watchful guidance of his sole companion, a deviant more shrewd and deceitful than Brandreth, and more dangerous.

Stuttering blue light from a video monitor sucked the life from the features of his mentor, lending him a corpse-like cast. The man wore a thick beard, and his hair to his shoulders. Brandreth's dishevelled appearance was through laziness and a lack of personal hygiene, but the other had purposely cultured his look, to help conceal his identity. Witnesses would recall the beard and long hair, not his true face beneath. For the 'Fell Man', as the press had dubbed him, was the subject of a manhunt stretching from the northern lakes of Cumbria to the furthest coastlines of the British mainland.

Brandreth was a simpleton, but he had his uses. He was easily manipulated through payment in alcohol or in depraved carnal acts. In exchange he'd allowed his mentor free range of his ancestral home to use it as he wished. In the sub-basement the man had retrofitted a video-editing suite where he churned out multiple copies of videotapes to supply his clients. Brandreth was engaged mostly in packing and carrying chores, because his technological savvy extended little beyond switching on an electric kettle. His appetites fed, Brandreth had become a servant in his own home.

His mentor tapped the nearest flickering monitor. 'She's awake.'

Brandreth exhaled through his nostrils.

'When did you last check her restraints?' There was urgency in the Fell Man's voice.

'When I was in earlier, emptying her piss bucket.'

'She didn't loosen that strap while she was asleep. Get in there and do it up again, and make sure she knows the consequences of trying to free herself.'

VCR machines whirred steadily in the background. The air was stuffy, charged with static electricity. The atmosphere was abruptly filled with a tangible buzz of annoyance from Brandreth. He wasn't mad at the command, but at the audacity of the girl. He stormed towards an access door to the basement, and threw it open with a wordless shout. He was still descending a small flight of steps when the Fell Man jolted rigid in his seat. On-screen, the girl leapt from the piled mattresses on which she'd slept, and darted away free of her leather restraints. A corresponding yell followed as Brandreth charged after her.

There wasn't a camera positioned to view where she ran, but there was another route from the basement, up a set of stairs to the kitchen. If Brandreth had been remiss in checking the girl's restraints, had he also forgotten to bolt the door from within after he carried out her slops bucket? The Fell Man was out of his seat in an instant, but he didn't pursue Brandreth. He exited the sub-basement, charging along a dank passageway and into the yard at the rear of the house. As he expected, the small figure hurtled from the kitchen less than ten metres away. She skidded on bare feet when she spotted him, emitting a gasp. The oval of her mouth was a raw hole. The girl turned and ran, pushing aside tendrils of bramble that encroached on the back of the house. Thorns snagged at the shapeless grey shift that covered her skinny frame from bony shoulders to knobbly knees, dug at her flesh and hair, but she fought past. Brandreth stormed out in pursuit, his boots slapping the broken paving. For a shambling giant he was surprisingly fast with momentum behind him. He almost had the girl in a few lunging steps, but then his momentum was also his undoing. Overbalanced as he reached for her, he tripped and went down hard. The girl slipped away from his grasping fingers, and Brandreth fought to stand. The Fell Man shoved past him, and didn't pause to check on him. Brandreth scrambled up and followed, cursing savagely.

Beyond the confines of the mildewed walls of her prison, their prey couldn't have had any prior idea of her surroundings. She fled without forethought: driven by terror she raced towards the rear of the grounds, with the Fell Man in pursuit. He'd easily run her down if she attempted to swarm up the nearest slope, a repository of tumbled boulders and snarled thickets of gorse. He was almost on her when she dodged to the right, and then she was between the branches of shrubs left to run wild years ago. The Fell Man crashed through them, and Brandreth rushed further to the right to hem her against the bank of a stream that bled from the fells above.

Driven by panic the girl plunged into the stream, grasping at exposed roots on the opposite bank to avoid being tumbled downhill by the rushing water. Muddy and dripping, she scrambled up the opposite bank, and fled up the slope. Cursing her under his breath, the Fell Man danced over slick stepping-stones in the stream. She had gained a few steps on him, but he was powerful and each step sent him higher up the slope towards a crown of stunted hawthorn bushes at the top. He was within a single lunge of capturing her but then the child was under the misshapen canopy, and between the close-knit branches she scurried like a rodent. He dropped to his hands and knees to pursue, and there she had the advantage.

She was a determined little rat. If she kept running she would escape, but the Fell Man had too much to lose to give up the chase. Brandreth, gasping at the unexpected effort, was somewhere behind him and couldn't be relied on to cut her off. Gritting his teeth, he bulled a passage through the stunted, but tough little trees and was abruptly over the crest, and descending into a valley. Twigs snagged in his beard and hair, caught in the neckline of his jacket and scored a weeping groove in his flesh above his collarbone. The trouble the little bitch was putting him to…

The girl emitted short bleats of fear, fighting forward through a cage of branches. The crackle of breaking twigs sounded like the popping of sparks in a bonfire. Her shift was held in the grasp of a thorny fist. She yanked and fell on her front, and the Fell Man grabbed at a grimy ankle. She kicked and squirmed and then scrambled forward, but got only as far as the branch would flex. Abruptly she broke loose and gaining a few feet, she threw herself towards where the copse thinned. The Fell Man rammed a passage after her. She halted unexpectedly. So did the Fell Man.

From below sounded the excitable squeals of children at play.

Moving forward with less urgency, he glanced down at his prize. Her hair was tangled, dirty, laced with broken twigs and leaves. Her shift was torn and filthy, and scratches covered her limbs. Her tiny shoulders rose and fell as she gasped for breath. She stood in a daze, unaware of the imminent danger. She raised a hand and he sensed her mouth opening. He clamped a palm over her face and dragged her backwards into the gloom beneath the trees. He crouched, his hand forcibly cupping her face and her squirms grew frantic as she fought for life. He ignored the dirty thing in his hands, concentrating instead on the two girls peering up the hill. Had they witnessed him grabbing the girl?

One child he disregarded. She was an androgynous little thing, with a thick thatch of coppery hair crowning a round boyish face, and even at a distance he was certain she was cross-eyed. The hem of a padded coat scuffed the tops of wellington boots designed for someone larger. But the second girl held his gaze. He almost forgot about the child perishing under his hand, while he stared at a vision. The girl was willowy, graceful, a beauty: when she turned away and bounded downhill, followed by her ungainly sibling, it was with elegance unmatched by any girl he'd taken before...and he coveted her.

The Fell Man advanced to the edge of the copse, dangling the wretch against his chest, one hand now clenching her throat, while watching every move the graceful girl made. Down below them at the very perimeter of the ancient estate he spotted a car, and a woman loading items into its boot. He ignored the adult, ignored the child chugging downhill in her ill-fitting boots, and ignored the now floppy girl in his arms; there was only one person worthy of his attention.

'Victoria,' he whispered throatily.

It was not the name of the graceful girl, but of one who'd similarly entranced him many years ago. It was through the dark desires Victoria had ignited in him that the Fell Man was born.

He backed into the deformed trees, still watching as the girls joined the woman by the car. They stood abashed, being scolded. There was no frantic pointing uphill, so he was satisfied he'd gone unobserved. Behind him, Brandreth forced a crackling path through the trees. The man's dependency on alcohol had sapped all vitality from him. He stood a moment, hands on his thick thighs as he gasped for breath. The Fell Man sneered, then aimed his derision at the wretch he still held suspended above the ground. She was as light as the filthy rag she resembled. He tossed her down at Brandreth's feet.

'Make up for your bloody stupidity and do something with *that*.'

'Is she dead?'

'What do you think?' The Fell Man had felt life slip from her as he'd crushed her trachea. 'It's no good to us now,' he said. 'Drop it in a deep hole like you did with the others.'

Brandreth didn't complain. Through his inattention it was his fault their prisoner had escaped, so it was down to him to clean up his mess. He reached and pawed up the dead girl, whose back arched over his bent elbow.

Her mouth fell open, a wet hole with only the stub of a disfigured tongue, from which escaped a wheeze of escaping air. Her last breath was sour. Brandreth glowered at her lax features, and his lips twisted in disgust. He preferred when their victims pleaded for mercy. He was secretly pleased she was done with, because he'd never fully enjoyed playing with the little dummy.

By the time he next checked, his mentor had gone.

Soon after he heard the belching growl of an engine, and formed an ugly smile. The Fell Man was hunting their next plaything.

1

The girl's hands were clasped as if in prayer, knees tucked tightly to her abdomen. Her eyelids were scrunched, her prayer fervent: begging for the agony to stop. It had gone unanswered except by death. Alongside the child, her dead mother also lay on her side. A hand reached as if to offer comfort, fingertips falling short by a few inches. The mother's face was rigid, contorted forever by grief. Ten-year-old Bilan Ghedi's death wasn't instantaneous; she'd died screeching, her body contracting around the bullet in her abdomen, while her mother Nala, blood pumping from a throat wound, strove to protect her children in her final moments.

Detective Inspector Kerry Darke caught only a snatch of the awful scene through the slim opening in the forensic tent. It was enough. She turned away, shuddering out a groan. Why did another little girl have to die?

'You still with me, boss?'

She blinked rain from her eyelashes. She was a transplantee to the capital since transferring to the Met's Gangs and Organised Crime taskforce, a northern lass used to rain heavier and colder than the showers currently washing over South Lambeth.

A concerned frown creased the olive skin of Detective Sergeant Danny Korba's forehead. His slicked black hair and the shoulders of his suit were sodden.

'I wouldn't say that, Danny.' She offered a weak grimace. 'Sorry...Bilan's death got me thinking, that's all.' She blew out her cheeks, tucked her auburn hair behind her ears and concentrated on the DS. 'What've you got for me?'

Korba read from a tatty pocket book. 'Two suspects, a driver and shooter. Car's a sonic blue Subaru Impreza, older model, with the airfoil on the boot. Partial license plate only.' He read it out.

'You've passed that to ANPR and the control room?'

He clucked his tongue. 'Course I have. You ask me, though, the plates have been switched. Those Impreza's rolled off the line back in the nineties, so it won't have a five nine plate.'

'Hoping for an ID of the shooter's too much to ask?'

Korba's eyebrows beetled. 'Still waiting to hear from the wooden tops,' he said – meaning their uniformed colleagues tasked with canvassing the area for witnesses.

'Let me know as soon as you get anything.'

She waited for clearance to enter the forensic tent. The pavement was greasy under foot, dotted with pigeon shit. It fronted a commercial strip, an eclectic mix offering everything from cheap mobile phones, fruit and vegetables, Moroccan coffee and budget dental plans. There were residential flats above the shops, and some locals leaned over their balconies for a better view of an abandoned pushchair and the corpses hidden a few feet away from it.

Other observers gathered beyond the police cordon. Uniformed officers diverted traffic around Larkhall Park, while others conducted a fingertip search of the road and kerbs. Three spent brass shells had already been recovered, photographed, tagged and bagged. On hands and knees constables continued a wider search, the rain pattering on their arched backs. A mother, her daughter and two-year-old son had been shot at. The victims were Somalian, and already the suggestion was that the gunman was white — an ember to be fanned into flames by racists on opposite sides of the colour divide.

A female constable coughed an apology at Kerry's side.

'What is it?'

At five feet six inches, Kerry wasn't tall. The constable was a couple of inches shorter, sturdy rather than overweight. Her round cheeks were florid. She

13

nodded at a tall black man cornered in the doorway of an Oriental supermarket. 'Funky said you'd better come and speak to him, ma'am, or he's leaving.'

Kerry recognised the gangling Nigerian, and his nickname. Ikemba Adefunke was on her radar, a footsoldier of Jermaine Robson's Nine Elms Crew. 'I'll be with him shortly.'

'He said the dead can wait, but he's a busy man.'

The gangster's rheumy gaze challenged her.

'Uh, he's a witness, ma'am.' The constable shifted foot to foot, staring over her shoulder at Funky. He inclined his chin. Kerry snorted, and the constable snapped to attention. 'Ma'am, Funky knows the gunman, but will only tell you who it is.'

'Alright,' Kerry said, 'I'll see him. You three stay close.'

The constable scurried to obey. Kerry ducked through the rain sluicing off the supermarket's awning. She shook drops from her hair, rubbed the back of her wrist across her mouth.

'Take your own fuckin' time, why don't ya?' Funky's head bobbed with each deep, mellifluous word. She closed in, invading his personal space. Funky's skinny neck bent like a vulture's. He studied her eyes, snapping from one to the other and back again. She had heterochromia, her left iris a light shade of amber, her right dark green. Some people were creeped out by her mismatched stare, and she'd learned to use it. His arrogance melted away.

'I hear you've got a name for me, Funky.'

'Mebbe I should keep it to myself, Detective Inspector *Darke*.' He made her name sound like urban slang for shit. 'Seein' as you don't look too interested in hearin' what a black man's got to say.'

'It's not like your kind to give anything to the Old Bill...expect lip.' She wasn't talking about his skin colour.

'I make an exception when some white boy tries to shoot me in the back.'

'How could you tell he was white if you had your back to him?'

'He was a shit aim. Hit that woman and her kid instead, then took another shot at me.' He snorted. 'I turned round and looked that fucker dead in the face and he still missed me.'

Three shots. Three spent shells found on the road. Maybe Funky was telling the truth, except she had an inherent distrust of his kind – meaning criminals. 'And you recognised the shooter?'

'Got a good look at him, yeah? You know Erick Swain, don't you?' Funky snorted. 'Yeah, 'course you do.'

She did. Jermaine Robson's patch included Nine Elms Lane, and the adjacent Patmore Estate all the way from Battersea Park as far north as the Kia Oval. Erick Swain was Robson's nearest rival, his gang controlling territory in Vauxhall and Lambeth, and was responsible for most of the drug trade through Newington, north towards the Thames.

'It was one of Swain's gang?'

'No, *Darke*, you ain't listenin' to me. I'm sayin' the shooter *was* Erick-fuckin'-Swain.'

'Oh, really?' Kerry abruptly turned away. 'Don't waste my bloody time, Funky.'

'Where the hell you goin'? You ain't ignorin' me like I'm a piece of shit.'

'I'm ignoring an obvious lie,' Kerry retorted. 'You're only saying it was Swain to stitch him up. I bet it'd suit Jermaine Robson to see his biggest rival behind bars.'

'Are you bent or somethin'?' Funky countered. 'Is that it? You takin' green from Swain to keep him outta jail, yeah?'

'Are you taking payment from Robson for setting Swain up?'

Funky snapped a long arm at the forensic tent. 'I'm tellin' you that Erick Swain killed *them*. And he tried to kill me. You're the detective. If you don't believe me, do your job and you'll see I'm tellin' the truth.'

'Can I count on you giving evidence in court?'

He rolled his neck. 'You know I can't go to court. I'd be puttin' a target on my back. This is off the record, yeah? That Subaru; ask anybody, I bet they've seen Swain toolin' around in it for years.'

'Did you get a look at the driver?'

Funky shook his head. 'I was too busy facin' down the bastard tryin' to kill me.'

'That was brave of you.' Her lips pulled into a tight line. 'You left innocent victims dying in the street next to a screaming baby while you hid in that shop. Yeah...very brave of you, Funky.'

'How'd I know that Swain wasn't gonna come back for another try?'

'Exactly.' She strode away ignoring a string of curses, satisfied that she'd shamed him.

She approached the forensic tent again, but stood a respectful distance from the entrance. Investigators worked around the bodies. Nearest to her lay Bilan. She thought of another murdered girl — her sister Sally. Her chest hitched, and it was a struggle to breathe. News crews had begun gathering beyond the cordon. Cameras trained on her as she clenched her fists at her sides. Police officers weren't supposed to be prone to public displays of emotion, but who could criticise her for being distressed by the senseless death of a child?

Funky sloped off in the opposite direction towards Larkhall Park. A barrier of blue and white tape was strung across the park's entrance. A girl stood just beyond the cordon, in the shadow of a nearby building. She stared directly at Kerry from beneath a mop of tousled hair, and her guts clenched in response.

Funky was suddenly between them, and Kerry sidestepped to keep the girl in sight. Except the girl crabbed sideways too. When Funky swiped his way under the barrier tape she had disappeared.

'Girl?' She took a faltering step.

'Kerry? Detective Inspector!'

The sharp voice brought her to a halt. She blinked her confusion at DS Korba.

'Something wrong, boss?'

She glanced towards the park's entrance. It was as if the girl had never been there. 'Uh, no, just thought I spotted…' She waved away an explanation. 'Never mind. It was nothing.'

He thumbed towards the forensic tent. 'Socco's ready for us.'

Kerry nodded, but couldn't resist another glance to where the dripping barrier tape swung in the breeze. Korba moved close, rested a hand on her forearm. 'Seriously, boss, you sure you're all right? You're as white as a sheet.'

'I'm…I'm fine.'

Korba wasn't perturbed by her heterochromia. He held her gaze, seeking a lie.

'I'm fine,' she repeated. 'Stop mithering, will you?'

'As long as you're sure,' he said conspiratorially. 'You look as if you've just seen a friggin' ghost.'

'A ghost, Danny?' She coughed out a laugh. 'You don't believe that sort of rubbish, do you?'

2

A tubular steel battering ram smashed the door open. Armed officers swarmed into the house on a residential street in the Vauxhall area of Lambeth, shouting and stamping, causing shock and confusion. A woman's shrieks and the barking of a dog elevated the racket, a man cursed savagely. Kerry and DS Korba waited on the front garden for Erick Swain to be cornered and forced to sit his arse down in the front room.

'We're secure.' Bob Grier, a uniformed sergeant, waved them inside. On the street a dog handler readied his spaniel to join the search.

The strength of Ikemba Adefunke's "off the record" tip-off hadn't been enough to secure a search warrant, but in the past hours three telephone callers to Crimestoppers, and one to an official police hotline, all insisted that Erick Swain was their murderer, and pinpointed where they'd find the murder weapon. The Subaru Impreza had also been found burnt out on waste ground alongside the Thames. The registration plates were missing, but the VIN on the chassis showed the Subaru had once been registered to Swain. Enough evidence to bring him in for questioning. If they didn't conduct a full search of the property before moving to the outlying garden Swain would possibly figure out his betrayer, and have him punished. If she had her way, Swain would never harm anyone again.

Clutching the warrant, Kerry squeezed past two constables in the hallway and entered the living room. The shrieking woman was on a sofa, dressed casually in pyjamas and slippers, in direct contrast to her styled hair, fudge-coloured tan and proliferation of gold jewellery: her large sapphire engagement ring could double as a knuckle duster. Both her knees were drawn up, protecting her surgically enhanced breasts. Two officers loomed over her, while she swore blue murder at them. As soon as Kerry entered, her rage switched target. She launched off the sofa, but was grappled by the officers. Kerry looked instead at Erick Swain who was seated in a matching easy chair on the other side of the room. He'd quietened down, but his calm rage was more worrying than his girlfriend's noisy tirade. Another two officers guarded him, thickset in their stab-proof vests.

Erick Swain wasn't physically imposing. He wasn't a squashed-nosed thug, bulging with muscles etched with tattoos. He was in his mid-thirties, a bit scruffy in faded bootleg jeans, Nike trainers and baggy tie-dyed shirt...an ordinary guy. Except in his case, first impressions were deceiving. Unconfirmed rumours fingered Swain for a litany of violent offences. There were victims walking around still carrying the wounds he'd inflicted on their flesh, but fear of further torture stilled their tongues. Kerry studied him for a second longer, taking in his shaggy blond hair, goatee beard, and single silver earring. He resembled a bohemian artist more than the aggressive leader of one of London's most notorious criminal gangs. She checked out the long, slim fingers digging into the arms of the easy chair. They were an artist's fingers...no; his were the fingers of a murderer. It didn't take a powerful hand to point and pull the trigger of a gun.

She approached within a few feet.

'Are you the one who's going to explain what the fuck's going on?' Swain sneered from between his guards.

'I'm Detective Inspector Darke.' She waved the slim stack of papers. 'I've a warrant to search these premises and adjoining property under section one four six of the Firearms Act nineteen-ninety-six.'

'Firearms? You're having a laugh, aren't you?' Swain glanced over at his girlfriend. She spat curses like a wildcat. 'Hettie! For fuck's sake, will you shut up? I need to hear what the hell this bitch is going on about.'

Hettie's eyes bulged. 'They've smashed down the fuckin' door, Erick! And trampled dog shit all over my carpets!'

Kerry had weathered similar accusations during the execution of other search warrants. She allowed Hettie to continue for a few more seconds, until she'd had enough.

'Get her out of here,' she said, and Hettie's guards led her to the kitchen, harangued the entire way.

'Hettie's a bit worked up,' Swain said. 'She's got a good right, though. If you'd knocked, I'd've let you in without you battering down the door. I've got nothing to hide.' He smirked, confident she'd find nothing incriminating.

'If you've nothing to hide, you've nothing to worry about. But if you—'

Before she could finish, Swain butted in. 'Listen. If you're talking about drugs, I've a bit of weed in my baccy tin, but it's for personal use. It's on the fireplace. Take a look.'

Kerry couldn't give a shit about a wad of cannabis resin. But for appearances sake she nodded at Korba to check it out.

'Like I said,' Swain went on, 'that weed's for personal use. What does that get me these days, a slap on the wrist?'

The searching officers ensured no stone – or bedside cabinet – were left unturned. In the adjoining kitchen Hettie swore at the family dog to stop it barking. Swain shrugged. 'What can I say? She's a passionate woman.'

The dog handler entered. His springer spaniel sped around like a battery operated toy, sniffing and discarding items as uninteresting. When it hopped up on the sofa, its demeanour changed. The handler commanded it to the ground, and while he praised the dog a uniformed constable moved in, dismantling the sofa cushions, and then feeding his gloved hands down the back. 'Are there any sharps down here, mate?' he asked Swain, concerned about jabbing a finger on a used needle.

'No. But if you find any cash down there, it's fucking mine.'

There was nothing down the sofa, but the constable turned it on its front to check underneath. The upholstery was factory fresh, all the original staples in place. Kerry shook her head. The dog must have given a false alert. The dog handler headed off to search rooms elsewhere in the house, and his assistant followed suit. Swain eyed Kerry with mild curiosity. 'You're wasting your time, there's no gun here.'

'So tell me where it is.'

'How should I know? I don't even know what gun you're on about.'

'Let's not play games, eh?'

His eyes abruptly clouded. 'If this is about those niggers getting shot, it had nothing to do with me.'

Kerry's features tightened. Not so much at his deliberate racism as his total lack of empathy towards the victims. 'We'll see.'

'Like hell we will! I'm telling you, Inspector Darke, you're not going to find a gun here.' He craned forward, and his guards jolted to readiness. 'I had nothing to do with that shooting, it's not—'

He halted, considering his next words.

'What? It's not your style? So help me out here, Swain. What exactly is your style?'

This wasn't Swain's first time around the block. 'That's *Mister* Swain to you. I was respectful with your rank and name; you should return the favour.'

'You also called me a bitch, what do I get to call you in return?'

'*Touché*, Inspector!' He rolled his tongue against his lower teeth while he decided. In the next instant his face morphed into something wolfish. 'Call me whatever you want, just not your fucking patsy.'

'Ma'am? A word please?'

In the doorway, Sergeant Grier jerked his head, indicating he'd prefer to speak in private.

'DS Korba,' she said, 'take over here for a minute.'

'Alright, boss.' He'd seized Swain's stash of cannabis, and was in the process of bagging it as evidence. He sidled over, nodded down at Swain as if they were old pals.

Swain sneered. 'So you're the famous Zorba the Greek I've heard about?'

'That'd be Korba, mate, and I'm Greek-Cypriot.' He'd been the butt of that joke for too many years for it to bother him now.

'Didn't I see you on *Britain's Got Talent* once?' Swain goaded. 'Stavros Flatulence, isn't it? You were quite nimble on your feet for a plod.'

'Mate,' Korba countered, and patted his tight abdomen, 'I didn't get this shape from dancin' towards the buffet table.'

Swain laughed, settled back in his chair. 'You're alright, *mate*,' he said with a wink. 'For a pig, I mean.'

Kerry left them to it. They were laughing, better that than trying to kill each other.

In the hallway, out of sight of Swain, Sergeant Grier jiggled the contents of an evidence bag. 'Thought you might want to check these out before speakin' to Swain.'

'What are they?' Before Grier could state the obvious, Kerry clarified: 'I can see they're bullets, Bob; I mean cartridge and calibre.'

Grier had served in the Army prior to joining the police and knew a thing or two about the subject of armament. He explained that specifically they were .38 Revolver Mk IIz cartridges. 'If you're too young to remember pounds and ounces, that equates to nine millimetres these days.'

'Same as the expended shells at the scene. Where were they found?'

'In the master bedroom. They were scattered on the floor under the bed.' He studied the bag's contents. 'You know somethin'? These are old cartridges, not readily available in the UK. If they're matched to the ones at the scene…'

'Aye. I'm confident they will be.'

'Yeah, well good luck with that,' he said enigmatically.

'I'd rather match the ones from the scene to the murder weapon. How're we getting on with finding it?'

'I've a couple of the lads out in the garden lookin' where—'

Kerry's palm shot up, stalling him. Swain was bantering with Korba, but she'd bet he had an ear on what she was up to. She nudged Grier towards the kitchen. Hettie was still there, now in control of a Border collie on its lead. Kerry glanced at the dog, and it peered dolefully back at her with eyes not unlike her own. It too had heterochromia, although its colouring was more vivid, one eye brown, one pale blue. She raised her gaze to Swain's girlfriend, expecting another outburst, but Hettie had eyes for something else. She sneered at the cartridges Grier carried. 'I see you've found my granddad's old bullets. He brought them back from Korea donkey's years ago.'

'Really?' Kerry said. 'Do you have a firearms certificate allowing you to keep live ammunition?'

'They're fuckin' antiques. And besides, I don't have a fuckin' gun.'

'You don't need one with a gob like that,' Grier pointed out.

Hettie snarled at him, but reconsidered his words: he might actually have been paying her a compliment. She turned her scrutiny on Kerry, lips pinched. 'Stupid cow, don't you know you've lost a contact lens?'

Nodding down at the collie, Kerry said, 'I'd have thought you'd have known better.'

'Eh?'

It was pointless explaining. A female constable bustled inside from the garden, a fixed grin on her face. She held up another evidence bag. 'We've got it, ma'am.'

'What you got there?' Hettie marched between them for a closer look. Grier jostled her aside as Kerry accepted the bag. Inside was an ancient looking revolver, clogged with freshly turned soil. *Yes, we've got him!*

Grier bent to inspect it, looked up slowly. 'It's a Webley mark four. It's an old school six-shot service revolver. Point three-eight calibre, just like those cartridges.'

'I think we also found your granddad's gun,' Kerry said to Hettie. 'Or maybe it belongs to Erick these days?'

'Ma'am,' Grier said *sotto voce*, 'I need to talk with you about this before—'

But Hettie piled in. 'Bollocks! This is some sorta stitch up! You bastards planted that!' She flew at Kerry, and Grier and the constable wrestled her aside, now fending off the nipping of the collie – the dog was terrified and its teeth didn't discriminate between the police and its owner. It was pandemonium. Another uniformed constable rushed in to help, and Kerry swerved past him for the living room. Time to go and get her man.

Hearing the commotion, Swain jumped to his feet. His guards barred him from rushing to Hettie's aid: all three pushed and shoved. Korba snapped a glance at Kerry, who held up the bagged revolver. A smile jumped briefly on his lips.

'What the hell's that?' Swain demanded.

Kerry took satisfaction in holding up the evidence bags. 'Erick Swain, I'm arresting you on suspicion of the murders of Nala Dahir Ghedi and Bilan Ghedi.'

'What? No fucking way!'

'You don't have to say anything but it may harm your defence—' As Kerry cautioned him, one of the constables reached for his cuffs, ordering Swain to turn around.

'You're not stitching me up!' Swain hollered directly at Kerry. 'You're having a fucking laugh, aren't you?'

Practically every criminal Kerry had ever arrested pleaded their innocence, and it didn't matter how stunned he looked, she didn't buy his lies. She continued cautioning him, while the two uniformed constables jostled him around. She was tempted to give them a nod, to cuff him extra tight, so he was in pain all the way to the nick — the least the murderous bastard deserved. She passed the evidence bags to Korba, freeing her hands so she could radio in the arrest.

Somebody roared in agony.

It wasn't Swain.

The constable on the left collapsed, clutching his knee where Swain had just back-kicked him. He rolled over, knocking into her and Kerry stumbled. Swain writhed out of the other constable's grasp — only one of his wrists was cuffed — and then snapped his head forward. Clutching his broken nose the constable reeled away, tripped over his fallen colleague and dropped to his knees. Swain barged into him, kneeing him solidly between the shoulder blades. He went down, under Swain, who stamped over the top of him.

Korba jerked into action, dropping the evidence bags on the sofa, and grabbing at Swain. Swain was nimbler, and determined to evade Korba's grasp. A minute earlier they'd been joking with each other but all pretenses at friendliness had evaporated. Swain swept his arm at Korba's face, and the rigid cuff locked around his wrist gashed his forehead. Blood ran into Korba's eyes. Still, he clambered after Swain, grabbing for his shirt, his hair. Swain stayed a few inches beyond his grasp though, and only Kerry barred his freedom. She lunged, trying to snatch hold of the rigid cuff, to lock his wrist and take him down.

Swain showed no hesitation in hitting a woman. His fist slammed her sternum. Beneath her jacket her lightweight stab-proof vest took the sting from his punch but little of the impact. She staggered, and he rammed her against the doorframe. He grabbed her, jerked her down to one knee, dodged past and was into the hall. Alerted by the commotion, other officers charged from the kitchen, but too late. Kerry was up in an instant, and after him, shouting at Korba to secure the evidence. Lurching into the hallway, she almost collided with Sergeant Grier and another constable. They skidded to avoid ploughing into her, Grier slamming into a wall, tearing loose a framed watercolour painting that crashed down and sent jagged slithers of glass into the carpet pile. From the kitchen Hettie cursed savagely, but this time it wasn't about the state of her carpet.

Kerry raced outside.

A bewildered copper was at the front gate, hand on his radio. Swain had hurdled past. Kerry didn't slow down to explain. The clatter of boot soles on the pavement followed her. She was unsure how many officers had joined the pursuit, and didn't have time to check.

An engine burst to life. Armed SC019 officers had conducted the initial entry to the house, but retreated outside once it was secured. If they could get ahead of Swain they could soon halt him in his tracks. For murdering Bilan Ghedi the bastard deserved a bullet between the eyes. The police vehicle roared along the street, whipping by, its blue lights flashing. Swain charged across the road in front of it and hurtled down a path between two residential houses.

The police car shot towards an intersection as the driver sought to cut off Swain at the next road over. Kerry pounded across the road, and also ducked into the alley. Behind her, feet slapped the ground, and then a younger bobby raced past, his elbows pumping furiously. He'd discarded his helmet and high visibility coat somewhere. More streamlined than his colleagues, he was gaining on the fugitive.

Without slowing, Kerry mentally goaded him on. Swain had already exited the alley, and was out of sight for a few seconds until she spilled out onto another residential street, rushing out from between parked cars. The bobby was about ten metres behind Swain as they both headed towards a tower block.

There were some affluent areas of Vauxhall. It was home to politicians who found the neighbourhood convenient for the short journey into Westminster. But the tower block wasn't home to any of them. It comprised of social housing, poorer families crammed into one- and two-bedroom flats. Perhaps Swain had friends inside and could find a hiding place with one of them; or worse, a weapon to hold off the police.

4

Erick Swain barrelled inside one of four tower blocks looming at opposing corners of an open plaza area, an expanse of uneven paving slabs, and flowerbeds devoid of any foliage but plenty of discarded cigarette butts, beer cans and fast-food wrappers. The tower stood eleven storeys tall, a concrete and glass monolith that looked as if it had been grabbed from the Soviet-era Eastern Bloc and dropped — with its trio of equally drab sisters — smack in the middle of their more upwardly mobile neighbours. There were good, decent people living there, but in a bad situation, and unfortunately surrounded by others at the far end of the spectrum.

The quartet of towers was well known to most members on the anti-gang task force. There was no visible signage declaring police were unwelcome but it went without saying. It wasn't unknown for them to have to dodge missiles dropped on them from above, and God help them if they were caught alone in any of the stairwells. Kerry knew all this, but didn't slow. She sprinted after her uniformed colleague who darted inside ahead of her. A squall of rain chased her towards the door.

Immediately inside was a bank of twin elevators, the scarred and battered doors displaying spray-painted gang fealties that would make Swain proud. Kerry ignored them, hearing the clatter of feet from a stairwell to her left. Breathless, she shouted an update on Swain's position into her radio as she pushed through the door and onto the first steps up. Other constables answered her call, some already converging on the tower, but thirty-or-so seconds behind her. She couldn't leave the constable to handle Swain alone. She clattered up the stairs, feeling blindly for her extendable baton in a harness buried under her jacket. Above her the young copper shouted, and Swain barked a curse. She doubled her effort, forgetting about the baton for the sake of speed.

Kerry kept fit. She swam and she attended a gym with her fiancé Adam when their shifts permitted. But it was one thing swimming a measured distance at a steady pace or completing reps on an exercise machine, another when it came to climbing a tower when her heart was jammed in her mouth. Her legs were leaden and bile scorched her throat with each gasping breath. Swain hadn't peeled off onto any of the floors; he was still heading up. She dug in, dragging herself up with one hand on the bannister.

Overhead a door banged open.

The voices dwindled, then disappeared completely as the door slammed shut again.

Kerry croaked an update into her radio as she spilled onto the tenth floor. On the landing stood a young boy in tracksuit bottoms, a baggy sweater, and filthy trainers. He was a scruffy kid, but he clutched a top of the range smartphone, angled upwards. He swung it on Kerry as she took a few seconds to suck in air, grinning at her feverishly as he lined her up on the screen. She took his direction from where he'd been pointing the phone a moment ago. Swain had made it up the next flight of stairs and onto the roof. Why he'd chosen to run all the way to the top escaped her, unless he knew of another route down where he could give his pursuers the slip. Grateful for her second wind, she powered up the remaining steps and slapped down the push bar. The door opened into a service corridor, lit only by dim bulbs. The uppermost floor was comprised of various utility rooms, some containing the machinery and electrical systems that controlled the building's beating heart. Swain might have hidden in any of them, except another door stood wide at the far end of the corridor, and beside it a silent day alarm flashed rapidly, a red light like the winking eye of a demon. The rain and wind competed to make the most noise, but couldn't disguise the grunting and scuffling of a struggle.

Kerry started forward, and came to a stumbling halt.

There was somebody in the corridor with her.

The figure barred her way.

It was a child. A young girl. She had straggly hair and a shapeless dress, stick-thin limbs and bare feet, barely discernible in a clot of shadows between two of the dim bulbs.

What was a young child doing out alone this late in the evening? Kerry thought of the boy on the landing below and remembered where she was. Spotting the chase, this kid had probably followed to watch the excitement. The last Kerry wanted was for another child to get hurt because of Erick Swain.

'Hey!' she called. 'Girl. Come away from there, it's not safe.'

There...she'd said it. *Girl*. It was the same girl she'd earlier spotted observing her from beyond the police barrier on Wandsworth Road. There was something indefinable about her, as if she was viewed through a haze of fog, but Kerry knew her. Nausea squirmed through Kerry's abdomen and the small hairs on her forearms and neck prickled. Subdued memories fluttered through her mind, a series of underdeveloped Polaroid photographs carried on a stuttering breeze. *Why now*, she thought. *Why have you come back now?*

The girl raised a palm.

Kerry took a nervous step towards her. 'What...what is it you want from me?'

Overhead the nearest bulb *pinked!* And went black.

'Girl?' Kerry croaked.

Except there wasn't a girl there.

Where she'd stood, there was only the wash of a bulkhead light, casting a meagre glow on the floor. Two silhouetted bodies wrestled past the open doorway. Her colleague emitted a pained cry.

Kerry started forward, but faltered. An uncanny sense of trepidation assailed her, made her fearful of passing through the space vacated by the spectral girl. She glanced everywhere, expecting a nebulous presence creeping through each dark recess and corner.

The young bobby yowled again, snapping her to attention.

There is no Girl, Kerry argued. *There never was a Girl. Concentrate on reality, Kerry. That officer needs you!*

Finally she found her baton, but only unclipped it. She groped for her incapacitant spray in its pouch on the harness under her jacket. All the while she scurried along the corridor, the fingers of unnatural dread playing down her spine, and stepped out the door over a raised stoop, and into the downpour.

5

They faced each other on the puddled rooftop, both breathless from their frantic race to the top. Exposed to the elements, it wasn't the best place for a stand off, though the rain-washed city formed a dramatic backdrop.

A chilly blast battered her, sweeping Kerry's hair off her brow. Steam rose from her wet shoulders. Raindrops gathered on her eyelashes causing her to blink. She daren't take her attention off Swain for a second; he was poised to move again. She desperately wanted to check on the constable lying in a puddle a few metres away. His silence was worrying. He needed medical attention immediately. The voices of her fellow officers were too distant to offer confidence. She was all that stood between the suspected murderer and his escape from the roof.

Swain sneered: how did a skinny woman hope to stop him? He had no respect for the law, and less for her rank than the constables he'd beaten up. He was taller than Kerry, outweighed her, and wouldn't care if she got hurt when he ran straight through her. In fact, she'd bet he would make certain of it.

She didn't stand aside. She raised her can of PAVA incapacitant spray, thumb poised over it. 'Don't move, Swain. You're under arrest.'

'Is that right?' Swain eyed the canister, her only visible weapon. Its threat didn't invoke fear in him. Besides, if Kerry was stupid enough to spray him, she'd get a face full of it too because the wind gusting over the roof was at his back. He tensed, ready to smash through her. 'How did that work out for you last time, Darke?'

'There's no way off this roof. Give up now and make things easier on yourself.' Perhaps she should get out of his way, and leave him to her colleagues, but no. She'd initiated his arrest, and it was her duty to go through with it. 'Come on Swain, you know how this works.'

'I'm not going down for shooting a couple of niggers.' His eyes were feverish, a similar flashing colour as the earring twinkling in his right lobe. 'Good riddance to them anyway!'

'You're talking about an innocent woman and ten-year-old child.'

'Fuck 'em. They don't mean anything to me. Give 'em another couple of years and they'd both be Robson's whores popping out more little black shits that our country has to keep!' Swain didn't hold his rival in high regard, and less those he perceived as unwelcome immigrants. 'Now get out of my fucking way or I swear to God...'

Kerry stood her ground. 'Don't try me, Swain. I won't be playing by Home Office rules—'

'You're kidding? You skinny-arsed bitch, what're you gonna do?'

'You're under arrest, and I'm taking you in.'

Kerry advanced, the PAVA directed at arm's length.

His head swivelled. Despite his bluster, he searched for a way out. A few rungs showed at the top of the parapet a few metres to Kerry's left, a service ladder of some kind to who knew where. Swain lunged for it and Kerry crabbed sideways, blocking him. He danced on the balls of his feet.

'Last chance, Darke. Move or I'll fucking move you. D'you want me to knock you out like your mate over there?'

She didn't follow his gesture at the unconscious bobby. It was a distraction, so he could push past when she was looking the other way. She had to hold him there a few moments longer, to allow her colleagues to arrive. 'Try it and I'll take you down like a bag of shit, you murderous bastard.'

Swain thought through his options, but they were few.

He charged.

Under perfect conditions, PAVA was effective up to four metres. These conditions were anything but perfect. Swain hurtled at her with his head down, an arm wrapped around his face to protect his vision. The stream of spray arched overhead, then rushed to fill the void in his wake. Kerry backpedalled, dropping the PAVA on its lanyard, and snatching instead for her extendable baton. She racked it open with a swift jerk of her wrist, swiped wildly...Swain battered into her.

He was a force of nature, a tidal wave of sinew and bone. She was picked up like flotsam, and then dumped on her back. Her skull rang as it bounced off concrete. Strength fled her, riding on a gasp of pain. But then she was dragged, and knew the fight wasn't over. Her left arm was entangled around his right knee, and she wasn't letting go. She was like a cloth rag, whipping in his back draft. No, she was being pummelled as he kicked to free his feet. She spilled loose, heard him slip and slide, and hit something solid. She swarmed up, but the PAVA cloud was in her face, and her eyes streamed. Through the blur she struck at Swain with her baton, and felt it land. He punched her, his knuckles raking her forehead. A white flash exploded through her skull, and she reeled, but grabbed at him in desperation. Found the loose ring of the cuff extending from his wrist.

With rigid cuffs a physically weaker person could control a larger one through application of leverage and pain control. Kerry twisted the loose cuff, and the opposite end bit savagely into his flesh. He shouted in agony, but he was high on adrenalin: pain in his wrist wasn't going to halt him now. He kicked a heel into Kerry's body. Her vest saved her again, but she was shunted aside. In desperation she dropped her baton, got two hands on the loose cuff and twisted as if closing a stopcock. Swain roared this time, and he flexed his arm to avoid further torture. It was where she wanted him:

Kerry hauled back and up, using the added leverage to lock Swain's arm and bend him at the waist. If she could now twist his elbow, and get his other hand secured she'd have a chance…

Swain rammed his shoulder into her, and she went airborne. She crashed against the parapet, her spine flaring in agony. Swain spun on her, and even through her bleary vision, she saw his wolfish face loom close as he barked a curse. He thrust out his free hand, forcing her backwards over the parapet. He was trying to throw her over the edge!

Terror added strength to her desperation. As he shouldered into her again, trying to force her up and over the parapet, she wrenched aside, twisting with all her might on the pinioned cuff. He struck at her with his other fist, catching her flush between the eyes. Stunned, she fell against him and heard his hoarse shout. There was a wild flurry of movement, a stuttering kaleidoscope of shadows and colours, and frantic yelling — the cuff was snatched from her hand with enough force to bark the skin from her fingertips — the sound diminishing to a keening whistle. And then she fell flat, half-blinded and dazed to the rooftop.

She struggled onto her front, her arms shivering under her. Her baton was lost. Her palms slapped at gritty wet concrete, and she pushed to her knees. Stayed there, trying to force lucidity into her spinning brain. Her eyes stung from the incapacitant spray. She spat a string of saliva, and lurched up. Searching for Swain through a sheet of tears. The empty PAVA canister rattled on the floor behind her, dragged on its lanyard as she took a loping step towards the roof access door. She pawed her face. Rubbing her eyes would spread the capsaicinoids in the solution further, but it was a natural reaction. Her eyeballs felt touched by fire and her nose dripped. *Where the hell's Swain?*

Officers pounded up the stairs. The lack of warning

shouts indicated they hadn't met him coming up.

She swiped her sleeve across her face again, swivelled around, expecting to find him racing around the rooftop, going for the service ladder.

She spotted the constable lying in the puddle. She groped towards him, dug fingers under his chin, seeking a pulse. Thankfully it beat strongly, but his breath rattled. She rolled him on his side, opening his airway. Searched again for Swain, and instead spotted the first armed officer to emerge from the stairwell. He checked for Swain before approaching her.

'Where'd he go, ma'am?'

Kerry spread her palms, even as her heart plunged.

She turned and peered through a wash of tears at the nearest parapet where they'd fought, recalling Swain's diminishing shout. A figure swayed there, indistinct, a blur through which the rain passed. Kerry blinked for clarity, and as her vision cleared the girl from the service corridor shook her unkempt hair in dismay, stepped off the roof and plummeted from sight.

'Oh, shit...no!'

Kerry stumbled to the parapet, bracing her grazed palms on the rough concrete to peer down.

A long distance below a single corpse lay spread-eagled on the uneven paving, but it wasn't the slight figure of a girl.

She'd warned Swain there was no way he was getting off the roof. She was wrong. He'd taken the fastest way down.

1997
Back O' Skiddaw, Cumbria

'Kerry! Stop that! If you don't behave, the Fell Man will get you,' Sally warned, one hand propped on her hip. With her colouring, her hair on the redder end of auburn, and a spray of freckles over her nose, and posing like that she was their mam's mini-me.

'Shut up, Sally! There's no such thing as the Fell Man.' Kerry stomped in the muddy puddle, and Sally shrieked, jumping to avoid the splash.

'Look at what you've done! You've got me all dirty now!'

'Ha!' Kerry crowed at the filthy water dripping from Sally's coat. 'Now you'll get in trouble and the Fell Man will get you instead.'

'No he won't. He only comes for horrible little girls.'

Kerry stomped again, and was forced to flee when Sally launched after her with a howl of indignity. Kerry's laughter was manic as her older sister chased her between stunted trees that had grown bent at an angle by the incessant wind. Running in ill-fitting wellington boots wasn't easy, and it was inevitable an exposed root would take her down. Kerry tumbled in the couch grass, adding more green stains to the knees of her jeans. She rolled onto her back, drawing up her legs protectively. Sally could have launched on her then, but unlike her little sister, she wasn't into all that rough and tumble boys' stuff. She bent over Kerry, both hands fixed to her hips. 'Serves you right, you little monster.'

Kerry made claws of her fingers and screwed up her nose. She growled. 'I'm not afraid of monsters.'

'Aye you are.'

'No I'm not.'

'You're scared of the Fell Man. It's why you have a

night light left on in your bedroom. Just like a little baby.'
Sally suddenly pivotted away, and she skipped off
between the trees, chanting in a singsong voice: 'Kerry
Darke's afraid of the dark, Kerry Darke's afraid of the
dark...'

Kerry was up and after her in seconds, the hunted
now the hunter. Sally shrieked in mock terror and ran
faster. She was six inches taller than her sibling, sapling
thin and long legged; it was no competition.

'Sally! Wait for me,' Kerry called when it was
apparent that her floppy wellington boots weren't
designed for running in.

Sally paused thirty feet ahead. She pointed back to
where the slate roof of an old building could barely be
discerned from similar coloured shale that had cascaded
down the hillside beyond. The decrepit ruin stood
alongside a stagnant pond, and was surrounded by
gnarly trees: the ancestral, but now abandoned home of
landed gentry, the Brandreth family, whose descendants
had fallen into financial troubles back in the eighties,
and allowed the mansion and grounds to go to seed. A
smelly tramp supposedly lived there; to the girls,
though, it was the home of a wicked witch or ogre from a
dark fairy tale. 'You'd better hurry up, Kerry! He's
coming. The Fell Man's right behind you!'

Now Kerry's shrieks of not-so-mock terror filled the
air, and she galloped, cumbersome and ungainly after
her sister who bounded over the tussocks of coarse
grass with the ease of a yearling deer.

'Girls! What did I tell you?' Their mother met them as
they burst out of the trees onto a gentler slope
overlooking a chuckling stream – a tributary that added
its water to the tarn in the valley below. Mam had one
hand propped on her hip, and her mouth pinched briefly
before she went on. 'I told you not to wander off, didn't
I? And what was the last thing I said? Don't get dirty.
Sally...look at the bloody state of your jacket.'

'It's not my fault!' Sally's face crumpled, on the verge of tears. She could be quick to cry, but her emotion was only for effect, to elicit sympathy. 'I warned her not to, Mam, but Kerry kicked mud all over me.'

Mam's accusatory gaze swept to Kerry. Guilty as charged, Kerry stood breathing heavily, her knees nipped together.

'Well, madam?' Mam demanded.

'I need a wee,' said Kerry.

Her mam shook her head at the deft way she'd changed the subject. 'Well you should've thought about that sooner. Come on, we have to go and pick your dad up at the train station.'

'I'll wet myself,' Kerry groaned.

'Serves you right for wetting me.' Sally smirked at her.

'Shut up, Stupid Sally!'

'Both of you shut up.' Their mam tapped her wristwatch in emphasis. 'And get a move on. Into the car and put your seatbelts on. Your dad's train gets into Penrith in an hour.'

'Ma-a-am,' Kerry whined, and her knees almost entwined.

Looking frazzled, her mam shoved her fingers through her copper hair. She cast a disapproving glare over the numerous grass and mud stains on her youngest daughter's clothing, but she wasn't genuinely annoyed: she'd grown used to Kerry's tomboyish ways, and had dressed her appropriately for a picnic on the fells, and for a girl who couldn't resist a muddy puddle or clump of dirt. At least she'd managed to avoid rolling in the proliferation of sheep droppings that dotted the hill. 'Hurry up then, you can go behind the car.'

'Somebody might see me,' Kerry moaned.

'Who wants to look at your skinny little bum?' Sally teased.

'No spying.' Kerry's nose scrunched in warning.

Sotto voce, Sally leaned in. 'It's not me watching that you have to worry about. Don't forget who the Fell Man's after.'

'Ma-a-am,' Kerry whined, this time with a nasal tone, 'Sally said the Fell Man's going to get me.'

'Sally, that's enough. Stop trying to scare your sister. You know the Fell Man's not real. Kerry, get a pee now or you'll have to wait till we reach the station.'

While Kerry protected her modesty alongside the car, she kept an ear cocked towards the conversation as Sally slipped in and buckled up her seat belt. She didn't really need to pee — that had been a ploy to distract her mam — so she only pretended.

'Mam, if the Fell Man isn't real, why do they keep talking about him on the telly?' Sally asked.

Carrying the leftovers from their picnic in a carrier bag, and loading the dirty plastic plates and empty flasks away in the boot, their mam said, 'You don't have to worry about what they're saying on the telly, Sally. That's another fell man altogether. He's not the same bogeyman that you're frightened of.'

'Isn't he?' Sally challenged. 'Because I heard he takes girls away too.'

'Well there you go then,' said their mam as she slammed the boot. 'You should both listen to me when I tell you not to wander off. You better hadn't've been up around those ruins like I warned, not with that horrible tramp supposed to be back living there.'

'We weren't. Kerry wanted to go and look, but I wouldn't let her.'

'Good girl, Sally. At least one of you is sensible. Kerry! Hurry up!'

Zipping her jeans, Kerry darted around and jumped in the backseat beside Sally. The sisters exchanged worried frowns. Sally whispered, 'The Fell Man sometimes looks like a horrible tramp. Told you he was real.'

40

This time Kerry didn't argue.

As their mam drove off the hillside and onto a track that followed a parallel course to the winding stream, Kerry peered back up the hill, searching the stunted trees for movement. Earlier, she thought, for the briefest moment, there was a small girl standing in the shadows beneath the trees, sadly watching her potential playmates leaving, before she was dragged backwards into the gloom. But then it could have just been the movement of a bush swaying in the breeze. When she was confident that no bogeyman lurked in any of the other shadows she leaned over and tapped Sally's wrist. Her sister looked at her open mouthed.

'Does that mean Santa Claus is real too?' Kerry asked facetiously. 'Because you told me parents just made him up to make sure little girl and boys behaved themselves.'

Their mother's eyes glared back in the rearview mirror. 'Sally! You didn't?'

'No, Mam, I didn't tell her. Honest!' To add validity to the outright lie, Sally yelped, 'I still believe in Santa!'

'Well that's OK then, otherwise who'd bring you the Tamagotchi pet you've been begging for?'

Sally huffed. She lived in hope that she wouldn't have to wait months until Christmas, not when all her friends at school already owned Tamagotchis and were busy raising their electronic pets to her envy. She'd hoped their dad would bring her one back as a gift from his business trip to Manchester.

'I want a Tinky-Winky for Christmas,' Kerry announced.

'The Teletubbies are for babies,' Sally reminded her.

'I don't care. I still want a Tinky-Winky.'

'Didn't you just have one before you got in the car?' their mam joked.

While the girls giggled and debated the must-have toys of the year, their mam pulled onto the track down off the fells towards the A66, where they could strike eastward for Penrith. When they reached the main road, they were oblivious to the battered old Land Rover that crept out in their wake and then followed all the way to the train station.

Sally never received the Tamagotchi her dad brought back from his trip, and come Christmas, eight-year-old Kerry didn't believe that Santa Claus existed, although she'd learned that the Fell Man was genuinely to be feared.

When Kerry arrived home in Fulham the bare-footed girl was waiting for her on the pavement. She was as nebulous as the last couple of times Kerry had spotted her that day, vague, ill defined, but unhurt by her jump from the tower. The rain spattering the windscreen, streaked by the wipers, didn't help to form a definite shape to her, but that wasn't it. Since the first time Kerry spotted 'Girl', she'd always presented as something insubstantial. She had never altered in form, always her straggly hair hung over her features and down her narrow shoulders; her grubby dress was barely more than a translucent shift that skimmed her knees, so thin and worn it outlined the bones of her hips and thighs as shadows through the material. She was best observed from the corner of the eye, because when viewed straight on she tended to melt or streak away. There was something important she needed to convey to Kerry, but throughout the two decades and more since she'd first been around, the apparition had proved mute.

Kerry didn't stop the car; she held her gaze resolutely ahead. Girl observed the car's progress from the flooded pavement. In Kerry's periphery she grew more solid, her face tilting up, but if there were any features then she couldn't make them out and the reaction to glance at her forced her to fade. Only raindrops slanted across the pavement where Girl had just stood.

'Shit, Kerry, you're in enough trouble as it is. Don't start with this ghost stuff again,' she admonished herself.

Although the reinsertion of Girl into her life was worrying, she wasn't fearful of the wraith as such. She'd driven past her because there was no available parking spot outside her house. Arriving home from work earlier than Kerry, her fiancé Adam Gill's Ford Focus had taken the last spot. In their neighbourhood, on-street parking was at a premium, and only the richer residents could afford private parking bays. Kerry found a space at the end of a row of vehicles on Favart Road, at an entrance to Eel Brook Common, and had to walk the couple of blocks back home, her collar up and head tilted down. She welcomed the rain, and the early hour, because it meant there was nobody else abroad. The last she wished was to meet a neighbour and have to dart past them to avoid their questions, be they well meaning or critical. She'd endured enough of both since Erick Swain's fall from the roof of the tower block.

With two decent incomes, Kerry and Adam could afford to rent an entire house, two storeys and a dormer attic. It was at the end of a terrace of similar quaint houses, all painted in pastel shades, next to a modern red brick apartment block that lacked all charm. They even had a front garden, though it was barely large enough to contain a couple of planter boxes and a path to the front door that could be traversed with a single stride.

Before she got her key in the door Adam pulled it open. It was almost 2 a.m. and because he was on a fast rotation his next shift was due to begin at HMP Belmarsh in only five hours. He should have been asleep long ago. His lack of rest had aged him; his brown eyes enfolded in dark smudges and wrinkles, and under the overhead light the fine growth of stubble on his head twinkled silver. He was a big man, fit and strong, but his shoulders slumped as he greeted her. He was only thirty-four, two years Kerry's senior, but right then he could have been her father's age. She had never been happier to see him.

'You're back,' he stated the obvious. 'I'm glad. Are you OK, Kerry?'

'It hasn't been the best of days,' she said.

'C'mon, let's get you inside. You're bloody soaked through.'

He took her right hand, helped her step over the threshold, then reached past to close and lock the door.

His closeness, his warmth, and even the scent of him were comforting. She leaned against his chest, and he cupped her head and kissed her scuffed forehead. She allowed him to walk her to their living room and collapsed in an easy chair.

'Here, I thought you'd appreciate one of these.' Adam pushed a glass tumbler into her hands.

She looked down at it, and the amber liquid sloshing inside. The smell was distinctive. Whisky. She wasn't a big drinker, and preferred gin, but any port in a storm. And he was right; she did need a stiff drink. She downed it in one gulp, without savouring any of its nuances, and held out the glass for another shot.

Adam fetched the bottle and poured. She met his gaze until the glass was almost full to the rim, and then blinked.

'Should help you sleep,' Adam said as he placed down the bottle on their coffee table.

'You should be asleep.'

'What? You didn't think I'd wait up for you after you called me?'

'I only wanted you to know I'd be late home. So you didn't worry.'

He exhaled, then dropped into the settee opposite her, reaching for his spectacles from the coffee table. He was dressed in a frayed *Game Of Thrones* T-shirt and oatmeal jogging bottoms. Feet bare. Hairy toes, like a hobbit. There was a rumpled blanket under him, so maybe he'd been snoozing while he'd waited for her, the reason why he'd set aside his specs. He sloshed whisky into a glass, only a finger because he didn't want to smell of it at work. He nodded at the muted TV. 'I saw you on telly earlier...after you telephoned me.'

'I dread to ask what they were saying about me.'

'They were talking bollocks.'

'Could you be more specific?'

'They implied you might have helped him to jump.'

Swain had caused quite a mess when he'd hit the concrete paving, but there was little damage to his left arm, except for the deep, bloody gouges in his flesh where somebody had "used excessive force" on the rigid cuffs. Anyone would think she'd forced him off the parapet by the overzealous application of his restraints.

'Your boss didn't help matters,' Adam went on. 'What's Porter's problem with you anyway? Why didn't he stick up for you instead of announcing you were on administrative leave while he conducts a review of your actions? The arsehole. He as much as said you were being suspended on suspicion of murder.'

DCI Charles Porter had a job to do. Protecting the Met's reputation came first, and if that meant pushing one of his detectives under a bus then he was the one willing to give them a shove.

'Do you think I forced Swain off that roof?'

'If you did, then the bastard must've deserved it.'

Light-headed, Kerry set her untouched second whisky by her feet. 'That wasn't the answer I was hoping for, Adam.'

His mouth bunched up at one side. 'Yeah, well I didn't mean it the way it came out. All I'm saying is if Swain was pushed, then it was just desserts.'

'I didn't push him, though. We were struggling and he fell. He was trying to throw *me* over the edge, not the other way around.'

Adam also set his drink aside, so that he could cross the room and go down on his knees before her. He grabbed both her hands in his, squeezing them with each word. 'I know you didn't, Kerry. But if you did, then I for one wouldn't blame you.'

'Jesus Christ.' Heat built in her throat, expanded into her skull like a mushroom cloud. She extricated her hands from his. 'A little support wouldn't go amiss, Adam.'

He reared back on his knees, hands spread. 'I'm on

your side.'

'But even you think I'd something to do with Swain's death. Where does that leave me when I've a chief inspector looking for a scapegoat?'

'He'll have to prove you pushed him, won't he? But there were no other witnesses?'

'There was a uniform there, too, but he was knocked out and didn't see a thing.'

'There you go then!' Adam grinned conspiratorially. 'If it's your word against Swain's, dead men tell no tales.'

She pushed up abruptly from the chair. 'For God's sake, Adam!'

He grasped for her, but she swiped his hands aside and lunged for the door. Her glass went spinning, sloshing whisky over the carpet. 'Oh, bloody hell! Look at—'

She bent to retrieve the glass, touched instead the sopping mess.

'Leave it, Kerry. I'll sort it.'

'I've got it myself. I don't need you—'

'Kerry. Come on. You're tired, you're—'

'I'm bloody disappointed! I thought of all people you'd be on my side.'

'I am on your side.' He knelt, reaching for the glass. Before he could pick it up, Kerry snatched it. He looked up at her. She glared down at him, her usually mismatched eyes uniform in their sadness. 'Jesus, Kerry, I'm sorry, OK? I don't think for one second you *deliberately* killed him...'

'You're not bloody helping! Not when *everybody else thinks I did!*' She stormed into the kitchen. The empty glass clattered in the sink. Kerry was back instantly with a tea towel in one hand, a roll of absorbent kitchen paper in the other. 'Get out the way. I'll do it.'

'Just give me the cloths. I'm already down here.' It was true; he hadn't made an effort to stand. As if by hemming it in he could stop the spread of the liquid through the carpet pile.

'I said, *I'll do it!*' Kerry pushed into him, and he only gave a little. She lowered to one knee, throwing down the towel. 'Shift, Adam, I'm in no mood for this.'

He didn't go away, he embraced her. She resisted, but he persisted, and strength flooded out of her. She almost collapsed over his knee, and he flopped back, drawing her with him away from the spillage. He ended up with his back against the settee and Kerry in his lap. He cupped her head to his shoulder, held her while she sobbed. She formed fists against his wide chest. Before making them she'd dug her nails into his flesh. Adam didn't flinch, or complain. He'd been an insensitive prick and deserved the discomfort.

If asked to explain her emotions, Kerry couldn't because they were conflicted. Swain's death — whether or not it was her fault — was still on her conscience. He was a vile, violent, racist thug, but still. She felt no pity for him, but was sorry he'd died. Her heart went out to the mother and child murdered because of the ridiculous dick-measuring contest Swain was involved in with Jermaine Robson. Erick Swain's premature death meant there would be no real justice for Nala and Bilan Ghedi and that wasn't right. For killing them, especially the child, he shouldn't have got an easy way out: he should've been left to rot in prison the rest of his stinking life. As soon as she was old enough, Kerry had joined the police for one reason: to get justice for Sally. By proxy any child harmed on her watch was a failing in the very thing she'd set out to do.

Erick Swain was Bilan Ghedi's Fell Man. Perhaps she deserved criticism for her mishandling of the arrest. If anyone knew how desperately she wanted to bring him to trial and watch him imprisoned for the rest of his days, they'd know she would have done everything to pull him back onto the roof. But she was blinded, stunned from his blows, and fighting for her own life at the time. Maybe if she'd fought harder…

She had no recollection of when Adam helped her to stand, or led her upstairs to the bathroom.

'Here. Let's get you out of those wet clothes,' he said, and began teasing her jacket off her shoulder. 'Have yourself a warm shower; it'll make you feel better. Then you can come to bed.'

Down to her underwear, she stood numbly as he reached inside the shower and turned it on. The patter of water reminded her of the rain on her car's windscreen as she'd arrived home — how long ago now? She glanced towards the open door to the landing, noticed a shifting of the shadows, as if someone small and silent had ducked away to avoid being spotted. She shivered and it wasn't because of the cool air on her bared skin.

'I'll take it from here,' she whispered.

'I was just going to—'

She stopped him with her fingernails resting on his cheek. Stared at him, imparting the seriousness of her words. 'I need some privacy, Adam. Close the door on your way out.'

His features tightened, and he exhaled sharply. Typical man, he'd thought he could turn her need for comfort to satisfying a need of his own.

'You take our bed, I'll have the settee,' she said. 'I don't think I'm going to be able to sleep tonight, and you have to be up for work soon.'

'You don't have to take the settee; I'm OK, I can get by on only a couple of hours…'

'Adam. Please. When I asked for some privacy…'

Now his entire frame tightened. Without comment he turned and stepped out onto the landing. But then he leaned back into the bathroom, his hand on the door handle. 'You know something, Kerry? Maybe you should look at this suspension another way. Use it as some thinking time; ask yourself if this is really the job for you, because it's getting to you in a way I don't like.'

'Really?' She tilted her head on one side, her vision sharper now. 'Well, Adam, it isn't all about you I'm afraid.'

'Yeah! That's my bloody point!' Before she could respond, he yanked the door shut and stomped downstairs cursing. Even over the patter of water she caught the words "obsessed about finding Sally".

She made sure the door was fully closed, and for good measure slid across the small brass bolt into its holder. It was the first time she'd used it since moving in with Adam. It was nothing to do with keeping him out, but everything about protection from other eyes. Not that a closed door had ever proven a barrier to Girl before.

When she entered the cubicle, slid down the wall, and hunkered under the spray from the showerhead hugging her knees, she was still dressed in her underwear.

1997

As it happened, their mother's urgency to reach Penrith railway station before their dad's arrival turned into a longer wait than she'd anticipated. A freight train had suffered mechanical failure in the valley below Shap, and dad's train held at Oxenholme for the line to be cleared. A railway station wasn't a safe place for two energetic girls to play, so she took them over the road to the grounds of the crumbling 14th century castle, built to defend the town from marauding bands of Scots. The girls had finished the picnic she'd put together when they'd stopped to play earlier, so before leaving the station she bought cartons of orange Kia-Ora and bags of cheese Quavers from a kiosk. They ate and drank sitting on the grass outside the castle walls, with the sound of traffic buzzing past on Ullswater Road. Finished their snacks, and boundless with energy, Siobhan allowed the girls to explore the ruins, with an explicit warning to stay clear of the road and *not to climb on the walls*. To Kerry, that was as good as adding petrol to a fire, and ignited her. She was off at a gallop conjuring knights and princesses and dragons in her fertile imagination. Fretting that she'd get them both in trouble, Sally followed her kid sister closely, hissing and prodding when the little tomboy got too close to anything remotely recognisable as sandstone. Sitting under grey, but thankfully dry skies, Siobhan grasped the few minutes' peace by burying her nose in a dog-eared Patricia Cornwell novel she'd picked up from a charity shop weeks ago and hadn't got round to finishing yet.

She could hear Kerry sword fencing imaginary ogres, and Sally primly attempting not to join in with the uncool fantasy, and becoming the target of Kerry's magic sword as a result. The girls giggled and chased, then giggled and chased some more. Soon their tinkling laughter and drumming feet became background noise along with the throaty grumble of engines, reedy tannoy announcements from the station, and the squawks of gulls fighting over fish and chip wrappers plundered from a dustbin, while Siobhan grew engrossed in the gory details of a post mortem being conducted under Kay Scarpetta's scalpel.

A single drop of moisture tapped Siobhan's wrist. Another dampened a tiny patch on her open page. She looked up, mouth open in dismay. The sky had turned to steel. Wind tugged at her. Siobhan marked her page by turning down a corner, and stood, shoving away her book into her handbag. An empty Quavers packet somersaulted past, caught on the breeze. She should have chased it, binned it, but already it was dancing out of reach. She was a country girl, and loathed litterbugs, but why have a puppy and bark yourself? She looked for Kerry, the obvious culprit, about to chase her after her crisp bag and put it in a bin. But then rain lashed down, and her shout to Kerry was for another reason.

Kerry charged over, wellington boots chugging through instantly soaked grass. Her face was screwed tightly, eyelids pinched against the solid raindrops peppering her, and her hands were filthy with dirt. The shoulders of her sweatshirt were damp.

'Where's your coat?' Siobhan demanded.

'It's in the car. I took it off before we got here.'

Siobhan clucked her tongue. 'Where's Sally?'

Kerry scanned back the way she'd just come from. 'Looking at something boring. She didn't want to play anymore, and went to read an old sign in there.'

'In the ruins?'

Kerry shrugged. 'I was with my friend digging for worms.'

Siobhan didn't react to her announcement, digging for worms and playing with imaginary friends were daily activities for Kerry. 'Go and give Sally a shout. Tell her to come now.'

Her puppy wasn't prepared to bark: with a whine Kerry buried herself between her knees, arms wrapped round her thighs. She grabbed Kerry's hand so she wouldn't stray, and headed to where a wooden bridge allowed access across the moat to the ruined castle. Both of them went bent over, the rain now battering their hair flat.

The castle hadn't fared well over the turbulent centuries, and now little remained beyond a fortified wall, and the remains of a couple of towers. Most of the castle's structure had been reduced to the foundations. There were few places to hide in its interior, although as they entered, there was some sort of ruined archway off to their right. It was the obvious place for Sally to shelter. Except a few strides in that direction told Siobhan her daughter wasn't inside. She scanned the rest of the ruins, and though some of the walls were tall enough to conceal a hunkered down child, she doubted Sally would hide. Kerry would have, but not her conscientious sister.

'Sally?' The hammering rain almost deadened Siobhan's voice. She hollered louder. 'Sally? Where are you? Come here now!'

Kerry stood mute, with rain dripping off her nose and her teeth clamped.

'Where was she last time you saw her?' Siobhan demanded.

'I was pretend-digging over there.' Kerry pointed in a random direction near to where she'd been playing. 'And Sally came in here to read the sign, but I wasn't interested in boring history stuff.'

There was a plaque on a wooden pedestal near the castle's entrance, relating its potted history. There was no hint Sally had ever been there. She grabbed Kerry tighter, and dragged her through the ruins, ducking, and stretching to see over, around and under any obstructions large enough to conceal a sylph-like ten-year-old girl. Sally wasn't in the ruins. They exited through a wide gap in the walls and on to the grassy embankment that overlooked the adjacent park. There was a bowling green, a few picnic tables, and a tennis court — all deserted in the teeming rain. Siobhan's anger was overtaken by mild concern, then by throat-clenching anxiety. Calling Sally's name repeatedly, louder and more high-pitched each time, she hauled Kerry along as she followed the decrepit walls back towards the grounds adjacent to the railway station. But her desperate wish that Sally had somehow followed another route back unseen was unrewarded. Sally wasn't there.

Had she crossed the main road and returned to the car in the station's car park? If she had, Sally was in for a bollocking, but also a hug of relief. Toting her bag, and towing along Kerry, Siobhan darted for the safest crossing at a point where three roads converged at a mini-roundabout. She checked the roads leading downhill to the market town. Sally wouldn't have wandered into town. Penrith wasn't exactly a metropolis, but Sally was a country kid the opposite of streetwise. To her any urbanization larger than a village was a scary concrete jungle. Siobhan caught a break in the traffic, and she grabbed Kerry and ran across the road, already craning to check the gaps between cars parked outside the station. Her five-year-old Vauxhall Cavalier was hidden from view by a white Transit van belonging to a local window cleaner. She charged around the van, bleating for Sally.

Their car was locked. Sally wasn't inside, and hadn't taken shelter nearby. If she'd returned to the car and found it locked, she could have ducked inside the station when the rain started. Still dragging Kerry she charged inside through the entrance and onto the platform, head spinning as she checked each direction. By now there was little volume to her croaks of alarm. She searched the waiting room, and the public toilets in seconds. Clutched by panic she rushed back out to the car park. By then she'd attracted the attention of one of the platform attendants. 'Summat the matter, lass?'

'My daughter,' Siobhan croaked, as if it should already be obvious. The man gave Kerry a confused look, which Kerry returned.

'My *other* daughter!' Siobhan screeched. 'She's missing!'

The attendant then did a full three hundred and sixty degree turn, all the while with no real idea of whom he was seeking.

'She's not here. She's *gone*.' Siobhan grabbed Kerry's hand tighter, terrified her second child would disappear as resolutely as the first.

'OK, lass, don't worry,' said the man. 'She can't have gone far. We'll find her.'

'I have to keep looking,' said Siobhan, and strode away. Kerry scuttled alongside her.

'Wait,' the man called out. 'We should call the police. Come back inside out of the rain. We've a direct line to the BT police...'

Siobhan halted. She was desperate to continue the search, but the more people looking for Sally the sooner she'd be found and safe with her mam again. She turned back to him, jaw quivering, her eyes pools of desperation. Behind her a battered old Land Rover puttered as it picked up speed, heading out along Ullswater Road.

Only Kerry noticed the vehicle. Its bearded driver grinned when she caught his eye. Kerry didn't like his grin, his teeth were big and yellow, and his friendliness didn't extend beyond his tightly bowed lips. Standing there, water sluicing from her, Kerry watched the old four-by-four recede, concealed by the falling rain and blue smoke belching from its exhaust. For a moment, she fancied that a rag of fumes hung in the air over the road, and it took on the form of a straggly-haired girl that stared with as much discomfort after the Land Rover, before the battering rain dissolved her.

In a huff, Adam had gone to work by the time Kerry finally vacated the bathroom. She'd deliberately waited him out, even when he'd knocked at the door needing access to the loo and to his toothbrush. She hadn't unlocked the bolt, so he'd stomped downstairs again, and she assumed he'd taken a pee in the backyard or he'd held it in and driven to work cross-legged. He deserved the discomfort, after being such an insensitive prick earlier. In hindsight, Adam had only tried to be supportive, but he'd gone about it the wrong way. Whether or not Swain had got what was coming to him, she didn't want Adam to commend her for his murder; she needed reassurance he'd never believe the accusation she was under.

She'd huddled under the pelting shower until the water turned cold, miserable. When she began shivering violently, her teeth clamped so tightly her jaw hurt, she struggled up and turned off the shower. Draped in a towel, she sat with the lid down on the toilet. In the shower she'd replayed the memories from her childhood — the day both the Fell Man and Girl entered her life and changed it forever — but as she sat hugging herself under the towel, she turned over yesterday's events on the rooftop, wondering what she could have done differently. Each replay ended with her standing over the steaming corpse of Erick Swain, with anger threatening to engulf her because another innocent girl had been denied the justice she deserved.

It was Sally's disappearance that led Kerry down the path to where she was now. Sally wasn't only her big sister, she was her best friend, and when she had been taken, the Fell Man also snatched a large chunk of Kerry's heart. It was a void very difficult to fill, and to this day there was a hollow spot where Sally should be. As an eight-year-old Kerry had sought comfort in a pantheon of imaginary friends, and yet the one she most wanted to lean on remained a silent, intangible companion. As she aged, the other imaginary friends fell by the wayside, and yet Girl — as Kerry christened her — was always around. Occasionally she'd come closer when Kerry was at her lowest ebb, to stand beside her with her head hanging in combined sorrow.

Her mam didn't offer much solace. Siobhan Darke blamed herself for Sally's disappearance, and so did their dad, Gary. They argued frequently — and sometimes things other than curses and accusations were thrown — and when they did it was to Kerry's exclusion. She would retreat to a private place, her room, or one of the barns on their property, with Girl keeping her silent company.

When she first mentioned Girl to her parents, her announcement was greeted by the sad smiles of indulgence of adults who thought they'd more to worry about. But when she persisted, their mild tolerance became disdain, then frustration, and shortly after she was the one being screamed at by both parties. Soon Girl was the only person not shouting at her, and Kerry spent more time with the silent phantom than was healthy for any child. When her obsession was finally recognised, her next stop was to Ronald Dawson's office, and he became her child psychologist. Doctor "call me Ron" Dawson reassured her parents that Girl was simply a manifestation of Kerry's grief, a coping mechanism on which she could draw the strength to get over the loss of her sister. Siobhan and Gary accepted his assertion that Girl was an imaginary proxy version of Sally, and Kerry made them none the wiser. The silent waif was not her sister, even if Kerry wished very hard that she were. Obvious mental health issues were ruled out to her parents' relief, and Doctor Ron prescribed regular grief counselling sessions with their daughter, where she'd be encouraged to accept and come to terms with her loss, at which point he was confident she'd move on, and leave such coping mechanisms as "Girl" behind. He was a gentle soul, kind and caring and Kerry had no desire to cause him difficulty, so she played along. By the time she was twelve, and on the cusp of teenage rebellion, she agreed with him that Girl was unreal, and had permanently been put behind her — all the while avoiding checking out the response of the bowed translucent figure in the corner of his office. The lie had come easy to her lips. Over the past four years she'd been party to similar lies made to each other by her parents. Not long after Kerry's final session with her psychologist, her dad abandoned them.

Mam blamed herself for his desertion.

Kerry didn't.

Her dad was supposedly so destroyed by the abduction of his oldest daughter that he was prepared to lose his wife and youngest daughter too? She didn't believe it. When she learned that dad had taken up with another woman, and she was pregnant with a half-sibling, Kerry accepted that he wasn't coming home. Perhaps her mam was slightly to blame — not for Sally's disappearance — because if she was as much of a cold fish to her dad as to everyone else, then it was inevitable that he had sought intimacy in the arms of another woman. It was laughable that Kerry sought similar attention from an invisible friend and was scoffed at by her parents, but hers was the lesser evil when compared to what Gary and Siobhan Darke tried to plug their Sally-shaped holes with. Dad took on a surrogate family, while Mam tried to fill hers with copious amounts of alcohol and prescription drugs.

With Dad gone and Mam barely capable of looking after herself, they couldn't keep the small farm that had been in Siobhan's family for generations; their mortgagors snatched it from under them as adroitly as the Fell Man had snatched Sally from the castle grounds.

By the time Kerry was fourteen she was totally out of her depth, living on a run down council estate in Carlisle's west end, and going to "big school" alongside fifteen hundred other kids, some from even poorer families than hers. She could have easily fallen by the wayside, embraced the behaviour and culture of some of her peers and gone lawless. But Kerry went the other direction entirely. Latching onto Girl was an indicator of her obsessive nature, and so was her intention to become a police officer.

In the intervening years Sally had never been found, dead or alive. Neither had another six girls also believed to have become victims of the serial abductor — and probably killer — that the press had dubbed the Fell Man. Their nickname for the child snatcher hadn't been as sinister as the local name they stole it from: they thought the Lakeland fells were evocative of his hunting grounds, and had a similar ring to it as the Moors Murderers on whose notoriety they could sell papers, but that wasn't the true source. The hills or high moorland referred to as fells in northern England took their name from the Old Norse *fjall* and bore no relationship to the name of the Cumbrian bogeyman. Fell, in his case, was used literally in its archaic Middle English sense, depicting something of "terrible evil or ferocity", and was related to the Old French word *fel*, the nominative of felon or wicked person.

The Fell Man was never identified, and obviously never caught, and it was assumed he either gave up his crimes, was imprisoned for unrelated offences, changed his *modus operandi* or he died. As other crimes shook the country, and the world in regard to 9/11, the unsolved abduction and killing spree was relegated to the cold files as the shape of modern policing changed to suit. But Kerry never let the case of her missing sister rest, although Girl visited less frequently than before, until finally Kerry barely noticed that she'd all but gone entirely. She joined Cumbria Constabulary, and was soon standing on full uniform parade at Hutton Police Training Centre near Preston, alongside other recruits from Greater Manchester and Lancashire Constabularies. There she told one of her tutors her reason for joining the police was to help those in need, and he'd contritely told her, 'No, PC Darke. Your duty's to uphold the Queen's law.' It was probably best that she hadn't admitted she'd joined up with the sole purpose of catching and punishing the Fell Man. To what end? Another fell man had escaped justice after killing a child, and her career was in serious jeopardy. And all she could do was sit there in wet underwear, huddled under a damp towel, waiting for the axe to drop.

A telephone rang.

It startled her out of the past.

She'd made it to her living room. It smelled of spilled whisky and Adam. His blankets were tussled on the settee, and so were his discarded T-shirt and joggers. She couldn't see her handbag containing her mobile, but thought she'd carried it up to the bathroom with her when Adam helped her upstairs. It was the landline that was ringing. Nobody she knew personally rang her landline, and for a second she feared that it was the press, attempting to get a quote from her they could twist out of proportion to suit their hysterical headlines. She was tempted to ignore it, but the phone kept ringing.

Pulling the towel around her, she padded to the kitchen where the phone was on a cradle on the wall. If it was a reporter calling, they could go to hell.

'Hello,' she said cagily.

'Mornin', boss.'

'Danny,' she responded. 'What're you doing calling me on my private phone?'

'Well, seeing as you ain't picked up on your mobile, or answered any of my texts, I thought you were maybe ignoring me. Tell you the truth, boss? I expected Adam to pick up, not you.'

'Adam left early for work.' She didn't add that he'd left earlier than usual, to avoid a second argument when she finally dragged herself from the bathroom. 'I was, uh, in the shower. I didn't hear my mobile.'

'Sorry if I dragged you outta the shower...'

Kerry was suddenly self-conscious. Speaking with Korba while semi-naked was almost tantamount to illicit behaviour, and she cringed at the images he might be formulating in his mind. Despite her landline being routed through a bog standard, technologically ancient press button phone, she rearranged the towel modestly.

'No, I've been up a while now, just thinking of having some breakfast.' Only the latter was a lie, so she carried it off. 'I guess today's going to be a long one and I'll need the extra energy.'

'Yeah. You ain't blooming wrong, boss. Are the news cameras outside your house yet?'

'I haven't checked,' Kerry said.

'If they're not there yet, it's only a matter of time.'

'Fucking vultures,' she growled.

'Yeah, they're that, but this time they're on your side, girl.' Korba checked himself. 'Uh, sorry, I mean *boss*.'

Kerry couldn't give a shit about his lapse in formal etiquette. She was more intrigued by what he meant by the media being on her side. Last night when she'd finally left the council estate crowds had already gathered, shouting foul and making accusations of police brutality and excessive use of force, and if anything the presence of the news cameras had made them more vocal. She'd expected social unrest by this morning, even localized rioting. Her silence prompted Korba to fill the gap.

'I take it Porter ain't managed to contact you yet?'

'No. Like I said, I was in the shower and didn't hear my phone...' She didn't go on, because it had struck her that there was a faint hint of triumph in Korba's question. 'What has happened, Danny?'

'Put it this way, ol' Porter's gonna have to eat humble pie 'cause of the way he handled this one.'

'Jesus, Danny, will you just tell me what you're going on about?'

'The camera never lies, does it? Well, hear this.' He chuckled to himself. 'You've become an Internet sensation overnight, Kerry. Some kid videoed you tryin' to arrest Swain on the rooftop and caught everything. How, despite Swain knockin' seven bells out of you, you tried to stop him escapin', and that bastard tried to chuck you off the roof. If he wasn't tryin' so hard to kill you, he wouldn't have tripped over his own feet and fallen to his death. Poetic justice, eh? Some scummy kid tryin' to make a few quid off monetizing his video on YouTube has exonerated you instead.'

Kerry recalled the boy with the smart phone she'd met on the landing. He must have followed her up to the roof and filmed her showdown with Swain, and took off before the first SC019 officer arrived. 'It shows I didn't force Swain off the roof?'

'It shows exactly what happened. He was tryin' his hardest to force you over the side, you had hold of his cuff and fell to the floor, and then he kind of…I dunno, he lost it and took a dive off the roof.'

'What do you mean by lost it?'

'Lost the plot, went ape shit. He was kicking and punching you, and god knows what else, then it was as if he lost his balance and took the long tumble. You're bein' hailed the right little hero, ain't ya!'

'I don't feel like a hero.'

'Ha! You will by the time you make Porter pucker up and kiss your arse…' Again Korba checked himself. 'Uh, figuratively speaking, boss.'

'Of course,' she said, and laughed. It was the first time she'd felt anything approaching genuine humour since before responding to Wandsworth Road the previous day.

'So will you be in today?' Korba ventured.

'That's down to DCI Porter.'

'Don't worry. I bet you he'll be on the blower in no time. You should come in and beat him to it. Let him know how much of a prick he was last night. Flaming jobsworth, he should've known better than treat you like that.'

'He was only following procedure, Danny.'

'Kerry, we're off the record, ain't we? So you're talking to me, your ol' mate, Danny Boy. You don't have to defend Porter when he made sure he chucked you under a bus to protect his own fat arse.'

'Yeah, you're probably right. But he had no option.'

'Yeah. We both know the score, Kerry. But Porter didn't have to make it so flaming obvious he thought you were guilty. If that kid wasn't up late on a school night, things might've turned out dodgy for you, especially when your commanding officer was in your opposite corner.'

'Huh,' said Kerry, 'you said I was being hailed as a hero, but I bet I'm not even flavour of the month with the DCI, right now.'

'So what's new there, eh? Anyhow, it might work in your favour. Maybe he'll be keener to green light that transfer you requested to the Murder Squad.'

'Detective Sergeant Korba,' she mock-scolded. 'If I didn't know better, I'd say you were trying to get rid of me.'

'Not me, Kerry.' She could almost picture Korba glancing around furtively, checking he wasn't being overheard, which happened to be a bit too late now. 'If you go, I'll be puttin' in a transfer request of my own. The job here just wouldn't be the same without you.'

'I think that's the nicest thing you've ever said to me, Danny,' she said, genuinely touched by his sincerity.

'Nah,' he said, 'what I meant was I wouldn't get away with half the bollocks I do with a different boss.'

He hung up before she had chance to reply, and perhaps it was best. Kerry could feel warmth in her cheeks. And it was only partly due to being exonerated of killing Swain. Had Danny Korba just flirted with her?

She went to dress, anticipating a return to work sooner than had seemed possible less than a quarter hour earlier. But she couldn't resist the pull of her computer. She logged on to a video-sharing site.

10

Detective Chief Inspector Charles Porter was a career copper. He was the type who always had an eye on the next rung up the ladder, and without any major stumbling blocks he was in line for promotion to Acting Superintendent of Gangs and Organised Crime, with a view to replacing the current Supt, Sandy Tinsley, when she shuffled off to the golf course or country club or wherever retired superintendents spent their golden years. Last night's unfortunate event was a possible stumbling block in his career path, a treacherous one indeed if it was mismanaged. He'd taken positive action to control the Erick Swain situation, diverting damaging accusations of unlawful killing away from the Metropolitan Police Service and onto one maverick inspector who could take the heat on their behalf. His impromptu sound bite to the press was designed to pacify the populace, the media and his superiors, but now he regretted the sanctimonious tone he'd taken when condemning Kerry Darke to the metaphorical firing squad. He'd dropped her in the shit, but she'd come up smelling of...not roses, but sweet satisfaction at his expense, all the same.

A video of her violent struggle with Swain had surfaced within an hour of DCI Porter's appearance on the news, and had gone viral on the social networks. Swain was the obvious aggressor, and his rage had looked blind when kicking and swiping at something that only partially included Darke, until he'd twisted away and lunged madly off the parapet to escape his imaginary attacker. The video's content negated the poorly concealed indictment he'd aimed at Darke, and made him look a complete fool. He'd appeared again on the news this morning, refuting everything he'd insinuated the night before in a single garbled response to the quick-fire questions hurled at him from a pack of reporters gathered outside the nick. He had employed double-negatives, obfuscation, party-line political mumbo jumbo, and sycophantic praise of the "courageous action taken by a valued member of my team in attempting to apprehend a violent criminal suspected in the shooting of an innocent mother and child, and to protect a fallen colleague without concern for her own safety or well being". It was quite a mouthful when he could barely work up the spit to unglue his tongue from the roof of his mouth. Maybe he'd have been convincing if he'd been sincere in his praise and made an apology. He'd watched the news feed in his office later and even he didn't believe a single word of it. It was time for damage control.

Seated opposite him in his office, DI Darke waited.

If she expected him to say sorry, she might be surprised.

'Before we begin,' Porter said, 'I'd like to remind you that you can have another colleague present, or if you wish, a Police Federation representative.'

'Will this be an official interview under caution?' Kerry responded.

'No. It's not an interview. Think of this more as a debriefing.'

'So I don't want or need either.'

Porter's feelings towards Kerry weren't personal. But he could tell from the steady glare of her odd eyes, the way her mouth was pulled fractionally to one side, the feeling wasn't mutual.

'That's fine then. I think it's best we put the unfortunate events of yesterday behind us and both move on from this a little wiser.' He sat back in his creaking leather chair, unbuttoning his jacket for freedom of movement. His shirt rucked up and his tie sat askew. 'I've spoken to Superintendent Tinsley, and it's our decision that your suspension is rescinded as of now and you can return to active duty.'

Kerry said nothing, but her mouth reset nearer the centre.

'I trust you're happy with our decision, Inspector Darke?'

'How much of the decision-making process were you involved in?'

'Pardon?'

'Was it your decision to reinstate me or did you just follow orders, sir?'

'I don't see why my input into the decision should be questioned. If you're asking if I'm genuinely happy that you're back, then I won't lie. I had my misgivings about your reinstatement until a full IPCC investigation and review of your actions had been completed, and your attitude now isn't doing anything to help assuage them. You sound as if you're displeased with the decision to allow you back so soon.'

Kerry shook her head. 'I'm not displeased. I'm only sorry I'm in a position where I have to be *reinstated*.'

'Well,' said Porter, removing his spectacles and placing them on his desk. 'If you expect an apology from me, it won't be forthcoming. I followed procedure, you didn't, Inspector Darke.'

'I was chasing a violent offender who'd already injured four of my colleagues; following procedure wasn't exactly the first thing on my mind.' She snorted. 'There wasn't an opportunity to conduct a dynamic risk assessment.'

'You were chasing a violent offender who you'd allowed to escape through your mishandling of his arrest,' Porter reminded her. 'Look, let's dispense with formality, Kerry. Before you get defensive, I'll remind you that I was a beat officer before I was a supervisor. I know how things are in the real world. The best plans and strategies work only until a third party refuses to play by the same rules. I've been there when things have kicked off, and what should've been a simple arrest degenerated into a full-on brawl. If I was the senior investigating officer conducting Swain's arrest, I can't swear that I'd have done anything different than you did. But that's beside the point. I'd expect to be criticised after everything went to pot. Kerry, a man died during a police pursuit, and unfortunately, as SIO, the buck had to stop with you.'

'As the senior investigating officer, if I'd been given an opportunity to give you a full report of the incident first, you might have handled the press more candidly.' Kerry stared at him again.

Porter retrieved his glasses, and fumbled them on. 'I handled the press the best way I saw fit under the circumstances.'

'By throwing me to the wolves?'

'It had to be done; we were facing growing civil unrest. Despite the fact Swain was hated, some of those living on that estate hate *us* more. They were looking for a reason to kick off, so I took it away from them.'

'You made them hate me more than they hated the police service? Wow! At least you haven't tried sugar-coating things.'

'You should know me by now, Kerry. I say it as it is, and I tell the truth. I place high value on personal integrity, in me and in those serving under me.'

'It's just a shame you don't place a similar value on loyalty.'

DCI Porter leaned on his elbows, his face looming across the desk like a flushed moon. 'Steady on, Inspector. I offered to dispense with formality, but that isn't to say I'll tolerate insubordination. Don't make me regret agreeing to having you back...I could soon turn things round again.'

Kerry raised both hands. 'I'm sorry, sir. But you must imagine how I felt being hung out to dry like that?'

He grunted, sat back again and undid another button. 'I'm sure you're professional enough to get over it,

Kerry. And I don't expect it to have a detrimental effect on your results, either. You have active cases on-going and I'd like updates on where you are with them all before the end of shift.'

He'd said his piece, and allowed Kerry hers, even if he'd largely brushed off her opinion. Now he was dismissing her. Kerry didn't take the hint.

'Was there something else?' he asked.

Kerry wormed uncomfortably on her chair. Then coming to a conclusion she met his stare. 'Sir, I get the feeling that you don't like me.'

'I don't think we need get personal,' he said.

'OK. But that means you don't respect me, or value me as a member of your team. I've a suggestion that could solve the problem. I'd like you to reconsider my transfer request to Homicide and Major Crimes.'

'I don't need to like you to recognise your abilities as an investigator,' he countered. 'Despite what you think of me, I *do* appreciate what you bring to my team. But—' he held up one finger '—as your supervisor I'm bound to hear your request. Put it in an email to me and I'll consider it.'

Kerry was under no illusion what he meant. He'd consider her transfer request, and promptly refuse it. He watched as disappointment sunk in, her chin falling, until she was staring at her hands in her lap.

'If that's all then...' Porter said, prompting her to get back to work.

Her head came up, and her mismatched gaze danced a moment over his features, while her teeth nipped at her bottom lip. Suddenly she focussed on a point slightly above and beyond his left shoulder, and startled, she yelped and threw her weight back in the chair. Her mouth and eyes made similar ovals and her head quivered.

Porter glanced over his shoulder. All he could see was his faint shadow and a certificate of commendation hanging on the office wall: he'd received it while still in uniform from the then Police Commissioner, and the certificate took pride of place. He looked sharply at her, and found Kerry on her feet, poised to run.

'What on earth's wrong with you?'

'Uh, nothing, sir,' Kerry said. Her voice was brittle. 'I just got a cramp.' She rubbed her right thigh vigorously, but it was an act. 'Excuse me...' she croaked, and was out of the door within two seconds. She didn't look back.

DCI Porter did. He turned and lingered over the area that had alarmed her and saw nothing...though there was something unusual about the atmosphere. Something weird. The short hairs prickled on the back of his neck.

She splashed cold water on her face, and rubbed furiously. Then, still dripping, Kerry gripped the edge of the sink, supporting her weight on braced elbows. Her reflection in the vanity mirror looked as rough as she felt. These days she wore her dark auburn hair short, but it still looked unkempt and stood up in tufts – throwing water at the problem hadn't helped. Her forehead was scuffed. She had a good excuse for her reddened sclera, and pale skin: except for zoning out for a few minutes under the shower in the early hours, she hadn't slept in the past thirty-or-so hours. But fatigue wasn't the cause for her red glare or pallor. *What the hell did I just see in Porter's office?*

As a child, when first informing her parents about *seeing things*, they'd worried that her heterochromia was affecting her eyesight. As a matter of course she'd been checked for neoplasm, where the melanomas can be lightly pigmented and the cause of an affected eye being paler than the other, but there was no sign of tumour or other abnormality beyond the lack of pigmentation. Her eyesight wasn't affected, but she'd since wondered if it allowed her to see into spectrums of light beyond the norm. She couldn't; she didn't have superhuman vision. What she had supposedly been seeing was "corner of the eye phenomena": a mote of dust or floater, sometimes even a swollen blood vessel in the orbit itself, taking on an unfocused shape in the peripheral vision as the muscles around the eyes tired. Whenever she saw Girl, she usually formed indirectly, and always fled or disappeared when viewed dead on. The thing looming over Porter's shoulder was different.

What at first she took for Porter's shadow grew denser. More shocking: the shadow moved independently of him. As crazy as it now sounded it was as if the shadow lunged at her – startling her enough to elicit a yelp and for her to scrape back her chair. Porter must have thought she was insane!

His prognosis might be right. But she'd rather find an explanation she was happier with. Hallucinations were a symptom of sleep deprivation and combined with the stress she'd suffered in the past day it was little wonder she'd fallen victim. She'd imagined that the figure lunged at her, and had conjured up details that weren't present in Porter's shadow. Surely her stretched nerves had added the wavy hair, and the rigid handcuff standing proud from the wrist of the hand that snatched at her. Considered rationally, the incident shouldn't be as alarming. She could put it behind her. So why the bloody hell was she still jittery with fear?

She challenged her mind to concoct spectres to appear in the mirror. There was nothing reflected behind her except for the institutional blue doors of toilet stalls. Relieved, she dragged out a handful of paper towels from the dispenser, and practically rubbed her cheeks raw, but tentative of her forehead where Swain had struck her. She dumped the wad of damp towels in a bin, just as the washroom door banged open. A sturdy young woman bustled in, unclipping her utility belt even before she reached a stall. Instantly recognising Kerry, the woman stumbled to a halt.

It was the same constable who'd delivered Funky Adefunke's demands yesterday. Kerry offered her a sharp nod.

'That was a bad show,' the woman said.

Kerry wasn't sure if she referred to the shootings, Swain falling off the tower, or the fact Kerry had been blamed for his death. Perhaps she meant all.

'It was a *terrible* show,' she replied.

The woman regarded her for a second longer, then nodded, and scuttled for the furthest away toilet cubicle.

Kerry left the washroom with equal haste. As she walked between rows of lockers two constables bantered together as they stripped off their protective kit, falling silent when they spotted her. As soon as she was out in the corridor she'd be the subject of discussion. Who knew what bollocks had already been spoken about her, but she'd bet there'd be more to come. Glossy celebrity magazines had nothing on police stations when it came to lurid gossip.

CID kept separate offices to the uniformed teams in the police station, and being a specialist branch, Gangs and Organised Crime had an office distinct from their other plain-clothed colleagues. It wasn't a case of preferential treatment, and they hadn't been afforded any extra space or comfort, the GaOC office was as stark and utilitarian as all the others. Because of the delicate nature of the intelligence shared in the room, it was a closed-door office, air-less and stuffy, with no natural light. Even in winter it was necessary to run fans to keep the place cool. The room always stank like a teenager's training shoe. The unpleasant odour had been added to; last night somebody had brought in their supper and the room was rank with the aroma of cold, greasy fried onions and burger meat. DS Korba was the first detective she spotted, and she wondered if the stench was coming off him. But who was she to criticise? Korba hadn't got to go home yet; he'd been left to pick up the pieces after DCI Porter dismissed her from the scene of Swain's death. He hadn't slept in thirty-or-so hours either, but you wouldn't know it from his beaming grin and clear gaze as he greeted her. He shot towards her, and for a second she thought he was going to hug her. She wouldn't unwelcome the sentiment, but Korba halted a foot from her. He made a half turn on his heel, and announced to the others in the room. 'Hey, you lot. D'you mind being upstanding for the hero of the hour?'

Three detective constables worked under her and Korba's supervision: Glenn Scott, Mel Scanlon and Tony

Whittle. Each of the trio was seated at individual workstations; shamed into action, they all began to rise.

'I think that's enough of the hero stuff,' Kerry warned before they made it to their feet. Glenn and Mel sat again, whereas Tony took the opportunity to stretch his lower back. Creaking and groaning, he settled his backside on the edge of his desk and braced his palms on his thighs. Despite her instruction to the contrary, Korba whipped the three into a round of applause. He even initiated a round of hip-hip hooray, until Kerry swore at him. They all laughed. If there'd been any discomfort about what had happened the previous evening, it had been put behind them in a few seconds. *Good*, Kerry thought, *let's get back to business as usual.*

Korba was dying to hear what had happened between her and Porter, but not in front of the others. He offered a conspiratorial wink, and then returned to Mel Scanlon's desk to retrieve a file he'd dumped there. Mel squinted at him. 'D'you still want me in the interview with you, Sarge?' she asked, making it sound as if it was no trouble.

'That's down to the boss.' Korba looked expectantly at Kerry.

'Who are you interviewing?'

'Henrietta Jayne Winters...Erick Swain's girlfriend.'

'Ah!' Kerry thought about the brash woman from last night. Hettie had more to trouble her now than a broken door and dog muck on her carpet. 'What's she in on?'

'Conspiracy to murder.' Korba shrugged in apology. 'I know, boss. She's just lost her fella. But Porter wanted her locked up.'

It made sense. Despite Swain's untimely death, there was still an open double murder investigation to conduct, and until she was cleared Hettie was as complicit in the evidence discovered at their home as Swain.

To Mel, Kerry said, 'I'll take it from here with Danny.' Then to all in the room: 'If you're up to speed with your files, leave them on my desk for me, then get yourselves home for some kip. It's—' she checked her wristwatch '—almost midday. I'll see you back here at six o'clock, OK?'

Nobody seemed keen to leave. There were employment rules that dictated proper rest periods between shifts, but rules meant nothing in the real world. Her team probably wouldn't sleep, but they'd get some time with their families if nothing else. 'You heard me,' she said, aiming a thumb at the door. 'Off with you, but don't be late back. Danny, my office please.'

Hers was actually an anteroom of the GaOC office. In fact *anteroom* was too generous a description: it had originally been designed as a stationery cupboard. She called it her 'cubbyhole'. Inside there was space for a chair, a small table and her computer monitor. It was stuffier even than its larger sister. But with the door shut it allowed a modicum of privacy for sensitive discussions. Korba joined her in the cramped space. The aroma of fried onions was coming off him. 'As soon as we're done here, you can get yourself off home too,' she promised.

'I'm good for a few hours yet, boss.'

'Sorry, Danny, but as your friend, it's my duty to tell you that you're honking. If you make me, I'll pull rank and order you home for a shower and change of clothes.'

'You don't like my aftershave?' Danny grinned, unfazed by criticism. 'It's *Eau de Grande Mac* with a hint of fag ash.'

Kerry clucked her tongue.

Korba changed tack. 'How'd it go with ol' misery guts?'

'Better than expected,' she replied, 'but not as well as it could have.'

'Porter didn't agree to your transfer, then?'

'Nope. Neither did he pucker up. But that's OK, I'm glad to be back.'

'What about the IPCC?'

'Their investigation will still go ahead, but at least I'm not suspended from duty. And from what I saw on that video, I'm not worried about their findings.'

'You got a look at it then? That Swain…the way he went mental at the last minute…' he halted, stared quizzically at her. 'Remember when you asked if I believed in ghosts? Well, maybe you should've asked Swain, cause the way he carried on, I'd say he saw somethin' that put the fear of God in him.'

'Yeah, he did act strange. It was probably drugs.' Only she knew the reason behind Swain's wild swipes and kicks, because the spectral girl had not been caught on camera. And yet, even as he fought to hurl her from the roof, Kerry now suspected the gangster had grown aware of her ghostly companion, and when Girl hurtled at him in a flurry of desperation to save her, he'd reared away and lost his balance. Never had Girl shown herself to anyone but Kerry before, but it wasn't something she was prepared to divulge to even her closest friend. 'I…I can't explain it any other way.'

'He didn't seem high when I spoke with him…yeah, he smoked weed, but not before we got there and everything kicked off.'

She shrugged, then leaned past Danny and forced the door shut over a ruck in the carpet. The DC's hadn't left the office as instructed, and she preferred to keep her latter words between her and Korba. 'Tell you what. It's a good job I was filmed from behind and the noise of the rain covered everything; I might've said a thing or two that could come back to bite me on the arse.'

'We all talk bollocks in the heat of the moment, boss.'

'I know.' Kerry's lips bowed briefly. 'Some of the stuff I said to Swain could be deemed unprofessional.'

'Good on ya.' Korba winked. He changed tack again. 'I've got the weapon and ammunition we seized from the house. You sure you want to be the one to interview Hettie? I mean, she might not be happy to see you after what happened to lover boy...'

'I've nothing to be ashamed of. He was the one resisting arrest.'

Her words felt hollow.

It was her turn to change the subject. 'Has she asked for a brief?'

'Yeah. She's got the duty solicitor, Dave Barnes.'

'I'm surprised. She can probably afford the best.'

'She's pleading innocence. Asking for a specific brief might make it look as if she's got somethin' to hide. She's in with Dopey Dave now, and I've already given him full disclosure.'

'OK. I'm taking it you've planned the interview?'

Korba coughed.

'OK, then. So we're playing it off the cuff. I'm good to go, then. You ready, Danny?'

He hadn't relinquished the file. 'Just have to grab the evidence, and let the custody sergeant know we're taking her to interview.'

'Right. So let's go hear what Hettie's got to say about her granddad's gun.'

Despite her good looks, there was something reptilian about Hettie Winters. Hers were crocodile tears, and her first response to Kerry's appearance was to clash her teeth like a crocodile ambushing a gazelle on a riverbank. Also, as in most reptiles she had a tough hide. She didn't come across as a woman who'd recently lost her partner. Anger was her overpowering emotion, but not the raw anger other recently bereaved people displayed; hers was more like pent up hatred finally set loose. She despised Kerry, but it wouldn't have mattered who interviewed her.

She didn't look crocodilian. If anything, a few hours in the cells appeared to have agreed with her, because she was more beautiful than she'd looked last night in her baggy pyjamas and slippers. Her blond hair was styled and set, and her make-up was flawless – false eyelashes, false nails, all perfect and in place, and her mascara was untouched by her tears. The tight T-shirt she wore made the most of her pneumatic breasts, and her designer jeans hugged her like a second skin. Even with her shoes off, she was a couple of inches taller than Kerry. She could be the beautiful star in a reality TV show: her language was crass, and added an ugly set to her lips.

While the equipment was prepped for the interview, Hettie bitched and snapped at Kerry and DS Korba. Even her legal brief, "Dopey Dave" Barnes wasn't immune to her sharp tongue. Then, as the tapes began to roll, and the introductions were out of the way, Hettie went "no comment" for the most part. It was a strategy many suspects played, often at the instruction of their solicitor.

'Before we continue,' said Kerry, with a lingering nod that included Barnes, 'I should remind you that we are conducting this interview under the *now* caution. In other words, it may harm your defence if you do not mention *now* what you later rely on in court. That means if you continue stating no comment, anything you mention in court might be ruled inadmissible in your defence. Do you understand what I'm telling you, Hettie?'

'No comment.' Hettie sat back, fiddled her sapphire engagement ring to a more comfortable position on her finger. The stone on Kerry's engagement ring was diminutive by comparison.

'Saying "no comment" is actually making a comment.' Kerry was facetious on purpose, to goad a response. Hettie sneered and spread her hands on the table. Displaying her engagement ring was a reminder to Kerry about whom she'd taken from her. Kerry ignored the dig, and glanced at the solicitor.

Despite his nickname Dave Barnes wasn't stupid. Plus, due to having been given forewarning of the evidence the detectives would reveal during interview by Korba, he knew what was coming next. 'It's OK to tell the inspector about your grandfather's military service...as we discussed.'

Hettie shot him the stink-eye, before switching her glare to Kerry. 'So what do you want to know?'

Kerry glanced at Korba, who was seated next to her. He delved inside a brown paper evidence sack between his feet, and passed its contents to Kerry.

She produced the Webley Mk IV .38/200 Service revolver, sealed in a translucent evidence bag, and placed it on the table between her and Hettie. Alongside it she set down another evidence bag containing the loose .38 200-grain cartridges seized from the master bedroom during the execution of the warrant. The four live cartridges found in the revolver, plus the empty brass shells from the shooting on Wandsworth Road were in other sealed bags, but had been held back from this interview, as had the projectiles removed from the bodies of Nala Dahir Ghedi and Bilan Ghedi during their respective autopsies. Those items were due for forensic and ballistic examination, and she wasn't prepared to risk compromising the chain of custody before the results were back if Hettie managed to rip open any of the bags.

'I'm showing exhibits DSDK-Two and SRG-One to Hettie Winters,' Kerry announced for the purpose of the audio record. 'Hettie, do you recognise these items, and can you tell me about them?'

'I already told you.'

'Yes.' Kerry had photocopied the page from her notebook where she'd made a record of Hettie's statement during the house search. 'In regards to exhibit SRG-One you said, "I see you've found my granddad's old bullets. He brought them back from Korea donkey's years ago." Is that a true account of what was said at the time?'

'Fucked if I can remember. It sounds about right.'

Still reading from her notes, Kerry said, 'I then asked if you had a firearms certificate allowing you to keep live ammunition, to which you replied "They're fucking antiques. And besides, I don't have a fucking gun."'

Hettie folded her arms beneath her breasts.

'For the tape please?' Kerry said.

'What? I didn't hear you ask a question.'

'Is that a true statement of what was said?' Kerry clarified.

'Sounds about right.'

'OK, then. So if you don't have a gun, can you describe what I'm showing you now...exhibit DSDK-Two?'

'Well it's obvious it's a fucking gun, isn't it?'

'This gun was seized during the execution of a search warrant at your home address. It was found buried in fresh earth in the back garden of your property. I showed it you at the scene and asked if we'd also found your granddad's gun, or if it was Erick Swain's these days. Correct?'

'You did, yeah, but I also told you it was bollocks, a fucking stitch up, and that you bastards planted it!'

Dave Barnes interjected, a raised finger of caution for Hettie's sake. She snorted at him. 'Yeah, well, nobody's putting words in my fucking mouth!'

Kerry went on undeterred. 'You didn't answer my questions at the time, and understandably because I wasn't clear. So I'll ask again now. Did this gun belong to your grandfather?'

Hettie frowned, figuring out if she was being led into a trap. 'No comment.'

'Did the gun belong to Erick Swain?' Kerry went on.

'No comment.' Hettie thought hard. 'Uh, no, wait. Yeah, the gun belonged to my granddad. He brought it back from Korea with him.'

'When did your grandfather return from deployment in Korea?'

'How am I supposed to know? Donkey's years ago, ages before my time.'

'To my knowledge the Korean War ended in nineteen fifty-four,' Kerry offered. 'Would it be fair to say that if your grandfather was deployed with the NATO First Commonwealth Division he probably returned home to the UK around that time? Around, let's say, sixty-five years ago?'

'I don't know. I'm not that good at maths.'

'Approximately sixty-five years,' Kerry repeated.

'Where are you going with this, Inspector?' Dave Barnes asked. 'My client has already told you she's unsure when her grandfather came back from war. If you've a specific question, can you please ask it?'

'I'm establishing a timeline,' Kerry responded, but without acknowledging him personally. She continued looking directly at Hettie. 'You said that the gun did belong to your grandfather.'

'Yes. How many frigging times...'

'So when did it come into your possession? Was it after your grandfather died?'

'I suppose so.'

'When did your grandfather pass away?'

'It was a while back. Ten years...eleven?'

'Before his death, did your grandfather regularly maintain his gun?'

Hettie's gaze swept from Kerry to Korba. He said nothing, his features giving no hint of where the questioning was leading. Hettie twisted to eye her solicitor. 'Do I have to answer this? How the hell am I supposed to know what my granddad did? I didn't live with him, did I?'

Dave turned the question back on Kerry with a simple rising of his eyebrows.

'So I'll ask a different question,' Kerry said. 'Have you ever maintained your grandfather's gun?'

'What? Like oiled it or something?'

'Yes. Exactly that.'

'Nah. I've never touched it.'

'Would you say the gun looks as if it hasn't been maintained for sixty-five years? Or even for ten or eleven years?'

'How would I know?'

'Despite being buried, and having a little dirt on it, wouldn't you agree that the gun looks as if it has been recently oiled and cleaned?'

Hettie sniffed. Leaned towards the evidence bag, and said, 'It looks shiny, if that's what you mean?'

'When the gun is forensically inspected, are we likely to discover your fingerprints or DNA on it, Hettie?' As she posed the question, Kerry studied her minutely, watching for the micro expressions that would indicate a lie.

'No chance,' Hettie answered, although her nostrils quivered as she thought about it. 'Like I said, I've never touched the bloody thing.'

Kerry ploughed on. 'Does anyone else live with you and Erick Swain?'

'Do you mean in the past tense, or have you forgot you killed my Erick?' Hettie smiled viciously – a *fuck you* to both Kerry and the audiotape. 'We lived together, just the two of us. *Lived*. But not now.'

In any other environment it would have stung her, but the accusation bypassed Kerry. 'So if there was only you and Erick in that house, whose fingerprints do you suppose we will find on the gun?'

'Who's to say you'll find any?'

'That remains to be seen. But what is the likelihood of Erick's being on the gun? If you didn't maintain it, then someone must have. And if Erick was the only person to share your house...'

'I don't know. He might've.' Hettie drew up in her seat, unfolding her arms and placing her hands flat on her thighs. 'Look. I said earlier I'd never seen the gun, and never touched it. Same goes for those—'

'For the tape Hettie has indicated Exhibit SRG-One, the cartridges,' Kerry quickly interjected.

'Yeah,' Hettie agreed. 'What I meant was I haven't seen them in years. They were stored with the gun in a box in the attic. Erick must have...'

'Erick must have fetched them from the attic if you didn't?' Kerry suggested, feeling victory was in grasping distance.

'Well it wasn't me. So who else could it have been?'

Kerry drew both evidence bags towards her, then moved them gently towards Korba. He placed them safely in the brown paper sack.

'Hettie. Can we make this clear? What you're saying is that it had to have been Erick who took the gun and ammunition out of the attic, and who subsequently dropped some of the cartridges in your bedroom and also subsequently buried the gun in your back garden?'

'Uh. Yeah. That's what I'm saying. It had to have been him, because it wasn't me.' Again Hettie's gaze swept from Kerry to Korba, then back again. 'But before you ask, I didn't know he'd touched them, or buried that thing. I had nothing to do with them.'

Kerry didn't acknowledge her plea of innocence. She asked, 'Can you tell me your movements for yesterday, please?'

'Movements? What, like where I was?' To Kerry's nod, she continued. 'I was at home all day. I got up about eight and watched some telly, had a coffee and some breakfast, then started cleaning. I'm house proud.' Her last was delivered with a hefty dose of pride, only dented by the memory of her ransacked home. 'Later on I watched Judge Rinder and Tipping Point and...' She opened both palms. 'I was there all day.'

'Can anyone corroborate your movements?'

'Huh. Erick could've.'

Kerry paused a moment. Slowly she closed and opened her eyes. 'Was Erick home the entire time?'

There was no denying her point, and Hettie squirmed while considering her options. 'Erick had to go out for a few hours, but I swear to you I never left the house.'

'When was Erick gone from the house?'

'I don't know exactly...maybe from eleven till about three.'

'That's eleven a.m. until three p.m.?'

'Yeah, give or take a quarter hour.' Hettie again squirmed, realising she'd admitted her partner's movements were unaccounted for over the period when the drive-by shooting occurred. Lamely, she added, 'He had some business to do.'

'What kind of business?'

'I dunno. He keeps his business private, and to tell you the truth, I don't ask.'

Kerry doubted Hettie could be honest if she tried. But again she switched focus abruptly, giving her no time to think. 'Erick was registered as the owner and keeper of a sonic blue Subaru Impreza.' She read off the correct license plate number. 'Is that correct?'

'Yeah. I know that car. It was Erick's pride and joy a year or two back. Why?'

Ignoring the question, Kerry posed another of hers. 'Do you know the whereabouts of that car, Hettie?'

'It's in a lock-up on our estate,' Hettie said quickly. 'If you want I can show you; I have the keys to the lock-up at home.'

'That won't be necessary,' Kerry said, 'although I would like to seize those keys.' She exchanged a glance with DS Korba. 'Anything to add, Sergeant Korba?'

'No. I've no further questions.'

'Thank you, Hettie,' said Kerry, and nodded briskly at Korba who was in charge of the tape recorder. 'Ending interview.'

'She's got more face than frigging Big Ben,' Korba announced after they watched Hettie Winters leave the police station. She'd flounced to where a sporty-looking red Nissan waited to collect her, summoned earlier as soon as the custody sergeant had returned her mobile phone. Hettie was returning home, to meet with DC Mel Scanlon, who despite Kerry ordering home was still in the nick when they left the interview suite. Mel was tasked with seizing the keys to the lock-up Hettie had mentioned, despite them all knowing that the Subaru was no longer there: it had already been impounded and was under forensic examination by the CSI team. She would also seek permission from Hettie to search the lock-up without need of a warrant.

'I didn't think you'd noticed, seeing as you rarely took your eyes off her boobs.' Kerry gently elbowed Korba in the ribs.

'You know me, Kerry. I'm not interested in fakes like Hettie. I prefer a *real* woman, with *real* curves, not ones blown up with silicone. They don't have to be that good lookin', only natural.' He glimpsed surreptitiously at her and caught another elbow, slightly harder, in the midriff. He gasped in laughter.

'Seriously, though,' he said. 'She's a walking cliché. She should wear a sign round her neck saying 'Gangster's Moll'.'

'Aye, she's a real wannabe.' She shrugged away the subject. 'Can you log the evidence back in, Danny?' The Webley required a full forensic investigation, and test firing. 'I need to phone the coroner's office for Swain's results.'

'Course I will, boss. You want me to grab you a brew on the way back? Dunno about you, but I've got a tongue like Gandhi's flip-flop.'

She squinted at him. 'A coffee would be good. I'll be in the office, OK?'

Korba headed off with his hands in his pockets, his rolling gait reminiscent of a Jack Tar on shore leave. Kerry returned to the GaOC office: deserted now her team had left. She used the landline at DC Glenn Scott's desk and punched in the Southwark coroner's office number.

Swain's cause of death wasn't the issue; it was whether or not any gunpowder residue had been found on him. Chances were that some kind of trace residue had been missed, even if he'd showered. Her mind flashed back to the search, and how the sniffer dog had acted on the sofa in the front room — it had possibly reacted to gunpowder residue. It was likely Swain sat on it not long after returning from where he'd burned out the Subaru, but before he'd changed clothing or washed, and residue had transferred to the cushions. In hindsight she should have had the settee seized and swabbed, as well as any unlaundered clothing. It was an opportunity lost.

Proving Erick Swain's guilt was important to Kerry. He wouldn't face punishment for his crimes, and it wouldn't bring back his victims, but at least there would be a modicum of resolution for the Ghedi family. Besides, proving Swain was their killer could lead her to his conspirator. Somebody had driven the Subaru while Swain took the shots at Ikemba Adefunke, and therefore complicit in the murder. Hettie had been released on police bail, to return to the station at a later date, when a decision to charge her would be made. She made a mental note to go and speak with Hettie, with an off-the-record offer of leniency if she pointed the finger at Swain's driver.

Her train of thought was broken by a voice on the other end of the line. It belonged to a coroner's office assistant.

'Hello, this is Detective Inspector Kerry Darke,' she announced, and gave her station identification number. 'I'd like to speak with Mr Bellows please.'

Nigel Bellows was an assistant coroner to Her Majesty's Senior Coroner for the Southwark district — which also encompassed Lambeth — and was the direct line contact in regards to both the Ghedi and Swain cases. Forensic pathologists under his direction would have concluded the autopsies of all three people by now, and the results collated by him.

'One moment please,' said the office assistant, and then shortly: 'Thanks for holding, Inspector Darke, I'm putting you through.'

'My, my, Kerry Darke,' Nigel Bellows said almost immediately. 'I feel a little star struck speaking with you. Quite the Internet star you've become.'

'You know me, Nige; I'm nothing special.'

'Oh, I don't know about that. Perhaps I was a little premature in dumping you…I could have lived off your fame and glory for decades.'

'Who dumped who?'

'Oh, that's right.' He chuckled. 'You were the one that stopped replying to my messages and tokens of affection.'

'You got so stalkerish I was tempted to take out an injunction on you.'

Nigel laughed. They had dated twice shortly after Kerry's arrival in London, once for dinner, once for drinks, but never with romance in mind. Nigel Bellows was a proud homosexual. They had remained friends, though, although their work commitments meant they rarely got time to meet socially.

'How are you, Kerry? From what I saw on that video that thug roughed you up before he slipped.'

Kerry hadn't given her aches and pains much thought in the intervening hours, but now that he mentioned it her forehead still throbbed where Swain struck her. She touched the sore spot. It felt swollen, but not too badly. 'I'm fine. A little achy here and there, but I'll live.'

'I'd love to see the state of the other guy. Oh! Wait a minute! I have!' Nigel had taken her call in a private location. It was that, or coroners got to laugh at dead scumbags the way coppers weren't allowed to. 'Seriously though, Kerry, that was a close call. My heart was in my mouth when I saw how near Swain was to throwing you from that roof.'

'I've watched the video,' Kerry said. 'My heart was in my mouth too. If he hadn't slipped...'

'Then the pavement pizza I'd the displeasure of inspecting this morning would've been you.'

Neither of them wished to contemplate that alternative.

'You personally conducted the autopsy?'

'No, of course not. I'm a lawyer, not a pathologist. But I did observe the procedure. Eew! Mr Swain was not a pretty sight.'

Out the corner of her amber eye, Kerry caught a blur of movement and colour. She thought Korba had returned with the promised cup of coffee. But when she looked, there was nobody there. Odd. With no windows, there was no reason to spot a shadow cast from outside. The door to the corridor was shut. An icy trickle worked its way the length of her spine. She shuddered, blinked a couple of times, and grasped for a rational explanation: she must have a floater in her vision. 'Do you have the results from his autopsy yet?'

'You're specifically asking about the presence of gunpowder residue? I had the samples rushed through the lab. Hair; fingernail scrapings; skin swabs from the hands and face. Sorry Kerry, they all came back negative. There were trace elements, detergents and capsaicinoids — the latter from your incapacitant spray — but none of the components found in modern or historical firearm propellants.'

'Is that unusual, if Swain fired a gun only a few hours earlier?'

'No. He could have been wearing gloves and a hat. The presence of detergent on his face and hands suggests he washed himself with something more potent than regular soap and water.'

'Bloody hell...'

'That isn't what you wanted to hear,' Nigel concurred.

'No. I was hoping we had Swain bang to rights.'

'You've the gun, the bullets, and a suspect so guilty he chose to run to his death rather than argue his innocence in court.'

'And we both know where those will get me.' Without tying Swain to the gun with irrefutable evidence, even Dave Barnes, the duty solicitor could rip holes in her case. Sadly, her only eyewitness to the shooting was hostile, and even forced to give testimony Funky would be deemed unreliable due to his allegiance to a rival gang. She was going to have to work on Hettie Winters harder than she had during her first interview. 'Hopefully the results from the test firing of the Webley will confirm it was the murder weapon,' she said. But still, for any hope of a conviction, and resolution in the deaths of the mother and girl, she must identify and catch Swain's driver.

'I hear that you're engaged to be married these days,' Nigel went on, in an awkward attempt at raising her spirits. 'To some brute of a man you met at Belmarsh prison of all places. Is there no hope left for us?'

'You'll always occupy a soft spot in my heart, Nige,' she assured him.

'Oh, shame. I was hoping to meet that hunk of yours, and steal him away instead.'

'You're shameless.'

Nigel laughed. 'I am indeed. But seriously, Kerry, if you'd like to bring along your fella I'd love for us to go on a double date. I've a man of my own I'd love you to meet, and my eye on a brand new cocktail bar that's just opened in Soho.'

'Adam's more of a lager lout,' she said — and he got the subtext.

'Then you should give him the slip and come away with a man of a more sensitive nature, and better taste.'

They both laughed, but Kerry's humour was tinged with morose. Nigel didn't know how right he was. Adam's display of insensitivity last night had been as subtle as hitting her in the teeth with a building brick.

She thanked Nigel, and promised not to be a stranger. Hung up. She rested her backside on DC Scott's desk, unconsciously touching the swollen spot on her forehead. The skin was hot; despite the air that was abruptly so icy she shivered. Between her fingers she glimpsed movement. Something loomed directly in front of her. She snatched her hand from her face, head snapping up at *whatever the hell it was*.

As before, it wasn't Girl.

The figure was ill defined, a hint of wavy hair, a twinkle of silver earring, a wolfish leer...

'Oh my God!' Every muscle in her body cramped. 'Y...*you* can't be here.'

'Can't I? Think again, bitch.' The disembodied words scratched at the inner surface of her skull. *'I can be anywhere I please, and do anything I want, and* you *can't stop me.'*

Breath shuddered from her, spurts of condensation visible in the frigid atmosphere. 'No. You can't be real. You...died.'

'Yes. I died. And we both know who's to blame.'

Erick Swain lunged, emitting a hiss that filled her skull, and his cuffed hand snatched at her hair.

With a squeal, Kerry jerked out of reach, tumbled off the desk. She cracked her elbow off the floor but ignored the pain, scrambled to make distance between her and the clutching hand of...

Nobody.

Swain had disappeared.

The breath caught in her throat, her eyes wide and dry. She stared, too afraid to blink in case she summoned *him* again. Her head shook as if palsied, and her breath wheezed out. There's bugger all there, Kerry!

If he'd ever been present, then Swain had left as abruptly as he'd appeared. A quake ran through her. It had nothing to do with the temperature this time, if anything the stuffy atmosphere had returned to normal. She grew aware of her unceremonious position on the floor. Grasping the desk for support she clawed upright, then sat on its edge. But seating herself went against her impulse to run away.

Her hands covered her face. Who are you going to run away from when there's nobody there? He wasn't real. Get a bloody grip, for Christ's sake!

She yelped as the door handle turned.

She scrambled back across the desk again expecting—

Korba backed into the room, juggling two large mugs of steaming coffee. With his hands full, he'd employed an elbow and hip to work the handle and nudge the door open. Thank God. It gave Kerry precious seconds to get composed before he turned and aimed one of the mugs at her. 'Just what the doctor ordered, eh?'

She knew her eyes were wide, her tongue wedged between her teeth, and how plain stupid she looked. She tried to smoothen the disbelief from her features, but Korba wasn't fooled. He wasn't a detective for nothing, and knew when something was wrong.

'What's up, boss?' He asked. 'You look rattled. Is it something to do with Swain?'

Oh, Danny, she thought, *why did you have to ask that*?

Baxter Court was mausoleum quiet. Even the drizzling rain failed to add any sound to the pall of sorrow hanging over the row of bleak apartments at the end of the cul-de-sac. All Kerry could hear was the movement of blood through her inner ears. She'd expected to find the press camped outside the apartments, hoping for a photo or quote from the distraught father, but they'd withdrawn so Suleymaan Ghedi could grieve the loss of his wife and daughter in peace. Then again she thought not. They'd probably got their pictures and story earlier, and quickly moved on to record the misery of other victims elsewhere in the city. She was relieved. Visiting Mister Ghedi was difficult enough, without first negotiating a crowd of insistent journalists.

Out of her car, she stood a moment on the pavement, feeling the drizzle on her exposed cheeks. There wasn't another living soul in sight, and more importantly nothing that could be defined as *undead*. The last she wanted was for Swain to follow inside the home of those he'd slaughtered. She was unsure if she'd be able to handle things any better than when he'd come at her in the office. She might have convinced Korba she was fine, even if she was in denial. She'd even persuaded herself that Swain had been nothing but a figment of her imagination, brought on by fatigue, and the blows she'd taken to her head. Blatantly she ignored the fact he'd also materialised in Porter's office before that. Also, she was relieved that Girl had backed off for now — being in the presence of the shade of a child could prove emotional considering the reason for her visit.

The Ghedis' neighbours kept to a respectful distance, their doors closed. Kerry approached the apartments without attracting attention. A short flight of stairs allowed access to a row of first floor apartments, and she counted down the doors. The Ghedi family home was modest. A blue door and one window, the drapes currently drawn to block out the world, were almost identical to their neighbours. A pink bicycle, with streamers of ribbons tied to the handlebars, propped against the wall under the window was the single unique detail. Her chest tightened: little Bilan would never ride that bike again. Kerry halted, took in a deep breath, and shivered as she expelled it. She'd arrived at Baxter Court despondent, but reminded of the act perpetrated by Erick Swain the embers of righteous anger were fanned. More determined, she knocked on the door.

The curtains shifted open an inch. She held up her warrant card, kept her features neutral. Suleymaan Ghedi needed reassurance that the detective on her case was professional. She could offer compassion but more so a dependable crux to rely on. The curtains dropped shut. A soft murmur of conversation filtered through the door. Finally the door edged open and an older, coffee-skinned woman, dressed in a conservative sash scarf and jilbab, greeted her politely with downcast eyes. Kerry identified herself, and accepted the invitation to enter and immediately saw Suleymaan, who'd risen from a chair at the centre of a small, but neat sitting room. He was a tall, slim man, his features sparse, his eye sockets scooped out with grief. Unlike the woman, he was dressed in western clothing, a shirt and necktie, and dark grey trousers, black shoes, and surprisingly a cross was pinned to his shirt. A matching grey suit jacket hung on the back of the chair he'd vacated. He'd clasped his hands against his abdomen, but lowered his right, cupped, and indicated Kerry to take his seat.

'Please,' Kerry said, aiming a gesture at the chair, 'sit back down, Mr Ghedi, I'll take the sofa.'

Suleymaan nodded, but didn't sit again. He turned his back and approached the fireplace: more likely the photos of his dead wife and child displayed upon it.

Kerry was unsure of Somalian tradition. Hopefully she hadn't committed a breech in etiquette by refusing his offer to take his chair. She sat on the edge of the sofa, her hands on her knees.

'Can I get you something? Tea perhaps?' The woman's English was heavily accented, but clear.

'Tea would be nice,' Kerry said, conscious of getting her response right this time. 'Thank you.'

The woman moved for the kitchen and Suleymaan turned to watch her go. A weak smile of affection rode his lips.

'My sister Filan.' His voice was brittle. 'She has come to help me with my son Taban. Would you prefer that she leave the house while we speak? I can have her take Taban out for a walk.'

'No. It's not a problem, Mr Ghedi. Besides, it's beginning to rain...'

The man nodded, looked at the floor. He visibly trembled. Maybe he was reconsidering the idea to send his little boy out: his wife and daughter had been murdered while strolling with Taban.

'How is your son?' she asked.

'Thankfully unaffected by what he saw,' Suleymaan said, 'but that is bound to change.'

Undoubtedly it would. The boy was young enough that he might not later recall witnessing the murders, but in the days and years to come he would begin wondering where his mother and sister had gone, and their loss would eat at him, the way Sally's disappearance had with her.

'You wish to see him?' Suleymaan suddenly asked. As if she'd a hidden agenda for visiting. 'He is perfectly fine. Filan put him down for his nap, but I can have her wake him.'

'No, let your boy sleep.' Kerry would have liked to see Taban, so that in some way she could import a message to him that she'd do everything she could to bring some kind of resolution to him, as she hoped to do with his father. But seeing the little boy might crack her professional veneer. It was difficult enough containing her emotions already. 'I imagine his routine has been...disturbed these last few days.'

Suleymaan exhaled sharply.

'It must be a difficult time for you too,' she added.

'My sister's a great help. She is a good person.' Suleymaan's bottom lip trembled. His eyes shone with unshed tears. Kerry guessed what he was thinking: Filan was helpful but would never be a replacement. He finally sat, lacking the strength to stand any longer. There was white stubble on his chin, and wrinkles in his shirt. His routine had not merely been disturbed but shattered. They sat in silence a moment, both lost in sadness, faces downcast, before she leaned forward a fraction.

'I wanted to pay my respects, to say how sorry I am for your loss.'

Suleymaan nodded at the floor, his fingers twining together in his lap.

'But this isn't just a social visit, Mr Ghedi. I'm the lead detective on your family's case.'

'I know.' Suleymaan looked up: his tears had glazed over. 'I recognise you from the news. I am a religious man, a Christian, and it shames me to admit it, but I have no forgiveness in my heart at this time. I cheered when I heard you avenged Nala and Bilan. Thank you for what you did to their murderer, Inspector Darke.'

Her abdomen clenched. Before, with DCI Porter, and with Adam, she'd defended the fact that Swain's death was accidental, and she was not to blame for his fall, but it was unnecessary to do the same with Suleymaan. It would be unseemly when offering his gratitude. Still, having him thank her for killing another human being was uncomfortable. 'My regret is that Erick Swain escaped proper justice. He should've been tried and punished accordingly.'

Suleymaan exhaled sharply again, and glanced towards the door. 'He will suffer the consequences of his sins in the afterlife. I am certain of that.' He suddenly leaned forward and reached across to grasp Kerry's hands. His gaze slipped once behind her towards the front door again, before he settled it on her. 'A greater power was at work on that rooftop, Inspector. You must know this, and accept it yourself. You were *protected*.'

He was referring to God, or maybe even to the vengeful spirits of his wife or daughter: yet she knew different, and was unsure how she felt about it. Accepting that Girl was real meant also accepting the truth of her most recent, and more terrifying visitations. 'There's nothing more I can do to punish Erick Swain,' she said, 'but I assure you I won't leave any rock unturned. Mr Ghedi, Swain might have been the gunman, but he wasn't alone when those shots were fired. I'll do everything in my power to ensure anyone involved in the murders of your family are brought to justice.'

'Catching these people will not bring back my wife or daughter,' said Suleymaan, 'but knowing they're suitably punished will bring a small measure of accord to their loved ones.' His words sounded hollow, as if he'd answered by rote, and had no belief that any peace would extend to him. 'Nala's parents and siblings are devastated; they wish to travel here to attend her funeral, but it's impossible for them. If I can tell them that her killers are all dead or behind bars, it will help them come to terms. At this time they know only loss.'

In her job Kerry had come across people in many stages of bereavement. Suleymaan was in one of the earliest, where initial shock could become denial. She'd noted more than once that his attention had flicked from her to the door, almost as if he expected Nala and Bilan to enter at any time. By diverting his grief to his wife's family, he could hold onto hope that this was all a nightmare he would soon wake from to find his loved ones safe and sound. It wasn't her place to bring him out of denial, not when she'd clung to a similar hope of Sally's return for decades. In truth they both understood they were grasping for the impossible, but it was easier coping with fantasy than reality.

He squeezed her hands gently. Then sat back, releasing her as Filan tentatively entered the living room carrying two small china cups on a burnished brass tray. Suleymaan gestured, Kerry should be served first. She accepted the delicate cup, and held it under her chin. The tea was weak, but fragrant. Nothing like the stewed brew she was used to back at the nick. Milk was absent from the tray, but there was a pile of brown sugar cubes on a saucer. Out of politeness she tried the drink without sweetening it, and was glad she hadn't. It tasted like honey as it were. Suleymaan dropped four cubes into his cup and stirred with a tiny spoon, but without drinking, he set his cup aside to cool. Filan returned to the kitchen and closed the door behind her. Kerry was grateful for the brief interlude as she drained the small cup. She placed it on a small table at the edge of the sofa, dug in her coat pocket. She held out her card. 'On here you'll find my contact details; if there's anything I can do, any question I can answer, please don't hesitate to call, OK? Also, I'll give you this...' She took out another card. 'This is the number for Victim Support, they will be able to assist you through the process of—'

Suleymaan took her card, but was uninterested in the second. He read her details, looked back at her and his gaze was earnest. 'I trust in *you* to help, Detective Inspector Darke. I said earlier I'm a man of faith; I believe my faith in you catching the others is not misplaced.'

She didn't know how to answer. Making bold promises was never a good idea, especially when so many variables could get in the way of a successful conviction. 'I'll do my very best,' she whispered. Her eyeballs were hot, and she steeled against shedding any tears.

He nodded, sat back, and Kerry took it as a sign to leave. She'd expected more questions, perhaps even recrimination and anger, and was thrown by Suleymaan's demeanour. He was in denial about Nala and Bilan's deaths, but conversely sincere in his belief she'd bring justice to their killers. She stood, and Suleymaan mirrored her. He extended his hand and she accepted it. He didn't shake it, only held her fingers in his, squeezing gently again. 'I can tell you too have lost someone dear to you,' he said, and for the third or fourth time his attention slipped past her to the door. She couldn't resist taking a furtive glance. Girl, for once, was caught full on. She stood in the shadows in the corner where the front door met the living room wall. Her head was tilted down, hair hanging loose over her features, and her hands clasped at her midriff: a similar pose to that adopted earlier by Suleymaan. The instant she realised she was observed, she jerked up her head, mouth slipping open. Kerry blinked, and in that fleeting moment, Girl wavered, then blinked out of existence.

Suleymaan looked back at Kerry. 'Do you believe in guardian angels?'

Taken aback, Kerry didn't answer.

He smiled sadly. 'So I'm not the only one refusing to accept the truth. Please, Inspector, whether you believe or not, consider this: there's a divine balance in the universe. For every act of evil, there are equal acts of virtue. My beloved wife and daughter died, but the only thing that gives me comfort is the knowledge that other lives will be spared in their place.' He gave her hand an extra squeeze. 'I mentioned guardian angels; not all are in spirit form.'

She coughed in embarrassment. 'You're thinking a little too highly of me, Mr Ghedi. I'm just a police officer...'

'Who, I know, would've fought as hard against the devil to save Nala and Bilan given the chance, as you did when you met his servant on that rooftop.'

Swain was not a pawn of the devil. He was a horrible human being, capable of evil acts, but driven only by his twisted psyche. That was as far as it went. There was nothing supernatural about him...*at least, not then*. The afterthought made her scalp crawl.

Suleymaan again looked at the door. Kerry checked surreptitiously, expecting Girl to have reappeared, but she was absent. Had Suleymaan seen her, or were his actions and words nothing but a strange coincidence? She couldn't bring herself to ask. Never before she had to Erick Swain had Girl appeared to anyone but her, and there was a part of her that wanted things to stay that way. While Girl was hers to see alone, she could continue fooling...if not herself, then everyone else.

She left the apartment, troubled by his assertion about a divine balance in the universe. To believe in angels you had to accept the existence of demons. Had Girl returned to level the playing field with Swain, or for some other reason? Nala and Bilan had died, but other lives would be spared in their place. What path had she set out on since attending the shooting on Wandsworth Road? She laughed without humour, and again tears threatened her eyes. 'You'll be on the road to madness if you keep thinking this way,' she whispered.

There was no illusive figure lurking on the pavement outside her house when she arrived home that evening, neither Girl nor one more sinister. Adam's Ford Focus was missing so she grabbed the opportunity to park before anyone stole the spot. As she got out the car, she felt a drip or two of rain, but the heavy showers of the past couple of days were finally passing. A warmer spell had been forecast, some laughingly predicting an Indian summer. Just then the skies were a uniform grey, similar to her mood.

It had been a long day, and, especially after her visit with Mr Ghedi, one that left her in a confused fog. By the time she went off duty, she was so tired that Korba offered to drive her home. She reminded him he'd been on the go as equally long, and ordered him to go home and rest, shower and change his clothing, although the latter two instructions with a hefty pinch of salt. Perhaps accepting a lift home wouldn't have been a bad idea. Twice she'd zoned out at red lights, with the genuine fear that on one of those occasions she'd taken a micro-nap. It took the blaring horns of impatient drivers behind her to get her moving. She'd earlier resolved to make amends with Adam, but she was thankful she'd beaten him home. In her near-zombiefied state she hadn't the energy. Hopefully she could grab a couple of hours' sleep before he got back.

She stumbled inside to a living room that stank like a distillery. The stink was cloying, but cleaning the carpet would have to wait. In her bedroom she plugged in her phone charger, and attached the lead to her phone. Visited the loo, then staggered back to her bed. It hadn't been slept in last night. She crawled on top of the duvet, fully clothed, kicking off her shoes and letting them fall wherever gravity took them. Sleep came instantly and it was absolute...but it didn't last.

At some point the depthless void began to take on shape and hues, and then she was standing at the apex of a tall tower. It bore no relation to the structure on which she'd cornered Erick Swain, but it was one and the same. This was more like a crumbling castle tower, with large, weathered sandstone blocks and Kerry stood in rain flattening her unruly auburn hair to her skull. She checked to her right for her mother, and spotted Siobhan reading a brass plaque screwed to a wooden trestle. Her mother wasn't reading the historical notes, she sought clues where Sally had gone. Kerry also looked for her sister, but in her heart there was a sense that Sally would never be found. Realisation took hold of her gut and gave it a sharp twist. She looked away from the past.

Erick Swain leered at her across the tower's flat roof. The crenellations either side of him were reminiscent of huge slab-like teeth. He stalked towards her, and though she matched each step backwards, he gained with astonishing speed until he loomed over her. Her perspective was that of an eight-year-old child, and he full grown. He bent to study her, his single earring twinkling under the same errant spark that flashed a highlight on an eyetooth. In this dark fantasy, Swain's hair was shaggier, his beard fuller, and his features not wholly his own.

'You're the Fell Man,' Kerry wheezed in a child's voice.

'I fell because you made me.'

Swain reached for her, and from his wrist drooped a rigid cuff.

Kerry backed away, looking for her mother to save her.

Siobhan was gone.

'Now it's your turn to fall, bitch!'

Swain lurched, and in desperation Kerry grasped at the dangling cuff, and twisted it with fingers so soft they split on the metal. Swain barked in laughter, yanked his

103

arm up, and still holding on, tiny Kerry Darke was plucked out of her wellington boots and flipped between two crenellations.

She fell headfirst towards a pavement dotted with chewing gum and bird shit. Way below her she spotted her adult self standing under pelting rain, having turned away from a murdered girl hidden beneath a white forensic tent. Elder Kerry fisted her hands at her sides while cameras flashed, and then as was the manner of illogical dreams, Kerry was within her older body, looking out through older eyes as Funky ducked beneath a string of barrier tape...and the girl was gone.

'Boss? Detective Inspector!'

The sharp voice brought her to a halt, and she turned round, and found DS Danny Korba eyeing her from beneath a frown.

She glanced towards the entrance of Larkhall Park, and then blinked her confusion at Korba.

He held up a flat white box, and raised the lid almost reverently. 'Just what the doctor ordered, eh?'

She didn't want to look, but something compelled her against her will.

The steaming contents were red and mushy, with tufts of wavy hair and a silver earring. Within the mess a lupine mouth split wide. *'What's wrong with you, bitch? Don't you want any pavement pizza?'*

Repulsed, Kerry cringed away, but Korba pursued her, shoving the box at her. 'Go on, boss. You know you want a slice.'

Kerry screeched and backhanded the pizza box away. But Korba came on, pushing it under her nose. She averted her face, snatched for the box and...

...Kerry grabbed her mobile phone off the bedside cabinet and dragged it towards her. It was plugged into the wall. Still partly snared in the nightmare, she fought with the cord before the connector yanked loose and she fell back on the bed. The room had fallen dark while she'd slept; the only light was from the phone's glowing screen. It cast moving shadows on the walls, sending a shudder of revulsion through her. If the caller was DS Korba telling her she wanted a slice of pizza she'd go insane!

It wasn't Korba.

'Kerry? It's me. Can you let me in?'

'Wh-who?'

'It's *me*. Adam. Who'd you think?'

Her ears felt stuffed with cotton wool, and the sandman must have fly-tipped a dump truck full of aggregate under her eyelids. 'Uh, I was sleeping,' she croaked. 'Where's your key?'

'In my hand, but I still can't get in past the security chain.'

'Sorry, uh, the chain's on?'

'I'd be in there with you instead of on my phone if it wasn't.'

She had no recollection of securing the door chain. But then, she'd little recollection of much since leaving the nick...even her nightmare was retreating to some hidden corner of her mind. She swung her feet over the edge of the mattress, and her toes found her discarded shoes. She didn't bother getting into them, just nudged them aside. She pushed up, and stood swaying in almost pitch darkness. The bedroom had blackout curtains, a necessity for those whose shift-patterns were as erratic as theirs. She tripped towards the door on remote control, and on the landing flicked on a light. She screwed her face against the glare, and told Adam she was on her way down. She fumbled her way down with one hand on the banister, the phone held to her ear with the other, updating Adam with her progress. 'Almost there...I'll just be a sec.'

The stairs were situated in the front hallway. Adam could hear her without the benefit of his phone. The front door was open the few inches to the extent of its chain, and he'd ended his call the moment she'd left the bedroom and switched on the landing light. She had to close the door first to disengage the chain. He shoved inside, almost in frustration. But then Kerry grew aware of the slashing rain outside and thought those who'd predicted an Indian summer should instead have forecast a monsoon. Adam shook himself like a dog, and beads of moisture flew from his shaved head. His spectacle lenses were misted over. He pulled them off, and blinked at her.

'Jesus Christ, Kerry!'

For a moment she grew defensive. Having to wait to be let in was no big deal. But then he leaned towards her and wrapped a big arm around her shoulders and pulled her into an embrace. She was still suffering a sense of dislocation, and was as rigid as a plank. He released her slowly. 'I acted like a dickhead last night,' he told her. 'I saw what that bastard tried to do to you on video and...'

'You weren't to know.' Kerry's tone was desultory.

Adam studied the graze on her forehead. Now it had had time to bruise, and the scrapes to scab, it probably looked worse than it had in the early hours of the morning. There was another swelling under her right eye that hadn't been apparent earlier.

'That bastard,' Adam growled. 'It's a good job he's dead or I swear to you, I'd rip his head off!'

His oath was pointless. But at least it held misguided sentiment. Kerry leaned into him, returned the hug, patting his back. Adam closed the door and followed her to the living room.

He wrinkled his nose at the smell.

'I haven't had time to clean,' she said.

'Doesn't matter,' he said, 'we'll sort it tomorrow. I've got the day off.'

'I'm working.' She slumped into the easy chair.

'I thought you were on suspension.'

'That was before everyone learned the truth. You weren't the only one too quick to judge me.'

Adam spread his arms. 'I wasn't judging you, I was trying to be supportive. I still am.'

'So where have you been?'

'What do you mean?'

'You know what I mean. You left for work in the early hours, it's what now?' She glanced at their wall clock. 'It's after eleven at night. Where've you been, because you certainly haven't been here supporting me.' She sniffed the air, for the scent of beer or perfume — there was neither — and she caught herself before making an unfounded accusation.

'Overtime. I had to pull a few extra hours to cover a staff shortage. You know how it is.'

'I thought that maybe you were avoiding me.'

He said nothing, and his silence was damning.

She closed her eyes and sighed. Rocking forward she cupped her face in her hands. 'I don't blame you, Adam,' she mumbled between her fingers. 'I was a bitch. Let's just put last night behind us, huh?'

'You've been back at work?'

'I had to face the music with Porter, and besides, I couldn't put off visiting Mr Ghedi any longer. Even if I hadn't been reinstated I would have gone to see him, to pay my respects. It wasn't easy an easy visit.'

'He was angry with you?'

'No. That's the thing. He was quite the opposite. He acted a little...I don't know. Strange. Well, some of the stuff he said was strange.'

'You should have let me know where you were going.'

'Why? Would it have made a difference?'

'Well, no, I suppose not. But at least I wouldn't have worried so much about you.'

She stared at him until he visibly squirmed.

'You made it clear you don't think I'm fit for police work,' she reminded him. 'I'd have thought you'd be more worried knowing I'd gone back to work.'

'I thought you wanted to put last night behind us?' Adam took off his jacket. Underneath he'd pulled a sweater on top of his uniform shirt. He began dragging it off too. Only partly done, he stopped, and stared back at her. 'You want the truth, Kerry? I do think you need to get out of the job. Now, I'm not being an arsehole. I know from my own job the kind of demands you're under. The death of that woman and kid has hit you hard, and visiting the grieving father wouldn't have helped. I don't care what kind of face you've put on for everyone else; I know that you're hurting. Especially about the girl getting killed.'

She shook her head.

'You aren't fooling me.' Adam snatched off the sweater, bundled it in his fists, then threw it down on top of the bedding on the settee. He pushed on his glasses, rough but determined to give her a magnified stink-eye. 'I heard you crying in the bathroom last night. Crying over Sally. That little girl's death has brought everything back that you've kept pent up about your sister.'

'Sometimes I wish I'd never told you about Sally going missing.' Kerry struggled up from the easy chair. Adam lunged at her. He caught her shoulders and held her, off balance. If he let go she'd fall on her backside.

'Well it's a bloody good job you did, isn't it? Otherwise I'd have no idea why you were jumping at shadows and speaking to yourself again.'

'What are you talking about? I don't...'

'It's getting worse, Kerry.' Now all anger had leeched from Adam, and in its place was genuine concern. 'It's your bloody job; it's doing you no good.' He shook her to force his point. 'You're losing the friggin' plot, love.'

'To hell with you.' Digging in her bare feet, Kerry twisted sideways, tried to escape. Adam held on. She yanked out of his grasp and headed for the stairs. He paced after her, not finished yet. He caught her at the bottom step, grabbed her wrist. And she swung for him, her features twisted into a knot.

'Don't!' he snapped.

Her slap had fallen short by less than a few centimetres. She withdrew her hand but kept it poised.

'Get off me, then!'

'Kerry, for God's sake! Look at the way you're acting. Do you think you're being rational?'

'Let go of me, Adam.' She turned over her hand, using an escape technique taught in self-defence classes. Adam only tightened his grip.

'You need to take some time off,' he instructed. 'You have to put some distance between you and this case. Jesus, Kerry, I'm only saying it for your own good.'

'I've a case to solve,' she snapped, thinking of her oath to Suleymaan Ghedi. She worked her wrist more forcefully. He let go. She didn't run up the stairs, but faced him. She hadn't the energy to maintain anger. 'I'm only tired, Adam. I haven't slept well in days. I managed a couple hours just now but even then...'

'You dreamed about Sally,' he finished for her. 'You're obsessed with finding her and — what did you call that nutter? — the friggin' Fell Man? That's my bloody point, Kerry. Taking on a case involving a dead girl isn't helping your mental health.'

'I'm not mentally ill.'

His head gave a tiny jerk to one side.

'And you're not equipped to diagnose me,' she went on. 'So don't even try.'

'You're right. I'm not a psychiatrist, but I am your partner. I know when you're not yourself.'

'If you know me so well, you should know when to shut the hell up. Jesus, Adam!' She threw up her hands in defeat. 'I'm going back to bed. You do whatever you want to do.'

'You should eat something,' he countered. 'You look as weak as water; I bet your blood sugar is low. I can call out for a take away? Chinese? Indian? Or we could order a—'

'Don't say *pizza*,' Kerry groaned as she plodded upstairs. 'Just please don't.'

'So what do you reckon, boss? Minty fresh or what?'

Kerry nudged DS Korba away. She was in the driving seat, and he was supposed to be seated in the passenger side. He'd leaned across to breath in her face. 'Ehm, you do understand the definition of personal space, right?'

'I understand it, don't necessarily mean I care.'

Kerry wiped a spot or two of saliva off her cheek. 'You can say that again.'

'Want one?' Korba rattled a box of Tic Tac breath mints.

'No. I'll pass, thanks.'

He rattled them under her nose. 'Go on. You know you want one.'

His words sent a flutter of panic through her: yesterday's nightmare was still in her memory. Brash humour was a good antidote to fear. 'Put them away, Danny, or you'll be minty fresh at the other end when I shove them up your—'

Korba barked in laughter before she'd finished the threat of involuntary enema. He stowed the breath mints in an inside pocket as Kerry parked outside the late Erick Swain's house. She wasn't looking forward to speaking with Hettie. It was one thing controlling an official interview at a police station, entirely different when on hostile ground. A brand new red Nissan Skyline was parked at kerbside: the same car used to collect Hettie from the nick. Danny's attention swept over it as if he was perusing a naked lady. 'Looks like we might not get Hettie all to ourselves.'

Despite being the girlfriend of a notorious criminal, Hettie Winters was also a human being. She was grieving the loss of her lover, and must contend with the arrangements for his funeral and internment once his body was released. At a time like this, it wasn't unusual to find she'd lean on others close to Erick. The car was probably owned by one of his lieutenants. 'Put it through PNC,' she said.

While he called through the details, she studied the house. The venetian blinds at the windows of all but one bedroom were closed. Weak daylight reflected off the window, but Kerry was certain there was movement in the bedroom. Hettie, she thought.

'No reports on the Skyline,' Korba said. 'It's registered to Zane McManus. We both know who that is.'

McManus was a known associate of Swain. Korba beat her to the punch asking the control room about him. 'No markers or outstanding warrants,' he announced. It was a shame. Arresting him for another crime would've allowed them to press him for information on the drive-by shooting. 'But what's he doing here? Do you think he could've been Swain's driver?'

'Him and about two dozen others.' Swain's gang numbered around thirty key players, and twice as many again if you counted the drug dealers and pimps Swain allegedly supplied with their wares. 'When I'm speaking with Hettie, why don't you get McManus to one side and see what you can squeeze out of him?'

Her gaze flicked up to the bedroom window again.

There was a face beyond the glass. It was indistinct, partially mottled by the daylight slanting inside through the open slats. All she could define was a few locks of wavy hair, a silver earring and the edge of a mouth that buckled up in a sneer. Erick Swain's face loomed into clarity.

'Jesus Christ!'

She almost kicked her way into the car's back seat.

Korba's head bounced off the ceiling, one hand gripping his heart. 'What the hell, boss? Are you tryin' to give me a heart attack or something?'

Gasping, Kerry craned for a better view. There was no face at the window. She blinked in open-mouthed apology at Korba. 'Sorry, for a second there I thought...'

'Thought what?' Korba checked back and forth, expecting an ambush. They were after all in Injun Territory, and less popular than the 7th Cavalry. 'What the bloody hell did you see?'

'Nothing.' How could she admit to seeing a ghost without sounding totally insane? Korba was more friend than colleague to her, but even he might question her fitness for the job if she admitted to seeing Erick Swain. She drew a hand across her mouth, and then quickly waved off his concern. 'Forget it. I didn't see a thing.'

Korba looked at her as if she'd grown two heads.

'Kerry?'

'Really. Forget about it, Danny. I just thought I spotted someone at the window. But it was only the shadows moving on the glass.'

He studied the bedroom window. The day had brightened a little, and it only reflected the sky. He chose not to immediately comment.

She waited him out.

But he was a stubborn sod.

'OK! For a second, I thought I saw Erick Swain in his bedroom.' She laughed at how ridiculous she sounded. 'But that's impossible, right?'

He shrugged, and, surprisingly, paraphrased Shakespeare: 'Nothing's impossible. There are more things in heaven and earth, Kerry, than I've ever dreamed of.'

'So you do think there could be such things as ghosts?'

'It pays to be open-minded,' he said, then added a wink and a caveat, 'as long as ain't so open your blooming brain falls out. I choose not to think Swain's ghost's hanging around. God help us, I saw bugger all and I still came close to crapping my pants.'

113

His crass humour broke the moment. Kerry laughed, shook her head, and before he could press her for her opinion on the spirit world, she got out the car. Korba mirrored her, but took a moment to unhitch his trousers from his backside before shutting the door. 'I'm telling you, that was a close call,' he added for effect.

Kerry didn't react. She put on her professional face and headed for the front path. To her right, she could see the tops of the quartet of towers, the one from which Swain had fallen two nights ago looming over the adjacent rooftops. Weren't ghosts supposed to haunt the location where they died? Not in her experience. When she glanced up at his house, she avoided the bedroom window, in case she spotted Swain again. She averted her face as she strode to the front door and rapped on it officiously. A temporary repair had been made to the door, but it couldn't hide a delve left in it by the battering ram, or the twisted aspect of the uppermost hinge.

Korba stayed a pace behind her, watching the living room window. He spotted fingertips widening a gap in the venetian blinds, as somebody checked them out. He held up his warrant card. From within there came muffled curses.

Kerry and Korba exchanged glances.

It took the best part of a minute, and another knock from Kerry before Hettie answered. 'You'll have to use the back door; this one won't open. You can blame the Old Bill.'

They followed a path between the house and a garden shed, to a gate that had been heightened to almost seven feet tall by the addition of extra wire. Many criminals made fortresses of their homes. Often it was to slow down the police, but also as defence against other criminals. Yet a bolt could be slipped from their side and the gate opened. More likely the gate had been extended to stop the collie dog roaming. Korba secured the gate behind him. As they walked around to the back, there was evidence of where the search team had dug holes in the flower borders around a neatly trimmed lawn. A yellow Frisbee and a red nylon bone looked incongruous on the verdant grass. Hettie stepped out the back door to meet them. A cigarette jutted from her right hand, unlit. She sparked up a lighter and touched it to the end of her ciggie. She stood, making no invitation to her home.

There were smudges of fatigue beneath Hettie's eyes, but otherwise she looked unaffected by her boyfriend's recent passing. But that was based on her good looks alone. She was fidgety, and when she drew on the cigarette it was as if it were an oxygen pipe and she had been submerged in the deepest of oceans.

'You know you're the last person I want to see?' She aimed the glowing end of her cigarette at Kerry. 'What do you want now?'

'I've got a few more questions for you.'

'Isn't the idea of police bail was so I have to return at a specific time and place to answer more questions? This is verging on harassment.'

'These might be questions you don't want to answer on tape.' Kerry nodded past her towards the kitchen. 'Visitors, Hettie?'

Hettie was reluctant to say.

'Look, we heard you talking to somebody when we knocked, and we know that's Zane McManus's car out the front. Is he here or not?'

'What do you want Zane for?'

'I don't. But you might not want him overhearing us.'

Hettie took another long drag on her cigarette. 'Zane called round to offer his condolences, yeah? Nothing else. You know he's my little cousin, don't you?'

The family connection had been lost on Kerry. But it made sense. Many criminal syndicates had extended families at their core. 'I'm not interested in Zane,' said Kerry. *Not unless I learn otherwise.* 'How about you and I have a word out here, and DS Korba can go in and keep Zane busy?'

'Fuck that.' Hettie flicked her cigarette stump onto the path and left it smouldering. 'Too many nosey neighbours to have a private conversation out here.' Without warning, she turned, leaned inside the house and hollered. 'Zane! Hey, Zane? Get your skinny arse out here.'

Zane had been lurking just out of sight, listening to their conversation. He was a tall, skinny youth with sticky out ears perfect for eavesdropping. As he appeared in the kitchen doorway, he made a show of innocence, eyes wide and mouth poised in question. 'Whassup, Hettie?'

'Do me a favour,' she said, in a tone that brooked no disagreement. 'Bring Tyke out on the back and throw his toys for him, will ya?'

'Yeah, right, will do...' Zane disappeared a few seconds, then came out leading the collie. It regarded the police with the same tentative looks as Zane did as he coaxed the dog onto the lawn.

'Right,' said Hettie. 'You two had better come in then.'

Korba pointed at the pack of cigarettes poking out of her jeans pocket. 'Can you spare one of those fags?'

'What, now I've to keep you fuckers supplied with ciggies?'

'Not unless you have any more cannabis lying around?' Korba grinned. 'I'm happy to chill.'

Hettie's nostrils flared a few times as she thought things over. She wasn't an idiot. She pulled out the pack, extended it to Korba and he slid out a cigarette. 'I bet you want a light now?'

'Would be helpful.'

She sparked her lighter and he drew in the flame to the cigarette's tip.

'*Efcharistó.*' Korba exhaled blue smoke, and received a bewildered scowl. 'It's an expression of thanks, but I bet it's all Greek to you, eh?'

'I haven't a clue what you're goin' on about.'

'I have the same problem with him most of the time,' Kerry added. It was a clumsy attempt at forming a common bond with Hettie, and earned her a snort of derision.

She raised her eyebrows at Korba as Hettie went indoors, with a sharp command to, 'Follow me.'

Empty cups and mugs were piled in the sink, but otherwise the kitchen was neat. Hettie had entertained visitors besides her cousin Zane that morning: visitors paying their respects to a man who didn't deserve the sentiment. With Swain gone, it would cause a void in their criminal operation, so arrangements other than which hymns to sing at his funeral were probably discussed.

'Do you want some tea or coffee?' Hettie flicked on the electric kettle.

Kerry had taken tea from Mr Ghedi, but that was under different circumstances. She was about to refuse, except there were occasions where accepting a hot cuppa helped to melt the ice. She nodded her thanks. 'I'll have a tea, please. Milk, one sugar.'

Hettie fetched two fresh mugs from a cupboard, and dished tea bags into them. 'Sit down.' She aimed a nod at a chair standing kitty-corner to the table.

'We're alone, right?' Kerry thought about the face she'd spotted at the bedroom window. A shiver of uncanny dread played the length of her spine and she squirmed her feet.

Hettie eyed her. 'I already told you. D'you think I want anyone overhearing us?'

No more than Kerry did. She felt as if malicious, unseen eyes scrutinised her from the open hallway door. Wanting no unwelcome surprises, she dragged around the chair so the doorway was in view. The light play in the hall remained steady.

Hettie kept her back to her while she prepped milk and sugar in the mugs and waited for the kettle to boil. Her shoulders were tense. 'This must feel weird to you, Inspector?'

Hettie had no idea how weird. 'I'm only doing my job.'

'Yeah. I know that. But sitting here, drinking tea with me after what happened to Erick? It's...*bloody awkward*.'

It was very awkward, and downright eerie, especially when the subject of their discussion could be lurking in earshot. However she wouldn't apologise. It was Erick's fault he fell from the roof, and Erick who'd murdered a mother and child in cold blood.

'I think it's important we speak straight, Hettie. I sympathise with you as a woman who has also lost somebody important. But I'm not here to offer fake platitudes. It's horrible for you, but I've to also think about a young family murdered by your boyfriend.'

Stirring furiously Hettie added water to the mugs. Kerry was on high alert. Being so direct when she was wielding boiling water wasn't such a good idea. Even when Hettie set aside the kettle she didn't relax. Having a mug of scalding tea thrown over her was still a possibility.

Hettie set down the mugs, slid one to Kerry and took the chair opposite. 'It's a shame what happened.' Her eyes glistened. 'I still can't believe Erick would shoot when those poor innocent people were in the way.'

Kerry stayed silent, busying her hands with spooning out the dripping tea bag. Her silence encouraged Hettie to fill the void.

'I'm not going to lie to you. Erick had his faults.' She laughed bitterly at the inanity of her words. 'He could be...well, not very nice. But it still shocked me when I realised what he'd done.'

'You accept that Erick was the one responsible for the shooting?'

Hettie fiddled with her mug of tea, her face downcast. When she looked up, tears made twin tracks down her cheeks. 'I can't deny that the evidence points at him. Not after you found that old gun hidden out the back.' She chewed her lips. 'I swear to you I'd no idea he'd taken it, or buried it in the garden. I've always tried to see the good in Erick, but I'd be a fool to think those were the actions of an innocent man.'

Kerry had prepared for an argument, a drawn out process of recrimination and denial before Hettie saw sense. But the evidence certainly pointed at Erick: had she wondered about her boyfriend's involvement even before the cops arrived? Had the anonymous tip-off to the police hotline about the gun's location come from closer to home than she'd suspected? She didn't get a sense of that from Hettie.

'Can I ask you a blunt question?'

Hettie's shoulders rose and fell.

'If Erick was still alive,' Kerry prompted, 'how would you feel about him now?'

Hettie tipped her mug and downed half its steaming contents. An action designed to give her some thinking time. Mirroring her, Kerry picked up her mug and took a sip.

'If you mean about him killing a kid, I'm not sure it's something I could forgive him for,' Hettie admitted.

Kerry was under no illusion. Hettie was fully aware of Swain's criminal activities. She had a beautiful home and lifestyle purchased by the misery of others. To most of what he'd got up to she'd turned a blind eye, and now and again possibly raised a glass in celebration. If Funky Ikemba were lying dead in a gutter Hettie wouldn't give a shit. But in shooting a little girl even she thought Swain had crossed a line.

'So you believe that he should be punished?'

'I don't know.'

'You said you couldn't forgive him, so don't you think he should be punished for his crime?'

'It's too late for that now.'

Kerry shook her head. 'It isn't too late for justice. Somebody helped Erick. Somebody was behind the wheel of the car when he shot Nala and Bilan.' She deliberately named the victims to humanize them, to give them back the life snatched from them during the senseless act. 'Whoever drove the car is complicit with Erick in the shooting.'

Out in the garden, Tyke barked with exuberance. Zane laughed and goaded the dog on. Korba laughed too. Hettie's attention slid to the open door. Kerry stared at her intently, until she caught her attention. Hettie gave a brief headshake. 'It wasn't Zane.'

'Then who?'

Another long gulp drained Hettie's mug. She stood and turned her back on the question. She dumped the mug in the sink with the others. Braced her palms on the kitchen counter, shoulders rounded as she thought. 'I admitted that Erick went out that day on business. But I also told you I didn't know what he was up to, or who with. I still don't.'

The day before, DC Mel Scanlon had seized the keys to Swain's lockup garage, and a search of it had failed to turn up any further evidence. The keys had been held onto, but whether they pointed to anything important was yet to be figured out. 'You know by now that Erick's Subaru was used during the shooting, and later found burned out. I've heard that car was his pride and joy. In fact, wasn't it you who said that?'

'It was once. But not for donkeys.'

'He hasn't driven it for a long time?'

'No. I'm surprised you haven't checked. He lost his license eighteen months back...accumulation of points for speeding, using his mobile and bollocks like that. The Subaru's been parked in the lockup since.'

'Which makes me think that he was being driven around by somebody else.'

Hettie sniffed. 'He has a lot of friends, and they all drive.'

'Surely he had a favourite? Somebody he relied on more than others? Particularly when conducting *business*?'

'I warned you once before. Don't try putting words in my mouth.'

'I'm not. I'm only trying to help you think.'

'I *think* I'm done with thinking.' Hettie was wiped out rather than angered. 'You should drink up and go. Im sorry, Inspector Darke, but I can't help you.'

'I can help you though,' Kerry said. 'You're possibly looking at a conspiracy to murder charge, or an aiding and abetting charge, at the very least. Help me, Hettie, and I'll make sure you're cleared of any involvement before anyone goes to trial.'

'I've nothing to be cleared of.' For the first time, Kerry noticed Hettie's sapphire engagement ring had been removed, as if she'd already began the process of disassociating herself from her child-killing boyfriend. It was something Kerry could work on. But before she got the opportunity, Hettie snapped her ring-free hand at the barely touched tea. 'C'mon, drink up. Or leave it. I want you to go.'

Kerry stood. She'd hoped for more, but it wasn't the right time to push. Hettie was at a fork in the road, angering her again would force her down the wrong track. 'Here are my details,' she said, planting a card down beside her abandoned tea. 'Use my mobile number. Don't contact me via the station if you want to speak to me more about this, we should keep it hush-hush.'

'That doesn't sound like police procedure to me.' Hettie crossed her arms across her breasts.

'Everything we've said today is off the record. Same if you come up with any names.'

Hettie promised nothing.

DS Korba took over the driving duties as they returned to the police station, allowing Kerry time to mull things over. She should have been thinking about the case, but her personal problems were more distracting. She was still fuming at Adam. They hadn't set a date for their wedding and it was a bloody good job too! If he was the type to try to dominate and control her this early on in their relationship she wasn't certain she wanted to be Mrs Kerry Gill. His assertion that her job was too much for her to cope with was plain wrong. She was a good copper, and he'd no right to say otherwise. She'd dedicated herself to becoming one of the youngest female detective inspectors in the Met, and hadn't reached that position by going down on her knees for her male superiors. Hard graft and determination were her pedigrees. And where did he get off insinuating she was losing her mind?

Maybe she'd acted a little irrationally, but people of sound mind could suffer temporary blowouts when stressed. Practically warning that she was going nuts wasn't the correct approach if he hoped to ease her worries.

Back when first she'd grown aware of Girl's presence, Doctor Ron had cleared her of any underlying mental health issues, so why should seeing her again now be any different? Admittedly, seeing Swain was another matter entirely, but what if it were part of a similar process? What if she did have some kind of heightened ability to see beyond the norm, what would Adam think then? On the face of it the idea was laughable, but who knew? There were swindlers and charlatans, but also people with genuine extra sensory powers. People who claimed to communicate with the dead and see into the future: they could be a bit whacky, but they weren't necessarily mad or frauds. And yet, Adam hadn't directly referred to any claim she'd made of seeing Girl, or *anything* else. His accusation was that her obsession with finding Sally and catching the Fell Man was unhinging her. She wished she'd never confided in him her reason for pursuing a law enforcement career. Every time the subject came up Adam found a way to use it to undermine her. His notion of tough love wasn't being helpful.

Bilan's death had affected her deeply. No denying it. But it wasn't the first death that had touched her while she'd been in the job. What kind of detective would she be if she didn't show compassion for the victims of crime? Having empathy with them ensured she tried her hardest to bring their attackers to justice. Normally her response was cold determination, and it drove her to catch the perpetrators. Bilan's death had hit her in a different way though: deep sadness. And then there was Erick Swain's horrible end, and her swift suspension from duty. Was it any surprise she wasn't acting herself? Adam should know better. He'd brought his work home with him before, and she had been a rock for him, not so much a shoulder to cry on — Adam wasn't prone to the gentler emotions — but a comforting presence. She had been *his* Girl.

He simply didn't understand her.

Her need to catch the Fell Man, and discover the fate of her sister, had become obsessive. In parts it had consumed her, but it had also shaped the adult she'd become. Throughout her police career it had possibly saved lives, and definitely led to the conviction of other criminals. It was an obsession yes, but for the good. And it was more than that. It was a personal quest. Well, if Adam didn't like it, he could lump it.

What are you saying? You'd choose your quest over the man you love?

She shouldn't have to choose.

Though Adam might.

Lately she'd had the feeling that he wasn't equipped to handle the baggage she'd brought into their relationship. *Well, that's his problem, not mine. If he isn't happy, he knows where he can get off!*

The thought hit her like a slap. Stomach acid bubbled up her throat. *Jesus, Kerry, is that what you really want?*

They had met when Kerry, at the time a Detective Sergeant, visited HMP Belmarsh to conduct follow up enquiries with a remand prisoner. Adam had been her assigned escort inside the prison. A big, smart, efficient guy, who was polite and attentive, and judging by his lingering eye contact found something in Kerry's mismatched irises mesmerizing. By chance they'd bumped into each other again months later, this time during a night out with some of her colleagues at a bar on Tottenham Court Road. She hadn't noticed him, but she was instantly recognisable to him. He'd made the first move, and they hooked up instantly. Totally out of character for her, Kerry had slept with him that night, and it had sealed their bond, and apart from where their alternating shift patterns dictated their lives, had barely been apart since. Was she prepared to lose Adam for the sake of...

She didn't end the thought.

It wasn't a debate.

Now you're being a selfish bitch!

No. This wasn't about selfishness. Her quest was as much a part of her as her heterochromia, her arms and legs, her heart and soul. If Adam wanted one part of her he must accept all. A person's faults were equally as important to their make-up as their virtues.

So cut Adam some slack for being an insensitive dick. Embrace his faults too.

Her train of thought fell silent. She could almost imagine the tumbleweeds rolling past. Almost. But apparently her imagination wasn't as fertile as it was when conjuring Girl, or...shit, she could deny the past few incidents all she wanted, but the shape lurking behind DCI Porter, then in her office and recently leering from Hettie's bedroom window was undeniable.

'You shouldn't dwell on Erick Swain.'

Kerry gawped at DS Korba.

'Sorry?' she asked once she'd caught her breath.

'Swain. You should put him out of your mind.'

It was almost as if Korba were the one with the extra sensory perception and had read *her* mind. She shook her head.

'What happened to him was horrible, but you don't have to carry any guilt,' Korba expounded. 'You ask me, well, it's guilt that made you think about him back there at his house. It wasn't a ghost, Kerry, just guilt.'

Kerry said nothing.

They were waiting at a red light, boxed in by black cabs and delivery vehicles on all sides. Ahead of them, a twin-carriage bus blocked the road, its extra length unable to clear the intersection. Horns blared in annoyance.

'I'm not dwelling on guilt over Swain's death,' she finally said, 'only on what he's responsible for.'

'You shouldn't carry that kid's death on your shoulders either.'

'She was called Bilan and she was only ten.'

'I know, Kerry. I don't mean to trivialize her murder. It's a horrible waste of a young life. But you can't let it get to you. You have to compartmentalize, put it away in a box so it doesn't eat you up.' Korba didn't look at her once.

'I'm not.'

Korba looked at her then. His eyebrows rose in question.

'Look, Danny, I appreciate your concern. But you don't have to worry about me. If I am dwelling on Swain it's only because we need a quick result on this case.' They both understood that it was only a matter of time before their superiors expected firm resolution to the case. More importantly she'd promised Bilan's father she'd do everything in her power to catch and punish her killers.

'Tell me about Zane McManus,' she said bluntly.

'He's an idiot.'

'Aye, well that's a given. Any suggestion he was the driver?'

'He's too stupid to have been involved. I ain't suggesting he doesn't play a part in Swain's activities, but in a less demanding role.'

'He drives. He has, what was it, a Nissan Skyline?' She didn't wait for Korba's confirmation. 'I don't need to be a petrol head to know a Skyline doesn't come cheap. How old's Zane...early twenties? A kid his age, and I'm assuming with no full-time employment and scrounging benefits, couldn't buy that car, let alone pay the extortionate insurance on it. You called him stupid, but he's obviously clever enough to do something for Swain that lines his pockets.'

'I ain't denying he's getting bunged a few quid, and the Skyline was probably an incentive to obligate him to Swain. But I had a good chinwag with him: he's a bit of a numpty. You ask me, the only reason he's been taken into the fold is 'cause he's Hettie's cousin. He's good for running a few errands, the odd street level drug deal, and keeping Tyke entertained. He's a glorified dog-sitter, and like I said, a numpty. He ain't somebody you'd trust to back you up on a drive-by shooting.'

Kerry rolled her neck.

The bus had finally cleared the intersection, but standing traffic still blocked them in. The lights had gone through their sequence twice in the meantime. Other drivers were growing impatient, and frustrated, and the sounds of horns were insistent.

'We don't rule Zane out yet,' Kerry decided. 'I want Mel to concentrate on collating the file, and doing follow up inquiries with witnesses at the scene. I could also do with her viewing the CCTV we've seized. We only need one clear picture of the driver and it should be enough to identify him.' Mel Scanlon had widened the ring in regards CCTV evidence, checking street cameras between Wandsworth Road and the bank of the Thames where the Subaru was later found burnt out. 'Glenn and Tony I want working their CHIS for any of Swain's associates we haven't already identified.' A Covert Human Intelligence Source was a police term for an informant, though they were often called by a more derogatory term. Occasionally a grass could be compelled to squeal simply through their hatred of the person they were fingering, or through monetary reward. It didn't matter how they got the intelligence, as long as she learned a credible name to follow up on. 'I'll keep working on Hettie, and I think another discussion with Funky's on the cards.'

The traffic abruptly started moving. They took a left and joined another queue of slow moving traffic. 'Did Bob Grier get back to you?' Korba asked. 'Once things quietened down at Swain's place, he told me he needed to speak with you about the gun.'

Grier knew more about weapons than her. He was a resource she should pull on. There was something troubling about the manner in which the gun was found, but what it was she hadn't worked out yet. Whatever Grier had to tell her could prove important. She took out her mobile and rang the control room, asked a dispatcher for Grier's personal line. It rang out. When she checked she discovered the sergeant was on his rest days. She rang his home number.

A sullen teenaged boy answered.

'Hello, can I speak with Bob Grier, please?' she asked.

Without answering, the youth placed down the handset. 'Dad! It's some woman for you.'

In the background Kerry heard soft muttering, clattering, then a gruff voice. 'This better not be another flaming market research survey.' The words were directed at the boy, who said something that could be deemed racist and sexist: 'It ain't a Paki, it's some Geordie bird.'

She wasn't a Geordie, but southerners often mistook her accent.

'Bob,' she announced as soon as he made a gruff 'hullo' down the phone. 'It's DI Kerry Darke. I hope I'm not intruding...'

'Oh, hi, Kerry,' he said, his tone brightening. 'Nah. It's nothin' that can't be put off. My missus has me assembling some flat pack cupboards. It's taken me bloody hours, so I'm due a break.'

'Those things can be torture,' she agreed. 'The other night at Erick Swain's place, you wanted to tell me something about the gun, but I didn't get back to you.'

'Yeah, you had your hands full at the time.' He chuckled. 'During the commotion I took an impromptu head dive into a bloody wall, so I forgot about it myself.'

'Danny Korba said you asked for me to get in touch after. Sorry about the slow reply.'

'Yeah, well, you can't be blamed for that either. That boss of yours...'

'Say no more,' she said.

'Yeah, that's maybe best. Look, something bothered me about that Webley we found.'

'Go on, Bob.'

'From what I know of the drive-by, there were three shots fired. Three brass shells found at the scene?'

'That's right.'

'Yeah. That's what bothers me. See, there were four bullets found in the gun.'

'And it was a six shot revolver. Aye, the numbers don't add up,' said Kerry, pleased she'd already noted the disparity.

'Swain could've easily reloaded an extra bullet afterwards. Why he'd do that if he intended burying the gun, we'll probably never know. But that's not what's been bothering me. You know how a revolver works, don't you?'

'I have the basic concept.'

'I wasn't trying to insult your intelligence, just some people unfamiliar with firearms make assumptions based on what they've seen in movies, brass shells tinkling round the gunman's feet. That's OK if the gun was a pistol. It doesn't happen like that with a revolver. After the bullet's been fired, the empty shell stays in the chamber while the cylinder rotates to set the next live round. For those expended shells to be found at the scene, they had to have been taken out the cylinder and dumped out the car window. Nobody with an ounce of savvy about forensics would do that, and they were savvy enough to burn out the getaway car. Who wastes time to dump the empties and load a single cartridge when there's still three live rounds in the gun?'

'It does sound implausible.'

'Or deliberate.'

'Get the brews in, Danny, and I'll see you all in the office in five.'

Korba flicked an aye-aye salute and sauntered towards the canteen, with the intention of rounding up the rest of their team en route.

Kerry made a swift visit to the loo, avoiding glancing at the vanity mirrors over the sinks and almost diving inside a cubicle. After she washed her hands, again averting her gaze from her reflection, she was in the act of drying her hands before realising how irrational her behaviour was. What exactly was she so afraid of? She should be inured to weird hallucinations by now. Girl's appearance was always eerie, but she'd never felt threatened by her. It was the *other* presence she was afraid of. *He* was sinister.

The problem with irrationality was that it was a self-propagating condition. The more she denied seeing Swain, the more she tried not to see him. But the harder she tried the more he remained in the forefront of her thoughts, and the more she feared he'd appear again. She almost fled the bathroom in panic. Mercifully the locker room was empty this time, so she was able to gather her shredded nerves before exiting into the corridor, and scuttling for the GaOC office.

She had the room to herself.

Thankfully DCI Porter was attending a Trident strategy meeting at New Scotland Yard. The reprieve was welcome. It was an opportunity to get her facts together before giving Porter a progress report. All she had was a disparity in numbers. Three shots fired, three spent shells at the scene, four live rounds in the murder weapon, a six-shot revolver. It didn't make sense. She couldn't act until she figured out *why* the numbers didn't add up.

Her team had collated a flow chart and pinned it to the office wall. It listed Erick Swain and his known associates. Corresponding mugshots had been added where available, but some of those named had little more than their dates of birth and last known addresses listed. She studied the board, hoping a name would jump out and demand further investigation. Henrietta Jayne Winters and Zane McManus were situated at opposite ends of the 'known associates' chart. Her attention drifted over the spaces between the two, absorbing names and faces. One of them was the person she sought. She took a step back, as if the bigger picture would become clearer if viewed from a distance.

'Look closer.'

She felt as much as heard those words. They were carried on a sharp exhalation that ruffled the hair around her left ear.

She spun around, her hand clasping down on the spot. Her skin was icy, clammy, and there was a residue of static electricity that crawled down her cheek on scuttling insect legs. Snapping her head about, she searched for who'd spoken. Nobody. Holding her breath, she twisted to face the chart again, briefly hoping she was the victim of a prank, and the joker had moved counter to her. Nobody.

The voice must have originated out in the corridor. The exhalation of cold air from...all the fans had been turned off while the office was empty; there was nowhere it could have come from! The office was its usual sealed tomb, airless and still.

Her fingertips played across her ear and jaw. The tickle of electricity was now the caress of an airborne spider's web. Goose pimples rose over her entire body and her short hairs stirred to attention. Uncanny dread clawed at her. She sought escape, lunged for the door.

A second icy breeze struck her face, halting her. This time the words felt tattooed into her skin by jabbing needles. *'I said look closer, you wall-eyed slag!'*

She swiped at the empty air, batting at invisible webs of energy, crying out. Stumbled backwards on rubbery legs. Her mind was chaotic, questions tumbling. What, where, how...*who?*

'You fucking know who!'

This time the voice came from her right. She cowered away. Didn't want to look, but she must.

The air directly in front of the flow chart rippled, as if disturbed by a wafting thermal haze. Snatches of colour dimmed then brightened, and there was a scattering of twinkling highlights: silver and pearl. Indistinct shapes and shades coalesced, and took on form. A wolfish visage jumped into clarity, framed by shaggy blond locks and a silver earring. *'Look closer, bitch!'*

Kerry shrieked, batted in horror at the face of a dead man. Her arms swept through the image, tearing it into translucent wisps and scattering them. She raced for the door.

Before she could reach it, she suffered a moment of stark lucidity. Stumbled to a halt. She braced her left hip against Mel Scanlon's desk, one hand covering her mouth, as she aimed a tentative glance at where Swain had appeared. She was unsure if the rippling haze in the air was genuine, or a result of her wet eyes. 'Neither,' she croaked into cupped fingers. 'It's all in your head. Adam was right: You *are* losing it.'

Girl — supposedly the product of a child's fertile imagination — had forever been a silent companion. Kerry had grown used to visual hallucinations, so much so that for years she'd ignored them entirely and Girl had faded into the deepest corners of her subconscious. Noticing her again only a few days ago, at the murder scene of a similarly aged child, was perhaps not entirely unexpected. But seeing Swain was unexpected and frightening. To hear his voice was terrifying. Whether his words were a form of auditory hallucination she couldn't ignore their consequence. This was an entirely knew level of craziness.

She balked against the notion.

Insane people didn't recognise their insanity...did they?

'I'm not mad,' she whispered. She was tired, stressed, annoyed, but not going insane. 'I'm not mad, I'm not mad.'

She straightened, staring directly at the shimmering atmosphere, challenging Swain to materialise again. Everything was as it should be. Scanning the entire room, she saw nothing out of place. The only sound was the low hum of the overhead lights, and the distant ambient noises of a busy police station muffled by intervening walls and doors.

'See...I'm not mad,' she confirmed with a little more backbone. And it wasn't a moment too soon, because the door opened and Tony Whittle held it open so Glenn Scott could enter, carrying a tray filled with five steaming mugs, Korba and Mel following. Kerry returned their greetings with individual nods, but didn't speak for fear her voice quivered. She was torn. Glad of their presence but wishing she'd had a couple more minutes to get composed. She could tell herself she wasn't mad, but judging by their frowns and glances, her team had other ideas.

Korba was last to have seen her, so to him her current dishevelled appearance was most obvious. Once Glenn set down the tray, the DS grabbed a mug of tea and offered it to her. Trembling, Kerry accepted it, grateful of something to do other than speak. Korba aimed a silent question at her. She shook her head gently, said, 'Some personal stuff I'm dealing with.'

'Swain again?'

'Adam.' Her fiancé was as good an excuse as any. She lowered her head and Korba got the message.

He took control of the briefing, and doled out the team's responsibilities as prescribed by Kerry earlier. Once he was done, he offered Kerry the floor, sensing she'd regained a grip of her emotions. Her instruction was short and pointed. 'You know what we need to do. So let's do it.'

Mel headed out to scare up the video evidence she was waiting for, while Glenn and Tony got on with contacting and arranging meetings with their informants. Kerry followed Korba through the nick to the canteen to freshen their cups. A trio of patrol officers was finishing up their fish and chips lunch, laughing and bullshitting, and once they'd dumped their papers and plastic cups in a bin, the two detectives had the canteen to themselves.

'How d'you feel about taking some advice from a lowly detective sergeant, boss?' Korba posed.

'Depends on whether it's about my love life. You're a confirmed bachelor, Danny; your advice might not be the best.'

'I know things ain't good at home for you,' he said, 'but avoiding the issue won't help. You and Adam need to sit down and have a heart to heart, get things straight between you again. This—' He touched two fingers to her upper chest, then immediately to her forehead '—has to be kept in line with this. One can't work without being in tune with the other, not if you want to stay balanced.'

'What do you mean by staying balanced?' I'm not going crazy if that's what you're suggesting.'

Korba forced a sad smile. 'See. That's exactly what I mean. Any other time you'd have made a joke of that, not got pissed off. You ain't acting yerself, Kerry. You're, whatchamacallit, off-kilter?'

'Nuts?'

'No. Not crazy, but acting out of character.'

'It's hardly surprising.'

'No. It ain't.' Korba took a furtive glance around to ensure they were still unobserved. 'But it is noticeable.'

'I'm just tired. I haven't slept well and...'

He sighed. 'The reasons ain't what's important, Kerry, the symptoms are. You know earlier, when we were comin' back from Hettie's place? If I didn't know better I'd swear you were high on speed. Your eyes were jumping all over the shop, and you were flinching at everything. Not just flinching either, it was as if you were expecting to be slapped or something. When I think about it, it started when we first got there and you thought you spotted Swain at the bedroom window.'

'Yeah, well, I told you then it was just the shadows on the glass.'

'And we both know you were lying, boss.' He held up a palm to placate her. 'Sorry, *lying* is a poor choice of word. I mean you were sparing me the truth, till you admitted you saw Swain at the window.'

'Spare me the semantics,' she said, attempting to make it sound like a quip.

He didn't respond with humour. He peered at her, his pupils darting from her amber iris to her green iris and back again before he came to a decision. 'What you thought you saw then is still troubling you. Did you see him again just now?'

'Danny, you're forgetting...I didn't really see him. I told you, it was just the reflection of the clouds.'

'Boss, you can call me all the names under the Sun, but don't call me cabbage-coloured. You're a tough girl, and brave as a lion, but what I saw...'

'What exactly *did* you see?'

'You were spooked, Kerry. Something put the willies up you, and we both know what. And I think it's still putting the willies up you now.'

'That's where you're wrong, then. It's you that's seeing things, Danny, not me.' She touched her pocket where she'd secreted her mobile. 'I'd just got off the phone with Adam. We were having a barney, and I was embarrassed that the others might've heard.'

'If you say so,' Korba said, unconvinced. 'But if that's true, you should still take my original advice. Go home. Speak with Adam, get your head sorted.'

'There's nothing wrong with my head. Now, I appreciate your concern. You're a good friend. But shut the fuck up, OK?' She gave him a friendly shove on his shoulder. He regarded her stonily, but two could play at that game. 'I'm not going home. I'm going to rattle Funky's cage. You can come with me or stay here and play Uri Geller with somebody who actually needs their spoons bending.'

There was never any question about the choice DS Korba made. He'd said his piece, been listened to, and Kerry had chosen to ignore his advice. Fair do. He'd let things rest at that. He wasn't the type to beat any friend into submission, and was also astute enough to know he'd be adding to her troubles if he did. As long as she understood he had her back, and was there to support her if she needed him, he was satisfied.

He liked Kerry Darke a great deal.

She fascinated him, and his opinion wasn't based entirely on her looks. She wasn't a classical beauty, or a fake like Hettie Winters who reminded him of biting into a fresh, crisp apple only to find a rotten core. To some people, those with heterochromia could appear odd, and maybe even a little creepy, but on Kerry the condition added to her allure. He could spend hours lost in her gaze, but was afraid she'd misconstrue his attention. Actually, who was he kidding? He was in love with her, but was terrified she found out, in case she laughed in his face. He wasn't a bad-looking bloke, but he wasn't tall and broad-shouldered like hunky ex-soldier Adam Gill, who was obviously her type. Besides, she was his boss, and he couldn't see how a relationship could work if he made his affections known and they were reciprocated. For starters, they wouldn't be allowed to work together, and it was unlikely Kerry would get the transfer she'd requested; he'd be the one kicked out of GaOC and shipped out to another station — the last thing he wanted. He wanted to be with Kerry, and if that meant keeping his feelings secret, so be it. He hated watching her go through this current turmoil, be it due to her fiancé or the aftermath of watching a man plummet to his death.

He was driving again, taking them across the Thames towards the Patmore Estate, a stomping ground of the

Nine Elms Crew. Respecting Kerry's silence he kept schtum, but couldn't resist an occasional glance to check on her. She was aware of his scrutiny, but refused to look directly at him. She struggled to keep a neutral expression though. Her fingers were constantly at play, even though she'd folded her hands in her lap. Twice he caught her flinching, as if in automatic response to a perceived danger, and catching herself in the act she'd coughed and exaggerated an itch on her face by scratching vigorously. Her bruised forehead was dotted with perspiration. He didn't comment. Waited her out instead.

They were on Thessaly Road, passing a huge fruit and vegetables market complex, when she finally spoke. It was only to confirm Ikemba Adefunke's last known address, a couple of streets over in the midst of the housing estate. As the crow flew they were less than four hundred metres from where Nala and Bilan Ghedi were gunned down on Wandsworth Road. He didn't need GPS to guide him in: he was familiar with the area. Funky lived in a decent neighbourhood, but as was the case with many estates it only took a notorious minority to bring it down. Jermaine Robson's crew numbered as many as Erick Swain's rival gang, and ruled their territory with an iron fist.

Funky's home was situated on the uppermost floor in a row of apartment blocks, part of a complex encircling a central garden. They found Funky standing out on the pavement, conversing with a couple of friends. They slapped palms and knuckles in flambouyant handshakes. Criminals had an inherent skill for spotting cops, and before either of them was out of the vehicle, Funky's pals sloped away, averting their faces. Funky pushed his hands in his tracksuit trouser pockets, and bunched them to hitch them up. He rolled his tongue behind his bottom lip as they approached, then dribbled saliva between his feet in greeting.

'Inspector Darke.' Once again her name sounded as if it was something to be reviled. 'What d'you want? The other day was a one time only deal.' He glanced around, checking he was unobserved. 'You're endangerin' me and my family by showin' up here.'

'Haven't you heard?' Kerry asked. 'You don't have to worry about Erick Swain coming after you again.'

'I heard. You did us all a service when you threw the bastard off that roof.'

Korba expected Kerry to correct Funky, but she didn't.

'Is there somewhere more private we can speak?' she said.

Funky shook his head. 'I don't speak with the pigs.'

'Only when it suits you, mate?' Korba said.

Funky strutted forward a few paces; Korba held his ground. He wasn't intimidated, even if Funky stood a head taller. The gangster bent his vulture neck to set his face a few inches from his.

'It would suit me better if you fucked off somewhere else, *mate*.'

'I've a better idea,' said Korba. 'How's about you turn out your pockets for me? I'd be interested in seeing what it was you were handing out to your bros when we got here. What do you say, Funky? Turn out your pockets or you'll be down to the nick for a full strip search.'

'You want to see what I've got?' He sneered, made a show of pulling out the empty lining of his pockets. 'Oh, would you look at what I just found!' He raised his balled fists, both middle fingers extended. 'Got one for each of you.'

Beside Korba, Kerry exhaled. He glanced at her, fully expecting her to order Funky's arrest, except she wasn't going down that route. She dabbed her fingertips across her forehead, mopping cold sweat from her brow. 'I haven't the time or patience for this, Funky,' she said calmly. 'I've a couple of questions for you, that's all. Then you can get back to whatever the hell you waste your life on. I don't have to remind you that we could be investigating your murder instead, and I'm pretty sure you'd want us to get to the bottom of it.'

'Swain was a shit aim,' he reminded her. 'Not sure you'd be investigating anyone's murder if that woman and kid hadn't got in the way.'

'Let's not argue semantics,' Kerry said — her word for the day.

Korba doubted Funky knew the meaning of the term, but who knew? You didn't get to be an inner echelon player in the Nine Elms Crew by being dumb, unless you were muscle, and Funky hadn't earned a rep as a fighting man.

'You said you recognised Erick Swain as the shooter...'

Funky rolled his neck in silent agreement.

'But you didn't notice the driver of the car,' Kerry went on. 'Do you recall how many shots were fired?'

'Three. Like I said. Shit aim. Or maybe the kiddie in the pram would have been dead as well.' He spoke as if Taban would have been a bonus prize. Korba had to hold his tongue, wondering at Kerry's approach.

She didn't rise to the taunt. 'You said you stared at Swain, challenging him to shoot.'

'That's right. It's how I got a good look at him and none of the driver.'

'You said the driver was white.'

'I got the *impression* he was white. He was in the corner of my eye.'

'That's funny, when I see something out the corner of my eye, they're only vague shadows.' Korba caught a brief glance from her, as if she was checking he hadn't read anything from her words. But before he could give it much thought, she continued. 'I can rarely define colour or shade in my periphery. How can you be certain the driver was white?'

'What are the chances that Swain was ridin' with a black man?' He had a point. Swain's gang was exclusively white. 'So maybe I glanced at him. Can't recall any features or anything else, but I saw a white face.'

'What else might you have glanced at?'

'I don't know what you mean.'

'OK. So let me clarify. You stared at Swain, counted the shots he fired at you — three of them — so what happened next?'

'They took off down Wandsworth Road like stink off shit.'

'Immediately?'

'Yeah.'

'And then you took cover in the shop in case they came back?'

'I took cover in the shop 'cause it was bucketing down, not 'cause I was afraid.'

'So you only went inside after the car was driven away?'

Funky threw up his hands. 'Am I fuckin' speaking Klingon here? How many times—'

'That's enough times for now.' Kerry turned away and strode to the car, wrong-footing Korba by her abrupt abandonment.

Funky gawped at him. 'Is she right in the head or what?'

'No, mate, she just can't abide being near arseholes for long.'

'I pity her then,' Funky sneered, 'seein' as you'll be getting back in that car with her.'

Korba winked. 'Takes one to know one.'

Funky raised an index finger again, and backpedalled away. Korba watched him retreat until he disappeared inside the apartment block. He headed for the car. Kerry was already inside, deep in thought. He slid into the driver's seat, frowning.

'I thought you wanted to press Funky for more?'

'We got what we wanted from him.'

'We did?' If they had, he'd missed the subtext of the conversation. 'Care to elucidate, boss?'

'Funky's a liar.'

'Goes without saying. But on what exactly was he lying?'

'Everything. Three shots fired, three brass shells at the scene.'

Korba's eyebrows knitted. 'Sorry, Kerry, you're gonna have to help me out here.'

'You heard what Funky said. He stood there like the big man challenging Swain to shoot. Swain fired three times then took off like quote-unquote *stink off shit.*'

'Yeah. So?'

'So when was Swain supposed to have unloaded the spent rounds, thrown them out of the window, and loaded a fresh bullet into the revolver?'

He'd overheard her telephone discussion with Bob Grier regarding the workings of a Webley Mk IV, and wasn't thick. He understood now: Funky was lying about the sequence of events, or had manipulated them to suit his narrative. 'He probably barely got a look at Swain, or what the hell really happened 'cause he was too busy running for his life. All of that stuff about staring down Swain, it's a load of macho bollocks.'

'I have to admit, there was one point he made that rang true. Swain's driver should have been white.'

'That doesn't help us. It was already a given, seeing as Swain was a racist.'

'Aye, right enough,' Kerry wheezed, her northern vernacular slipping through. 'But not what I mean.'

She lapsed into silence.

'You don't feel like sharing, eh?' Korba asked.

'Not yet. There's something I need to check first.'

'There's no harm in saying...' he pressed.

'Not yet.'

Korba started the engine. But they didn't move.

A sleek white Mercedes Benz pulled up alongside them. Korba met the studious gaze of a black man seated in its driving seat. He had a statuesque face, with strong high-cheekbones and deeply set grey-blue eyes, his hair in woven cornrows. A smile played across his full lips. Korba held his attention a second longer before he craned forward to peer past him at Kerry. He held her gaze for a few seconds too, before he offered the briefest nod of displaced gratitude and drove away.

'Jermaine Robson,' Korba stated.

'One and the same.'

Funky hadn't had the opportunity to alert his boss about their presence, but the two younger black guys who'd skedaddled earlier had. Robson had announced his presence rather than driving past, but for what reason? 'The smug bastard,' Korba said. 'He didn't come over to check on Funky. It was to see who he owed thanks to for doing away with Swain.'

Kerry clucked her tongue. 'Now you sound like Adam.'

'You know what I mean, boss.'

'I do,' she admitted. 'And you're probably right. With Swain out of the picture we've opened a void in the power structure. If we're not careful, Robson will fill it.'

During the return drive to their station north of the Thames, Kerry received a summons to DCI Porter's office. The going was slow, and it was half an hour before Korba parked their vehicle in the station's secure parking basement. As they entered the station, Korba's phone rang. Mel Scanlon updated them with where their investigation was. Good news: the ballistics report confirmed the murder weapon and Swain's Webley was a match. Kerry had never been in doubt, but the confirmation needled her.

'What about forensics?'

Korba relayed Mel's words. 'Fingerprints matched to Erick Swain were found on a bullet in the revolver, and also on the rounds seized from his bedroom. The shells at the scene were clean, and the gun had been wiped clean before it was buried.'

'I'd best go and give His Nibs the news,' she said with little enthusiasm.

'D'you want me to come with you, boss?' Korba shoved his hands in his trouser pockets. For a second she waited for him to pull Funky's trick, draw out his fists and flip her off. But his offer was genuine.

'No. It's best I see Porter alone.'

She sounded defensive, and she was. He'd earlier raised the subject of her acting out of character, and her behaviour in the past couple of hours wouldn't have allayed his concern. He'd been aware of her flaky mood, and the way she flinched at shadows, and couldn't hide the fact he found her sudden curtailment of the talk with Funky odd, to say the least. Was his reason for volunteering his support about keeping a close eye on her, to ensure she didn't do or say anything crazier in front of the DCI? No, she was doing him a disservice. Danny was a colleague, but more than that he was a friend, and he cared for her more than he openly admitted. Paranoia *was* getting the better of her.

'Can you give Glenn and Tony a shout and see if they've anything new for us?' She made her request sound like a concession to fobbing him off. 'And see if Mel needs an extra set of eyes going through the video evidence. If there's anything, and I mean *anything*, useful, I don't need to wait until the end of the meeting to hear about it, OK?'

'Got ya.' Korba flicked a salute and headed for the GaOC office.

A funeral dirge would have made a fitting soundtrack to her walk to DCI Porter's office. Irrational as it were, she wasn't afraid of seeing Porter, but who else might be waiting in his office. It was there, after all, that Erick Swain's incorporeal spirit had first made its presence known to her. *So what are you going to do, Kerry? Avoid the GaOC office too, because that's where he finally spoke to you?* If what she'd witnessed was more than a hallucination, then nowhere was safe. Ghosts weren't constrained by the place of their death. And if the sightings were figments of her imagination, then there was no escape from something dwelling inside her head.

For a second she hoped Swain's ghost had visited her. The alternative was far scarier than being haunted by a restless spirit.

She laughed aloud.

Instantly she wished she could retract it, because it was a cackle, and it didn't go unnoticed. Porter's office door swung open, and the DCI was in the act of showing somebody out with a hearty handshake. Both faces turned at the sound of lunacy, then they regarded each other. Porter offered an "I told you so" grimace as they released their handshake. The other man, as severe and grey in his demeanour as in his choice of suit, was a stranger to Kerry, but she knew *what* he was.

'Sorry, sir,' she said. 'I was just struck by a funny thought.'

'There's no rule against happiness.' The grey-haired man offered a smile that added a touch of colour to his cheeks. He turned his smile on the DCI. 'Having a happy team is the mark of good leadership, Charles.'

His comment to the DCI was a welcome distraction, and Kerry was grateful. By the time they both regarded her again, she'd regained a modicum of professionalism. The man approached her with his hand extended.

'Superintendent Harker,' he said in introduction. 'I'm glad we got the opportunity to meet, Inspector Darke, and I would like to chat longer. Though you must now excuse *me*; duty calls back at The Yard, I'm afraid.'

His handshake was brief, but warm enough. Except a dribble of icy water ran the length of her spine. Superintendent Graeme Harker: she knew exactly who he was. He also knew her name, which was bad news. She flickered him a smile, and trying not to sound ironic said, 'Another time then, sir.'

'Indeed. Charles, be seeing you too.'

The Superintendent strode off down the corridor, his leather-soled brogues beating noisily on the thin blue carpet underfoot. He was a contradiction. Officers working in the Department for Professional Standards were referred to as 'rubber heelers' after their propensity for sneaking around and eavesdropping private conversations. Perhaps by the time you made Superintendent of DPS the necessity for silence was replaced by the thunder of the firing squad you headed.

Kerry watched him until he'd disappeared around a corner some distance away.

'Kerry. I haven't got all day.' Porter held the door open. 'Come in.'

She aimed a thumb at the space in the corridor vacated by Harker. 'Was he here because of me?'

'If he were, it wouldn't be right to admit it. Now, come in, Kerry, you've kept me waiting long enough.'

As she entered his office, Porter stayed at the door. He studied her reaction – watching if she had a similar response to the area where his commendation hung on the wall as before. She rested a hand on the back of the chair she'd previously sat in, glanced at him. Porter's mouth pinched briefly, then he closed the door securely and hustled past to his side of the desk. As he sat, so did she. She deliberately fixed her eyes on his neatly knotted tie. Again she sensed his scrutiny, and lifted her head. The overhead light washed out the lenses on his glasses; his return stare was inscrutable. The silence was palpable.

'I'm sorry I took a while getting back, sir. I was conducting follow up enquiries with a witness.'

He sniffed away her excuse. 'Tell me that you've got something actionable.'

'Nothing concrete, I'm afraid.'

'Then get something concrete. Erick Swain's death doesn't mean we've dodged a bullet.' He paused, considering his poor choice of words. 'By that I mean we still need a successful conviction. The media can posthumously try and convict Swain for the deaths of the Ghedis, but it's an unsatisfactory result for the Met, and for my team in particular. I want a live suspect on the stand, Kerry. Where exactly are you with identifying Swain's driver?'

She quickly related the actions taken, and that her team was conducting pro-active enquiries with CHIS, and interrogating CCTV evidence. She told him about the ballistics report confirming the murder weapon and the one seized from Swain's garden matched, and that Swain's fingerprints had been lifted off a bullet loaded in the revolver and also those seized from his bedroom, though not from the spent shells found at the crime scene or from the gun itself. Next she mentioned her recent discussions with Hettie Winters and Funky, and how neither of their versions of events rang true with her.

'On what level?'

'They're both liars.'

He tilted his head, and his glasses flashed reflections off the polished desk. 'So find out the truth.'

'I'm working on it, sir.' Earlier, she'd avoided mentioning what was on her mind to Korba, but she was in a pinch under his stern expression. 'I have a theory—'

He held up a hand. 'I'm not interested in theories. I want facts, proof and evidence. I want to see arrests and convictions.'

'I'm working on it,' she repeated. 'I'm only waiting on a single piece of corroborating evidence that I can act on.'

'What kind of evidence?'

'I don't know for certain. But I'll know it when it arrives and I will give you the arrests and convictions you expect.'

Porter grunted.

'I could do without empty promises, Inspector Darke.' He studied her closely for a moment. Changed tack entirely. 'I'm wondering if in lieu of what happened to Swain you're the best person to head this investigation. Would it be unreasonable to suggest that you were affected by his violent death?'

'I'm perfectly fine,' she said.

He pursed his mouth. Sat back. He'd taken off his suit jacket earlier, so didn't need to unbutton it to make room for his belly. Instead he fiddled with his tie. Then slowly — deliberately, she suspected — craned around to observe the framed certificate on the wall. Sensing the trap, Kerry didn't follow his prompt. When he gave her a sidelong look she was still facing forward. He turned back to her with a smile ghosting across his lips.

'If there's any support I can offer, you need only ask,' he said.

'I have DC Scanlon tied up with going through hours of CCTV footage if...' She didn't finish the request for extra manpower, because it dawned that was not his meaning. 'Sir, if you mean therapy, I'd like to politely decline. I don't need it.'

'Maybe you're not the best person to judge.'

Kerry scowled. 'Has somebody said something about my odd behaviour?'

'About what?'

Idiot! She'd almost sprung a trap for herself. 'I don't know. I only wondered why you'd think I'd need it.'

'You were involved in a violent incident that ended with a man's death. Police officers aren't soulless robots, Kerry; we do have feelings. It's why we have the robust support of an occupational health department.'

'Have any of the other affected officers been offered therapy?'

'No. But two constables injured by Swain are currently on sick leave, one whose leg injury is quite serious and could disqualify him from future active duty: as and when the time comes, both will be offered, and encouraged to accept, assistance from Occupational Health.'

'That's fine. Their injuries are more serious.' She touched her grazed forehead. 'As you can see, mine is already on the mend.'

Again Porter pursed his lips. It was in his power to order her to attend sessions with a force therapist, but couldn't do so while she was on active duty. If she wasn't careful another suspension could be heading her way. 'Sir, honestly, you've nothing to worry about. I'm fine. I'm a little tired, a little under pressure, but hey, aren't we all?' She raised her hand, holding her thumb and forefinger a hair's breadth apart. 'I'm that far from getting something concrete for you. I'd rather spend my time investigating than being analysed.'

'I'd be a poor supervisor if I didn't care about my team,' he said enigmatically. He said no more.

His silence was her cue to leave. She stood, straightening her clothes.

'Sir,' she said, uncertain if she was saying goodbye or asking his permission to go.

He continued staring at her, inscrutable again behind the glare on the lenses of his spectacles. She couldn't meet his gaze and felt her own slip beyond him. It was almost a physical effort to drag her eyes from the spot where a semi-translucent Erick Swain mimed a lewd act of sexual self-gratification over the DCI's shoulder.

'What a sanctimonious tosser *you work for,'* Swain crowed, for her ears only. *'All he cares about is how much you embarrass him!'*

Kerry didn't know whether to laugh or cry as she hurried away without a backwards glance.

Sloshing an inch of whisky into a glass, Kerry collapsed on the settee in her living room. When she'd arrived home in the early evening, the stale smell reminded her she'd neglected her share of the domestic chores for a couple of days. Adam's attempt at mopping the spilled whisky had been in his usual bullish-style: throwing down a few sheets of absorbent kitchen towel and stomping up the residue. The carpet had dried, but the stain and aroma hadn't shifted. Resolved to do something about it, she collected a basin of warm water, bicarbonate of soda and white vinegar from the kitchen, as well as a scrubbing brush and cloths. She got as far as picking up the abandoned bottle of Scotch, and decided cleaning the carpet could wait.

Food hadn't crossed her lips since breakfast, and when the whisky hit her stomach it cramped. Alcohol fumes burned a trail up her throat, and she hiccoughed, felt sick. Hair of the dog, she thought, and poured another measure. She took her next drink tentatively, this time appreciating the oily warmth in her gullet. Alcohol had led to the ruination of her mother, and watching her slow destruction had tempered Kerry's response to hard liquor. These days she drank only on odd occasions, and usually only to the point of experiencing a fuzzy glow, not stupor. Right then, she was content to drink to senselessness if it helped. Gin was her tipple of choice, but there was none in her larder. She poured more whisky.

Peeked under her lashes at the easy chair opposite.

A semi-opaque Swain aimed a smarmy grin at her.

'Drinking to forget, Inspector Darke?'

Kerry closed her eyes, shivering.

'Please leave me alone,' she whispered.

Since his appearance in DCI Porter's office she couldn't shake him off. He'd been an unresponsive stalker most of the time, dogging her movements in the GaOC office, moving between her team and in and out of Kerry's cubbyhole, before hanging over Mel Scanlon's shoulder as she worked through a video file on her computer. None of the others were aware of his presence, but it was no comfort to Kerry. It suggested he was solely in her head, and the more worrying because of it. Almost she wished that he were capable of physical touch. If he swept a file from a desk, or prodded Korba in the neck, or even flicked off the overhead lights, she could accept that he was there, had some kind of tangible solidity and she would punch him in his smug face. He was incorporeal, though, a figure of refracted light and shadow, conjured into recognisable shape by her mind – her unhealthy mind, she might have to accept.

She'd refused Porter's offer of therapy. It was a kneejerk reaction. Accepting a problem was the first step to recovery, but she was still caught in the murk of denial. Not only denial, also fear. If she was diagnosed with mental health issues her rank — not to mention her career — as a detective inspector could be deemed compromised. She'd be out on her ear, and what then? She'd worked hard to get where she was, in the hope that one day she would lead the hunt for the Fell Man and find Sally, and finally lay them both to rest. Kicked off the job she'd never give up searching, but without the resources of a modern police force it could prove a hopeless task.

Mel turned up nothing fresh from the video evidence, and Glenn and Tony were playing a waiting game to hear from their sources. Kerry hid in her office, completing administration chores and signing off on other crime files submitted by her team, aware constantly of Swain's presence and trying her hardest to ignore him. Escaping the nick, she drove home. She half expected an unwelcome hitchhiker, but he left the confines of her car alone, only appearing to her as reflections in shop windows or waving from street corners as she passed. The usual parking situation arose when she arrived back at her street, and she had to again abandon her car a couple of blocks over near Eel Brook Common. Her walk home was completed with her head bowed, hands stuffed in her jacket pockets. Swain was waiting on the front step, and refused to budge when she unlocked the door and hurried inside, passing directly through him. She'd slammed the door, but doors were no obstruction to hallucinations. Before she entered the living room Swain had already made himself confortable in her easy chair, his ankles crossed.

Cleaning the carpet had been intended as a distraction, but the whisky would do a better job.

'You can neck the full bottle; it won't make me disappear.'

'Maybe not, but I'll be too drunk to care.' It struck her that her madness was growing more acute when she was answering him back. She closed her eyes again, shutting him out. 'Just go away, will you?'

'Sorry, Inspector Darke, but you're stuck with me.'

'You're not real.'

'So not only do you make me fall off a building you're also happy to hurt my feelings?'

'You fell.' She snapped open her eyes to glare at him. The heat of her anger should burn him up like sunlight on morning mist. 'You were trying to throw me over the side, not the other way around!'

'You were the one that smacked me round my head with your truncheon, and got that spray in my eyes. Or have you forgotten?'

It was apparent that *he'd* forgotten any part Girl had played in defending her...or perhaps Kerry kept the memory from him. 'I arrested you; it was your choice to try to escape. Don't dare blame me for your death!'

Swain returned her stare. He raised his right hand from which hung a facsimile of the rigid cuff he'd died wearing. He pointed a finger, was about to say something, but shut his mouth with an audible snap. He disappeared.

Shaking, raising the glass to her lips was difficult. The whisky tasted sour. She dribbled it back into the glass and set it aside.

'Holy Christ, Kerry, you do realise you're arguing with yourself?'

She was more prone to cry at happy moments. Sadness had been an aspect of her life so long that it rarely reached her on a physical level anymore. Yet tears rolled down her cheeks as she scanned the room for a sign of him. Hopefully he was gone for good, and she'd exorcised him by stating the obvious.

Damn him! He hadn't left, only moved from the chair to stand in the doorway, arms folded across his chest. His gaze roved over the walls and ceiling, one side of his mouth curled up in disapproval. *So crime doesn't pay, eh? If that's the case why did I live in a palace and you squat in a shit hole? Bloody hell, Inspector, if you expect me to hang around here you'd best think about redecorating.'*

Kerry gawped. Not only was she being haunted by the shade of a violent gangster, he was also a bloody snob! She almost laughed at the absurdity, but was more outraged. 'If you don't like my place, you're free to bugger off out of here.'

She struggled off the settee. The whisky was yet to have any affect on her; her lack of coordination was more to do with indignation. She went to her knees, grabbing the basin of warm water, and shoved it towards the spillage on the carpet. The bowl sloshed as she grabbed for a cloth.

'That's where I like to see my women,' said Swain from directly behind her. *'Down on their knees, and I don't care which way they're facing.'*

If she'd been outraged before, Kerry was volatile now. With a throaty cry, she snatched the bowl of water and twisting at the waist she hurled the contents, and the bowl, at Swain. He dodged aside, though there was no reason to, because the water couldn't cling to a figment of the imagination. The water splashed up the far wall, and the bowl clattered against the blinds on the front window. Kerry swivelled on her knees. In a moment of distaste, Swain checked his clothing for wet spots. Then he faced her, raised up the tail of his baggy tie-dyed shirt. *'Did you have to kill me when I was wearing these old things? For Christ's sake, Inspector, I've to exist for all eternity dressed like Shaggy off Scooby-frigging-Doo!'* He rattled the handcuff on his wrist. *'And what the hell's this meant to signify? Are these cuffs symbolic? Do they mean we're going steady or what?'*

Kerry struggled to stand. Where was Swain's indignation coming from? If he was a hallucination, then she was the one that clothed him, so why be upset at his funeral garb? And she certainly wasn't the one putting those misogynistic words into his filthy mouth. She craned forward, challenging him.

'What are you?'

He dropped the tail of his shirt. *'What am I?'* His voice was pitched low. He raised his hand and fingered the silver earring. The handcuff tapped against his shoulder, apparently to his distraction. He snapped down his hand, and his tone of voice held a rasp. *'What am I? What the hell do you think I am, Inspector Darke? I am...FUCKING ANGRY!'*

He flew at her – literally. One instant he was standing near the front window, the next hurtling through the intervening space. Only his face and grasping hands were definable, the rest of him a streak of insubstantial colour. His eyes shone like fire, his fingers were claws as they went around her throat. Kerry pitched backwards in shock, falling on the stained carpet. Swain followed her down, his features creased in rage, teeth bared, fingers now gouging to scoop her eyes from their sockets. But for a tingle of static electricity on her skin, Kerry felt no actual pain. The knowledge he lacked the power to physically harm her didn't alleviate her horror. She fought back, her own hands grasping and flailing. Swain's intangible form was ripped and broken in one instant, but reformed the next. He clubbed and pounded, strangled her, but Kerry scrambled up, passing through him as she had when he'd blocked access to her front door. She lurched away, kicking aside the scrubbing brush that ricocheted off the base of her easy chair. Ten feet away she spun round to confront him, hands coming up defensively, fully expecting another flying assault.

He'd reformed to a figure equating an entire human being, though still only partially visible in places. Swain knelt on the carpet with his back to her, head lowered. He held up his cupped palms, the handcuff drooping from one, and she watched as his back shook in a series of sobs at his limitations. As if sensing he was the object of study, he twisted at the waist, holding out his cupped hands. His fiery gaze had dimmed; the sparks of ferocity leeched from them. *'What did you do to me?'*

'I didn't do a bloody thing, Swain. If you are real, this is your punishment...for what *you* did.'

He stood, slow and deliberate. He held up his cuffed wrist, and his lips twitched, curled up at one side and displayed an eyetooth. *'This is what? A twenty-first century version of Jacob Marley's chains?'*

Kerry didn't have another explanation for him – the cuff was symbolic of his sins, the way Marley's chains and locks were of his. It was better he come to that conclusion than be told.

MATT HILTON

He grasped the rigid section of the cuffs with his other hand. Twisted, yanked. To him the cuffs were tangible. The steel bracelet nipped his flesh, blanched the colour from his skin. Discomfort wormed across his features. *'You'd better have a handcuff key, Inspector Darke.'*

'You know I can't release those cuffs from you. They're *your* burden, for what *you* did.'

'Yeah? Well there's the supreme fucking irony, then. What's the point of lying now? I've done wrong, Inspector. Worse shit than any copper knows about. But I don't deserve this*!'* Again he twisted the cuff, but it refused to open or move more than a fraction. *'I'm not being a pussy. If you can't do the time, don't do the crime, right? I was always willing to pay the price. But this—'* he yanked the cuff a third time *'—this is* fucking bollocks*!'*

'You shot and killed a mother and child,' Kerry reminded him. 'You murdered them, Swain, an innocent little girl and her mum in cold blood. You deserve far worse than what you got.'

He cocked his head on one side. *'Is that what I did?'*

'You know fine well what you did, you bastard. What was it you just said; what's the point of lying now? Accept that you're a murderous piece of shit and maybe those cuffs will fall off your wrist, and then you can go to hell where you belong.'

'I'm a murderer, am I?' He gave a brief shrug, and his mouth twitched. *'Well, yeah, I can't deny it; I've killed more than once. But the mother and kid?'* He shook his head.

'Liar.' Involuntarily, Kerry stepped towards him. 'We've got the murder weapon, and bullets with your fingerprints on them. We've got your burnt out car.'

'You've got jack shit.'

'You ran, and you tried to kill me. Tell me those weren't the actions of a guilty man.'

'Those were the actions of an innocent man unprepared to take the rap for somebody else's crime.'

Kerry was tempted to spit on him; if it would have any effect on him she would. 'Liar.'

'You keep calling me that. But am I really lying? Think about it, Inspector Darke. Tell me the truth now. Isn't there something that doesn't sit quite right with your detective's intuition?'

'If what you're saying is true, help me out here,' she said. 'Who was your driver?'

Swain wagged a finger at her. *'It isn't as easy as that.'*

'Why not? You're pleading your innocence. If it wasn't you, tell me who really fired those shots. It had to be the other person in the car if it wasn't you.'

'Disappointing.'

She said nothing. If he was a figment of her subconscious mind, how could he tell her the identity of the driver if she didn't already know it? She sighed into her cupped palms.

But Swain wasn't finished with her.

'There are no secrets in the underworld,' he said.

She lowered her hands.

'And by the underworld I'm not talking about fire and brimstone,' he went on.

'You mean the criminal underworld?'

Swain eyed her with scorn. *'For a detective, you take some catching on. The thing is, I know who shot the Ghedis, and it's for you to find out.'*

'Tell me then.'

'No. You need to find out for yourself, and when you do, you'll realise you were wrong about me. When that happens, there's something I want from you, and it isn't a bloody apology.'

'I don't owe you a bloody thing.'

'Not yet.'

'What do mean by *yet*?'

159

'*You do something for me,*' he said, '*and I'll do something for you.*'

She shook her head.

'*You don't know what I'm offering...*'

'I'm not religious,' Kerry admitted, 'but I know enough not to make bargains with the devil.'

'*Don't worry.*' He laughed at the notion. '*I'm not interested in your immortal soul. I want* something else*.*'

'I'm doing nothing for you.'

'*Not even if I tell you who the Fell Man is?*'

'What? How do you know about him?' If she could she'd grab the front of his shirt and shake the answer from him.

'*I know stuff.*' He tapped the side of his nose. '*Secrets.*'

'I don't believe you.' How could Swain know about her obsession with catching the Fell Man, unless he was a manifestation of her subconscious mind? 'You have no idea who he is or what he did to—'

'*To Sally,*' he finished for her. '*Yes. I can tell you what happened to your sister, too.*'

Knowing her name didn't change a thing if she were the one subconsciously feeding the information to him. But was that a chance she was willing to take?

'Tell me then,' she said, on the verge of pleading.

'*Steady on, Inspector. There's the small matter of you delivering on your side of the bargain first. Scratch my back and I'll scratch yours.*'

Her fists clenched, and she stood shivering. 'You have to give me something first. You have to convince me you know about *him*.'

'*No. You need to think. You have to decide if helping me is worth getting what you want most.*'

'Tell me and I'll do—'

'*Anything?*'

Her mouth nipped down on a false pledge. Instead she said, 'There are boundaries I'll never cross.'

Swain rocked his head. *'Yeah, well, we'll see about that. I'll tell you what, Inspector Darke. You think I'm a despicable man, a right bastard, and you're correct. I make no apologies for my nature. But I'm not unreasonable. I will give you time to think about my offer. When you come to the only decision I'm interested in hearing, give me a shout.'*

'No. Wait I'll—'

Swain was gone.

'Come back!' Kerry rushed forward into the vacated space, again swiping at air, as if she could claw him back into existence.

'Come back. I'll give you my decision right now!'

She waited, breathless.

Swain was a no show.

'Come back, you bastard,' she hollered. 'Where are you? You've haunted me all day and now...' She was shouting at thin air. She sank to her knees, hands fisted against her sternum. 'Come back. Please?'

There was movement to her left, a brief darkening of the doorway to the entrance hall.

'Swain?'

But it wasn't Swain.

Girl wouldn't be viewed directly. She swept to the right, and Kerry tried to follow her. Girl darted. Kerry understood the rules. She forced herself to stare dead ahead, and in her peripheral vision Girl took on more solidity. She stood, as grey and morose as ever, hair hanging lank across her undefined features, and shook her head.

If Girl's display was one of reproach, warning or regret, Kerry couldn't tell. And when she couldn't resist checking for clarity, Girl disappeared as resolutely as Swain had a minute ago.

There was a long, drunken, rambling voicemail message on his mobile phone when Adam finished his shift. Because of the strict security procedures he worked under at HMP Belmarsh, prison officers weren't permitted to carry their personal phones while on duty. Once he'd checked in his radio and other kit, and returned to the locker room beyond the security barriers to change out of his uniform, he found the message from Kerry. He waited until he was seated in his car before listening to it, rather than while fielding goodbyes and banter from other officers going off duty. He couldn't believe the sheer insanity she was talking.

Ghosts. Hallucinations. Making deals with the devil.

She'd bloody lost it!

He drove home at speed, but the closer he got to their house the less enthusiastic he grew for a confrontation. He circled the block twice before finding a parking spot for his Ford, and it wasn't due to there being no closer spot — some of the residents had already left home for morning shifts — more that he was using the excuse to think. He trudged to the house, and let himself in. The place was silent. After getting pissed, Kerry must have passed out. His instinct was to leave her to it, let her sleep it off: maybe when she woke she'd be less inclined to babbling about supernatural nonsense.

He took off his jacket and hung it over the end of the banister. Wan early morning light leaked onto the upper landing through the open bathroom door. Their bedroom door was shut. He sucked in a steadying breath. Moved along the vestibule for the kitchen. A strong coffee or two, maybe something stronger, wouldn't go amiss. But he'd the feeling Kerry had wiped out their stock of alcohol last night. As he passed the living room he glanced inside. Saw an upturned basin, a scrubbing brush, some cloths and other cleaning items scattered on the carpet. He saw Kerry.

She wasn't on the settee or easy chair, but seated at the small table they used for dinner on special occasions. She'd discarded her jacket, and shoes, but was otherwise dressed in the clothing she'd gone to work in yesterday. Her ankles were crossed under the straight-backed chair, her upper body slumped over the table, head nestled on her folded arms. Her hair concealed her features, but a single lock rose and fell with each exhalation. She was asleep, or had fallen unconscious. He'd bet on the latter judging by how drunk she'd sounded on the phone. Directly in front of her was her laptop computer. A screen saver danced on the screen, since it had defaulted to sleep mode. He didn't have to be a detective like Kerry to figure she'd fallen asleep while surfing the net.

He moved tentatively towards her. Spotted a fan of wet carpet, an empty Scotch bottle, some crumpled lager tins, even a depleted bottle of dark rum, although she normally loathed the stuff. The room stank worse than it had after the spillage the other day. He checked his wristwatch. She was supposed to be at work in less than two hours. She was in no fit state, and that was before he considered her manic rambling of last night. He would phone her in sick if it came to it.

He was tempted to leave her be, but the longer he put off the inevitable, the worse things could get. He reached to touch her shoulder. The computer screen caught his attention. He checked his partner wasn't about to wake suddenly, and instead touched the track pad on the laptop. The screen came alive, but demanded a four-digit password. Adam knew it, Kerry's collar number from when she first joined Cumbria Constabulary. By sheer coincidence it was the month and year in which her sister Sally was born: 1187. Adam gently tapped it in and the computer reverted to the last website she'd perused.

Adam exhaled in disappointment.

Displayed on-screen was the contact page to a bullshitter claiming to be a paranormal sleuth and demonologist. The man's name was enough to tell he was a charlatan — Elias Tiberius Price was a theatrical *nom de plume* if ever Adam had heard one — and that was without the posed photo caught in dramatic night vision, vivid greens and shades of grey, and reflective eyes, and not to mention an archaic wooden cross studded with iron nail heads that Price wielded directly at the camera.

Adam read the legend on screen, written in a typically eerie font that dripped green ectoplasm. *To book your consultation or spiritual house clearance, contact Britain's pre-eminent multi-faith exorcist via the form below. All major credit cards and PayPal accepted.*

'For God's sake, Kerry,' he whispered. Adam was agnostic to the belief in ghosts, the supernatural, and things that went bump in the night. But he believed in crooks and con men, and could recognise a scam when he saw one. 'Tell me you didn't contact this dick-head?'

He wasn't computer literate enough to tell if she'd emailed Price or not, but he wasn't having any ghost buster coming around their place splashing holy water and talking gibberish. Pulling the computer around, he began typing.

His message was short and sweet.

Ignore any previous emails you've got from this account i've realised your a scumbag fraudster who prays on vunnerable people.

He didn't bother signing off, just hit send and hoped that would be the last of it.

He'd stabbed the send key too hard, because Kerry flinched at the sharp noise, murmured, and pushed upright with a groan of self-pity. She stared through bleary eyes as he repositioned the laptop in front of her. Her sclera was red, and her right eyelid drooped. Dried tears had left scum in the corners of both eyes and formed salty patches on her cheeks. She didn't immediately comprehend what, never mind who, she was looking at. She reared away and had to catch herself on her left elbow to avoid spilling off the chair. She righted herself, placed a hand on her forehead, and smacked her lips to work up some moisture. 'Uh…Adam,' she croaked, 'you're home.'

'Yeah. Look at you. What a bloody state to get yourself in!'

'Please don't start with me,' she moaned, and cradled her head in her arms again.

'So you don't want my help? That isn't what you said when you phoned last night.'

She snorted into the table.

'I can't hear you,' Adam snapped.

She pushed up again, and this time managed to focus on him. 'I said you took your time getting here.'

'You rang my personal mobile. You know if you need me you have to go through the proper channels. I didn't get your bloody message till this morning.' He snatched up the empty lager tins off the floor. 'Maybe it's a good job. I wouldn't have been pleased if I'd come home early and found you pissed up.'

'What? I'm not allowed a drink?'

'Not if it sends you off your bloody rocker, Kerry. For God's sake, do you even remember what you were raving about on the phone?' He coughed in disbelief. He made a quick trip to the kitchen, dumping the empty cans in a wastebin. He bustled back into the room as if there'd been no break in their conversation. 'I doubt you even remember making the call.'

'I remember.' While he was out the room she'd somehow righted herself in the chair. She rubbed some life into her features. Her hands flopped down on the table, suddenly stricken. 'If you'd suffered what I did yesterday, you wouldn't be as judgmental.'

'I hardly think I'm being judgmental.' He grabbed the empty scotch bottle, grasped for the rum. He shook the half-empty bottle at her. 'I just don't think getting sloshed as bad as this can be any good for you. Have you seen the time?'

'Oh, shit!'

'Well, there's no way you can go to work in this state, is there?'

'I have to.' Pushing up, her knees betrayed her. She sat down hard again.

'Yeah. Sit down and stay put. You're not going anywhere, Kerry.'

She glared. 'So first I'm not allowed a drink, now you're telling me where I can or can't go. Stuff you, Adam.'

'You're not fit to go to work. Look at you. You're still drunk.'

'I'm not. I'm just hung-over. A shower—'

'Would be a great idea,' he agreed. 'You're bloody stinking. If you walk in the nick smelling like that, you'll be out on your ear in two seconds flat. Oh, and by the way, you can forget about driving there. Do you want to lose your licence, or worse still, kill somebody? Then you'll know all about it, when you've got another bloody vengeful spirit haunting you!'

She gawped. 'I told you about Swain?'

'See! I knew you wouldn't remember the message you left me.' He hoisted a bottle in each hand. 'I'm not talking about these kind of spirits, am I? Yes, you frigging mentioned Swain. You said he's following you around, tormenting you, offering deals to tell you where to find the Fell Man. Have you any idea how insane that sounds, Kerry? Jesus! Then when I get home, I find you've been contacting some dick-head claiming to be an exorcist! How bloody gullible can you get?'

Kerry peered at the laptop. It had only occurred to her that the screen was uncharacteristically lit when it should have fallen into sleep mode hours ago. 'You snooped on me?'

'I didn't need to snoop. You left the last page up that you were looking at.'

'But my password...'

'Like I don't know it?' He used the neck of the Scotch bottle as a pointer. 'As if you don't know mine?'

'I don't snoop around your computer; you've no right to spy on me, Adam.' She stood, and tried to force past him. Adam stood his ground.

'I wasn't spying. Just seeing what the hell's been giving you these stupid ideas about ghosts.'

She jabbed a finger at the computer. 'I went on there *after* I saw Swain, not before. I was only looking for some kind of explanation for what I'm experiencing.'

'Well you sure as hell won't get it from Elias-fucking-Price! Bloody hell, Kerry, you're supposed to be a detective! I'd've thought you'd be able to spot a bloody scammer when you see one. What do you expect to get from him? I'll tell you what. He'll come in, roll his eyes, speak a few words in Latin and proclaim your house haunted by demons or some such bollocks. Then he'll hit you with how much it's going to cost you to get rid of them. Jesus wept!'

On the face of it, in the cold light of day, she had to accept how ridiculous the notion of vengeful spirits sounded. And if she admitted how crazy it was then those proclaiming to be experts in the occult had to be as equally stupid. 'You don't need a witch doctor,' he snapped, 'you need to see a real one.'

'I don't need a doctor.'

'Really? So this all strikes you as the behaviour of a sane person?'

'You don't know what you're talking about.' Kerry was growing strident, but Adam was prepared to match her.

'I know that you aren't being haunted, Kerry. Not by Swain and not by your imaginary friend.' He slammed down the bottles on the table, jabbed a finger at the side of his shaven head. 'It's all up here. You're stressed out, not well. I've told you before. Your bloody job is going to do your head in. In fact, forget I said that. *It has done your head in.* Now sit down, and don't move. I'm going to phone your boss and let him know you won't be in until you've sorted yourself out.'

'Don't you bloody dare!'

'I'm *bloody* well going to.'

'You'll get me the sack!'

'Would that be a bad thing?'

'You bastard!'

'Kerry,' he said with less vitriol, 'I'm only trying to help you. I'm telling you, love, you need to take some time off, see a doctor and get your head sorted out, or better yet, pack in the job altogether.'

'Or else what? What are you going to do if I refuse? Because I promise you this, Adam, there's no way I'm quitting, and no way I'm jeopardising my career by admitting to seeing ghosts.'

He'd tried, but he was reaching the end of his rope. It was time for hard fact. 'You want to know what I'll do? Well here's the truth, Kerry, and you're not going to like it. I spend enough time looking after nutters at work, I don't intend coming home to one too.'

'If London's one of the most surveilled cities in the world, why the hell can't we find one camera with a clear image of Swain's Subaru?'

Kerry's frustration was manifesting as anger, aimed wrongly at Korba as they sat over their breakfasts. After her early morning spat with Adam, her fiancé had decided to end their argument with his ill veiled threat, then stormed off to the kitchen where he rattled around for a few minutes before stomping upstairs and throwing himself in bed. Although she'd personally questioned his commitment to their relationship before, it still hurt when he was having similar doubts about her. Tempted to follow him, to reason with him about his sensible — but impossible — demands, she'd proven too stubborn. Having spent the night in an alcohol-induced fog, it was easy to now believe that the events of yesterday were figments of a dream she'd allowed to leak into her waking thoughts. She was sleep deprived, stressed, and whether she'd admit it openly, was suffering from repressed guilt over Swain's death, and the murder of Bilan Ghedi had re-ignited her obsession, her desperation, to find Sally's abductor. She *should* see a doctor. But what could conventional medicine do for her? When she was a child, struggling to deal with her sister's disappearance, Doctor Ron had counselled against the use of medication. He'd suggested to her parents that instead of worrying about their daughter's need to drift into fantasy they should allow her to find a safe place in her imagination to work through her troubles. As an adult she wouldn't be given the same leeway to heal in her own time and place. A doctor would prescribe anti-depressant or anti-psychotic drugs, plus time off work, and they were the last she needed.

The only way she could exorcise Swain was to solve the case. He wasn't real. He couldn't be. He was the manifestation of her detective's intuition, telling her she was missing the obvious to prompt her on to the correct investigative path. She had a layman's knowledge of the way the human mind worked, and thought that her current demeanour could be explained by Sigmund Freud's tripartite psyche theory being out of balance. In Freud's opinion, the human psyche, or personality, comprised of three parts, the id, ego and superego. Broken down the id was the primitive part, generating impulsive and unconscious responses, based on instinct and hidden memories, while the superego operated as a moral conscience. The ego was the realistic component charged with mediating between the id and superego, and supposedly coming to balanced decisions. The interaction of each part dictated an individual's behaviour. The id operates on the pleasure principle, where wishful impulse demands immediate satisfaction, regardless of consequence, and right then she believed she was caught in its thrall. Popular culture had pictured Freud's theory in simplistic terms: a devil and angel on each shoulder. Swain was her devil, and Girl — as Suleymaan Ghedi might have it — her guiding angel. Unfortunately Swain was proving the more vocal.

Expecting an immediate response from Mel Scanlon's laborious examination of the CCTV network was possibly a wishful desire of the id too.

'Swain knew the neighborhood well, and probably plotted his route beforehand to avoid detection from the street cameras.' Korba posed his suggestion more like a question: it was a valid theory.

'That makes sense,' she concurred, 'but he couldn't've avoided every private camera system, or mobile phone or whatever. Surely someone caught a clear image of the Subaru on its way to or leaving the scene?'

'It's a probability, but they're unaware of it. We need to put out another request for information.' Korba shrugged at his idea. 'It'd mean throwin' it past Porter, but I'm happy to do that.'

'He'll welcome a few more minutes on camera,' she said. 'An opportunity to put his last appearance behind him.'

'You going to eat that, boss?'

Kerry glanced down at her plate.

They were seated in a quiet corner in a family run café on Museum Street, a stone's throw from the British Museum. Despite the owners being Greek Cypriots, and relatives of Korba, he hadn't requested Greek food but ordered them both a full English breakfast – the best cure for a hangover in his opinion. Kerry had pushed the items around on her plate, and couldn't recall taking a single bite. 'Take what you want, Danny, I haven't the appetite.'

'No. Get it down you. You need to line your stomach. Get a bit of colour in your cheeks before you show up at the nick.'

'I need more tea.'

'Eat something. I promise you'll feel better.' He checked over her plate. 'Mind you, if you're not keen on sausage...'

She stabbed his object of desire off her plate and transferred it to his. Korba immediately set to it, cutting it into manageable chunks that he mopped at some egg yolk with. Kerry was close to heaving. 'Fancy the bacon as well?'

Korba's eyebrows danced a jig.

Once she'd vacated her plate of recognisable meat products she gingerly began picking at the eggs, tomatoes, baked beans and toast. Each mouthful went down a little easier, and soon she regretted giving away the most succulent items. She ordered another mug of tea and round of toast, butter and jam.

'That was a lifesaver,' she said, finally setting down her cutlery on her cleared plate.

'Told you.' Korba spread butter on the last surviving triangle of toast. 'Uh, do you want this?'

'No. Go for it. You've earned it, Danny.'

Adam was right when advising her against driving. Even hours later she suspected she'd fail a test, but the food and tea would help metabolise the alcohol from her system. After showering, dressing in fresh clothing, and going overboard with perfume and deodorant, she'd summoned Korba to her rescue. While waiting for him, she brushed her teeth three times, gargling with mouthwash between each go with the toothbrush, before she was reasonably confident her breath wouldn't strip the paint off the walls. Sympathetic to her cause, Korba had suggested waiting until later before making an appearance at the nick, and had driven her to his cousin's café for some "restorative medicine". En route to Museum Street he'd called the control room with a white lie that they were conducting follow up enquiries.

'While you're in the mood for sharing, boss...'

It took her a moment to realise Korba wasn't talking about toast.

'Me and Adam are going through a rough patch. But you don't have to worry. We'll get through it.' Which she feared *was* a lie. Some things you couldn't come back from unmarked, and Adam hurt her with his parting threat. As far as she was concerned, wedding vows included a commitment to your spouse through sickness and health, and Adam had clearly stated his position there. Well, in her case it was warts and all, or he could forget it. She loved Adam, or thought she had, but now she wasn't as certain.

'I'm not one to pry,' Korba said tentatively.

'Come off it, Danny. You're a detective. Prying's in the job description.'

'Not into your private life it ain't.'

They eyed each other for an uncomfortable moment. For once she didn't see fascination in his gaze as he studied her eye colouring, only sadness.

'Say what's on your mind,' she said.

He gathered himself by tearing open a sachet of sugar and dumping it into his second mug of tea. Concentrating on his cup as he stirred, he asked: 'Would it offend you if I said there's something off about you?'

'Apart from my smell?'

He looked up at her from beneath his brows. 'I thought you were acting odd when we went to see Hettie...all that stuff about ghosts. But after, when you were back in the office...'

'Aye,' she sighed. 'I was a little off. You can blame that on Porter.'

'He giving you a hard time?'

'When doesn't he?'

Korba exhaled with enough force to move the empty sugar sachet a few inches towards her. He trapped it under his fingers.

'But that's his job,' Kerry went on. 'He demands results, and it's my job to give him them. He made that clear.'

'Wouldn't be the first time. But that's what I find so odd. He pisses you off, pisses me off too, and I've seen you annoyed before. But, well...'

'Go on. Just for a minute forget that I'm your boss, and see me as your friend. Tell me what's on your mind.'

'OK.' Korba spread both his hands on the table. 'Friend to friend, I've never seen you shit scared like that before.'

'I'm not afraid.'

'Sorry *friend*, but you were. Correction, you *are* scared. Even while we've been sitting here you've been on pins. As if you're expecting the worst to happen.

What are you so afraid of...imagining Swain's ghost again?'

There was no possible way she could admit to being haunted by a foul-mouthed spirit, despite his caring approach. 'It's another kind of spook I'm bothered about. Do you know who Superintendent Graeme Harker is?'

'I know of him. Thankfully I've never had the misfortune of meeting him, seeing as he's the Lord of the Dark Side.' A shadow passed behind Korba's features. 'Aah, I get ya.'

'When I went to see Porter, I almost walked in on a meeting they were having. Porter wouldn't confirm it, but I think I was the subject of discussion. Danny, I am afraid, but it's because I'm worried I'm under investigation by Professional Standards.'

'Fucking rubber heelers.' Korba's reaction was similar to most she'd heard concerning the DPS. 'They've nothing better to do than cause trouble for good coppers. But why would they be after you, boss? You ain't given them cause...'

He paused, and Kerry wondered if he was reconsidering. The Department for Professional Standards wasn't only concerned with rooting out corruption in police ranks, it was also there to avoid any employee bringing the force into disrepute through other means. Had her erratic behaviour grown so noticeable that she'd raised Porter's hackles to that level? Unfortunately the answer was yes.

'There's, uh, nothing they can use against you, is there?'

'I'm surprised you even have to ask, Danny.'

'Yeah. I know. Sorry.'

She waved off his apology. 'Unless you include *this*. Grabbing breakfast to cover up the fact I'm too pissed to go to work.'

Korba glanced around quickly. The only other person in the café was an octogenarian woman, almost asleep over her own breakfast. 'I think we're safe,' he said, and offered a strained grin. 'Unless Mata Hari over there has some kind of directional microphone stashed under her headscarf.' They shared a chuckle. Korba touched his nose. 'Don't worry, your secret's safe with me.'

Unfortunately, his action soured the humour for her, because Kerry pictured an ethereal Erick Swain similarly tapping his nose. *'I know stuff. Secrets.'*

She fully expected the bastard to show his face again, maybe leering from behind the elderly lady at the corner table, performing a lewd act to salt her breakfast. *Jesus, Kerry, that's disgusting! You're beginning to think like him.* 'Maybe we should get out of here?'

Korba stuffed the last piece of buttered toast in his mouth, chewing as he approached the counter, digging his wallet from a hip pocket.

'There's no charge, Danny,' said the server, an older version of DS Korba: more weight, less hair on his head, but a similar height and colouring.

'Cheers, Cuz.' Korba began jamming away his wallet.

Kerry placed a twenty-pound note down on the counter, said, 'Keep the change.'

His cousin glanced at Korba for permission to accept the money, then at Kerry, and finally nodded his thanks. He spirited the note into the cash register, then waved goodbye as they exited. There were tables on the pedestrianized section of the street, and a couple of smokers had taken up residence at one of them. Tourists taking a well earned break from trudging around the nearby British Museum, or undercover DPS officers staking them out? Kerry's bet was on the former, but she'd been particular about paying their way for their breakfasts...just in case. A freebie offered to coppers was seen as a possible route to corruption, and she didn't want to give Porter or especially Superintendent Harker any grounds to question her integrity.

Their car was in a "permit holders only" parking bay on Little Russell Street, outside a shop front museum dedicated to the history of cartoons. Korba had stood a laminated card on its dashboard, identifying it as being parked "on official duty". He saw the parking privileges it afforded as a perk of the job, rather than a misuse of their official status. Under the current situation, Kerry wasn't sure they should take any liberty. She took a prolonged look over her shoulder before getting inside.

Before driving off, Korba dug in his jacket pocket and held up a clear plastic box. 'Breath mint?'

'I still stink of alcohol?'

'Kerry, you smell like the angel's share,' Korba told her. She was briefly complimented until she recalled where she'd heard the term before. It was what distillers called the amount of alcohol that evaporates through a barrel during the whisky maturation process.

Sighing, she held up her cupped palm. 'You'd better give me the full box.'

DCI Porter was on the warpath when they finally rolled up at the nick. He was dressed in his number two uniform, as opposed to the civilian suit he normally favoured, suggesting he'd been out at New Scotland Yard again, and wasn't happy that they were AWOL when he'd returned.

As they entered the Gangs and Organised Crime office, toting paper cups of coffee from a nearby Starbucks, he was standing over DC Scanlon at her workstation like a scavenger waiting for her to perish. Glenn Scott and Tony Whittle were elsewhere, conducting enquiries of their own. Korba was first through the door, and skidded to a halt. Kerry almost spilled scalding black coffee down his back.

'Where the bloody hell have you two been?' Porter strode out from behind Scanlon's desk. 'I've been calling you both for the past hour.'

Korba offered a disarming shrug of confusion. 'Called us how, sir?'

'How do you suppose, Sergeant, with bloody jungle drums? I've called you both and neither of you have picked up.'

'We were conducting follow up enquiries, sir. We did inform control that we'd be unavailable on comms for a while.'

'It's not good enough. But forget that for now. We've a more urgent matter to deal with.' He snapped a command to join him behind Mel's desk. Mel angled her computer screen so it could be viewed from the room. 'Look,' Porter said. 'While you were off gallivanting, DC Scanlon made a break through, and had to call on me for instruction. This is not how I like to see my team run, Detective Inspector.'

Before the DCI could go on complaining, Kerry moved in to study what was on the computer screen. Excitement jolted through. It was time and date-stamped CCTV footage of Swain's blue Subaru Impreza caught only a few minutes after the fatal shooting of the Ghedis. Unlike most footage they usually had to contend with, grainy black and white images filmed on archaic surveillance systems, this was HD sharp and in vivid colour. Only the angle of the camera denied them a clear shot of the faces of the car's occupants, but one thing was proven: Ikemba Adefunke was a downright liar.

The CCTV evidence threw everything they thought they knew about the shooting of the Ghedis on its head. For a start, Erick Swain wasn't in the getaway car at all. There was the small possibility he'd been dropped off somewhere between the shooting and the side street where the Subaru was filmed, but Kerry wouldn't credit it. Swain was a racist, and his gang comprised entirely of equally prejudiced white guys. The driver and passenger were both dark skinned, though positively identifying them could prove difficult.

The revelation stunned all four detectives into silence. Having had more time to absorb it though, DCI Porter was first to speak. 'I'd like to know why this is the first time I'm hearing we got the wrong man.'

'I mentioned yesterday I had a theory, sir, but you didn't want to hear it. You said you wanted facts, proof and evidence.' Kerry indicated the screen with the back of her hand. 'This confirms some of the misgivings I had about Swain's supposed involvement.'

'Facts, proof and evidence are what gives me the arrests and convictions I also demanded,' said Porter. 'At least now you've something to work on instead of roaming around aimlessly. I want the two men in that car identified and brought in, do you hear me?'

'They'll do for starters,' Kerry agreed, 'but if I'm right, there'll be more arrests.' Before Porter could reply, she caught Mel's attention. 'Good work, Mel. Now you have a reference point, widen the net between the Subaru's current position and where we know it ended up on the riverbank, see if you can find any clear images of their faces.'

'No problem, ma'am.'

Korba leaned in. 'Before you do that, Mel, can you run back that image? If they used a particular route to avoid known camera placements, they might've approached Wandsworth Road the same way.'

Without answering, Mel got to it with a few deft strokes on the keypad. The tape counter began a high-speed reverse, as did the onscreen images. Various other vehicles zipped in and out of shot, travelling backwards. After eighteen minutes had counted down a familiar car appeared.

'There,' said Korba.

Mel halted the recording, and began shunting the images forward in slow motion. When it appeared on screen this time the Subaru was being driven the opposite direction — towards the shooting — so there was no clear image through the windscreen. There was a decent view through the side windows, and subsequently through the back windscreen, at a third person riding in the backseat. In a court, the images wouldn't convict the backseat passenger, but both Kerry and Korba had had personal contact with the gangling figure, Kerry on two occasions now. There was no doubt in her mind about who the vulture-necked individual was.

Not only was Ikemba Adefunke a liar, he was also complicit in the murders!

'Who is that?' Porter demanded.

'Funky,' Korba said, his voice hoarse.

'Ikemba Adefunke,' Kerry clarified for the DCI, 'the alleged target of the drive-by shooting. Known as Funky to other members of the Nine Elms Crew.'

Porter was familiar with the name, and also the gang he belonged to. 'Adefunke was driven to the scene at Wandsworth Road, and chose that family to stand alongside while his friends shot them in cold blood. The bastard...'

In his opinion on Funky they were all in agreement.

'I want him brought in,' he said.

Korba nodded in agreement, but Kerry stood her ground.

'Sir, I don't think that's the best thing to do.'

'Get him arrested,' Porter stated. 'Work on him. I don't care how you do it, threats or promises. Do whatever it takes, but get the names of his conspirators and arrest them too.'

'If we do that, fine. We might get those responsible for carrying out the shooting, but not the ones that set it up. If we grab Funky the others will go to ground, and he'll clam up for fear of his life. All we'll have is another scapegoat.'

'*Another* scapegoat?'

'Erick Swain,' she said.

'He must have still had a hand in this,' Porter said, but there was doubt in his mind too. Who in their right mind set himself up to take the fall for a murder he didn't commit? He shook his head. 'We're under pressure to get results. Bring in Funky and let the dominoes fall where they will. In the meantime, I'm going to have to spin the reason why an innocent man died during what now might be seen as a false arrest.'

'Swain wasn't an innocent man, he *was* a murderer.' Kerry was adamant. Perhaps he hadn't been involved in the shooting of the Ghedis, but he was a killer.

'I'm sorry?' Porter straightened up. 'One second you're calling him a scapegoat, the next he's a murderer. On what evidence are you basing the latter?'

'I've done wrong, Inspector. Worse shit than any copper knows about.' Swain had told her to her face. *'I'm a murderer, am I? Well, yeah, I can't deny it; I've killed more than once.'*

'He admitted it to me.' The words were out of her mouth before she could stop them.

'Told you when? When you were on that bloody rooftop fighting with him?'

'Yes,' she lied.

'You never mentioned this in your statement.'

'He was dead by then. Besides, he didn't give me any specifics, only that he'd killed a number of times. Mentioning his confession in my statement wouldn't have helped us solve any of those cases.'

'No, Inspector Darke, but it would've put a completely different spin on the way we subsequently handled his death.'

She was unconvinced. Porter would still have thrown her under a bus to save his own arse. She didn't argue, she'd no grounds. Swain's confession had come to her after the fact, and she wasn't even sure it was real, only her intuition given voice. It certainly wasn't something she wanted to go into now. 'Sir, if you only give me some time, I'll get to the bottom of this. Funky's a footsoldier; he takes orders. He—'

Porter's palm snapped up. 'He obviously understands the concept of orders better than you do. I want him arrested, do *you* understand what I'm telling you?'

'Sir, with respect I'd—'

Porter stiffened. Then ignoring her, he directed his next words at Korba and Mel. 'May we please have the room?'

As usual the GaOC office was as stuffy as a tomb, but it was as if the temperature had dropped below freezing, and this time it wasn't due to a supernatural manifestation. Embarrassed for Kerry, the two detectives vacated the room.

'The door please, Danny,' Porter said. 'And do not let me catch either of you loitering in the corridor.'

After aiming a piteous grimace at Kerry, Korba closed the door behind them. The click of the latch was ominous in its finality.

'Sir, I—'

'Stop,' Porter snapped. 'I don't want to hear it. All I want when I give you an express order is that you obey it. Am I clear, Inspector?'

'I'm only suggesting an alternative course of action, sir. One that will give us better results.'

'Didn't I warn you I wouldn't tolerate insubordination?'

'I'm not being insubordinate; I'm only trying to do my job to the best of my ability. I think arresting Funky's the wrong move if we hope to get the others too.'

'And I don't care what you think.' Porter's heels were dug in as firmly as hers, and superiority gave him the trump card. 'When I give you an order, I expect it to be obeyed *to the best of your ability.*'

'Respectfully, sir, I do not expect to be shouted at as if I'm a naughty child.'

Porter's hands made fists. It was a struggle to contain his anger. When he replied, his voice was still too loud, and it held a quiver. He'd overstepped the mark, but it was difficult coming back. He changed tack, wrinkling his nose. 'Are you drunk, Inspector Darke?'

'Pardon?'

'I think my question's clear enough...without shouting. But let me rephrase it. Have you been drinking alcohol?'

'No.'

'Did you drink to excess last night?'

'No. Why do you ask?'

'I'm responsible for those under my command, as are you. If one of your team smelled as strongly of alcohol, and were quite obviously hung-over, I'd expect you to ask questions of them too. I'd expect you to make a decision on how fit they were to carry out their duties.' He eyeballed her, allowing his threat to sink in. 'You see, I'm wondering if your argumentative behaviour's a result of still being drunk, or for some other reason.'

'I'm not drunk.' Even as she stated it, she knew he wouldn't be convinced. The angel's share still seeped from her pores. 'Sir, I'll admit to having a nightcap, but

I've taken all precautions to ensure I'm fit and capable of carrying out my duties in a professional manner.'

'I'm doubtful. And it's not the first time I've had similar misgivings in the last few days. Your refusal to carry out a direct order isn't helping.' He faltered, and an expression danced across his features that approximated sympathy. 'I know you've been through a difficult time, but it's no excuse. You're either fit for the job or not, and in my opinion, in your current state, you're proving to be a liability. Get your act in order, Inspector Darke, or else. I can easily find a replacement who is, and who will carry out an order without argument.'

She didn't reply, couldn't.

'Go and arrest Funky.'

When she didn't argue Porter nodded brusquely, and strode for the door without looking back. His message was crystal clear. As the door slammed behind him, Kerry lowered her face into her palms, and groaned in misery at...well, *everything*.

Funky was absent when Kerry, supported by DC Scott and two uniformed constables, attended his flat on the Patmore Estate. Secretly she'd never been as relieved at her inability to arrest a suspect. Only she and Glenn had entered the apartment block, with the others staying out of sight a block away — ready to bring in the van once Funky was in cuffs — but before they were on their way down the stairs, she suspected that alerts were flying up and down the estate that the Old Bill was on the hunt. It was doubtful Funky would return to his flat any time soon, going to ground at the hangout of one of the other gang member's instead. Criminals were suspicious by nature, sometimes to a level of paranoia. It wouldn't surprise her if he'd left immediately after she spoke to him the day before, ordered to go into hiding. She couldn't ignore the fact that Jermaine Robson had shown up, and the probable reason was to contain a troublesome situation.

DCI Porter demanded a quick win.

Arrest Funky and throw the book at him.

She would arrest Funky, and he'd pay for his part in the murders. The bastard had specifically targeted the Ghedis so the Nine Elms Crew could implicate their greatest rival in the murders. He'd chosen the victims by their skin colour, to add validity to the attack, and incite public anger over the racially motivated killings. Or was told to choose a certain type of victims by the brains behind the plan. Three footsoldiers of the Nine Elms Crew hadn't come up with the scheme in order to curry favour with their leader; they'd acted on his orders, as they always did.

She wanted Funky, and the two in the car, but she wanted Jermaine Robson more. Getting to the leader would prove tricky. There were layers of protection between him and the killings. If arrested, Funky and his pals would be coerced by promise of death or reward to take the rap for him. Direct evidence of his involvement was needed before she could arrest him, and that would never happen if Porter got his quick win.

As they retreated from the Patmore Estate, she updated the control room with the negative result, and pre-empting Porter asked for a citywide bulletin to be issued requesting Adefunke's arrest. In the meantime she hoped she got to the bottom of things before Funky was captured, and the key players got away scot-free. Players in its plural sense, because Jermaine Robson couldn't have set up the scheme without insider help from somebody close to Swain. Back at the nick, she had Mel Scanlon fetch a certain piece of evidence from storage. It was the key for Swain's lock-up where his Subaru Impreza had allegedly been stored since his disqualification from driving.

Kerry didn't need to hold the key, but seeing it helped concentrate her mind.

'The garage was locked when you went to conduct the search?' she asked Mel.

'Yeah.'

'New lock or old?'

'Newish. But if you're asking if it was brand new, put on after a previous one was cut off, I'd say no.'

'What was the garage interior like?'

'A regular lock-up, but with very little in it.'

'Any suggestion that the Subaru was previously parked there?'

'I'd say yes. I took photos of the interior if you'd like to see them.'

Kerry nodded, and Mel fired up her computer. She brought up the appropriate digital file, and the dozen photographs she'd taken at the scene. It was unfortunate Kerry's weird ability didn't allow her to see the ghosts of cars. Yet she could see an open space where a car the size of a Subaru could have previously sat. Assorted cardboard boxes and sundry pieces of junk were clustered around the three walls, but the central area was bare. The floor was scuffed by tread marks in a film of fine concrete dust.

'We only have Hettie's word that the Subaru was ever parked there,' Mel said.

'I believe her,' said Kerry. 'The issue for me isn't if the car was there, it's how it was taken from the lock-up by the Nine Elms Crew without Erick Swain's knowledge. When you went back with Hettie to collect the keys, did she invite you inside?'

'Yeah. I followed her in and she went to where they were hanging on a hook in the kitchen.'

Kerry sucked air through her teeth. 'No pause, no trying to remember where they were first?'

'No. Went straight to them. But that doesn't tell us anything. I could take you to my house and walk you directly to where I keep my keys too.'

'Hettie handled the key when she passed it to you, so that means hers will be the most prominent fingerprints we'd find if we looked.' Kerry believed Swain's fingerprints would also be on the key, seeing as he would have used it on other occasions. But the person that had used the key so the Subaru could be removed from the lock-up, then relocked the door and returned it to its peg in Swain's kitchen, would have worn gloves. They'd want Swain's fingerprints on the key, to implicate him.

The detectives looked at each other, both of them ruminating over the possibilities.

'Hettie gave the keys to somebody in the Nine Elms Crew?' Mel finally posed. 'Then had them returned to her later? Do you really buy that, ma'am?'

'No. In interview she told me she didn't leave the house, but Swain did. Gave me a story about doing some housework then watching TV. She offered no witness corroboration, said she was home alone. Do me a favour,

Mel. Run Hettie through PNC, and check her driver status with DVLA. Then, if my suspicion's correct, I'm afraid it's back to reviewing CCTV evidence for you.'

It took Mel less than a minute to confirm Kerry's inkling.

'Hettie doesn't hold a driving license.'

Kerry called Korba and put the phone on speaker.

'When we were at Hettie's last, Zane McManus had his car outside...'

'Yeah. Nissan Skyline. The dog's bollocks for boy racers.'

'You ran a PNC check on it, did you happen to note down the reg number?'

There followed the sound of the DS scratching through his notebook. 'Got it here, boss.' He read out the number.

'Thanks, Danny.'

'That's all you need?'

'For now.' Kerry hung up. Mel had already brought up the car's details on the computer.

It made sense now why Zane owned a car that was normally way out of the reach of a kid like him. With Swain disqualified, and being driven around, Hettie also required a personal chauffer. And Hettie wasn't the type to be seen dead in the kind of crappy motor the likes of Zane could ordinarily afford. She was keeping it in the family, using a car to her taste and by employing her younger cousin as her driver.

'Do you know what a Skyline looks like?' Kerry asked.

'Got a good idea, ma'am. But hang on.' Mel typed the make and model into a search engine, and brought up the images. Kerry pointed out a Skyline the same colour red as Zane's.

'I want you to look for his Skyline in the neighbourhood of Swain's lock-up in the hour or two before the shooting on Wandsworth Road, OK?'

'Bloody hell, I'm square-eyed already,' Mel groaned, but it was for effect. She didn't object to sitting through however many hours of video footage it took to find what Kerry was after. 'Shouldn't take too long actually, Swain's lock-up's in a secure compound. It never occurred when I was there to ask, but I'd bet it's protected by cameras.'

She should have thought about that too, Kerry realised. Footage of the compound would show who collected the Subaru as well. But her mind had been on *other things* that had made her miss the obvious.

'I'll take a run out and see if I can find who monitors the site.' Mel could discover the information she needed via her computer, but Kerry didn't begrudge her some freedom from the office. She needed some too.

'Can you drop me at home before you do that? I didn't bring my car to work this morning.'

Mel grinned. Porter wasn't the only detective with a nose. Surely by now, hours later, the incriminating smell had faded?

'I've a couple of things to do at home, and then I'll drive myself back here,' she explained, to prove she was now sober enough to be behind the wheel. 'Hopefully by then you'll have something to show me.'

Mel checked the time. 'I'm supposed to be off at six, ma'am.' It was less than two hours away. 'But I don't mind hanging on if you're happy to approve the overtime.'

'Take as long as you need, Mel. I'll be back as soon as, OK?'

'Let's get you home then.' Mel closed down her computer. 'I'll go drop the key in evidence and then join you outside.'

While she waited beside Mel's vehicle, Kerry peered around the subterranean parking garage. It was the domain of light and shadow, a breeding ground for a fertile imagination. Erick Swain was conspicuous by his absence. His non-appearance gave her hope that by following her intuition, she'd banished the need for his prompts for good.

Hope, unfortunately, was wishful thinking, and another desire driven by the id. The devil on her shoulder wasn't finished with her yet. Not by a long shot.

Adam was out, and it suited Kerry. Returning home, it wasn't with making up with him in mind. She wished to be somewhere beyond the reach of DCI Porter's beady eyes and flapping ears. Adam's presence would only complicate matters while she made a call she'd put off for too long, even if he were responsible for pushing her into it.

She had to do some digging to locate the number she was after. It was two decades since last she'd spoken to Doctor Ronald Dawson, and for all she knew her psychologist could be dead. In a child's perception, Doctor Ron had looked ancient, but could have barely been into his forties. If that were the case then he would be now be around retirement age.

There was no listing in Carlisle for a practicing psychologist of his name, and none in the wider Cumbrian region either. But she didn't give up easily. She put his name through a search engine and it threw up a few historical newspaper reports where Ron had been quoted. The most recent article spoke about the publication of the retired psychologist's debut novel — not a psychology treatise but a crime thriller — and gave details of his website. Apparently Ron had aspired to write for most of his adult life, and after retirement had taken the plunge and finally put his keen mind to another use. He wrote under the pen name Don D. Rawson: not exactly a household name, but Kerry felt she'd noticed the author's name on books in remainder bins and wholesale discount shops. She wasn't certain if the proliferation of discounted books was due to his success or a failure to gain a readership. She followed the link to his website. He'd been busy in the past four years, turning out six novels, the latter of which was exclusively available in eBook. Again Kerry's knowledge of the publishing model didn't give her a clue as to his success. A mega successful author might have an agent or PR team handling his communications for him: she didn't want to go through any third party. As it were, Doctor Ron was an approachable author, and had added an email contact page to his site, and, helpfully, a phone number.

She dithered before ringing. For starters, by ringing Doctor Ron, it was confirmation she needed help. By reaching for help it was an admission she was ill. Being ill could destroy her career and hopes of ever solving her sister's case.

No. She couldn't think that way. If she was ill, she needed to get well. And that wouldn't happen without support.

She tapped in his number.

The line rang out, so she hung up.

She felt watched. Standing in the corner of her living room was Girl, silent and still. Kerry avoided looking, but could almost sense despondency washing over her.

'Don't worry,' she said gently, 'it isn't you I want rid of.'

Girl moved towards her, head down, but hands held palms up. Kerry glanced at her.

Girl was no longer there.

Maybe she had never been there. If she hoped to banish Swain, then she must accept that Girl didn't exist either. Only she wasn't sure she wanted to.

She lifted her phone, about to redial, and it rang. Unknown caller.

'Hello?'

'Hello,' replied a voice she hadn't heard in decades. 'You just rang me, and I'm returning your call.'

'Doctor Ron?'

A moment of quiet reflection followed, before Ron Dawson chuckled. 'It's been a while since I've gone by that name. Have we met, young lady?'

'We have. I'm Detective Inspector Kerry Darke.'

'Detective Ins—' Ron suddenly grew guarded. 'Is there something I'm supposed to have done wrong?'

For a second or two, Kerry felt awkward. 'It isn't like that; I'm not calling in my official capacity. It's more a...well, a personal matter.'

'Personal? Of course it is. I'm old, these days, but thankfully senility hasn't set in. Of course I remember you, Little Kes.'

The nickname thrust a pang of nostalgia through her. She hadn't heard it in, well, as Hettie Winters might say, donkey's years. During their earliest sessions, when the psychologist had encouraged her to call him Ron, she'd agreed with the caveat he called her Kes. Nobody, not even her family called her that, but she had seen a book that Sally was reading before going missing, about a poor boy rearing a kestrel he'd named Kes, and if she could be a bird, Kerry had thought, it would be a hawk. When she'd insisted on referring to him as Doctor Ron, she had become Little Kes: it was their pact to always tell the truth during their sessions, though as an adult Kerry knew she'd betrayed their deal as many times as Ron had.

Little Kes. She found it difficult to wipe the sad smile from her lips.

'So you're a police detective these days?' said Ron.

'And you're a famous author.'

'I wouldn't go that far.'

'I've seen your books in lots of places,' she told him, taking care not to mention where.

He chuckled. 'But not in many readers' hands, I'd bet.'

'Maybe if I buy one you could personalize it for me?'

'It'd be my pleasure.'

Even as they made the agreement, they both suspected it would never happen.

'But you didn't call me because you have a problem getting your hands on a signed copy of *The Immolation Killer*,' said Ron. 'I'm pretty sure if you go online you'll get a copy of any of my novels for a few pennies. Ha, I've a box full in my garage I can't even give away.'

'You must be kidding me,' she said, feeling that his ego required a little massaging. 'There aren't many people capable of writing a book, let alone getting it published, and by all accounts you've done it half a dozen times.'

'You've certainly done your research, Little Kes. Pardon me. You probably cringe when I call you that, Detective Inspector.'

'Not at all. In fact, it helps.'

'As I suspected. You haven't made contact after all these years for advice on writing your own novel then?' He went silent, and she wasn't sure if he was reminiscing, or something else. His next words didn't help clarify either. 'It's such a sad business.'

When she didn't immediately respond, Ron went on. 'But I can imagine how it must've brought all those memories flooding back.'

'I, uh, sorry,' Kerry said. 'You've lost me, Doctor Ron.'

'The girl,' he said.

Immediately she thought *Girl*, but that wasn't it.

'The little girl that has gone missing in Cumbria?' he prompted.

'What? A girl has gone missing?'

'Well, I'd've thought you would be aware being as you're...'

'I live and work in London these days.'

'Oh, I assumed you were a detective with Cumbria Constabulary. Please excuse my assumption: I based it on my own inability to escape the cold, wet north.'

'A little girl has gone missing?' Kerry asked again, and once more a wave of despondency engulfed her. Girl was a shadowy mote in the corner.

'It's all over the local news channels. I'm guessing that the story hasn't made its way to civilisation yet.'

'No...no it hasn't.' In truth, she'd been too caught up in her own problems to spare a second on anyone else's. 'Is it...is it *him* again?'

'Him?'

'The Fell Man.'

'The beastly creature you believed took your sister? It's highly unlikely, Little Kes. I mean, how long ago was that now?'

'Twenty-something years.' She could have told him the exact number of days if he was interested.

'Yes, it was a long time ago. No, if this poor girl, Hayley, has been abducted then I fear it's by a different monster. Little Kes, uh, Kerry...Detective Inspector...listen. The media might be jumping the gun again, as I might be by telling you this. But I'm pretty sure that as a police officer you're aware that most abductions occur between family members. This little girl's parents are going through an acrimonious divorce; you can bet one or the other is responsible for spiriting the child out of the other's hands.'

'It happens. Not in every case.'

'No. Of course not. That was a tad insensitive of me.' To change the subject, he said, 'So if you're not calling for writing advice or about this latest missing child then I can only assume there's something from the past you'd like to talk about.'

As soon as she hit the answer button on her phone she'd resolved to be forthright. 'I wanted some advice, but, like I said, on a personal issue. Doctor Ron, if I was suffering a mental breakdown, would it be something I was aware of myself or would I be ignorant of the symptoms?'

'Now that would depend a great deal. But, I must remind you that I'm no longer your psychologist. Perhaps I'm not the right person to ask.'

'I'm asking as a friend.'

'Oh.' Her remark hit him in a soft spot. 'Then I shall make every effort to answer as your friend. As long as you drop the 'doctor' and call me Ron as I asked all those years ago.'

'Deal,' she said.

'Deal,' he echoed. 'OK, so how'd you like to start at the beginning and tell me how you've come to the notion?'

She did, admitting to him that as a child she'd hidden the fact she'd never truly shaken off her silent companion, although Girl had somewhat faded for most of her adulthood until the moment a few days ago on Wandsworth Road. Of course, it wasn't the presence of Girl that she'd reached out to Ron for an explanation; he'd tried two decades ago and failed. She narrated the tale of Erick Swain's death and subsequent resurrection in spirit form.

'Well,' he said after some thought, 'it's quite a fantasy you've become embroiled in.'

'More like a nightmare.'

'Or a waking dream,' he suggested. 'When you're suffering insomnia, as you probably are, it's not unusual to dream while awake. Some people have even been known to achieve a REM state while for all intents and purposes they think they're awake. It's the subconscious' coping mechanism; it works through your fear or grief. It can feel real, but only to the dreamer. It doesn't exist in the actual world.' He paused, made a decision. 'Kerry, it's best we speak as friends, so you can trust me. What you're seeing is not real...I know you've struggled with this problem since you were a child, but it's as unreal now as it was then.'

'Girl was there,' she answered, stoic in her belief. 'She has always been with me. To me she's real, Ron, as real as you are.'

'*You* genuinely believe that.'

'Yes I do, because it's *my* truth.'

'It wasn't a question; I was stressing an important point. Belief in itself is a contradiction, because we can be fooled into forming false beliefs. When the mind's in emotional turmoil it will grasp at anything for comfort. After the trauma of Sally's abduction, you needed to feel better. You, and your parents, were in emotional distress. It made you all susceptible to false beliefs. In that delicate frame of mind, you can be encouraged to believe in almost anything. Think of a faith healer who says they can take away your pain simply by waving his hands over you. If you believe strongly enough, he can wave his hands and — Hey presto! — the pain will disappear. But it's not a miracle; it's what's known as a placebo. It's a feel-good, make-believe pile of poop. When you're in emotional pain, or grief, you will sooner embrace magic, and ghosts and any other fantasy if it helps ease your mind, than deal with your actual feelings. On occasion, all of us turn to symbolic crutches to lean on. You're imagining Swain because you need him to soothe your pain. There is no Swain, Kerry, and there is no Girl. There's only you.'

'So I am going nuts?'

'No. As I said, you're only grasping for support, but Swain — especially Swain — is not what you should cling to.'

'You can say that again. So...what do I need to do?'

'As your friend, I'd say you only need a firm hug and a sympathetic shoulder to cry on. But that wouldn't be good enough, and I'd be doing you a disservice. As a psychologist I'd advise you to seek medical treatment; I'd say you're suffering a mild form of depression. A prescribed course of medication from your GP will make the hallucinations go away so you can heal on real terms. Untreated, what you're dealing with could grow worse, to a point where you could suffer a psychotic break. And to answer your original question, you would be ignorant of the symptoms because you'd already be too deep in its grip.'

'Well, how did that work out for you?'

Swain directed a puissant grin over Kerry's shoulder as she straightened from the bathroom washbasin and looked in the mirror. She yelped, as much in indignation as surprise. Her elbow jabbed into his ethereal face, then as she swept around her wet hand slapped at empty air. Injuring him was impossible, but he jolted in response to the attack and backed out of the bathroom into the hall. She grabbed the door, slammed it shut and threw the bolt.

'Feisty bitch!'

'Stay away from me! You've no bloody right invading my private space!' She jammed her bare shoulders against the door. 'What are you, some kind of pervy creep? Do you get your kicks spying on half-naked women?'

'Now, now, Inspector Darke, don't be selfish. Surely you wouldn't deny me the perks of my current situation?' Despite the presence of the door between them, his words could have been crowed in her ear.

After ending her call with Ron Dawson, she'd visited the bathroom to freshen up. She was confident most of the alcohol was out of her system by now, but a lot of it was deposited in her clothing. She'd dumped her blouse and trousers in the laundry hamper, and stood at the washbasin in her underwear. Taking Ron's words on-board about Swain being of her own making, she'd been careless: and the bastard had crept up on her.

'Let's get something straight right this second,' she snapped, 'you *must* respect my privacy.'

'There's nothing I must *do*. What exactly are you going to do if I refuse? Arrest me?' He laughed nastily. 'Think that door's any kind of barrier? Haven't you heard? Ghosts can walk through walls.'

'Show your face in here again and I swear to God I'll...'

'Slap me again? Yeah, how'd that work out for you? About as useless as your little tête-à-tête with Doctor Ron? What was his deal with all that Little Kes *shit? He sounds like a kiddie fiddler. Did he used to give you* therapy *with you sitting in his lap? Did he get you to suck his purple lollipop?'*

'You're a sick-minded bastard,' she snarled.

'It takes one to know one. If I'm only an expression of your repressed guilt, then who's putting these words into my mouth?'

'You were eavesdropping our conversation?'

'Would I need to if I was only in your head?'

All reassurance given by Doctor Ron was wiped out. She still had no idea what was real or not.

'If you're only in my head,' she challenged, 'tell me what I'm thinking right now.'

'Oh, that's too easy! Rather than being in your head you'd prefer me in your knickers?'

'You sick-minded—'

'Yeah, yeah. I'm a pervy bastard. But you did ask. So what does my answer tell you?'

'That you're not in my head. I'd never want you anywhere near me. I don't want you near me now!'

'Don't worry, about that, Kezza. I told you, you're not my type. I like a woman with tits I can get hold of, not somebody with two backs and a boy's skinny arse.' Again he directed nasty laughter at her. *'Truth be told? I wouldn't touch you with your pal Korba's greasy dick, never mind my own. Now there's a bloke who really would like to get into your knickers.'*

'Shut up you sick-minded...' her words faltered.

'Yep. You're beginning to repeat yourself. Kind of loses its impact once you've been called a sick-minded pervy bastard more than once.'

'It doesn't make it any less true.'

'And you're a stuck needle. Last time I was a liar. Now I'm a sicko. Change the record, Kezza.'

'Stop calling me that.'

'Must I?'

'Yes. It's not my name.'

'See, I find saying Detective Inspector Kerry Darke a mouthful. What do you suggest I call you?'

'Nothing. Just go away and leave me alone.' She lunged across the bathroom, snatching a towel she wrapped around her like a shroud.

'I'm sorry, Kezza. No can do. I made you an offer, and need to hear what you've decided.' He waited. *'Do you need a prompt?'*

'I remember exactly what you offered.'

'So what will it be? Is helping me worth getting what you want most?'

'All I want is to be rid of you.'

'Well, here's the bonus,' he said. *'Do what I ask, and I'll tell you what I know about your sister's disappearance, and the paedo-bastard that took her. Yeah, you probably got from my comments regarding the good Doctor Ron that I've no tolerance for nonces; I'll happily grass on a kiddie fiddler.'*

'Doctor Ron's a good man.'

'Yeah. Whatever. Do what I ask, Kezza, and once it's done, you have my promise you'll never hear from me again.'

'There are boundaries I won't cross,' she reminded him.

'Boundaries are like lines on a map. They mean fuck all when you can just step over them.' Like that, Swain was back in the bathroom. Kerry tightened the towel around her, and crushed back against the washbasin. He pointed at the shower cubicle. *'Unless you want me in there with you every time you shower, or holding my nose beside you every time you take a dump — for the rest of your miserable life — you'd better accept my offer.'*

'What do you want from me?'

Swain fiddled with the handcuff dangling from his wrist. *'You know now that I didn't shoot those niggers.'*

'Language like that doesn't endear any pity from me.'

'I don't want your pity. I want revenge.'

'On me?'

'No, Kezza, on the bastards that set me up.'

'I'm already working on that.'

'Not diligently enough for my liking. I had to push you to look closer at that flow chart in your office, to force you into seeing the obvious staring you in the face.'

'Why not just tell me what I need to know if you're so fucking omnipotent?'

'I never claimed to know everything, but even I could see there was something wrong with the scenario with who was driving my car. But then, fair enough, I had the hindsight that I wasn't the one in the passenger seat either.'

'I know now that you weren't involved,' she admitted, 'but it doesn't make me think any better of you. You're still a criminal, a murderer. And I feel no guilt over your death when that was your own fault.' Now was his opportunity to raise the subject of Girl coming to her rescue, but apparently he had no recollection.

'Yeah, keep telling yourself that, Kezza. To be honest I don't give a shit how you feel about me. I don't blame you for my death; I blame the ones that set the ball rolling that ended up with us both fighting on that rooftop. And we both know who they are. But it's down to you to prove it.'

Briefly she wondered if Mel Scanlon was back at the nick yet, and how far she'd got with the CCTV evidence she hoped to find.

'I'm working on a lead that might prove the conspiracy. If it pans out I'll be making arrests soon.'

'Arrests! I don't give a shit for arrests!' He raged towards her, and stopped only inches from her face, his

teeth bared. ' *I want him. I want Jermaine Robson DESTROYED!'*

'Destroyed how?'

'You know how! Robson did this to me. And do you know why? Because he wants what was mine, *but he didn't have the balls to try to take it from me in person. Now I'm out of the way he wants to move in and take over my patch, my business...everything that was mine. Everything I fought and worked hard for all those years. Well you have to make sure he gets none of it. Do you hear me? Do you understand what I want now? If you want me to uphold my side of the bargain you have to give me what I ask.'* He glared at her, waiting for it to sink in. *'I'll give you the Fell Man, but I want Jermaine Robson's head served to me on a fucking plate.'*

'You're asking for something I can't give you.'

'It's your choice, Kezza. Say ta-ta to the Fell Man, bitch, and say hello to your new bosom buddy Swain-o.'

'I'm a police officer, I can't just—'

'What, chase someone onto a roof they just happen to accidentally-on-purpose slip off? Come on, you know as well as I do that unfortunate accidents *happen all the time. I'm sure there's enough nounce up in that detective's brain of yours to come up with a plan.'*

'No. I won't do it. I'm not capable of murder.'

He snorted in disbelief. *'Tell me that again once I set your hands on the Fell Man.'*

This time, she didn't argue.

Swain allowed her the privacy to complete her ablutions, a huge relief on one hand, but it also suggested the decision to go along with his demand was a foregone conclusion to him. She hadn't agreed to his terms, never would. Not to the extreme length he expected. Yes, she'd do everything in her power to solve the case and ensure the culprits were punished. She owed as much to the Ghedi family, but not to Erick Swain. She would not, no way, no how, be pushed into committing murder for him!

Interestingly, when mentally making her stand, Swain had not reappeared to rant and rave, but stayed wherever it was he retreated to when not spying on her. If he was a product of her unconscious id, then surely there was no thought she could keep from him? Or she was the victim of a double bluff of her own machination. Maybe he thought his argument was strong enough without further haranguing, because when he'd suggested she would happily murder the Fell Man she hadn't experienced the same sense of discomfort as at the thought of killing Jermaine Robson. In fact a thrill had tingled through her body and left her hot and slightly breathless at the possibility. Where she held the towel she'd formed fists so tight it had been an effort to uncurl her fingers after Swain vacated the bathroom.

Adam didn't return before she left the house. It was dark, and the wind swirling down her street held a promise of winter. She pulled up the hood on her duffel coat, donned over a fresh trouser suit and blouse, and clutched her handbag under her left elbow. She approached Eel Brook Common kicking through drifts of fallen leaves as she made for her car, already holding her key. Broken twigs and leaves had accumulated on its bonnet and windscreen, wet and shiny under the dim glow from a nearby lamppost. Overhead the branches of a tree swayed and groaned in the breeze, scattering more autumnal detritus on its roof.

Inside the car it felt damp, and a film of condensation immediately coated the windows when her breath hit the colder glass. She started the engine, turned the blowers to their highest setting and the windscreen wipers going. The wipers picked up the mulch of leaf and twigs, streaking dirty arcs over the windscreen. She turned up their rhythm and the leaf litter was thrown aside. She wiped the moisture off the windscreen with the back of her hand, and immediately regretted it. Now the glass was smeared inside and out. She'd have to wait before driving off, because with the lack of visibility she could end up crashing, or worse, knocking over a pedestrian. While she waited, she pulled out her phone and rang Mel Scanlon.

'I was just about to ring you, ma'am,' Mel announced the instant she answered the phone. 'You won't believe what I've got to show you.'

'You found something?' In that moment all thoughts of Erick Swain, Girl, the Fell Man, and even Sally, were cast by the wayside. She hadn't given voice to her suspicions, but throughout all the distractions she'd suffered, her detective's mind had been working away in the background, piecing together clues, formulating a theory, and all the while clinging to the hope that something concrete would present as evidence. 'Did you get the Skyline on tape near the compound?'

She only required one CCTV image showing Zane McManus meeting with Funky and his pals to tie the plot together. For the scheme to frame Erick Swain to work, Jermaine Robson had needed an inside man. Somebody with free access to come and go to Swain's house must have supplied the key to the lock-up, then returned it to its hook in the kitchen, as if Swain had absent-mindedly returned it after burning out the getaway car. Somebody must have been given the murder weapon to reload with bullets daubed with Swain's fingerprints, bury the incriminating evidence in his garden, then make that anonymous telephone call informing the police where to find it. Swain had never been expected to die, but on such damning evidence, he'd have been looking at a lengthy prison sentence. With Swain out of the way, it would be a simple enough task for Robson's Nine Elms Crew to steamroll their way over Swain's territory and for Robson to take it for his own.

'Ma'am,' said Mel, and Kerry heard the victorious chattering of her team in the background, 'You wanted some actionable evidence, well we might just have hit the mother lode.'

'You can see Zane meeting with Funky and the others?'

'Better than that,' said Mel.

What could be better? 'Don't keep me on tenterhooks, for Christ's sake. Just tell me.'

Danny Korba's voice broke in. 'Are you coming in to see what we've found or not? We need your input on this before we do anything else.' He was like a conspirator, cajoling her under false pretences to attend her own surprise party. 'You have to see this with your own eyes, boss.'

'I'm on my way now.'

She turned from a cautious driver worried about getting in a wreck, to a speed freak prepared to take reckless chances with red lights and the narrowest of gaps between slower moving traffic. What would ordinarily take her twenty minutes to drive was accomplished in under ten. She hit the ramp into the subterranean parking garage so fast that the front bumper scraped the concrete before her car levelled out. She abandoned her car in a space reserved for visiting SCO19 vehicles. Jogged through the nick, ignoring startled or bemused looks from her uniformed colleagues and shouldered open the door to the GaOC office. Wild-eyed and windswept, she stared expectantly at her team who'd all clustered around Mel's workstation: somebody had got the brews in, the on-duty copper's celebratory drink of choice, with the foresight of grabbing her a mug of tea too. They all grinned so hard they'd need their jaws slackened with a crowbar afterwards.

'Let me see,' she ordered without preamble.

Mel had already prepped her computer screen, angling it out the way she had earlier. Tony Whittle danced aside to make way for Kerry, sprightly for a stockily built bloke. Korba leaned in alongside her, and when she glanced at him he waggled his brows to build anticipation. She returned her attention to the screen, even as Glenn Scott pushed a mug of tea into her hands. She ignored the steaming brew.

'This footage isn't from the compound's official security system,' Mel quickly explained. 'A renter, Mr Torrance, installed his own cameras after his adjacent lock-up kept getting vandalised, and the images from the compound's security cameras proved too distant and grainy to identify the culprits. He mounted a hidden camera he could remotely access from his laptop to keep a discreet eye on the place. I'd bet Swain originally chose that lock-up because it was far from the security cameras and had no idea this one was there. This little bunch of scumbags certainly had no idea of its presence. Torrance was reticent about giving me a look at his recordings when he heard I was a detective, but...' Mel stopped, realising she was babbling. 'Well, here it is.'

The quality of the footage was superb, in colour, and importantly it was date and time-stamped. The angle of the camera didn't give a direct view of Swain's lock-up; it had been placed for maximum coverage of the one rented by Mr Torrance. Yet the angle actually helped when Zane McManus's Nissan Skyline drew to a halt directly below – purposefully leaving clear access to

Swain's lock-up so the Subaru could be driven out. Before he was even out of the driving seat, a tall dark-skinned man — unmistakably Ikemba Adefunke — moved into shot. Zane got out his car, and they bumped knuckles, clenched hands and gave a one-armed shoulder hug, like old buddies.

'No audio?' Kerry asked.

'Picture only,' Mel said.

'It'll do.' Adrenalin flooded through Kerry, making her shiver.

On-screen Zane and Funky exchanged words, but even the best lip reader would be thwarted by the angle. Kerry didn't need to hear them talking, the images were enough to prove the conspiracy. Two black men moved into frame.

'Recognise them, boss?' Korba still maintained a manic grin.

'I do.' It was the two young gang members they'd witnessed meeting with Funky outside his apartment block.

Glenn Scott placed two printed sheets of paper on the desk. Her team had been productive rather than waiting until her arrival before getting on with identifying the gunman and driver. She only glanced at the mugshots, before returning her attention to the video footage. A fifth man had joined the small gathering of plotters. He was cooler about greeting Zane, only offering a swift dip of his chin.

'Jermaine Robson.' Kerry's whisper barely carried beyond her lips. 'Christ, we've got him…'

Korba touched her wrist. 'It's not over yet, boss.'

Gloved-up, Zane handed over a car key and the one currently in an evidence bag down the hall, and Funky and one of the younger guys hurried off-screen. Their shadows painted the ground. From their shadows Kerry could tell they were opening the adjacent garage door. While they were busy moving the Subaru, Zane and

Robson exchanged words, then the briefest of handshakes. Their display of friendship didn't extend to their facial expressions or body language. Theirs was a deal based on mutual need. Funky must have locked the door after the other guy drove out the Subaru. He returned the key to Zane, who pushed it into an inside pocket — to be returned to the hook in Hettie's kitchen — then Funky disappeared out of sight. The other young gangster joined Robson, and walked around the Skyline and stood by the front passenger door.

There was no view of the person inside the car, but evidently they had powered down the window. A gloved hand emerged, holding out an object bundled in a cloth. Without taking it, Robson unwrapped the cloth and Kerry's view of the Webley Mk IV .38/200 Service revolver was excellent. Robson avoided touching the gun. He nodded at the young man beside him, who took it in his gloved hands, and quickly transferred it to his waistband. The gunman sloped off-screen towards where the Subaru Impreza waited for him. Robson directed some instructions towards where the Subaru must now be, before he leaned towards the passenger window of Zane's Skyline. Even from the sharp angle, he could be seen smiling. He leaned deeper towards the window, intimately.

From within the car emerged a hand now devoid of gloves, and Kerry caught her breath. The sapphire engagement ring on her second finger was very identifiable. Then, as Robson ducked inside the window, that hand curled around the back of his neck to pull him into a lingering kiss. There was a hint of blond locks spilling from the window. On the other side of the car Zane shifted uncomfortably and turned his back on the show of affection. It was one thing plotting Erick Swain's fall with their enemies, quite another to openly fraternize. Watching his cousin locking lips with Robson was asking too much of him.

'Hettie?' Kerry wondered aloud.

Who else could it be except for Hettie Winters?

When Kerry thought about it, the sniffer dog had reacted to the settee where Hettie had been sitting when the search warrant was executed at her home. It was she who'd probably reloaded the gun, while seated on the settee, after it was subsequently returned to her for burying, and she who had scattered the incriminating cartridges in the master bedroom. As she'd stated during interview, Hettie was 'no good with maths'. Hearing that only two victims had been killed, she'd made the fatal miscalculation of reloading a single bullet, without first removing one from the cylinder: the three shells deliberately emptied from the revolver and dropped at the scene bore Swain's fingerprints, as did the one she'd fed back in the gun. She trusted that Hettie had manipulated Swain into handling those bullets beforehand. Ensuring his prints were prominent on them, so they could be used as evidence to convict him.

On the occasions she'd spoken with Hettie, both in official interview and subsequently at her home, she'd found her cold, and had put down her behaviour to mild shock at her boyfriend's death, and the dawning understanding that he was a child killer, but that wasn't it. Hettie was a cold-hearted bitch, full stop. She had plotted with Swain's rival to get rid of him. For what reason though: she and Robson were secret lovers?

'*No. Not* my *Hettie.*'

While the others in the room waited for Kerry to absorb the surprising denouement, she had done the same with Erick Swain.

At some point he'd materialised to stand behind Mel Scanlon, as Porter had stood earlier. The DC was totally unaware of his presence, although Mel shivered a couple of times as if chilled. The look on Swain's face was unrecognisable. Before this he had either been smarmy, cock-sure of himself, or snarling and snapping his teeth in rage. Now his expression could only be described as bereft. His mouth hung open, drooping at one side, and his eyes were, ironically, haunted. Slowly, he reared back, his eyelids screwing tight. Kerry tensed for the inevitable explosion.

It didn't come.

Swain dematerialized, and again the only hint he'd been there was in the way Mel ran her palm over the short hairs on the back of her neck.

It was a relief that he'd left, because she wouldn't be able to concentrate with him storming up and down the office, ranting about his betrayal. Hopefully discovering who was involved was enough to chase him off to wherever dark spirits like his belonged, expect she had one regret: he hadn't given her the answers she wanted yet.

She'd previously wondered if once a person passed, if they became party to all the secrets of the universe. She'd entertained the notion that Swain could indeed point her at the Fell Man, and reveal to her Sally's fate, through some metaphysical all-knowing, all-seeing talent. But Swain had never claimed to wield unearthly powers. All he'd claimed was that he knew things: *'There are no secrets in the underworld. And by the underworld I'm not talking about fire and brimstone.'*

Well, apparently he wasn't as connected as he'd boasted, when he'd failed to notice that one of those plotting against him was his lover. Accepting his lie was wishful thinking, she had to consider if he'd been manipulating her to get what he wanted, without ever intending upholding his side of the bargain.

That was fine. She didn't need Swain.

It was intuition that had led her to follow a different investigative path, and the work of her team under her determined guidance, that had discovered those behind the murders of Nala and Bilan Ghedi...not through being steered by a bloody ghost!

Paired up, her intuition and determination should lead to the capture of the Fell Man too. Erick Swain could go to hell.

She realised her team were still watching her. Who knew what emotions had played across her features in the past few seconds?

'I take it DCI Porter's unaware of the scale of this?' She nodded towards the computer screen, on which Mel had frozen the picture.

'We wanted you to see it first,' said Korba, 'so you can thumb your nose at him when you break the news.'

'I'm not interested in one-upmanship.' She placed down the mug of tea she'd forgotten she was holding. 'I want every last one of those bastards arrested, but we still have to go at it the right way.' Their arrests needed coordinating so none of them were tipped-off that she was coming for them. She took a quick glance over her shoulder, checking her boss hadn't sneaked in the office. 'He's a pain in the arse, but we need Porter onside to organise things. Do we know if he's still in the nick?'

Korba raised his wristwatch. 'Are you kidding? It's after seven. He's at home with his feet up in front of the TV by now.'

She smiled and reached for the nearest phone. She didn't mind disturbing his privacy. After all, everyone in the office faced a long, sleepless night ahead, so why should Porter be spared the inconvenience?

Knowing who she was after was one thing, but catching and arresting them all was another. It proved a logistical and resource heavy nightmare in fact. Six suspects required six different teams coordinating simultaneous raids on their individual home addresses, despite nobody expecting an arrest at each. Funky wasn't home. Neither was Kingston James, identified as the driver of the Subaru Impreza, or Derrick Lewis, the man who'd accepted the gun from Hettie Winters, and most assuredly the slayer of the Ghedis. Jermaine Robson wasn't home either. So, of the six, only two were grabbed in the initial raids. Zane McManus and Hettie were both found at her house, but bundled into separate vehicles for transportation to the nick to stop them colluding prior to their interviews. Searches were conducted at the home addresses of all six individuals, to turn up any evidence of the plot. All the while, Kerry was nervous. The minute the police descended on the first of those dwellings the news that a manhunt was underway flashed through the criminal networks and sent Robson and his cronies into hiding. With DCI Porter's support she pulled from teams based at other stations throughout the city, and a second wave of raids was set in motion where the homes and premises of known associates of the Nine Elms Crew were targeted, though with no success.

She would like nothing better than to personally arrest the individual conspirators, but that was asking for too much. As it were she ensured a member of her team accompanied a raid where possible, and it pleased her when Korba informed her that Hettie and Zane were en route to custody: he deserved the collars. She'd love to have seen the look on Hettie's face when he snapped on the cuffs but out of necessity, she'd joined the team targeting Derrick Lewis, the gunman. It turned out to be a bust.

Porter shocked Kerry with his response to the news that Hettie and Robson had conspired to bring down Swain. He actually admitted he'd been wrong, when demanding Funky's arrest earlier, and gave what might have been an apology, if he hadn't then twisted the narrative, where it was his motivational guidance that had driven Kerry to solve the case. She didn't care who received the kudos; she only cared that justice would be done as she'd promised Mr Ghedi. Besides, any congratulations were premature. She needed another four criminals in custody, and charged.

She was run ragged for hours, attending six different scenes, and three police stations including New Scotland Yard, before she returned to her own nick, and was bombarded with questions and requests from all sides. Throughout, she kept a clear head, professionally directing the operation to locate and apprehend those still out standing. At first opportunity she went to the custody area.

She approached McManus's cell first, and lowered the flap on the door. Zane was curled up on a thin blue PVC mattress, his back to the door, and his arms wrapped over his head. He was awake, aware he was being observed, but refused to acknowledge her. Kerry said nothing. He wormed across the mattress, jamming up against the wall as if he could escape her ire. She counted to twenty in her head, then slammed shut the flap.

Hettie was the only woman presently in custody, locked in the furthest cell away from her cousin's.

Kerry paused. She drew in a steadying breath, before lowering the flap. When her face wasn't a target for Hettie's manicured fingernails, she leaned closer to the letterbox-sized slot. Hettie was seated on her mattress, with her knees drawn up to her chest, arms wrapped around her shins. The incriminating white flesh where her sapphire ring used to be was bold against her perma-tanned skin – Korba had seized the ring in evidence from her jewellery box at home. She rocked back and forward, until Kerry caught her attention.

Neither woman spoke.

Words were unnecessary, because their expressions said everything. They held the tableau for a long time.

Kerry was first to glance away, except it wasn't a victory for Hettie.

Erick Swain hunkered against the opposite cell wall, dressed as before, still adorned with the cuff jutting from his wrist. His expression differed significantly though. He was no longer bereft. He glared at Hettie with a depth of hatred Kerry had rarely witnessed. Kerry stared at him, long enough for Hettie to follow her gaze, to what was to her a blank wall. Again their gazes clicked, and now Hettie's was quizzical. Kerry ignored her, looking again at the dead man.

How long had Swain been in the cell? Possibly the instant he disappeared from the GaOC office yesterday evening he'd gone directly to Hettie, to punish her betrayal, and had later accompanied her to custody in the rear of the police van. He must have quickly realised he was physically incapable of harming her, but still exhibited his wrath. Apparently Hettie was immune to his threats and curses because she remained totally unaware of his sinister presence. Swain — in life — was a person unused to being ignored, in death he would have to get used to it.

If only that were true. There was one person who couldn't avoid him.

He finally looked at her.

There was no obvious transition from Swain crouching, to flying at her. Kerry jerked, but didn't fully retreat. He came up short, his eyes locked on hers through the observation slot.

'I'm not speaking to you here,' Kerry said.

Hettie misconstrued her meaning. 'I'm not speaking to you either, you bitch. So you might as well piss off till my brief gets here.'

Swain turned to regard her. *'Shut your fat mouth, you slag!'*

'You're wasting your time,' Kerry said.

'We'll see about that when he gets here,' replied Hettie, meaning her solicitor. She stuck up two fingers. 'Now shut it and fuck off.'

Swain swept across the room voicing a wordless roar, began slapping and kicking Hettie. She was unmoved, apart from wrapping her arms tighter round her knees and shuddering as if chilled to the bone. She turned on her side and adopted a similar foetal position as Zane, as if unconcerned. She'd no idea of the videoed evidence Kerry had against her, and fully expected Dopey Dave Barnes to have her released the moment he arrived. Kerry couldn't wait to see the look on her face when it dawned on her it'd be many years before she enjoyed freedom again.

Swain loomed over his ex-girlfriend, chest heaving — did ghosts breathe? Perhaps the mechanics of rage were carried across from the physical to the ethereal body, a memory performed by the shade of the once corporeal form. Kerry supposed they would breathe, as would a hallucination given life in her mind. Maybe Swain's assault on his ex was Kerry manifesting her own hatred of the woman through his actions.

'You're wasting your time trying to speak to her I mean,' she said. 'She can't hear you, any more than she can sense you beating the shit out of her.'

Hettie's face turned towards her, though her blond locks concealed her expression. 'You what?'

'Do me a favour,' Kerry said, this time for Hettie's ears. 'Just shut your fat mouth, you slag!'

Swain's attention shifted to Kerry. He slow-clapped her choice of words.

'That's the first and last time I'll be your voice box,' Kerry promised him in a harsh whisper.

Hettie muttered under her breath, but she was largely ignored now. Swain moved for the door, even as Kerry raised the flap. Then he was before her in the corridor, and offering her a conspiratorial grin.

'Don't know what you're looking so bloody happy about,' she said.

'You're right. I've every reason to be seething, and I am. But you know something, Kezza? For a copper you aren't a complete twat.' He jerked his head at the cell door. *'I've been trying to let Hettie know how I feel about her betrayal, and what you just said to the slag, it felt kind of satisfying. Not as satisfying as ripping her lying tongue out, but,'* he thumped his balled fist repeatedly against his sternum, *'it got me right here.'*

'I didn't say it for your sake.'

'I know. But I don't care. That bitch needed to hear it; she did, and that's good enough for me...for now.'

Kerry led him a few paces from Hettie's cell. They were unobserved — rather *she* was unobserved — but she couldn't take the chance of being witnessed effectively talking to herself. 'I need your help,' she whispered, 'but not here. Can we go somewhere more private?'

'Bloody hell! This is a turn up for the books. I thought all you wanted was to be rid of me, now you're begging for my company.'

'I'm hardly begging. I need your help to catch the others. It's in your best interest if you help me.'

'And if I do, you'll uphold your end of our bargain?'

'I have to catch Robson first,' she said, taking care not to agree to his extreme wishes. 'And when I do, you'll tell me what you know about the Fell Man?'

'I should have you kill every one of those bastards for setting me up,' Swain said. *'But, yeah, I offered a deal. What kind of man would I be if I went against my word?'*

'The exact same piece of shit you always were?'

Swain laughed. *'I'm beginning to like you, Kezza.'*

'The feeling isn't mutual. And stop calling me that.'

He checked all around, hamming up the clandestine nature of their discussion, then whispered out the corner of his mouth. *'So where do you want me?'*

'Meet me in the parking garage,' she said, 'in five minutes.'

He nodded. *'You'll know it when I'm there. I'll be the one wearing the handcuffs,'* he said and jiggled them for effect. He offered a wolfish smile as he faded from existence.

He disappeared not a second too soon.

Janice Beverley, a member of the civilian custody staff entered the corridor, making her rounds. If she was curious why Detective Inspector Darke was standing mid-corridor facing an empty cell, she didn't mention it. She'd assume that Kerry had checked on their sole female prisoner, but she'd a box to tick too. She lowered the flap on Hettie's cell door and looked in. 'Everything OK, love?'

'Piss off and leave me alone,' Hettie snapped.

'Cup of tea or anything?'

'Fuck off.'

Janice closed the flap, looked at Kerry. 'Just charming,' she said, and gave a low chuckle as she continued her rounds.

As Kerry arrived at the custody desk two burly coppers struggled in with a prisoner — a skeletal man in shabby clothing. A rank unwashed stench wafted off him, a comingling of sweat and sour alcohol with an undertone of tomcat piss. He swore savagely at the custody sergeant, who dispensed with formalities and commanded the coppers to immediately put him in a cell. They dragged him away, still swearing madly, to a cell set apart from the others, reserved for obnoxious drunkards.

'Another day in paradise,' the custody sergeant moaned, as he reached for a can of air freshener.

And people wonder why coppers grow cynical, Kerry thought.

'I'll have my guys come back shortly to do interviews,' Kerry informed him.

'Take your time,' he said, spraying the area, 'they aren't going anywhere. It's that stinking git I want shot of.' He meant the drunkard, whose belligerence was now aimed at the officers currently searching him in his cell.

Kerry buzzed herself out of the secure area, into the nick. It was jumping with activity. She paced along a corridor, avoiding the notice of her colleagues, and found the stairwell to the subterranean parking garage.

She fully expected Swain to be waiting for her, lurking in the shadows where he belonged.

But he was unaware that she was setting a test. Not for him, if he were of her making he'd do as she imagined. The test was to determine if she was going out of her mind or not. If she was nuts, he couldn't help her.

The basement car park was dimly lit. The overhead lights were sparse and dusty, netted with grimy cobwebs. Concrete stanchions upheld the upper floors of the building, throwing slanting shadows across the floor, and doorways were nestled in shaded alcoves. The atmosphere was redolent with exhaust fumes, perished rubber and the damp smell of standing puddles. Not a place where anyone hung about for long, so ideal for Kerry's purposes.

It was cloak and dagger stuff, but necessary to set her thoughts at rest. If she could determine the truth behind her visions, she could at least begin to manage them — through intervention or otherwise. If she was losing her mind, she'd a responsibility to seek care with her issues. Despite her life being governed by her quest, she was still conscientious, still a detective who'd pledged to uphold the law, and she hated lying to everyone around her; her superior officers; her closest colleagues; her lover; and especially to herself. It was a situation she couldn't, or shouldn't, maintain.

Doctor Ron explained that the construct of *belief* was a contradiction in terms. He'd largely convinced her that "seeing was not believing", because the mind often grasped at false beliefs because they were easier to come to terms with. Erick Swain's ghost was a construct she'd built in response to contending with a number of traumatic experiences. Nothing about her encounters with Swain's ghost should convince her otherwise. Even the way he'd attacked Hettie, and those vile names he'd called her…Kerry wished she could do the same to the bitch. So, was Swain her puppet? If so then she wasn't beholden to his demands, though he could still prove useful in leading her to the Fell Man. If he was a manifestation of her suppressed guilt, then there was something more powerful waiting to lead her to her sister's abductor.

As if she was given life by thought, Girl materialised, flitting between two of the upright columns. Her footsteps were soundless and left no trace of her passing through a dirty puddle that had settled at the mouth of a blocked drain. Kerry didn't follow her movement, convinced that Girl would secrete herself in a dark alcove to watch while she played tit-for-tat with her id.

'Where are you, Swain?' she whispered.

He was a no show.

'You keep turning up like a bad penny, so where the bloody hell are you when I need you?'

She completed a full turn, checking all the darker corners of the basement. Some of the bays held parked vehicles, but most were empty.

'Swain?'

'Peekaboo!'

She spun around sharply at his voice. She still couldn't see him.

'Stop pissing about, Swain.'

'Cooey, cooey! I'm over here, Kezza!' Swain rose from a crouch behind her car. He dangled the handcuff. *'Don't you recognise me?'*

She bit down on a response. Nodded at the car. 'Get in.'

He didn't move.

'What, you need me to unlock the door first?'

'Just wondered where you were taking me.'

'We're going nowhere. I just want some privacy. I don't want anyone overhearing us...' Why the hell did she bother explaining? 'Just get in, and stop messing about. I've another meeting to go to soon...'

'It's a bloody cop car,' he said, *'I have an aversion to sitting in them.'*

'I bet this is the first time you've been allowed in the front. Get in, Swain, and be quick about it.'

She aimed her electronic key, disengaging the locks, as she approached.

Swain was inside. Seated in her place. 'Shift,' she snarled, as she dragged open the door. She began climbing in before he moved, and felt a mild electrical charge crawl across her skin: a psychosomatic response? Despite the mild discomfort, she settled in the driving position, happy he'd drifted to her left. She scowled at him.

'What? You didn't specify where in the front I could sit.'

'You're just being a dick. Now pack it in and listen up.'

'It turns me on when a woman gets bossy with me,' he said.

'And we both know where your choice in women got you.'

His forced joviality dissipated. *'That's a low blow, Inspector Darke.'*

'But it's also the truth. Apparently Hettie's sense of loyalty was as fake as her plastic boobs. You never suspected she was plotting to ruin you?'

'No. She's the last person I'd expect betrayal from. I don't expect any sympathy from you, but it hurts. Worse even than when I hit the ground that time. When I smacked into the concrete, it was over in an instant, this is...well, it's tearing me up inside.'

Kerry studied him. His words sounded heartfelt, and seen in profile, without the smarmy grin, he appeared pitiful. She could forget for a moment that he was a despicable creature. Almost.

'I think I've enough on her to prove she was involved in the murder of the Ghedis, and conspired with the others to frame you for the crime. She'll get her comeuppance, Swain, but she's not the only one responsible. We have Zane McManus too, but...'

'Yeah, the big-eared shit. After everything I did for him too.' His face had grown sharp again, his jawline tightening.

'In my opinion he was being used by Hettie. It doesn't diminish his involvement, but I'm doubtful he played any part in the planning, and was coerced into it by his cousin.'

'*Don't underestimate Zane,*' Swain warned. '*He acts like a dope but he's sly. Trust me, he won't have taken much convincing by Hettie to betray me; a handful of cash, a snort of cocaine and a blow job, buys the likes of him. Still, I'm surprised he went over to Robson. He hates niggers more than I do.*'

'Stop with the racist crap, will you?'

'*I'm not being racist. They call themselves niggers these days, don't they?*'

His question didn't deserve an answer.

'I was about to say that I need to find the others from the Nine Elms Crew. They've gone under the radar.'

'*You and me both,*' he concurred. '*I want Jermaine Robson dead and buried.*'

'So you can continue your feud with him? Surely there's more to the afterlife than carrying on the same bullshit you did here?'

'*Who knows what happens in the afterlife? You'd think I'd have an inside track, but I've no clue. I'll tell you something for nothing: I didn't see any white light or Saint Peter, or ol' Nick with a toasting fork, either. All I know is I'm still here, and I won't be happy until Robson's messed up as badly as I was. Before you do him, you should ram your truncheon up his arse and let him feel what it's like to be eternally fucked!*'

'Before I can do anything I need to find him.' She stared at him intently. 'That's where you can help me.'

'*How?*'

'By finding him and telling me where he's hiding.'

'*And how am I meant to do that?*'

'You know stuff. Secrets.' She curled up her lip as she quoted his words back to him. 'There are no secrets in the underworld. Well, if that's true, then you'll know his safe houses, the places where he holes up in times of trouble. I want you to check them out, see if you can locate him and his cronies. And don't forget—' This time she paraphrased his words '—even the doors to a safe house are no kind of barrier. Ghosts can walk through walls.'

A look of doubt crossed his features.

'What's wrong? Not up to the challenge?'

'It's not that. Every other time I thought about visiting one of Robson's cribs, it was to put an axe in the back of his skull. Now you want me to...what? Sneak inside like a coward and not do a thing except report back to you?'

'That's exactly what I want. You scratch my back and I'll scratch yours. Now where did I hear that before? Right! Come on, out of the car, Swain.'

He stayed put. Offered her a grin. *'Who'd have ever thought Kezza and Swain-o would become partners, eh?'*

'Don't get above yourself. We're only partners out of necessity. You need to prove you're not totally useless, or you can forget about any arrangement we made.'

'You don't think I can do it?'

'Swain,' she said, and held his gaze, 'I don't even think you exist.'

'That's just charming.'

'So prove to me I'm not going insane. There's no possible way I could know where to find Robson and the others. Show me and...well, just show me.'

'I'll show you. But there's something you have to promise me first.'

'I won't hurt anyone for you.'

'That's not it. Tyke. My dog. With Hettie and Zane locked up, who's looking after my boy? I want him to go to a good home.'

She had no idea what had become of the Border collie after Hettie's arrest. But she'd find out. 'I promise he'll be looked after,' she said, and wondered why the issue of the dog's welfare had entered her mind. It surprised her that a violent thug could have empathy towards a pet: so maybe — in her changing opinion — Swain wasn't as irredeemable as she'd first thought.

He surprised her again. *'I trust you,'* he said.

Then he was gone.

What began quietly the next afternoon, with officers converging stealthily on the location, grew noisy very abruptly. A plain-clothed SCO19 Tactical Support Team bolstered the raid on a warehouse on a business estate off Queenstown Road. Secured doors were rammed, and armed officers spilled inside shouting warnings and commands. The Nine Elms Crew employed various buildings and houses throughout the region as bases for their operations, but the police had never before identified the target of this raid as one of theirs. An 'anonymous' tip-off to Detective Inspector Darke had allowed her to gain RIPA authorisation to conduct covert surveillance on the warehouse, and within a few hours, Derrick Lewis had been spotted. As the suspect in the shooting of the Ghedis, and possibly armed and willing to shoot, the inclusion of the TST in the raid was mandatory.

Kerry, accompanied by Korba and DC Tony Whittle, entered the warehouse on the tail end of the tactical officers, each of them wearing ballistic vests, and police decal similar to those worn by the plain-clothed SCO19 officers.

The warehouse was an Aladdin's cave of contraband goods, ranging from high-end motor vehicles to counterfeit cigarettes and alcohol. It also contained upward of a dozen gang members, and also innocents coerced into manual labour, most of them Eastern Europeans and illegal immigrants from further afield.

None in the warehouse offered resistance to the small army of cops, but some tried to flee, and there were running scuffles where the use of force became a requirement, but none critical. However, in an adjoining annex block to the warehouse, the opposition proved tougher. Funky Adefunke, Derrick Lewis and Kingston James, and four of their gang mates, weren't for coming quietly. They fought their arresting officers, both Lewis and an unidentified gangster choosing the lethal option. They weren't armed with antique weapons like Hettie's grandfather's Webley, but with modern semi-automatic handguns.

Kerry took cover against a doorjamb as the gangsters opened fire, bullets striking the wall a few inches from her face. The response from SCO19 was immediate, and pinpointed, and the unknown gangster fell – shot three times in quick succession. Derrick Lewis charged away, hurdling unmade cot beds they'd been using as a home away from home, taking wild shots behind him. Funky threw up his hands in surrender, but Kingston James tried to flee by throwing himself through a window. He'd watched too many Hollywood action movies, because in reality he rebounded from the toughened glass into the arms of DC Whittle, who rugby-tackled him to the floor. A firearms officer assisted Whittle on with plastic restraint cuffs. Funky and the other three were soon all face down, surrounded by grim-faced cops armed with MP5 Carbines, while they were searched and secured.

Kerry charged after Korba, who in turn was on the tail of a duo of SCO19 officers pursuing Derrick Lewis. Of all of the conspirators Lewis had most to lose, and wasn't prepared to do the time for his crime. In an adjoining room, he barricaded himself behind an overturned desk and prepared to take on the world. He was shot in the upper chest, and sprawled out dead on the floor, within a matter of seconds.

Seeing her prime murder suspect die — and escape lawful justice — Kerry was gutted. But apparently one person was overjoyed at the gangster's abrupt end. Erick Swain, an unwelcome addition to the raiding party, loomed over him, bent at the waist, arms thrust out to his sides, as he roared in celebration into the dead youth's face. He spied over at Kerry who rested wearily against a wall, and fist-pumped in exhilaration. She took great care not to respond to him. She rested a hand on Korba's shoulder as the sergeant exhaled deeply, and shuddered out some of the nervous energy he'd contained since before the green light to storm the warehouse was given.

'At least we've got Funky and Kingston James alive,' Korba said, as they observed the SCO19 officers securing Lewis's weapon.

'But no sign of Jermaine Robson,' she responded.

'We'll get him. Just you wait and see.'

'Zorba's got a point,' said Swain, drifting over to her. *'I told you you'd find De-Lew and those other fuckwits here, didn't I? Trust me, Kezza, I'm going to give you Robson too, and that's how I want to see him end up.'* He jabbed a translucent finger at the corpse.

Kerry ignored him.

It was regretful Derrick Lewis went down fighting, but when all came to all three of the four fugitives had been rounded up – it was a huge success for the GaOC team, but she was torn by mixed feelings.

Swain had passed her test, and she'd no logical explanation for how, other than she genuinely was being haunted, a terrifying prospect.

She returned to the adjoining building. By now, Funky and Kingston James were in full restraints, kneeling alongside their other gang members. Officially they'd been arrested and cautioned, but she wanted a private word in Funky's ear.

'You,' she said, leaning to challenge him an inch from his nose, 'are lower than scum. You are responsible for the deaths of a mother and child, you made a widower of Nilan's husband, and an orphan of her baby, Taban, and you will pay fully for your crimes.'

Funky couldn't hold onto his arrogance. He looked despondent. He lowered his face and tears dampened his cheeks. His remorse wasn't for the family he'd helped destroy, it was because he'd been caught.

'Not such the brave man now are you, you piece of shit? Those lies you told me about staring down your would-be killer, when you're nothing but a spineless coward, a baby killer. You make me sick to the stomach.'

A blur of movement from her left startled her, and she jerked back.

Swain was poised to kick Funky directly in the face, but it would be a pointless conduit of his rage.

'OK. That's enough,' she sighed, and to her surprise, Swain backed off, and waited for instruction.

Funky and Kingston James were loaded in a police van. Before they were locked inside, Kerry nodded at Swain and he got the message. He slipped inside the cage with them and sat on the bench alongside Funky, listening to every word they exchanged.

Once all the prisoners were out of the way, and the scene managed, Kerry headed for her car. Korba and Whittle had travelled with her to the scene, but they were given lifts back to their nick to begin the custody process. She couldn't return to base yet: the warehouse required a full search, and there were witnesses and possible illegal immigrants to deal with. SCO19 stayed on site, securing it, and also making safe the firearms they had seized. Ambulances were called, but it would be a while before the bodies of Derrick Lewis and the other dead gangster were moved, and CSI and the coroner were en route. A full review of the fatal shootings would be conducted, and again Kerry could be criticised.

She didn't care.

She'd more on her mind.

Sitting in her car, she did what she'd put off days ago. She pulled up a webpage on her smartphone and noted the contact telephone number. Alongside her window, she was aware of a dim shape. She didn't look directly at it. There was no need in order to tell Girl nodded encouragement.

She called Elias Tiberius Price, paranormal sleuth and demonologist, Britain's pre-eminent multi-faith exorcist.

The night before the raid on the warehouse, Kerry had gone home and found Adam waiting for her. He'd made supper, and poured glasses of wine. He didn't bring up the subject of their recent fights and Kerry was grateful. There was an uneasy undercurrent, but their truce held, and later they slept together for the first time in days. In the early hours Adam reached for her, and she'd snuggled into him, thankful of the embrace. But when Adam tried to take things further, hands roaming and kneading, she gave him the cold shoulder, and he abruptly turned over on his back with a curse: how could she tell him she was embarrassed to have sex when somebody could be watching? It would reignite their fight, and who knew where it would end. Kerry fell asleep with tears dampening her pillow, and when she woke, Adam had already left the house. Erick Swain had greeted her at breakfast with the location of the fugitives, and things had been all go since.

When she finally arrived back at the nick, her team had got the interviews underway, and already Hettie Winters — despite Dave Barnes' assertion she was not a flight risk — had been remanded in custody and was due to be taken to HMP Holloway before appearing before a magistrate the following day. Zane McManus had also been charged, and remanded, but wouldn't be joining his cousin, he was off to HMP Belmarsh, along with Funky and Kingston James and other Nine Elms Crew members arrested at the warehouse: she'd bet that their uneasy alliance had ended so things could prove tricky for Zane. Poor Zane, she thought sarcastically.

To her surprise DCI Porter appeared ebullient, buoyed by her apparent return to form. He sought her out in her cubbyhole in the GaOC office, and asked her to join him for coffee. There was no vending machine slop for him: Porter had a coffee percolator in his office. She took the same seat as on previous occasions, but Porter kept things informal, brewing them fresh drinks. He placed her steaming mug on his polished desk, and his alongside it. He perched his backside on the desk too, and Kerry couldn't help feel intimidated by his proximity. It was difficult meeting his gaze, and she knew she looked flaky glancing everywhere except at him.

'Relax, Kerry,' Porter said. 'If we've been a little off with each other these last few days, then it's over now. Let's put it behind us and move on. Go ahead, drink your coffee.'

She squeezed out a smile, and took her cup in both hands. It tasted pretty good. But she put it down again.

'I'm impressed with your results,' said Porter.

'I only did my job,' she retorted, unnecessarily snappy. 'It's all I ever wanted to do.'

'Yes, and I see now that you were right. Catching those suspects so quickly, well, it is damn impressive. Superlative detective work.'

She suspected there was an underlying *but* waiting in the wings, except he wasn't ready to slap her with it yet.

'Things dropped into place once I knew what happened, and who was involved. Like I said, going after Ikemba Adefunke first would've made things more difficult for us.'

'Yes. Like I said. You were right, I was wrong.' He took a long gulp of his drink. Set it down and leaned forward. His coffee breath was hot and moist on her face. 'You've delivered a real coup for my team, for which I'm grateful.'

Again she waited for the inevitable *but*.

When it didn't come, she said, 'I'll be happier once Jermaine Robson's in custody.'

'And you'll get your man. I've all confidence in you, Kerry.' He took another long sip, and his glasses steamed over. He took them off and wiped the lenses on his shirt.

As he replaced them, she glanced at his magnified irises. He was acting friendly, but his eyes lacked any lustre. He hit her with what was actually on his mind. 'You know, I'm curious. Just how did you manage to locate the others so quickly?'

'Information from a CHIS, sir,' she lied.

He nodded; it wasn't an unreasonable explanation. 'Who?'

'I'm sorry, sir, but I have to protect my source.'

'You can tell me, their identity won't go beyond the two of us.'

'Sir, you know we have a protocol in place, to protect informants from repercussions. I can't tell you, and if I do I'll be the one responsible if any harm comes to him.'

'He must've been an insider in the gang?' Porter prompted, although he'd already made up his mind. Who else but an insider could have known where the Nine Elms Crew was holed up? 'Hopefully he can also give you Robson's whereabouts.'

'That remains to be seen,' Kerry admitted. 'I'm hoping he gets back to me soon with something actionable.'

'I do too.' He drained his cup, then aimed it at hers. 'Drink up. I can make you another if you'd like?'

'I'm wired on adrenalin as it is; more caffeine's probably not a good idea.'

'When do you expect contact from your CHIS?'

'That's down to him, sir,' she said.

'You can't usher things along? It'd be a rare success if we could collar Robson before the day's out.'

'It'd be great, but if I hear anything it'll be in my CHIS's time.'

'He's doing this for reward?'

'Pardon?'

Porter pinched his thumb and forefinger together, rubbed the tips in circles. 'Is your informant being paid from our budget?'

Kerry didn't respond.

'The only reason I ask is that I'm prepared to authorize an extra incentive if your man delivers in good time.'

Kerry sighed. 'Thank you, sir, but the arrangement I have with him is that he contacts me. I've no way to reach him directly. I can't promise he'll be in touch until he's ready.'

Porter made a humming noise in the back of his throat.

Kerry pursed her lips, waiting for the axe to drop.

'There's something you're not telling me, Inspector Darke.' He was back to formal names again.

'CHIS rules,' she reminded him. 'We must protect their identities at all costs.'

'OK. I'm not going to press the issue.' He abruptly changed tack. 'Your team members are conducting the prisoner interviews?'

'Yes. They're formalities, to get the suspects charged and in front of the court. I'm confident Danny and the others have everything in hand.'

'I agree,' said Porter. 'You should get yourself off home. Get some rest, Inspector Darke, before this informant of yours comes through, otherwise who knows when you'll next get the chance.'

She didn't argue.

She left his office, but didn't walk away. She took out her phone, pretending to check her messages, and listened to a one-sided conversation. 'Hello, yes. This is DCI Charles Porter for Superintendent Harker...Oh, I see. Well, if you could ask him to give me a call at his first convenience I'd appreciate it. Thank you. He can reach me on my extension number...'

Kerry strode away, frowning. It might have sounded like paranoia when she told Korba she was worried she was under internal investigation, but why else would Porter call Graeme Harker the instant she left his office?

She must be more careful with her interactions with Swain.

Once she'd finalised some notes, signed off on the crime files stacked in her inbox, checked with Korba how everything was going, and left the running of the investigation in his capable hands, she headed home.

Adam had beaten her to it, but had gone out again, though to where he gave no clue. He'd left a hand-written note propped on the coffee table in their living room, short and to the point. WE NEED TO SORT THIS, KERRY XX. The inclusion of the kisses meant he was hopeful of a peaceful reconciliation. She crumpled the note and threw it in a waste bin in the kitchen. It wasn't spite. The situation wasn't something they could sort between them, only she could.

She logged onto her laptop and opened her emails. The reply she'd hoped for was in her list.

When she'd rang Elias Price earlier, her call had gone directly to his voice mail. She'd asked Price to contact her as a matter of urgency and left her email address. In his brief reply Price gave implicit instructions of where and when to meet him, and no offer of an alternative. Kerry typed a response, thanking him and promising she'd be on time. He didn't acknowledge her response.

She showered, ate supper, then sat in her living room with the TV off, waiting for Swain to show up. He didn't appear by midnight, so she retired to bed, and dropped into a depthless sleep, and wasn't roused until her alarm clock shattered the calm the following morning. Adam was beside her, his back to hers, snoring soundly and smelling of beer and kebab. She didn't wake him, only prepped for what would prove to be a day of contradictions, and left the house, closing the door gently behind her.

Hettie Winters and Zane McManus appeared before a magistrate to tender their pleas. The court hearings were private affairs; they were formalities to ensure both suspects were remanded to custody pending trial, to allow the Met to prepare cases against them. Kerry would have liked to go to both appearances, except her workload was gigantic. Besides, Korba attended, being the respective arresting officer, and she was confident his remand requests would be granted and they were. Later in the day DC Whittle was also due in court, this time as Ikemba Adefunke's and Kingston James's arresting officer, and Kerry asked Korba to accompany him to ensure everything went the Met's way.

She was kept busy all morning, coordinating and managing dozens of police and civilian staff, each of whom wanted her time and input. All the while, she kept a discreet watch for Swain, but he was conspicuous by his absence. Ordinarily his desertion should have been cause for celebration, but not under the circumstances. As lunchtime approached, and the nick grew busier, she slipped away, and grabbed a taxi into central London, watchful for a tail. Sneaking off, and acting counter surveillance savvy, could prove detrimental if she was under DPS investigation, but there was nothing else for it. She left the taxi at Covent Garden, and took the tube to Charing Cross. Emerging out on The Strand, she was carried on a tide of shoppers and tourists towards Trafalgar Square, not the ideal location for a covert meeting, but she hadn't set it. She entered a chain eatery on Northumberland Avenue, with ten minutes to spare, and looked for a man toting a massive iron-studded crucifix.

Of course Elias Price looked nothing like his online persona, and she didn't really expect him to. There was little to distinguish him from the other lunchtime diners, and she'd have been hard put to spot him if he hadn't described where he'd be seated. The eatery was laid out on split-levels. Price had chosen a table at the back right corner of the upper level for its modicum of privacy in the busy restaurant.

As she approached, Price glanced up from an open laptop, alongside a half-eaten plate of sausages, eggs and chips. He stood, and was much shorter than she'd expected, a small, narrow-shouldered man with greying, receding hair. Perhaps a sturdy physical body wasn't necessary for a spiritual fight. Price extended a hand, indicating the seat opposite him, all the while studying her heterochromia with mild curiosity. 'I'm assuming you're Kerry Darke?'

'I am.' She hadn't mentioned she was a detective inspector, and had no intention of doing so until she was sure he could help. 'And you're Elias Price.'

An embarrassed smile flickered across his mouth for a second or two. He glanced again at her mismatched eyes, appearing bashful in her presence, then quickly rallied, again indicating she take a seat.

She allowed her arms to drop by her side, as it appeared his habits didn't extend to shaking hands in greeting. She sat, and he mirrored her. While she took a long check over her shoulder, he lowered the screen of the laptop so it wasn't a barrier between them.

'I'm going to be upfront with you, Miss Darke,' he said. 'After you made contact with me I was dubious about accepting this meeting, because I'm a little suspicious of your motive.'

Taken aback, she blinked at him in a state of brain freeze.

'I didn't piece things together when first I typed my response to your voice mail message,' he went on. 'It was only after I received your reply that I noticed your email address was the same as one I received an inflammatory message from a few nights ago.'

Kerry's eyelids screwed shut and she exhaled in realisation. Adam hadn't only snooped on her computer usage, he'd gone and sent Price a nasty email from her account! As she slowly opened her eyes, she noticed he was appraising her, his bashful smile flickering in place.

'It's OK, Miss Darke. I also noticed the distinct disparity in writing styles between your subsequent message and the first. If you don't mind me saying so, the person behind that first message could do with a little schooling in grammar and spelling.' He chuckled to himself. 'Well, at least he managed to spell "scumbag fraudster" right, eh?'

'Oh, God, I'm so sorry. I'd no idea...'

'A concerned husband?'

'My fiancé,' she said. 'I'm sorry, Mr Price, if I'd know Adam had sent you an email like that I'd have apologised sooner.'

He waved away her concern. 'In regards to some of the accusations aimed at me, your fiancé's was mild by comparison.'

'It doesn't matter. He'd no right doing that.'

'I'm pretty sure his intention was to protect you; perhaps you shouldn't be so angry with him.'

'He's sceptical of all this...'

'Spooky stuff you're experiencing?' He smiled again. 'It's actually healthy to be sceptical, Miss Darke. And I can tell by your body language that you're uncomfortable with your conclusions too.'

'I'm going to be upfront with you, too, Mr Price. I'll admit that for a while there I thought I was losing my mind.'

'And something has changed that tells you otherwise?'

Something had changed. How could a self-induced hallucination know where to send her to find Funky, James and Lewis?

'You could say that.'

The eatery was buzzing with activity and conversations, although in their corner she felt insulated from everyone around them. She leaned forward conspiratorially, about to blurt out that she was being haunted. Price stalled her. He straightened up, and directed a smile and nod over her shoulder. Kerry glanced up at a young female server, approaching with a menu in hand.

Kerry ordered a coffee and a slice of carrot cake, and the server left.

'They allow me to work here as long as I wish, but only when ordering food and drinks,' Price whispered. 'I'm surprised I'm not as fat as a whale by now.'

Kerry glanced at his plate. The food on it was in the process of congealing. He forked up a chunk of sausage and nibbled it, before returning it to the plate.

'I make it last,' he told her with a wink, 'otherwise the use of their free Wi-Fi would end up costing me a bomb. Yes, the food comes at a cost, but I have to keep up my energy. A case of killing two birds with one stone, eh?'

Abruptly, Price sat back and regarded her with sudden clarity. 'You're a police officer,' he proclaimed.

Kerry ran her tongue over her lips.

'I thought you looked familiar,' he said, and thankfully he didn't appear perturbed by her occupation. 'With your eye colouring, I'd almost convinced myself I was thinking of the actress Jane Seymour, but that isn't it: hers were blue and brown. You were featured in some news reports very recently, weren't you?' Before she could answer, he clicked his fingers. 'Yes! That was it. You were the detective involved in that horrible incident where that obnoxious criminal fell to his death.'

She nipped her lip between her teeth.

Price's eyes were deep blue pools. Dawning lit them, like submerged lamps rising to the surface of a pond. 'Is your trouble related to that criminal's death?'

'Yes,' she said, her voice barely audible. 'Among other things.'

'To what extent?'

'I don't know how you measure these things.'

'Bad dreams, hearing disembodied voices, strange apparitions?' Price asked.

'All of the above,' she said.

'Sensations?'

'I've felt temperature drops, and something like a static charge on my skin…as if I'd walked through an electrified spider's web.' She danced her fingernails across her opposite wrist as a visual aid.

'Any physical harm?'

She shook her head.

'He's tried attacking me, but is unable to touch me.'

'You have no unexplainable scratches, welts, or bruises?' He curled his thumb and pinky finger under his right palm, extended three fingers like a bird's talons. 'No repeated pattern of the number three?'

Kerry frowned, wondering where he was going with his questioning.

'That's good. There's no mocking of the Holy Trinity.'

'I'm sorry. I don't follow.'

'We can discount supernatural activity in your case,' he announced. 'Usually when a victim is suffering a demonic attachment they display physical manifestations, usually in wound patterns of three, where the demon displays its hatred of the Father, Son and Holy Spirit. I'm pretty confident that your activity is paranormal in nature: the supernatural is connected with the gods, angels, demons, but you're being troubled by a human spirit, and not an agent of the devil.'

Kerry caught herself open-mouthed. 'Are you psychic, Mr Price?'

He lifted his fork, and the chunk of gnawed meat. 'I'm as psychic as this sausage, Miss Darke. Uh, should I call you detective?'

'I'm not here as a detective. Call me Kerry.'

'Yes. It's so much easier. You can call me Elias…if you wish? But getting back to your original question…I don't need to be psychic. There's only one reason for you to seek out my services. Seeing as we can dispense with my skills as a demonologist, I'd say you are concerned you're being haunted by a ghost?'

'I haven't even told you what's happening yet,' Kerry said.

'And now's your opportunity.'

She described the prolonged and disquieting visitations from Swain she'd endured. At no point did he appear sceptical she was being anything but truthful. 'But even after everything,' she said, 'I've still doubted my senses.'

'You mentioned having bad dreams, hearing voices, seeing apparitions, being assaulted by incorporeal hands, unexplained temperature drops and unusual sensations on your skin, they're all ghostly phenomena, Kerry. All symptoms of a haunting.'

'Or they're all easily explained by science,' she countered.

'And yet you haven't sought the assistance of a scientist. You've come to me.'

'Actually, I have spoken to a scientist, a psychologist.'

'Who obviously didn't satisfy your concerns, because—' he spread his arms, the fork and speared chunk of sausage meat still in one hand '—here we are.'

Yes. There they were.

The server returned with Kerry's order, and placed a copy of her bill on the table with instruction to pay on the way out. Kerry thanked her, and caught the young woman giving her a conspiratorial wink and nod at Elias. He was obviously a familiar face in the eatery, and the subject of some mild ridicule. By virtue of the company she kept Kerry could be thought of as a crank too. She couldn't care less. She cut off a wedge of carrot cake and put it in her mouth, chewing slowly.

'Did your experiences begin immediately following the death of this...what was his name?'

'Erick Swain,' she said, and couldn't avoid a glance around to check her spectral companion wasn't spying on them.

Price raised a finger in affirmation. 'Swain. Yes. I remember now. So? He began appearing to you immediately after his death?'

'Within a day or two,' she said. 'At first he was elusive, I only got a glimpse of him, and wasn't sure what I was looking at. Then he...well, he grew bolder.'

'I can imagine how frightening that was.'

'Terrifying,' she said. 'He says some horrible things, creepy stuff, but in a perverted way. He hasn't physically harmed me but I still feel...*violated* by him. He appears at the most inappropriate times.'

Price thought. He forked the morsel of sausage in his mouth and chewed. Kerry ate more cake. Finally Price raised a finger again. 'You asked me if I was psychic. Is that because you're wondering if you have the ability, a sixth sense, so to speak?'

'I'm not psychic,' she scoffed.

'There are different forms of psychic ability. They differ wildly.'

'Yeah, but, I'm like you, as psychic as a house brick.'

'Forgive my rudeness, but I'm assuming that you're in your early thirties, yes?' She inclined her head at the question, and he went on. 'Usually psychic abilities become apparent at a young age. Is this the first time you've experienced any phenomena like this?'

'Yes,' she lied, and had no idea why she didn't come clean about Girl...or the *other stuff* from her childhood.

'Have you suffered any recent head trauma, had a near death experience, anything at all that might have triggered a latent talent?' He stared at her, and she felt he was studying her micro expressions for the truth.

'I watched a man fall to his violent death,' she said contritely.

'That in itself is horrible, but I doubt it'd be enough to kick start your ability to see and hear the dead.'

She tapped the side of her head. 'But it could mess this up, right?'

'I don't think you're mad, Kerry.' He laughed. 'But I can tell you're still trying to make up your mind about me.'

She smiled with him. 'I have to admit that I struggle with the concept of demons and exorcisms.'

'Because, quite simply, what you know about them are misconceptions promoted by horror movies for cheap thrills. In all my years conducting deliverances I'm yet to see anybody spew green pea soup.' Again Kerry smiled along with him. 'Demon is a term we've all grown used to. But it's a catchall phrase used worldwide for various differing phenomena. Every culture has its own demons, but in each they differ vastly. I won't bore you with a full treatise, only to say I prefer the scholarly explanation that our demons are down to our collective psychology: we conjure an embodiment of evil to torment us as deserved punishment for our wrongdoing. Every culture has unique visual representations for demons, and ours relies heavily on medieval Christian iconography: the reason why I use crucifixes and holy water to banish them. But we must remember that the Christian church labelled all the pagan gods and spiritual deities evil. Our image of a hooved, goat-headed devil is most certainly a representation of a satyr, or Pan from Greek mythology. Ironically the ancient Greek term *diamon* is the etymological forerunner to *daemon*, or demon, but originally translated as 'divine power' or 'god'. In Greek mythology, the daemons were intermediaries between humankind and the divine, and

242

could be good or bad depending on the individual they'd attached to. In Islamic tradition, Muhammad alleged that every man has an angel and demon as guides, the angel towards goodness, the demon to evil.'

'Yeah,' she concurred. 'Freud said something similar, but gave his demons and angels different names, id and super ego.'

'Ha! So you've been conducting your own research?'

'I'm a detective, Elias.' She smiled conspiratorially. 'It's in my nature.'

'OK, so let's dispense with the little sprites with horns and get down to how I choose to approach the issue of the demonic. What are your beliefs on positive and negative energy?'

'I didn't pay much attention in science class at school.'

'Then I'll keep things in layman's terms for you. Instead of good and evil, think light and dark. One cannot exist without the other. Light and dark are determined by energy. And, as we've learned — through quantum science — energy can be transformed but it can't be destroyed. If we think in terms of humans as spiritual beings, powered by energy, then after our corporeal bodies fail us what becomes of our energy? It can be transformed into something else, surely, so why not a ghost? When an evil person dies, what happens to their life force? Swain, by definition could not be described as a good man, and it's doubtful that if his spirit were visiting you, then it's with a sense of bonhomie, I'd bet. He was a shit in life, and a shit in death, right?'

Kerry chuckled. 'You've hit the nail on the head there.'

'And you said he torments you?'

'Regularly.'

'He blames you for his premature death?'

'That's the thing. He claims he doesn't.'

'And yet he wants something from you?'

Kerry pushed aside the remaining chunk of cake. She picked up her coffee, to be doing something with her hands. 'I can't go into specifics, but yes.'

'And is this something that you can deliver?'

'Yes. But I'm not prepared to.'

'Ah!'

Kerry peered at him. 'What?'

'It's my belief that Swain's spirit, an embodiment of his negative energy, has attached to you, because he perceives you as his nemesis – despite what he tells you to the contrary – and he'll stay attached until he gets from you some kind of appeasement.'

'He wants revenge,' she admitted.

'On you?'

'On others.' She paused, but the only way she'd get the answers she needed was to be truthful. 'He wants me to hurt somebody on his behalf.'

'And you won't?'

'Definitely not. But he claims he won't leave me alone until I do.'

'Hmmm. Then I'm afraid you might have to get used to having him around. By their nature, spirits are timeless; he can wait you out. Are you prepared to do the same?'

'I'm not prepared to do what he asks. Isn't there something you can do to get rid of him for me? I'll pay—'

Elias shook his head morosely. 'I can clear negative energy through rituals based on my clients' personal religious beliefs, but I can only help cross restless spirits over when they're ready to go, once they've found closure on the earthly plane. Appease Swain with what he wants, and sure, then I can cross him over, but until then...well, you'd be wasting your money, and I'd be wasting your time and mine. Despite what your fiancé thinks of me, I'm not a fraudster preying on the vulnerable, Kerry.'

'I appreciate what you're saying. All I meant was I'm prepared to reimburse you for your services...if you can get rid of him. But what you're saying is that I'm asking for the impossible?'

'Nothing's impossible, of course. You could do as he asks, but answer yourself this question: do you genuinely believe you can trust him to deliver his end of the bargain once you do?'

'To leave me be after? Yes, I suppose I do. But about...' she faltered.

Again, Price studied her closely. 'There's more you're not telling me, isn't there?'

Kerry said nothing, only met his gaze.

'You said he wants you to hurt somebody on his behalf. We're not talking about giving this person a fat lip, are we?'

'Put it this way; what he wants doesn't only go against the grain as a detective, it goes against my humanity.'

'Aah, then you're in quite a pickle,' he said.

'Isn't there anything you can do to help?'

'Not yet. But there's something you can do to help yourself.' He leaned forward, reaching for her hand. He gave it a reassuring squeeze. 'You are alive, Kerry. Your energy is contained in its corporeal vessel, and therefore more powerful than his. It's been proven to you already in his inability to harm you. He understands that your power is greater than his, otherwise why try to bully you into acting out his wishes? Stand your ground, enforce your boundaries, and tell him you do not grant him permission to bother you without invitation.'

'And that will work?'

'I couldn't possibly say,' Price said, 'but it's worth a try, isn't it?'

'I've told him to go away and leave me alone before. It had no effect on him.'

'It's because you were frightened of him then, and he knew it and fed on your fear. Now you know that by comparison he's a weakling, you have nothing to fear from him.'

Kerry nodded at his logic, but something still troubled her. 'Why would I grant him an invitation?'

Price shrugged his narrow shoulders. 'Because, Kerry, I think there's still more you haven't told me, and you need something from him too.'

Kerry returned to work too distracted with competing thoughts to care about counter surveillance tactics. She flagged down a taxi on the Strand and headed back to the nick. She wasn't gullible. It took more than Elias Price's prognosis to believe a restless spirit energised by the negativity of his life was haunting her. Where was the proof that ghosts actually existed? Price was convinced that ghosts were real, but recently Kerry had also been convinced she could get into a pair of size 8 skinny jeans until she'd tried to pull up the zip. To be honest, she had more faith in Doctor Ron's assertion that "Belief in itself is a contradiction, because it can be fooled into forming false beliefs", than in the argument of a man that allegedly banished demons to hell for a living. Before she left the eatery he had noted her uncertainty.

'Kerry,' he'd said, as she stood to leave, 'you can accept what I've told you or not. That's totally your prerogative. As a police officer, to ensure a conviction you need evidence and proof, but I'm betting there are times you can't get what you need, and yet you're certain of a suspect's guilt. It's the same when I approach the supernatural and paranormal. These things are ineffable. It means they can't be explained. But you know they're genuine. You feel it here—' he touched his heart '—and you know they are real, despite there being no logical way of scientifically proving them.'

She had a logical mind, and that was what made her a good detective. She was able to extrapolate, connect the threads, and come to conclusions based on lucid and rational lines of thought, and from there find the evidence to prove her point. In England, the standard required in a criminal trial was that proof was beyond reasonable doubt. Yet, the civil standard required only that the proof be based upon the balance of probabilities. On the latter measure she thought her ghostly companion could be judged probable. She'd set her test of Swain based on the same question: On the balance of probability had pure luck led her to the exact warehouse where Funky, James and Lewis had gone into hiding, or had she been the recipient of spiritual guidance? Well, if her luck was that good, she should begin playing the lottery again, because she'd be a multi-millionaire in no time.

Price encouraged her to accept the ineffable, and go with her heart over her mind, but he'd have been better encouraging her to trust her gut instinct. It wasn't the first time that she'd worked a hunch to a satisfying conclusion, and probably wouldn't be the last. So why not go with what her copper's sixth sense was telling her: Swain was the real deal.

And if she accepted that, then what?

Have him as a millstone around her neck for the rest of her days, or do what he asked and be rid of him for good?

The latter was out of the question.

She was not a murderer. Full stop.

Could she reason with a vengeful spirit?

Price had been mesmerised when she'd explained the extent of their discourses. Ghosts, in his belief, were largely mute or confused. You got little from them by way of conversation apart from the occasional moan or a random and often ambiguous statement. He'd told her about EVP's, or Electronic Voice Phenomena, where he'd captured the alleged voices of spirits on digital recorders, but they were always invariably difficult to hear and open to individual interpretation. That Swain was not only talking, but at length and in the manner he'd spoken in life, suggested he was incredibly sentient for an incorporeal being. She got the impression that Price was desperate to investigate her case further, and hopefully share and record a conversation with Swain, but she shot down that idea before it gained traction.

So, as she sat in the rear of the taxi as it hustled through the congested streets towards the nick, she conceded there could be truth in it. Swain was real. He'd directed her to the Nine Elms Crew's safe house, and three of the four fugitives had been captured. But if he was real, where the bloody hell had he got to since climbing inside the police van with Funky and Kingston James? It was approaching twenty-four hours since she'd sent him on the clandestine mission, so what was keeping him?

Spirits are timeless, according to Elias Price.

If they were eternal, did that mean they had no concept of the passage of time? Well, that wasn't conducive to fast results, exactly what was expected from her by Porter. She wasn't sure what was most uncomfortable, a ghost or the DCI breathing down her neck.

Who was she to complain about the tardiness of a ghost?

What she'd originally planned to take less than an hour had eked into the day, and by the time she paid her taxi fare, and made it back inside the nick to the GaOC office, she'd been gone for the better part of three hours.

DS Korba was the bearer of bad tidings. He'd just taken a phone call from DC Scott.

'Funky squealed like a pig in interview,' he announced. 'For a deal he's stitched up the others.'

'What do you mean by a deal? Funky isn't getting out of this, Danny. No way on Earth.'

'Tell that to the boss man,' Korba said and shrugged in apology. 'You weren't here, so Porter put his oar in. He sent Glenn over to Belmarsh to offer Funky leniency if he grassed on his pal, Robson. Don't worry, Funky's going to do time, just not at as a category-A inmate.'

'We don't need a deal with Funky! We've already got them all bang to rights with the video and forensic evidence.'

'We had them all on conspiracy,' he reminded her. 'But we hadn't positively ID'd the murderer. Funky's confirmed it was Derrick Lewis who pulled the trigger on Jermaine Robson's command.'

'Bloody hell! That was already a given.' Throwing up her hands, she almost turned full circle. 'What the hell's Porter playing at? I only need a little more time and I'll have Robson. I told him that already, but he can't keep his bloody nose out of my business!' She emitted a string of un-lady-like curses, and a promise to shove Funky's deal up the DCI's backside.

Korba's jaw hung slack. Mel Scanlon and Tony Whittle kept their heads down, pretending to be too busy to eavesdrop.

'Well?' she demanded, throwing up her hands again.

'Steady on, Kerry,' he cautioned her. 'Wall's have ears.'

'Yeah, you can bloody-well say that again!' She stomped away to her cubbyhole. Suddenly she spun on her heel and eyed Korba suspiciously. 'Actually,' she said, 'do tell, Danny. Have the rubber heelers asked you about me?'

'What?'

'The frigging Dark Side, the suits, the bloody DPS! You know who I bloody-well mean. Harker's lot!'

Korba expelled a snort. 'I know *who* you mean, but do you really think I'd go behind your back like that?'

'Why not? It hasn't stopped Porter, has it?' She glared at the backs of Mel and Tony's heads. 'What about you two? Anybody been asking about me?'

They didn't have anything to say on the subject, and she realised she was being unfair to them. Especially to Korba, who'd proven his loyalty time and again. She slapped a palm over her mouth and fled for her office.

After a respectful few minutes, Korba knocked gently on the door.

Her elbows were propped on her desk, her face in her hands. Kerry didn't move.

'Boss? You alright?'

'I'm OK,' she said through her cupped hands.

Korba paused, choosing his words. 'Boss...uh, Kerry, you don't sound OK. Is there anything I can...'

'Just leave me alone for a while,' she groaned, and sat back in her seat. Her hands didn't leave her face, though. 'I just need a minute or two, OK?'

'Yeah, course, but...'

'Danny? Please? Just do as I ask.'

She knew what was wrong, but how could she explain? Admitting that Swain was real, it had given her hope that he would soon lead her to Robson, and she would break the case with the gangster's arrest. As soon as she did that, she could demand the answers she really wanted from him. The identity of the Fell Man, and what the bastard did to Sally was finally within her grasp. But Porter's meddling jeopardised everything! With more pressure on him to stay hidden, Robson might flee beyond her reach, and she'd never be able to fulfil her side of their bargain. For a second there she had almost imagined the elusive Fell Man tittering at her, knowing his secret would remain safe. Fight or flight, her response to panic was anger.

'Danny, I'm sorry I blew up at you like that.'

'Ah, it's nothing, boss.' By his tone her accusation had stung him. She owed him an apology.

'You didn't deserve it. Tell Mel and Tony...' her words faltered. She should personally tell them she was sorry. She got up and steadied herself against her desk. Approached the door. The stubborn thing wouldn't move. 'Danny, give the door a shove, will you?'

It took only a swift nudge to push the door over the rucked carpet. He stuck his head in the narrow gap. 'Seriously, boss. You alright?'

'Just keep me away from Porter for the next hour or two or I swear to God I'll punch him in the face.'

'Want me to go get him and hold him still for you?' His grin flickered off an on like a faulty bulb.

She smiled at his offer, but shook her head as she stepped out the door. 'Maybe I shouldn't go saying things like that, eh? Like you said, walls do have ears around here. But,' she gripped his forearm, 'I know there are no loose lips in here. Just forget I ever mentioned it, OK? You guys too?' Mel only squeezed out a smile, while Tony shrugged and continued, as if he wasn't bothered. Nevertheless, she'd done what needed doing.

She needed to speak with Swain next, and the GaOC office wasn't the place for that.

'Actually, Danny, I'm feeling not too well,' she said. 'Something I ate at lunch didn't agree with me. Can you hold the fort again? I need to go home for a while and pull myself together.'

He was no fool. He didn't buy that a queasy stomach was enough to send her home sick, and that there was something else troubling her. But he didn't press while they were in company. 'You don't look too good,' he pointed out, 'and you don't need to be here. Want me to drive you?'

'No, no, it's OK. I've got my car with me.'

He exhaled softly. Stared at her intently for a few seconds.

She winked at him. 'Quit worrying, will you? I'm going to be fine. I promise.'

He nodded, though it was obvious he wanted to accompany her, and be a sympathetic shoulder to lean on.

'If anything comes up, ring me,' she said.

'Will do, boss.'

There was a danger that by going home, she was throwing herself outside the loop. Porter was already making decisions without her input, or even against it, and by making off she was offering him opportunity to make more. But what else was there for it? She couldn't exactly hang around the nick and have a conversation with her ghostly spy in full view and hearing of her team.

She drove home at speed, hoping that Swain had thought the same and waited in private for her return. Not that he'd ever been considerate to her before.

Unfortunately, Swain wasn't there, but Adam was.

'I know, I know. It sounds insane, but please listen to me, Adam. Hear me out. It's all real, and I can prove it if you just give me a chance!'

'Give you a chance? I asked you to sort your head out, see a doctor, but no! You went to see a friggin' fortune teller!'

They were in the kitchen. Circling the small dinner table, like prizefighters in a ring.

'Price isn't like that. He's not a fake. He actually knows what he's talking about.'

'Anybody can be an expert about shite if they talk it enough times! Jesus Christ, Kerry! Ghosts? Demons? You sound like a complete idiot! Fraudsters like Elias Price thrive on ripping off gullible fools like that.'

'He didn't ask me for a penny.'

'Not yet, he didn't. But mark my words. As soon as he's got his claws in you, he'll have you signing up to a monthly direct debit.'

'Don't be so bloody ridiculous!'

'Oh? I'm being ridiculous? Who's the one running around like she's one of the Ghostbusters?'

Kerry swept an empty cup off the table. It clashed against a kitchen counter, shattering. 'Just stop it, Adam! Stop for one minute and listen to me!'

'What? Or the next cup hits me in the head?' He stormed out of the kitchen, with Kerry in pursuit.

'That's unfair! I wouldn't hurt you. It's just that you aren't listening to me. I need you to stop and listen!'

He spun to face her in the living room doorway, his face blazing.

'No! You need to stop and listen. And I don't mean to the bloody voices in your head. I'm talking about listening to me! This isn't right, Kerry.' He stabbed his finger repeatedly against his skull. 'You're going on like some kind of nutter. A ghost told you where to find his killers? For fuck's sake!'

It was wrong confiding in him. At first he'd listened, even been sympathetic, pleased when she told him she was feeling much better now that she was achieving good results at work. But then came the flashpoint. She mentioned how she'd discovered the whereabouts of the fugitives, and the colour drained from his features. When she admitted forming an alliance with the ghost of Erick Swain, who promised to deliver the Fell Man's identity to her in exchange for Robson's life, he lost it. And little wonder. She never got the opportunity to explain she'd no intention of hurting Robson on Swain's behalf, because Adam flew into disbelief-induced panic. Telling him that Elias Price had validated Swain's existence, as had the test she'd set the ghost, well...there was no hope of a rational discussion afterwards.

'How could I know where they were? Tell me that, Adam? Did I just pluck a random location out of the air, and lo and-fucking-behold, they just happened to be there?'

'You're a copper. Coppers find criminals, don't they? You must have had an idea, some intelligence about them or...I don't know! But I know for-frigging-certain that a ghost wasn't behind it.'

'I had no idea where they were. I was told, and they were exactly where Swain said they'd be.'

'Swain? You even call him by his name? Swain's dead, Kerry. Swain fell off a building and smashed his brains in. How can he speak to you when his teeth are rattling around in the back of his skull?'

'He doesn't look like he did after death. He looks like he did just before it.'

'What?' Adam shrieked, waved his arms around like something demented, his face contorted in terror. 'Like that? Just before he hit the pavement?'

Kerry snorted in disgust. She spun away heading for the kitchen, and this time Adam charged in pursuit.

'Go on,' he demanded. 'Explain to me why he looks the way he does. From what I hear, the headless horseman doesn't look like he did before he got the chop. So why doesn't Swain? Why does he look as fresh as a daisy when every other ghost look as if they've dug their way out their own graves?'

'What do you know about the subject? You have no idea what you're talking about.'

'Oh and you have? Suddenly you're an expert, are you, because Elias Price schooled you in the art of ghost busting? Pity he didn't tell you how to spot a bloody conman while he was at it. Go and take a good look in a mirror, Kerry. Tell me what you see isn't the face of a gullible idiot.'

They faced off across the table again, her fists braced on it. 'One thing I do know is how to spot a pig-headed son of a bitch! Why is it because you don't believe in ghosts it's me who's wrong?'

'Because I am right. And if you looked at it clearly, you'd see I'm right. Jesus, you're a copper. How can you believe any of this shite when you've seen what you have in the job? There's no such thing as *evil spirits*, Kerry, only people doing *evil things* to each other.'

'What does being a copper have to do with it? Plenty of other coppers are religious. They believe in God and Jesus and angels, and in other religions. Are they wrong to believe, just because it doesn't fit into your version of reality?'

'That's different than believing you're being haunted.'

'Why is it different? If you accept God's real, then why not His angels? If angels are real then why aren't demons? And why stop there: if the supernatural's real, then why the hell am I a lunatic just because I happen to be experiencing it? Go on. Explain that, you bloody know it all!'

'I'm not going to explain because it's a load of bollocks. Any way, you'd better keep your mouth shut about hearing voices, Kerry. You know what happened to Joan of Arc, don't you? They burned her at the bloody stake!'

'So now you just want to make a joke of it?'

'Dead right,' he snapped. 'Because it is a joke.'

'Oh. So that makes me a joke, too?'

'I didn't say that.'

'You don't have to.' Kerry shoved off the table. Its wooden legs squealed across the floor. Adam gave it an angry shove back at her.

'OK! So if Swain's real, let him prove it to me. He's here now, is he? Where?' Before she could answer, Adam slapped his hands on his chest and threw back his head. 'Come on, Swain. If you're here let me know. Come and whisper sweet nothings in my ear, you bastard. Come on then!' He waited, for about three seconds, before he thrust out his chin at Kerry. 'Well? Did that wake the bastard up? Is he here or what? Yeah that's right. He's a no show. That's because he never was here. He's only in *your* head.'

'So I'm a joke and a delusional nutter?'

'You're not a joke,' he growled, 'but you're acting like you've lost your mind. I told you before, you need help, Kerry.'

'So help me.' She screwed her fists against her sternum. 'Help me by listening to me, Adam. Please? Give me the benefit of the doubt. Once I catch Robson, Swain will give me what I want, and it will be all over.'

He shook his head. 'Sorry. I can't. I warned you I can't live my life like this. It won't end with Robson, because next you'll be chasing Sally's abductor. It'll never end. Kerry, this obsession you have with the dead...I can't handle it.'

She'd wilted momentarily, desperate for his understanding, and held out an olive branch. All he had to do was reach for it and everything would have been fine between them. But no, that wasn't Adam's style. Instead of simply taking the branch he'd slapped her in the face with it.

Anger, disappointment, frustration: they were the emotions driving her argument, and they melted from her. With cool clarity, she worked her engagement ring off her finger and placed it on the table. Adam stared at it, then at her face. His head shook gently, but that was the extent of his response.

'You can't live your life like this,' she said, then flicked the ring away. It hit his abdomen and fell to the floor. He didn't retrieve it. 'Well, I'm sorry, Adam, but this is my life. Not ours.'

She left the house with nothing more than what was in her handbag, her phone and the clothes she wore.

He was about to summon DI Darke to his office, when his phone rang. He hit the speaker button.

'DCI Charles Porter,' he announced.

'Hello, sir,' said a woman with a soft Scottish burr he instantly recognised. Alisha Graham was the civilian staff comms supervisor. 'I have an Adam Gill on the line who'd like to speak with you about his fiancée, uh, Detective Inspector Darke.'

Porter wasn't in the habit of receiving personal calls from the respective partners of his team. The one time he'd met Adam Gill, he'd found the man to be a brash lout with little endearing about him. He'd wondered what a bright, attractive young woman like Kerry found likeable in the lager-swilling Neanderthal. It had come as no surprise to later learn that Gill was a guard over at HMP Belmarsh, having apparently failed to pass the stringent testing process to enter the Metropolitan Police Service, despite his background in the Royal Marines. Porter had no particular desire to speak with him, but his curiosity was piqued.

'Did he give any hint about what he wants, Alisha?'

'He only asked to speak with you on a private matter regarding Kerry.'

Porter thought for a second longer, then picked up the handset and cancelled the speakerphone function. 'OK. You can put him through.'

There was a brief pause while Alisha transferred the call, and again Porter announced his rank and name in full.

'Hello,' said Adam, his voice sounding hoarse. 'Thanks for speaking to me, Chief Inspector. But I'm going to warn you. You might not be too happy with what I've got to say.'

'Well,' he said ambiguously. 'We'll have to wait and see.'

'I'm calling about Kerry. DI Darke. I'm her fiancé, or, well, I was till about an hour ago.' Adam fell silent, but Porter was certain he could hear a faint crunching noise. Was the man grinding his teeth?

'I'm sorry to hear that, Mr Gill. I take a keen interest in the welfare of my team, and it pains me to hear that a valued officer is experiencing relationship problems.'

'Yeah, of course you do. Look, Chief Inspector, can we just speak man to man without all the formal bollocks? We both know you don't give a shit about our relationship, only how it might affect Kerry's performance at work.'

'If you intend being rude, I won't put up with it. Be civil, Mr Gill, or I'll hang up.'

'I wasn't being rude.' Adam sounded genuinely surprised he'd been taken out of context. 'I just don't want us dancing around each other. Just want us to say things as it is so there's no confusion.'

'Yes, well, we can speak plainly, but there's no need for bad language.'

'Fair enough, I'll watch my P's and Q's.'

Porter nodded, without answering.

'You're Kerry's superior, her immediate line manager, aren't you? You have a duty of care to her?'

'That's right, Mr Gill. What are you getting at?'

'Well, you must have noticed...'

'Noticed what?'

'Come on, Porter. You know what I'm talking about. Her bloody behaviour!'

'Kerry's been under some stress lately and—'

'Stress you didn't help alleviate,' Adam butted in. 'But it's more than that. We all have stress at work; I'm betting you have too? But things with Kerry have gone beyond the joke.'

'In regards the recent incident with Erick Swain, I offered Kerry counselling with one of our occupational therapists.'

'Yeah, and she refused. Surely, as her superior officer, you could've ordered her to attend therapy?'

'She convinced me she neither wanted nor required therapy. Pushing her into attending counselling might've had a detrimental effect at the time.' Porter racked his brain, trying to recall if he'd made an official record of Kerry's refusal to accept his offer of help: yes, he had.

'And you don't think she needs it now?'

'In the past few days she's shown a fine—'

'You're kidding me, aren't you? She's on the verge of a break down, man. If you haven't noticed, you're bloody blind or you don't take as keen an interest in the welfare of your team as you make out.'

Porter wasn't blind. He'd noticed all right. And despite what Adam said, he did care about the individuals in his team: it worked best only when they were at their best. But he couldn't deny he'd neglected to act on Kerry's erratic behaviour, except for sharing his concern with his old friend Graeme Harker. It might surprise Adam to learn that he was actually giving her a break, in not following disciplinary procedures for what could be perceived as neglect of duty — a sackable offense. She'd arrived at work drunk, ignored his direct orders, grown resentful and insubordinate of his leadership, and now — reading between the lines — had sneaked off home for a row with her boyfriend when she should've been on duty. He didn't appreciate the insinuation he was being unsupportive when she could be suspended from duty, pending disciplinary action.

'She has been notably distracted,' he admitted.

'Little-bloody-wonder. She needs help. All this stuff with Swain and Robson—'

This time it was Porter who cut in sharply. 'Which she is not at liberty to speak to you about.'

'Come off it. You don't go home to your missus and tell her what's going on at work?'

'I certainly do not.'

'Bollocks. Besides, she isn't giving away state secrets. Anyway, that's not what I mean. I'm talking about how obsessed she's grown with catching this Robson character. And what she'll do when she gets her hands on him.'

Porter's chest felt constricted. 'What exactly are you getting at, Mr Gill?'

'Nothing,' Adam said too quickly. 'I just don't think she should be on the case. It isn't helping her state of mind, and it isn't going to end well. Look, I feel like a swine even calling you like this. It sounds as if I'm just being bitter, because she's dumped me. But, I'm worried about her. You need to pull her off this case, Porter. Hey, you know about what happened to her sister, don't you?'

Porter was aware that Kerry's older sibling had been abducted as a child, but beyond that he hadn't given it much attention. Many officers had personal reasons for entering the police service. If her sister's abduction had been the catalyst for Kerry joining up he wouldn't hold it against her, she should be applauded. 'What has that to do with anything?'

'The trauma's had a lifelong impact on her,' Adam stated. 'When she was a kid, she had to attend psychotherapy sessions. After that kid got shot on Wandsworth Road, and Swain fell to his death, well, I think it's all come back to haunt her...uh, come back on her again. Now there's this stuff with another girl going missing up in Cumbria. She's a lit fuse, and she's going to blow. Porter, no, *Detective Chief Inspector Porter*, you have a duty of care to her. You have to help her before something really bad happens.'

'Do you have any idea where she is now?'

'I was hoping she'd returned to work. I haven't seen her since she threw her engagement ring back at me, and to tell the truth, I'm not sure there's anywhere else she could go.'

'Hmmm.' Porter frowned deeply, then on impulse craned round and peered at the point on his office wall where his commendation hung, thinking how it had perturbed Kerry and left him creeped out by her reaction. 'You mentioned that Kerry was once under psychiatric care...'

'Well I know she saw a child psychologist. I'm unsure if that's the same thing.'

Porter didn't bother clarifying the difference. 'Do you know the name of her psychologist?'

'Kerry only ever told me she called him Doctor Ron. He had a practice up north in Carlisle, back in the late nineties. I was going to ring him before I decided to call you, and I did a bit of digging. I found him in Kerry's browsing history on her laptop. He's called Ronald Dawson. He's retired now but, well, do you think he can help her?'

'Possibly,' said Porter. 'Did you get a contact number for him?'

'Yeah.' Adam read it out, and Porter jotted it on a notepad on his desk. 'Will you call him, Porter?'

'Doctor-patient confidentiality exists,' Porter explained. 'But I believe Doctor Dawson will be more inclined to answer my questions than those of Kerry's ex-fiancé, don't you?'

'Yeah. You've probably got a point. It'd be best coming from you, and I really hope you can help, because I'm at my wits end here. I only want what's best for Kerry. I didn't call you to stir up any shit for her. Only so she gets the help she needs before...' he faltered and went silent.

Before she gets her hands on Robson, Porter thought, *and something really bad happens.*

If she asked him, she was reasonably confident Danny Korba would let her crash at his place for a few nights until she found somewhere more permanent to live, but she wasn't going to ask. It was difficult enough staving off his overly protective attention as it were, and it could become unbearable — and impossible to hide her state of mind — if they shared a house, as well as an office. Mel Scanlon had adult kids at home, and both Glenn and Tony had toddlers, and girlfriends who might not be keen on them living in such close quarters to another woman. It was the problem with being a transplantee in the city; she had few friends and no family there to reach out to in times of need. Nigel Bellows, the coroner's assistant, was a friend of sorts, but not close enough to ask help from. With nothing for it, she found a room at a hotel near Euston Station, where the overnight parking cost almost as much as the basic, though clean and comfortable, facilities. She picked the hotel as a snap decision. The first time she'd travelled from Carlisle to London, she'd spilled out of Euston Station clutching an overnight bag, and an online booking to the nearest affordable accommodation, and had stayed there for three weeks while she settled into her new role with the Met. There was nothing sentimental about her return. Her room was exactly as she remembered — Spartan and uniform — but the hotel boasted a restaurant with good food and a coffee shop she planned on making regular use of again.

Being in her room reminded her of her first arrival in London, when she'd been excited, anxious, and also maudlin for home. Transferring to London she'd effectively said goodbye to her mother. Siobhan's alcoholism and dependency on prescription drugs had replaced any necessity for keeping her only remaining child close. Her mother had abandoned her as acutely as had her dad, without ever having gone anywhere but inside her own self-pity. Thinking of her mam, she was tempted to give her a call, but resisted the urge. No good could come from talking to Siobhan, considering the reason for her current predicament. Siobhan had formed a low opinion of men since her dad left, and when Kerry rang her with the news of her engagement to Adam, she'd been met with a wall of indifference bordering on animosity. Hearing that her daughter's relationship had failed wouldn't change her opinion any, and would earn Kerry only an unwanted 'I told you so'.

She lay on her side on the hotel bed. It was huge, and its wide expanse exaggerated her loneliness. She needed a hug, but even a metaphorical one was out of the question, especially from Siobhan. She'd no close friends back home in the north, none that knew her well enough to lend a sympathetic ear, definitely not a shoulder to cry on. What she wished for was her older sister. She pulled up her knees and wrapped her arms around her shins, feeling even smaller and alone.

She wasn't.

Girl had accompanied her to the hotel, and had taken residence in a corner of the room, in the unused space behind a tub chair sitting kitty-corner to a long counter holding the few accoutrements, and pamphlets supplied by the hotel. Kerry watched her from under her lashes, and for once Girl didn't race for cover. She remained nebulous though, indistinct, and unresponsive under her scrutiny. As ever, Girl hung her head, sorrowful, stringy hair concealing her features, and yet Kerry sensed a change in her demeanour. There was mournfulness as usual, but this time Kerry was certain it was due to hers and not Girl's troubled existence.

'Why won't you speak to me?' Kerry whispered.

Through the veil of her eyelashes, she was certain Girl's head raised a fraction in response, but she didn't speak. She never spoke.

'You and Swain are alike,' Kerry went on, and this time Girl flickered and appeared poised to run. 'You're not like him in nature. That's not what I mean. You're his opposite. But you are like him in one way. You want something from me.'

Girl's head rose and fell again, and Kerry could define enough of her to see her small hands clutch at the insubstantial fabric of her shapeless dress.

'Unless you tell me what to do I can't help you. Girl. I don't even know your real name. I've called you Girl for...well, forever. You've never objected to it, but neither have you hinted it's wrong. Who are you? I mean who are you *really*? And what is it you want from me?'

Girl turned her back. Kerry allowed her eyes to widen a fraction more, and for the briefest of moments saw Girl's shoulders hitching, as if she sobbed, but then she darted, and as Kerry tried to follow the movement, Girl disappeared, though not completely. There was a swirl of shadows as she fled into the en suite bathroom. To pursue her inside the tiny room was pointless, there was no cornering a wraith that could come and go from this world at will.

'I'm sorry.' Kerry meant it, but frustration was killing her. 'I shouldn't press you, I know. But I'm at a loss here! How am I meant to know what you need if you won't tell me?'

She angled for a clearer view of the bathroom's interior. If Girl was in there, she'd taken refuge in the shower.

'Girl? If you can't speak, is there some way you could show me?'

No reply, and no hint of movement. Kerry stood, and took a step closer to the open door and craned for a peek.

Girl rocketed past, this time for the corner beyond the bed. Kerry made the mistake of turning with her, and

Girl never slowed when she reached the corner, only dematerialized through it.

'No! Wait! Come back, Girl!'

She swore under her breath, at herself, not the recalcitrant sprit.

What was it with her personal coterie of ghosts that they were reluctant to show when she bloody well wanted them to?

Where the hell was Swain?

The ringing of her mobile phone startled her.

She delved inside her bag, and sat down heavily on the bed as she brought up the glowing screen.

There was a number displayed, no contact details, because she hadn't assigned any yet. She recognised the number though, it was one she'd rang only days ago.

'Doctor Ron?' she asked, surprised that he'd called her.

'Yes. Hello, Little Kes.' He gave the prompt for straight speaking in those few short words. 'Ehm, are you alone?'

She glanced around. Yes, she was alone all right.

'What I mean,' Ron went on, 'is are you able to speak in private?'

'Aye,' Kerry said, feeling a knot form in her stomach. 'I'm the only one here. Is...is there something wrong?'

'Well I genuinely hope not. I hope I didn't talk out of turn...'

'Ron. What is it?' She stood, paced half the length of the room.

'I just received a rather impertinent call from a chap claiming to be your commanding officer?'

'What?'

'A chap called Charles Porter? He said he was a Detective Chief Inspector, and your immediate supervisor.'

The knot in her gut twisted tighter. 'What did he want?' Her voice was a croak, and swallowing was difficult.

'He asked me about our relationship, and I confirmed I was your assigned psychologist when you were a child. But I also reminded him that was as far as I would go. I might be retired but I still respect patient confidentiality.'

'Why'd he want to know about you?'

'He wasn't interested in me, Kerry. He wanted to know about you.'

When she first applied to join Cumbria Constabulary, she'd declared her medical history, but the fact she'd undertaken grief counselling as a child had never been an issue. Her current mental health and acumen had been deemed well through the psychological testing she'd been subjected to during the recruitment process. Did Porter hope to use her childhood issues against her in whatever agenda he was working?

'It wouldn't matter if you divulged everything from our sessions,' she began, but sensed there was more to come. 'But that isn't what he was digging for, was it?'

'He asked if we'd been in contact more recently.'

'What did you tell him?'

'Well, Kerry, I assure you I had no need to lie on either of our behalf. I admitted to speaking with you regarding a private matter, of which he'd no business enquiring.'

Kerry exhaled, and it was probably audible at his end of the line too. It sounded too much like a sigh of relief. 'I bet he didn't leave things at that, though?'

'No, he was persistent. He mentioned having some concerns regarding your current state of mind and if you'd shared any similar concerns with me.'

Kerry waited.

'I reminded him we spoke about a private matter. But, Kerry, that was as much as an admission to him. I tried dissuading him from pursuing matters any further by telling him you're not mentally ill, if that was his concern. I told him you were only dealing with a recent trauma in your own fashion, and all you needed was a little time to process and come to terms with it.'

Her eyelids screwed shut.

'Like I said, I hope I didn't speak out of turn?' Ron knew he'd said too much. His call wasn't a warning, it was an attempt at gaining forgiveness for blabbing and soothing of his guilt.

'No...it's fine.' Her tone hinted that it most certainly wasn't. She caught herself, though. Doctor Ron, the sweet man, had only tried to protect her, and she couldn't be disappointed, let alone angry with him. She opened her eyes. 'Honestly, Ron, it's OK. I don't know what he was angling for, but I'm pretty sure he didn't get it. Did he...' Something troubled her more than the fact Porter had contacted Ron, it was how he knew whom to contact. She'd never included Ron's personal details on the forms during the initial police recruitment process. 'Did he say how he knew you were my psychologist?'

'He didn't. I assumed it was something you'd shared with him...'

'Hmmm. That has to be it,' she lied, because she wanted Ron off the phone, and feeling no guiltier about betraying her confidence than before. Beyond her parents, and neither of them would have been as helpful to Porter, there was only one other person who could have given the DCI his name. 'He didn't...by any chance...mention my fiancé did he?'

'You have a fiancé?'

'Yes.' She *did* have, past tense. 'Adam Gill?'

'No. That name wasn't mentioned.'

Kerry sniffed. It didn't clear Adam of betraying her. She'd left him because he told her he couldn't handle her life. So why bloody meddle in it? Why couldn't he just leave well and good alone?

'Can I now be an impertinent caller?' Ron said, and without waiting for permission, continued any way. 'I just read the sub-text in your last question. Are the hallucinations you told me about having a negative impact on your personal relationships?'

'Things are a little strained,' she admitted.

'Little Kes. Kerry. I'd never do anything to harm you on purpose; if I've hurt you by opening my big mouth to your boss, I'm sorry. But hopefully there was something good I did do for you. Do you remember when last we spoke? I advised you to see your GP, who could prescribe you a course of mild antidepressants. Did you take my advice and see someone?'

'Yes.' She thought about Elias Price. 'I spoke to a specialist and it was a great help.'

'That's a good thing then. I'm pleased you did that, Kerry. Stick with it, and I assure you things will get better soon.'

'Don't worry,' she said, mentally crossing her fingers, 'I intend sticking out the full course.'

Ron wished to say more, but she didn't want caught in the lie. If he asked what kind of medication she'd been prescribed she couldn't even hazard a guess. She made a quick goodbye, hung up.

It was early evening. She'd been gone from work far too long, and sneaking back in was going to be difficult enough without Porter snooping on her. But returning to the nick was unavoidable if she hoped to further her case. The only way she could divert Porter from whatever messed up agenda he was following was by catching Jermaine Robson, and handing him over as a trophy to the DCI.

She didn't make it to the nick before Swain leaped out from the roadside directly in front of her car. He was semi-translucent, but a figure diving in front of a moving vehicle ensured an instinctive reaction. Kerry hit the brakes, and the car slewed, almost striking a parked van. Swain's lower body was engulfed within the engine compartment of her car. He was unaffected, and rushed across to the driver's side.

'I've been waiting for hours. What the bloody hell kept you, Kezza?'

'Are you bloody stupid? You almost made me crash!'

'Think yourself lucky I've no animosity towards you, or I'd have jumped out when you were going much faster.' Instantly, Swain swept through her and into the passenger seat. She felt the itchy tingling of his passing, and shivered at her core. *'Turn round,'* he ordered bluntly. *'You don't want to go in the nick. Your arsehole of a boss is on the war path.'*

'I have to go in. I need to report—'

'If you want to get Robson, we have to go right now. It's been hours! I've waited long enough!'

'I thought spirits were supposed to be timeless?'

'What? Are you kidding me? It's the flaming opposite! Every second feels like an eternity to me right now! Turn around, get moving. I'm telling you, Kezza.'

The police station was in sight. One more right turn and she could be down the ramp into the basement car park. If she hoped to save her career, she should report to Porter, explain her domestic situation and blame it for her recent erratic behaviour, and promise that now she'd ditched Adam she would get her act together. Surely Porter would give her a break under the circumstances?

The car was already almost sideways across the street. She threw it in reverse and pulled a quick Y-turn, and sped away from the nick.

'Where are we going?'

'I'll tell you when we get there.'

'Tell me now, Swain.'

'Why? So you can call in the cavalry? Fuck that! I'll show you where to find him, Kezza, but if any other filth shows up, the deal's off.'

'Just tell me where he is, right now, or the deal *is* off!' Elias Price told her that her power was greater than Swain's; otherwise why would he try bullying her? He told her to stand her ground, enforce her boundaries, and…well, more or less he'd encouraged her to show the bastard who was boss. 'You need me more than I need you, Swain. If we don't get Robson now, well it's inevitable another of my colleagues will in the next few days. You've promised to tell me about the Fell Man, and what happened to Sally, but if you don't, well, I'll be no worse off than I am now. So here's the new deal, *Swain-o*. You show me where Robson is, or you can bugger off.'

'Take a right turn,' he said, wafting his cuffed hand at the windscreen.

She was unsure if he was surrendering to her demands, or was still the arrogant piece of dirt he'd always been. It didn't matter. Kerry took the right turn.

'Keep going. Don't you have a siren you can use to get us through this traffic?'

'This is my own car,' she reminded him, 'it doesn't come with lights and sirens.'

'So put your bloody foot down, and hit your horn. Bull your way through, Kezza. Trust me, they'll get the hell out of your way.'

He was right. In life he'd driven without the benefit of blues and twos, but nobody would ever have held him up, she'd bet. She flicked her main beam on and off, repeatedly hit the horn. Vehicles moved aside. They soon forced a path through the early evening traffic, and Kerry realised they were heading for Blackfriars Bridge. Swain kept quiet, staring intently through the windscreen until they were over the Thames. *'Take a right on Stamford Street, and keep going till we get to Waterloo Station.'*

'Back towards your old stomping ground?' She took the right turn as instructed. The road ahead was quieter, and she stamped down on the throttle. Typically, when she wanted to see a police car, there wasn't one in sight. If she was pulled over, she'd flash her warrant card, and demand the patrol car follow hers, whether Swain liked it or not.

Once they were beyond Waterloo, and on Lambeth Palace Road, Swain directed her along the Embankment.

'Are we going to Nine Elms Lane? Just tell me, and I'll get us there.'

'Where'd you expect Robson to be?'

'Yeah, well, it took you long enough to figure it out, didn't it?'

'I don't need your criticism. I was the one who had to listen to those whining bastards for hours before they slipped up.' He was talking about Funky and Kingston James. *'They didn't say where Robson was, cause they didn't have a clue. But they mentioned names of other Nine Elms tossers, so I paid them a visit. Took ages before one of them mentioned going over to the Power House. I hitched a lift and found the bastard, then came back for you. I didn't expect to be stood up like that, Kezza.'*

'Robson's hiding at Battersea Power Station?' Kerry glimpsed his sly sneer. For years the iconic twin-chimneyed power station had been a landmark on the London map. It had sat obsolete, but in recent years the riverside Victorian power station had undergone radical reconstruction, to house luxury flats, shops and dining and entertainment venues. It wasn't a location where a fugitive could lie low these days. 'He'd be better suited to a kennel at the dog and cats home,' she said, and was rewarded with a wider sneer from Swain.

'Speaking of which,' he said, *'when you get past the dog pound, take a right on Prince of Wales Drive and under the railway.'*

It took minutes to get there, and once they were out of the underpass, and at Queen's Circus, Swain told her to go right on the roundabout. He had her park the car on double yellow lines on a side street between some recently constructed executive class apartment buildings on Queenstown Road, in sight of Chelsea Bridge. At first Kerry suspected Robson had taken refuge in one of the vacant flats, but that wasn't it. Swain alighted the car, without needing to open the door, and headed down the side street, and she hurried to keep him in sight. As she jogged, she dug in her bag for her phone, considering calling Korba and asking him to meet her ASAP. But before she called for back up, she should check Swain hadn't brought her on a wild goose chase.

More construction was in progress. Hoarding and scaffolding surrounded her. Plastic and canvas sheets snapped in the evening breeze coming off the nearby river. There was a brief view of two of the massive chimneys on the power station, red lights blinking at their tops, but then she took another right, and an immediate left onto an old cobbled road in need of resurfacing. Directly ahead was the raised embankment of the railway, and she went right where a row of Victorian bridge arches had been converted — decades earlier by the dilapidated state of them — as retail units. Swain, twenty feet ahead, abruptly halted, and waved urgently for her to duck. There was nowhere to hide except in a shallow alcove at the beginning of the bridge. Underfoot there was a bed of trash, and the stench of urine billowed, overwhelming her. She flattened herself in the alcove, craning so she could see what had alarmed Swain. At first she saw nobody else, but from Swain's body language — bent at the waist, fists clenched — he was poised to attack.

She knew of this place from intelligence gathered on the Nine Elms Crew. One of the arched units once housed a gymnasium, old style, where hulking men pumped actual iron. It had been a recruitment ground for doormen when Jermaine Robson took command of the local clubs and pubs, and also an outlet for the sale of anabolic steroids and cocaine. It bore the unoriginal name of the Power House, being in the shadow of Battersea Power Station's chimneys. After several successful drug raids, the gym had been closed down but apparently the derelict building was still used by Robson's gang for other reasons.

Two young men emerged from the Power House. On the back street, hidden by the glistening bulwarks of the ultra-modern luxury apartment blocks, no expense had gone into repairing the street lighting. A lamppost cast a dim glow over the men, but not bright enough to identify them. Kerry was familiar with Robson's face. She'd studied his mug shots plenty of times, and had seen him in the flesh a few days ago when he'd arrived to check her out outside Funky's flat. From what she could tell of the two men exiting the unit, neither was Robson. They looked youthful, dressed in the ubiquitous gangster uniform of baseball caps, hoodies, baggy pants and trainers. They spoke rapidly, in gang patois that was difficult to follow, to somebody still inside the arched unit, before strutting across the street to a car parked in the shadows. The engine roared, and the lights came on, and the car shot towards Kerry's hiding place. It swept directly over Swain.

With nowhere to go, Kerry could only avert her face, and hope. Thankfully the two men in the car failed to notice her, and the car continued to the corner, took a left and sped up the incline between the new apartment blocks. Taking a peek towards the unit they'd emerged from, Kerry could see nobody else. Nobody alive. Swain had survived being ploughed over. He was tilted forward, his hands clenched at his sides, head extended on his taut neck. He thrummed with hatred, reminiscent of an aggressive pointer dog.

She still didn't have eyes on Robson, but Swain's reaction was enough. She pulled out her phone and rang Korba.

He replied, but she cut him off immediately. 'Danny, listen to me. Don't ask questions; just trust me. I've got Robson, but I need back up to bring him in. I'm on a backstreet off Queenstown Road, next to the railway lines alongside Battersea Power Station.' Korba butted in for clarity, and she spoke over him. 'Yes, outside the old Power House gym. But you have to come in via Queenstown Road where the construction site is. Get a TPU over here now.' A TPU, or Trojan Proactive Unit, was the name given to the armed response vehicles on high-visibility patrols in crime hotspots. She couldn't swear Robson was armed, but it was a high probability, so having the support of armed officers was a prerequisite before arresting him. Korba bleated at her to wait for back up, promised he was on his way too. But as with every arrest scenario, the situation was fluid.

Jermaine Robson stepped out from under the arch, puffing on a cigarette that lit his face with a red glow with each inhalation. He was totally oblivious of Erick Swain.

Expecting Swain to launch at his enemy in a frenzied attack, Kerry made the mistake of leaning out of the alcove. Had she intended warning Swain to stop, to back off...what? It didn't matter, because Robson caught a glimpse of movement, and swung towards her on high alert. He was a fugitive, and suspicious of everyone. He began walking slowly towards her, head tilted as he tried to make her out in the dimness. If she was cornered she'd be at his mercy, and it would be minutes before the TPU arrived, enough time to be severely injured or worse. She was equipped with handcuffs and PAVA, and they were both on the sling harness she could conceal under her jacket. Unfortunately her harness was in the GaOC office, along with her radio and extendable truncheon. Her only tool of officialdom was her warrant card, buried in her handbag, and Robson wasn't the type to pay it any respect.

She stepped out of hiding. 'Police! Stop right there, Robson, and get down on the ground! Now!'

He halted, dropping his cigarette at his feet.

He was a very dangerous man, suspected of as many gangland slayings and beatings as his rival, Swain, and physically Kerry was no match for him. He was controlled by primitive instincts, and when cornered that meant one of two responses: fight or run. To her relief he sprinted, angling directly at her, swiping out a long arm to shove her aside. She jerked backwards, avoiding impact, and then Robson was past her and hurtling for the side street between the new apartment blocks.

Her relief was short lived.

He was escaping, and it was her duty to pursue.

The side street where she'd parked her car hadn't felt as steep jogging down it, but racing up towards Queenstown Road, flashes of pain in her knees accompanied every step, and her breath was ragged in her throat. Galvanised by adrenalin, Robson didn't seem to be as hindered. He flew up the hill; each long stride gaining him a lead on Kerry. As she ran, she juggled her phone, attempting to update Korba, but it was a frustrating task. She managed to hit his number, but running, gasping for breath and issuing new directions was almost impossible. In the end, she left the line open, and ran, shouting now and then and hoping the DS could make sense out of it all.

Robson could have turned around and beaten the crap out of her long before an armed response vehicle could arrive, but he was under the impression he could already be surrounded, so didn't as much as pause. He charged across Queenstown Road, at the same time that Kerry pounded past her car. She was tempted to jump inside it and give pursuit, but if Robson got off the main route she'd lose him in seconds. She ran on, trying to drag in the oxygen needed to energise her straining muscles.

On the far side of Queenstown Road was Battersea Park, an expanse of grass and trees and ponds, and a million hiding places. A tall fence surrounded the park, metal railings topped by ornamental spearheads. There was an entrance down at Queen's Circus, but none she could spot on the street within hundreds of metres. Robson continued up the main road, and hopefully he'd meet a TPU coming the other direction.

History repeating. She'd chased Erick Swain on foot, and now Jermaine Robson. Perhaps it was a sign that instead of swimming she should take up running as a pastime, so when it happened again she would actually be fit enough to catch somebody. Chance would be a fine thing. With his long-legged gait Robson was leaving her standing. She put down her head, pumped her elbows, and the effort was felt in her chest as if each lung had instantly shrivelled to the size of a walnut. She hollered at her phone, but her voice was a foreign language even to her ears.

In the distance blue lights flashed as a police car streaked towards them over Chelsea Bridge. Kerry didn't spot the responding patrol car at first, only heard the tempo of Robson's clattering footsteps alter, and she looked up in time to see him slide to a halt. He was caught in indecision, stepping one way, then the other, before he spun and glared at her. Kerry also slowed, but continued striding towards him, one palm held out flat towards him. 'Stop right there,' she shouted. 'You're under arrest, Robson.'

He launched at the railings surrounding the park. Swain, appearing from nowhere, attempted to stall him. He wrapped his arms around Robson's throat and tried hauling backwards. Robson slipped the gossamer noose, and swarmed up the railings. There was no easy way of scaling them. He had to crouch on top, balanced with his hands on two spear heads, feet crimped between them and on a narrow cross bar, then make a flying leap to clear them. Haste was his downfall. The cuff of a pants leg snagged on one of the spearheads. He jumped, and his left leg was yanked backwards before the material tore loose, and Robson went down to the dirt headfirst. Kerry raced to the spot, and saw Robson gathering his feet under him. He turned towards her, grimacing in pain. As he pushed up, he limped heavily on his left leg, and cradled his right arm against his ribs. 'Give it up,' she snapped.

He swung his back on her and took off at an awkward, agonised lope.

Kerry shoved her phone in her pocket and sprang for the railings. She was perched on the top like a church gargoyle when the TPU screeched to a halt alongside her. She waved urgently at the armed response officer in the driving seat, sending him to the park's entrance on Queen's Circus, then jumped. She landed, didn't bother checking the car had sped off to enter the park by the distant entrance, and charged after Robson. In the few seconds it had taken to scale the railings, darkness had engulfed Robson. She couldn't see him, but she could hear. He crashed through some bushes twenty metres ahead. She plunged forward, aware of the darkness folding around her.

Pursuing a desperate criminal into the park was risky. If he turned on her, even injured, he'd still easily overpower her. But it was a risk she was willing to take. Now she had back up converging on the scene, all she need do was keep an ear on his location, then direct her armed colleagues to him. Robson was making so much noise as he blundered through the bushes that she'd get plenty of notice if he came after her. Now he limped on a twisted ankle, and was struggling with an injured arm, she was confident she could evade him, while still keeping close tabs on him. If he tried to hide, she'd have him surrounded and captured in no time. She moved through the shrubs with more care, following his crashing progress.

Swain was at her side, his face set in a rictus. He stabbed his cuffed wrist at the darkness.

'He's going to get away from you!'

'He's going nowhere. Except to jail.'

'No! You have to go get him. Now! Before it's too late!'

'He can't escape. Chill out, Swain.'

She forced her way through some broken twigs, caught sight of movement ahead. The line, remarkably, was still open on her phone.

'Danny? You still there?'

'I'm here, boss!' Behind his strident voice, sirens howled. She thought she could hear their fainter echo somewhere in the distance. 'Where are you?'

'In pursuit of Jermaine Robson. I'm in Battersea Park, the east side.'

'I'm a few minutes out. Kerry, for God's sake, don't try grabbing him yourself.'

'I've got back up.' She glanced at Swain's tormented face, but didn't mean him. 'TPU are here. They're coming in the park by another entrance. I just need to keep an eye on Robson, see where he goes and we've got him.'

Swain coughed out a curse and flashed ahead.

'You're alone?' Korba suddenly asked. 'TPU aren't with you yet?'

'No, they're still a few hundred metres away. They're coming though.'

'So who were you talking to a few seconds ago?'

He'd overheard her speaking with Swain. Shit. Hopefully he hadn't heard her referring to him by name.

'Nobody. I was shouting at Robson, that's all.'

He was unconvinced, but she didn't really care at that moment. Robson had changed direction; his crashing advance had switched to her left. She swung after him, telling Korba Robson was heading parallel to Queenstown Road. 'Let my back-up know.'

Through the tree trunks she spotted the flashing blue lights of the TPU, but it hurtled past her, speeding along one of the park's carriage driveways. She spilled out from under the trees just as heavy raindrops showered down. The tumult briefly deafened Robson's progress.

A deserted sports stadium was to her right, and dead ahead a serpentine jogging trail wound between more trees. She picked up speed, again feeling the exertion in her knees. Fifteen metres ahead, Swain waved impatiently for her to catch up.

'For Christ's sake, Kezza! Get a frigging move on, will you? He's going to get away.'

'Show me where he is,' she hollered, and conscious of the phone in her hand, she slipped it back in her pocket, and slapped her hand over it to muffle her voice. 'Swain, where did he go?'

'This way. Come on.' He shot away, a ragged streamer of colours, lit by some inner illumination. Kerry followed as if he was an elusive will-o'-the-wisp.

The jogging path met the same carriage trail the TPU had sped along moments ago. The patrol car's lights flashed among the tree canopy a few hundred metres to the north, but Swain continued dead ahead, towards a circular building surrounded on one side by wooden picnic tables: some kind of café, there to serve park goers during daylight hours. Out of season, the café looked as if it had been sealed shut until next spring. She briefly wondered if Robson had tried to force entry, to hole up inside, but Swain swept by, and she ran, glancing across at where the patrol car was well out of hailing range. Other blue lights converged on the park's main entrance. There was a choice of two trails through a copse of trees to the left, but the nearest headed too close to the main gate where the other police cars were arriving. Without her ghostly guide's insistence, she took the second trail.

'Jermaine Robson,' she shouted, 'stop running. You're surrounded. Just stop where you are and get down on the ground.'

She heard the scuffing of feet and wheezed curses, as Robson grew more frantic to escape. She charged towards the sounds, and came to the convergence of three snaking trails. Robson was on none of them. He clattered through low tree limbs to her right, swiftly pursued by Swain. She yelled, and plunged after them.

Rain pattered in the canopy. Then it was as if a boulder fell from the sky and hit the boating lake. Wild thrashing followed, and a croak of alarm.

Kerry forced through a tangle of bushes and branches, and skidded out onto a muddy embankment. Robson was already waist deep in water. In a blind panic, he'd staggered from the path and into the large lake that dominated Battersea Park. The lake was dotted with tree crowned islets, and in his desperation to escape Robson waded for the nearest. But with each step his feet were dragged into deeper mud, and in the next instant he was chest deep, and his arms began clawing for something to grab on to. He slipped, went under the surface. In the darkness he disappeared completely. Then he exploded up again, crying out in horror, and his arms thrashed the surface into froth. Swain, baying at his enemy, clung to his head and shoulders.

'Kerry! Come and help me push this bastard under! Come on. He can run like a whippet, but he can't swim for shit!'

Robson sank under again.

Next time he exploded up, his mouth was wide and he gasped, stricken with terror, and began slipping under again.

'Drown you bastard!' Swain crowed in delight. He snapped his gaze on Kerry. *'What are you waiting for? This is your chance. Drown him before the other coppers show up and they'll never know who did it. Do it now, Kerry, and I'll give you the Fell Man's name.'*

He was right. There wasn't another police officer in hundreds of metres. She could swim out, add her weight to Robson's shoulders and let him suck in the murky lake water. Swain would get what he wanted, and she would get the answers she was desperate for. Who would ever know she'd assisted in Robson's drowning? Did the man who'd ordered the slaying of a mother and child for his own gain deserve any better? Even Suleymaan Ghedi, a devoutly religious man, could find no forgiveness for those responsible for his wife and daughter's deaths, so why should she show any pity?

It took her all of a second to decide.

'Danny, Robson's in the lake,' she shouted as she plucked out her phone. 'He's drowning!' She looked once at Swain's gloating visage, and said, 'I'm going in.'

She threw her phone down, pulled her handbag from around her shoulder and cast it aside too, then plunged into the lake, diving, so that she wouldn't also be caught in the mire.

'Drown him! Drown him!' Swain raged over Robson, his colours flaring as if the drowning man was engulfed in flames. Robson's thrashing served only to sink him deeper, and he could now barely crane his head back far enough to suck in a last breath. *'Push him under,'* Swain screeched at Kerry, delirious with delight. *'Stamp on his fucking throat. Kill the bastard!'*

Kerry grasped hold of Robson's jacket. Robson erupted out of the water again, buoyed by her grasp, but he fought, grabbing and pulling at her. She slapped his hands aside and forced him around so she was behind him, grabbing at both his shoulders, and she levered down.

'Yes, push him down. Go on. Do it. Push him down, keep him down, keep him under...' Swain's commands were almost hysterical, the words rushing from him in ecstasy at his rival's doom. *'DrownhimKerryFuckingmurderhim.'*

She kicked out with her feet, into the backs of Robson's knees and he fell backwards against her. Her left arm she wrapped under his chin, elevating his face from the water.

'Wait! What?' Swain was in Kerry's face as she plunged backwards, towing the semi-conscious fugitive with her for the nearest bank. *'What are you doing? Drown him, before the Old Bill get here.'*

Kerry ignored him, too encumbered with the effort of dragging Robson to the safety of dry land.

'What are you doing?' Swain demanded, but this time there was a different timbre to his screech. 'Are you fucking kidding me?'

She struggled through knee-deep mud. Almost fell flat under Robson. He outweighed her, and could have flattened her into the muck if he wished, but he was almost senseless, gasping, crying in relief. Kerry rolled him over and he went on his hands and knees, spluttering. She grasped his collar with both hands, backing for the bank. He scrambled after her, and when finally his torso cleared the water, he collapsed face down in the dirt at the edge of the lake. He lay gagging up filthy water. Kerry forced a knee on his shoulder, held him in place, but there was no need. He wasn't going anywhere.

'Jermaine Robson,' she said, 'you are under arrest.'

Kerry looked out across the churned up water.

Swain stood waist deep, his mouth working silently as he glared at Robson, then up at her.

'Why didn't you do it?' he croaked. 'You had a chance and you didn't take it.'

'I warned you there was a line I wouldn't cross,' she reminded him.

'You've ruined everything,' he moaned. 'Everything!'

'I've caught the ones that destroyed you,' she countered. 'All of them. They'll all go to prison for a long time. Isn't that enough for you?'

'No. No it isn't. Noooooo!' He howled like an injured animal.

Then he was gone, and others were there. Armed police officers rushed to assist her, Korba crashed through the nearest bushes, face stretched wide in concern until he spotted her kneeling on top of her prisoner and he almost sat down in relief.

And Girl was there too, watching the proceedings morosely around the crooked bole of a nearby tree.

In the days that followed, Kerry's life went from complicated to chaotic. Not all of the uproar was bad, only some. Suleymaan Ghedi wept when she informed him that all the plotters had been captured, and suitable punishments would follow: his tears were of gratitude, and he held her hands briefly, kissed her on the cheek and again called her an angel. She was hailed as a heroine in the press and on TV; the downside being packs of baying journalists pursued her whenever she showed her face outside the police station. Her colleagues and superiors alike applauded her — the latter at least in public — and DCI Porter was happy to share in the plaudits, though every time she was in his presence she experienced an uncanny crawling of her skin. There was nothing supernatural in her ability to sense his feelings regarding her. She could almost imagine the tendrils of suspicion coiling off him to prod and poke at her as he delved for something useful to knock her from her lofty perch. He didn't accept her assertion that she'd been following a lead when she'd located Jermaine Robson's hideout, especially after she again refused to name her intelligence source. There were procedures in place to protect the identities of CHIS from repercussion, but they didn't extend beyond the request for clarification from a superintendent, and Porter got Alexandra Tinsley onboard. Charles Porter and "Sandy" Tinsley were not golfing buddies, or members of a secretive brotherhood, but they were firm friends. Back in the day, when Porter was a lowly DC, Sandy was his sergeant, and — if the rumours were true — his lover. They'd both gone on to marry other partners, but affection persisted, though these days in a purely platonic fashion. Whenever Porter chose to throw his weight around, he preferred Sandy in his corner.

Three days after arresting Robson, Kerry was invited to the superintendent's office, and she refused the offer of having a Police Federation representative accompany her. The office was similar to Porter's, though slightly larger, and with more framed commendations on the walls, and a larger window that let in natural light. There was a desk at which the superintendent could work, but at the room's centre chairs surrounded a large table, where policing strategy meetings were conducted. Sandy took the chair at the head of the table, Kerry the one at the foot, while Porter had his choice of any of the other six ladder-backed chairs. He decided to lounge against the wall to Sandy's right, as if overseeing the proceedings rather than taking an active role.

'Would you like some spring water?' Tinsley offered.

Kerry declined politely. Besides, it was doubtful water would sufficiently unglue her tongue from the roof of her mouth.

'Would you prefer coffee? I can have some fetched.' Tinsley glanced at Porter, as if he should see to the refreshments, and he frowned. Kerry saved him the humiliation of waiting on her.

'I'm fine, ma'am.'

'Are you, though?' The superintendent didn't waste any time getting to the crux of things. She could be sharp-tongued, but Kerry had more time for her than for her immediate supervisor — normally. Tinsley sat, her deep brown eyes sparkling with intensity behind the rectangular lenses of her designer spectacles, a Mona Lisa smile on her lips.

'Never better, ma'am.' Kerry glanced up at Porter, who failed to conceal a snort of disbelief. In fact, he hadn't slipped, but snorted on purpose. Tinsley's response was to lift her hand off the table an inch, but that was all. Porter crossed his arms, and stayed quiet.

'I'm impressed by the results you've had lately,' Tinsley said. 'Charles has also expressed how pleased he is with how you handled the Ghedi shooting. However, it hasn't escaped his notice that your methods might prove questionable when the defendants come to court. He's yet to see a report, redacted or otherwise, regarding the chain of events that led you to the original arrests. I haven't seen such a statement either.'

Procedure meant a full and concise evidence file should be collated and presented to the Crown Prosecution Service. Any sensitive information would be censored — redacted — prior to copies being supplied to the respective defence teams, thus ensuring the anonymity of those at risk of repercussions if their personal details were leaked. Kerry didn't enjoy special dispensation from legal process.

'My source wishes to remain anonymous, and I promised they wouldn't appear in any statement, censored or otherwise.' Heat grew in Kerry's throat. Her answer plainly wasn't good enough.

'So if I ask how you happened to locate not one but two hiding places, what would you tell me?' Steepling her hands on the table, Tinsley waited. Her enigmatic smile slipped, her mouth forming a tight line.

'All I can say is I followed tip-offs from an anonymous source, and both played out.'

'In the first instance, at the warehouse off Nine Elms Lane, you organised and implemented a raid. Yet you felt the need to go after Jermaine Robson alone. It's not the behaviour I expect of an inspector under my command.'

'Ma'am,' said Kerry, 'I was under a time constraint with Robson. There wasn't time for obtaining a RIPA authorisation, or organising the resources to control the location he was found at. If I'd delayed, Robson would've slipped away. It's since come to my notice that he was lying low at the Power House until transportation could be organised to get him out the city.' She was stating fact. Following her arrest of Robson, he'd admitted he was only hours away from skipping out of London, with a plan to escape to the continent and from there fly to a country with no extradition treaty with the UK. It mattered not if he was telling the truth, it still added to her case. 'If I hadn't gone there when I did, he would've escaped.'

'You were on a tight timescale,' agreed Tinsley, 'I can accept that. But for one point.' She looked at Porter, and he nodded. Obviously the two had rehearsed prior to Kerry's arrival.

Porter strode forward, unfolding his arms, and stopped halfway down the length of the table. He rested his hands on the back of a chair, peered at Kerry, and exhaled, as if it pained him to make the accusation. 'You claim to have been constrained by time, but you found the time to go home first.'

'I was still waiting for contact from my source when I went home. I'd no idea if he'd come through with information or not. I told you that beforehand, sir.'

He didn't validate her answer. 'It has come to *our* notice,' he said, using her words against her, 'that whilst you made this unscheduled visit home, you ended up arguing with your fiancé, and as a result you broke up with him. Your wedding engagement's off and you're currently no fixed abode?'

Glancing at Tinsley, Kerry got no sympathy. She concentrated on Porter instead. 'Our personal relationship isn't really any of your business.'

'It is when it affects your work,' he countered. 'Before you argue, I must remind you that your trip home was taken during a particularly busy period where you abandoned your team, forcing them to take up the slack.'

'I hardly think abandoned is the right word,' she snapped. 'Everything was under control; I delegated tasks to the more than competent members of my team, and with DS Korba overseeing them. By then I'd been on duty for a long time, and needed to go home to freshen up for what I anticipated would be many more hours on duty. I think we can all agree that my suspicions were born out. After locating, chasing and not only arresting Robson, but saving his life in the process, my day didn't end there.'

'Nobody's denying you had an eventful day,' Porter said. 'The issue that you returned home isn't what concerns us most. It's the fact that you lied about being ill. Before you deny it, I was looking for you, only to be informed you'd gone home sick. Now I trust that was your lie and not DS Korba's?'

'I told Danny I felt unwell, and I did. But I also told him I fully intended returning to work, and to call me urgently if anything came up. I bet you he told you that too?'

Again Porter chose not to confirm, doing so undermined his point.

'The thing is,' he said, with a quick glance for support from Superintendent Tinsley, 'you've had issues with your health for some time now. Is that correct?'

Kerry sat back, a knot of anger growing in her chest.

'It's not something to be ashamed of,' Porter said.

'What isn't to be ashamed of, having an upset stomach?'

'Your *other* illness,' he said.

'No. What you mean is my supposed *mental* illness. That's what this is really about. I know that Adam telephoned you, sir. Can I point out that it was immediately after we had a blazing row and he wasn't exactly my greatest fan at the time?'

'A second source corroborated Adam's concerns,' he said.

He meant Ron Dawson.

'Oh? Really? And who would that be, sir?'

'I'm not at liberty to mention the name of my source,' Porter said, and immediately grimaced, realising his *faux pas*.

She sneered. But being facetious wasn't the best move for saving her career. She opened her hands like a supplicant. 'I don't see what the problem is here. Yes, I went home with an upset stomach; yes, I broke up with my fiancé, but as soon as I had a lead on Robson I worked it, and everything turned out great in the end.'

'Everything except for your domestic arrangements,' Tinsley put in.

Kerry closed her mouth.

Since their break-up she'd lived out of her hotel room on Euston Road, but accepted it was a stopgap measure. She was still at odds with Adam: after blatantly grassing to Porter about her mental instability, she was unsure if she could ever forgive him.

Porter stood up straight, allowing his hands to fall by his sides. Tinsley also stood, straightening her uniform shirt. It was so white and unblemished it was difficult to look at. Kerry raised her gaze to Tinsley's face. The lenses of her glasses reflected the overhead lights. She gave no clue about what was coming.

Excruciatingly, Tinsley made her wait. The superintendent walked to the window and peered outside. Her office was on an upper floor of the station, and wasn't overlooked. There wasn't much of a view, just the bare brick walls of an adjacent building, and if she stood on a chair and craned far enough she might get a glimpse of St Paul's Cathedral on a bright day. Outside, rain lashed down, the promised Indian summer never having transpired. Without looking at her, Tinsley said, 'I don't think you need to be here, Inspector Darke.'

'You're suspending me, ma'am?'

'No. This is not a suspension. I'm authorizing a two weeks period of paid leave.'

Kerry shook her head.

Tinsley turned to face her. 'My decision isn't up for debate, Inspector. It's final. Full stop. Think of the time off as a period of compassionate leave, if you prefer. An opportunity to sort out your personal problems without having to worry about how it will affect your ability to do your job.'

Kerry stood. 'I've just cleared one suspect's name of murder, and arrested the conspirators who put Derrick Lewis up to shooting Nala and Bilan Ghedi. It was unfortunate Lewis died during his arrest attempt, but that was unavoidable when he chose to shoot his way out. I don't see where my supposed personal problems have affected my ability to do my job. If I hadn't been on the ball, an innocent man would've taken the rap for a double murder he didn't commit, and all those others would have got away scot free.'

Tinsley's eyes narrowed. 'When I say my decision's final, I don't expect to repeat myself. Neither do I expect to explain myself, but I will. Despite what you think, I'm actually doing this for your benefit. Charles is in agreement with me. We both feel that you've been under undue stress since Erick Swain died and need to take some time out to come to terms with what happened.'

Porter must have repeated Ron Dawson's advice to the superintendent *ad verbum*. And now Tinsley was quoting it back to her. It surprised her, because she truly had felt that Porter wouldn't be happy until she was drummed out of the station. She frowned at him, but his features remained impassive for the time being.

'I appreciate the offer,' she said, looking again at Tinsley. 'But I can't do it. I've too much to do. I have more than the Ghedi case ongoing and need to—'

'It's not an offer, Inspector Darke,' Tinsley snapped. 'It's an order. Don't make me regret my decision to take this route with you. You said you delegated tasks to your team before, and that's what you'll do now. I've already arranged cover by an acting DI to allow you to take time off, and DS Korba is fully conversant with your caseload and can help steer the ship. We will manage fine without you. I don't want to see you back here for two weeks, do you understand?'

'Yes, ma'am.' Kerry stared at her folded hands. Her gaze latched on the faint pale ring of skin where her engagement ring used to be. 'Maybe some time off will do me good,' she murmured.

'This,' said Tinsley, and gestured at the table, then the room in general, 'is between the three of us here. You don't have to worry about it appearing on your service record. As far as anyone else needs know, you requested leave and I granted it.' Tinsley raised her eyebrows, waiting for gratitude.

Kerry nodded, said, 'Yes. Only the three of us.'

As she left the office, Erick Swain followed.

Once Kerry was out of earshot, Superintendent Tinsley regarded Porter. His eyebrows rose and fell, and he shrugged.

'I don't understand why she's so adamant about protecting her source,' she said. 'How does revealing a name to us harm her?'

Before Darke's arrival at Tinsley's office, Porter had intimated his concern about the inspector's approach to the case. After Swain's untimely death, it was almost as if it had become a personal quest for her to prove the man's innocence in the shooting. Admittedly, her doggedness had gone on to prove the wider conspiracy, and secure a PR success for the Gangs and Organised Crime taskforce and the Met by association, but he couldn't shake the suspicion that there was third party motivation at play.

'All I can think of is that her source gains from her silence,' he said.

'Not a scenario I care to think about.'

The original plot to dethrone Swain was Jermaine Robson's attempt at grabbing control of a larger territory. He'd conspired with Hettie Winters to replace Swain not only as the head of a wider and more lucrative criminal empire but also in her bed. On Robson's arm, Hettie would enjoy a level of riches denied her by Swain, who was proud of his working class roots and had no intention of living the lavish lifestyle she craved. By her own admission, her relationship with Swain had been a loveless one, and she required a more attentive and virile lover: the boobs, the Botox, and all the other enhancements, hadn't been for Swain's benefit. Robson and Hettie each had a different end result in mind, but both were motivated by greed. There had to be loyal members of Swain's gang who were not party to the plan who would do anything to ensure it failed. Kerry Darke was a solid detective, not exceptional by Porter's measure only decent enough, and she couldn't work miracles. She had to have been given the key information she needed to find the fugitives — which she'd admitted to receiving through this elusive Deep Throat character — but for whose benefit? Her erratic behaviour, bordering on manic at times, meant she was under some kind of duress, but was it of her making? Was her burden of guilt not because an innocent man had died, but because she was receiving *favours* in return for her services, and was terrified of being found out? Had someone paid her to ensure the truth came out, and Robson's and Hettie's plan collapsed? With Robson and Swain out of the picture it left both their territories ripe for a take-over.

'As you know, I've talked this through with Graeme Harker...'

'Yes. I'm aware. And I thought you were jumping the gun, Charles. You began these talks with Professional Standards before Kerry's unexpected successes, though.'

'Because I'd a suspicion there was something off with her before then,' he reminded her. 'When I spoke with her that day in my office her behaviour...well, it was more than odd. Let's just say she left me feeling thoroughly creeped out. When there's a sudden shift in somebody's demeanour it often means they're struggling to contend with something.'

'Corruption, bribes?'

Porter blew air out the corners of his mouth.

'Charles,' Tinsley said, 'you were a complete bastard with her after Swain died. It's unsurprising her behaviour was off after you used her as a scapegoat. Name me any detective who'd have been any less angry at the way she was mistreated. You can't.'

'I was doing what was required at the time,' he countered, puffing out his chest.

'And I'd have done the same. I'm not criticising your actions, only pointing out that I can see why Kerry was so pissed off. At you.'

Porter deflated.

'What's Graeme's take on things?'

'Ambivalence.'

'So he's discovered nothing to say Kerry's dirty?'

'There's nothing unusual in her financial records, but that isn't to say she isn't receiving payment in cash or in some other commodity.' There were instances when he'd wondered if Kerry was high on something, and one time where he was positive she was drunk, but there was no evidence of drug or alcohol dependency. 'If she's being paid it's in hard cash she can keep under her mattress.'

'Or you're wrong and she's totally above board.'

'Yes. There is that. Except for…I don't know. There's something the matter with her. You did notice how she kept looking around, as if watching another person in the room with us? It was almost as if she was trying to convince *them* as much as us that she followed the correct course of action. I don't believe in ghosts but…' he chuckled, shook his head at the absurdity of where his mind was leading him.

'I noticed. But then again, I find it difficult holding her gaze. Perhaps I was glancing everywhere but at her too. I can easily put her behaviour down to nerves: she came in this room expecting the worst.'

'Her fiancé, Adam Gill, warned me she was on the verge of a break down. He was worried that…I don't know…she might try to harm Jermaine Robson if she got her hands on him? I think he was talking about murder.'

Tinsley snorted. 'Except that didn't happen, did it? Quite the opposite: Kerry saved Robson's life. If she intended him harm she could've let him drown. Perhaps Gill's concerns about her were as unfounded as yours are, Charles. It's like Kerry pointed out, Gill only rang you after their argument, maybe he was trying to cause trouble for her, to get back at her for dumping him.'

'He claimed her behaviour was getting out of control…and I saw evidence of it.'

'She was out of control? Were those his words or yours, Charles? Really?'

'She obviously had concerns of her own to track down her childhood psychologist,' Porter countered.

'Who promptly told you she was only coming to terms with a traumatic experience. It's why I granted her some time off, so she can do that.'

Porter spread his hands.

'So do I ask Graeme to drop his investigation into her or not?'

Tinsley went to the table and reached for a bottle of spring water. She uncapped it, and poured a measure into a glass, deep in thought. Finally she took a sip, and smacked her lips. Her gaze drifted back to Porter, and her smile quirked. 'I see no harm in keeping Graeme on her for now. Perhaps his findings will convince you she's incorruptible, after all.'

'I hope you're right,' he said, and it would have surprised Kerry to hear his sincerity.

Emotions flooded through her as Kerry took the lift down to the ground floor. But one feeling rode roughshod over the others and quelled them, totally unexpected to her. It was relief.

In hindsight, taking some time off wasn't such a bad thing. When she'd entered Superintendent Tinsley's office, she'd been prepared for the worst. She believed that disciplinary procedures would be initiated, because although she'd subsequently argued the toss with her superiors, she had been in the wrong going maverick like that and for withholding pertinent information regarding her source. Leaving the office on compassionate leave was far preferable to an actual dismissal. It was as Tinsley said, nobody but the three of them need know she hadn't requested the time off. The rumour mill would generate another opinion of course, because there were no worse gossips than coppers, but they could get on with it. The journalists chasing her for quotes and photograph opportunities might make a meal of her sudden vacation. They could speculate, but officially she was on leave and that was as far as the story could progress.

On her way down to the basement car park, she called into the GaOC office, to apprise her team of her decision to take a holiday. They weren't idiots, they knew the decision had been forced on her, but her secret was safe with them. In her private cubbyhole, she did a handover with Korba, and told her an acting DI would cover for her, but she expected him to keep things running her way. It wasn't as if she was setting off on an around the world cruise that'd take months to complete, she'd be back in a fortnight, and didn't want any interference with the way they ran their shop. She gave him a brief hug.

For a moment, Korba's eyes welled up and she thought he was going to blubber.

'Hey, what's up with you? I'll be back,' she reassured him, then gave him a gentle punch to the shoulder. 'So you'd better watch out!'

'Aah, don't mind me, boss. I'm alright.' He winked, showed her a trembling smile.

She suspected what was wrong with him. He feared her enforced break was a sign of sweeping changes to come. Hopefully he was right, but for a different reason than he was worried about.

She went down to the basement and got in her car. Only then did she turn and appraise Erick Swain seated alongside her. Sullenly, he ignored her. He'd ignored her for the past three days, moody and scowling, sometimes muttering curses under his breath. After dragging Jermaine Robson from the lake, she'd worried that he'd disappeared for good — admittedly her end game desire. Saving Robson from drowning wasn't only a moral act, or one of duty as a police officer, because there had been a part of her that wanted him to gag to death on the muddy water, but also a selfish act, one to ensure Swain remained beholden to her. If she'd forced Robson under water, to perish, Swain would have got exactly what he demanded, and she didn't trust him to deliver his side of the bargain. He'd have been off, crowing his pleasure at his enemy's demise, as he skipped towards the white light. By saving Robson, she'd kept her devil on a short leash. If Robson's eventual conviction brought justice, and with it enough satisfaction to Swain to set him free then so be it. But before then she wanted the information he'd promised.

'Stop acting like a spoilt child,' she said.

He flipped her the middle finger without looking at her.

Clucking her tongue, she started the engine and pulled the car up the ramp. It was a ten minutes journey back to her hotel. It felt much longer, accompanied by his baleful presence. After parking again, she went up to her room. When she pushed inside, and sat on the bed to pull off her shoes, Swain was already waiting, seated in the tub chair, behind which Girl had taken to standing. Not while Swain was present though, she never showed then. Kerry had wondered if Swain was even aware of her other spectral companion, as it didn't appear to be the case, and never had since the moment she helped startle him off the roof to his death. Girl though was aware of him, and cared not to share a space with him.

Undressing in front of him wasn't as humiliating as before. He'd leered at any show of nakedness at first, but familiarity was breeding contempt. When she began stripping off her work clothes, he snorted in disgust, and dropped his seething gaze to the handcuff dangling from his wrist. Two days ago, Kerry had returned to the house she'd shared with Adam, after checking first that he was out, and loaded what personal belongings she could fit in two suitcases, and brought them to the hotel room. With a lack of storage, she was living out of those suitcases. She chose fresh underwear, jeans and a T-shirt, and went in the bathroom to shower.

Swain had once threatened to torment her during her most intimate and private moments, but apparently he'd lost his appetite for it. If he could leave her alone completely, she suspected he would. Except, they were indelibly linked together. She, in one respect, had become his jailer. She showered, luxuriating in the act for the first time in ages, satisfied that she wasn't being ogled. Once dried and dressed casually, she evicted Swain from the tub chair while she dried her hair at the counter. He stood in the back corner, bottom lip working silently.

'Go and stand in the bathroom if you don't want to see me,' she commanded. 'Instead of standing there like the ugliest lampstand ever.'

'You're stuck with me.'

'Oh, so it can speak?'

'I've nothing to say to you.'

'That's good. There's nothing I want to hear from you.'

'Liar. I know why you spared that piece of dog shit's life. It's because you're afraid you'll never learn the truth about the Fell Man.'

'For having nothing to say you enjoy flapping your lips, don't you?' She switched the hairdryer to its highest setting, drowning him out.

He swept alongside her, leaning to growl directly in her ear. 'You were supposed to kill Robson.'

'No. You asked me to kill him and I told you I wouldn't.' She switched off the dryer, set it aside and turned to look up at him. His shaggy hair hung over his face, limp and dull. Even his silver earring had lost its sheen.

'You said you couldn't. Wouldn't and couldn't are two different things. I gave you the opportunity, but instead of drowning the rat you dragged him to safety.' He leaned so close she could sense his electrical discharge on the tip of her nose. She jolted from her seat, forcing him to back away.

'I've warned you about boundaries before,' she snapped, and her double meaning wasn't lost on him.

'We made a deal,' he growled.

'No. You tried to force a deal on me. And repeatedly I told you it was something I couldn't promise. I told you I'd arrest Robson and the others, and that's what I did. Well, almost all of them. Derrick Lewis died. Isn't his death enough for you?'

'His death means nothing to me.'

'He was the one who pulled the trigger. He killed that mother and child, the ones you were originally blamed for. The reason you ran and fell to your death.'

'He was Robson's puppet.'

'Robson and Hettie's puppet,' she reminded him. 'So here's a question for you, Swain: why not demand that I kill Hettie too? They were equally involved in trying to destroy you. If I were you, I'd feel more betrayed by Hettie than by a rival gangster. I mean, you'd expect something like that from Robson, but not your girlfriend.'

He stared at her. Confused.

'You have no idea why, do you?'

His mouth writhed, but he said nothing.

It occurred to Kerry that his rage was centred on Robson, as it had already existed within him in life, before she'd uncovered the truth and depth of the conspiracy against him. It was also why he couldn't raise any genuine ire towards Derrick Lewis, or any of the others. 'You have no idea why you want Robson dead, before you can move on. What do you expect will happen then?'

Again confusion reigned over him.

'He needs to die.'

'Not by my hand.' Kerry rolled up the hairdryer's cord and set it aside on a tiny corner shelf.

Swain hurtled at her, his bunched fists hammering her. She blinked in reaction, but his flurrying assaults had grown commonplace to her, and hardly surprised her any more. 'Are you finished?'

'I was only proving a point!' Swain backed off, throwing up his hands. He held them under his nose, studying them in detail. *'If I could do it, I'd kill Robson myself. But I can't even ruffle your hair! So that means you have to do it for me.'*

'And I won't. Besides, I can't. He's on remand at Belmarsh, on a high security wing, safely out of my reach. The next time we're in the same room it'll be when he appears at court.'

'You're the lead detective on his case; you can visit him in jail, doing follow up interviews or whatever the hell it is the Old Bill do. You could get at him then.'

'You've watched too many American cop shows, Swain...'

'Are you telling me you can't arrange a visit with him...bollocks! Your ex works there for fuck's sake! He can get you in. When I've been locked up before, I had plenty visits from CID after info on outstanding crimes.'

'Yeah, ordinarily I could. But the thing is, right now I'm not on duty, and won't be for a fortnight at least. I'd have no official reason to visit Belmarsh, so would be refused access.'

He sneered at the poor excuse. 'How the hell would anybody at Belmarsh know you're on leave?'

'Listen to me, Swain. You can try convincing me, but I'll save you the breath. It isn't going to happen. If I kill Robson, who do you think will end up in prison for his murder? What good will it do me to know who the Fell Man is then? You see; the deal you're offering is worthless if I'm in a cell for the next fifteen years.'

'So find a way to do it without implicating yourself.'

She clamped her lips together, gently shook her head.

Swain threw his hands in the air again, and paced back and forward. He halted, glared at her. 'If you don't kill that bastard you're stuck with me,' he snarled. 'Forever.'

'Yeah, well, that goes both ways doesn't it? You're stuck with me too. So here's the thing. You may as well tell me now what you know about the Fell Man, otherwise I'll be the one mithering you forever.' She returned his glare, and his attention switched from one different coloured iris to the other: they both held the same promise.

Abruptly he sat down on the end of the bed. He had less substance than it took to ruffle the purple comforter spread across the foot of the mattress.

She waited.

He wafted his cuffed wrist.

'Stick the TV on,' he said despondently. *'The lunchtime news is about to start.'*

His instruction came out of left field, but Kerry didn't argue. She found the remote control and turned on the power. The TV was on an adjustable bracket suspended on the wall above the multi-purpose counter. Kerry stepped back far enough so craning was unnecessary to see the screen. She flipped to a BBC channel, turned up the volume. The picture was naff, the digital image breaking up and pausing. But there was enough of a picture to make out the gist of the report: politicians animatedly debating something or other in Westminster. Kerry gave Swain a sharp look for clarity. He waited, nonplussed, then waved at the screen again.

'The picture's terrible; I'll change the channel.'

'Leave it. It won't get any better.' His proximity to the TV was affecting the local electromagnetic field, and disrupting the channel.

'What am I meant to be looking at? The bloody Muppet Show?'

'Just give it a second or two.'

The picture froze, broke up, before it flickered to a newscaster in the studio. The picture froze again, shattered into zigzags of static. Then the scene was different. It had been years since she'd been home, but the scenery was timeless. Aerial footage taken by a drone swept the length of Derwent Water, towards the town of Keswick. Looming on the near horizon was the saddle formed between Skiddaw Pike and Blencathra, two of the most recognisable North Lakes fells. It was the landscape of Kerry's childhood, before Sally vanished and she'd relocated to Carlisle with her mother. The footage segued to mountain rescue volunteers trudging up a muddy path, then to police officers in high-visibility jackets picking their way across a scrubby field in a skirmish line. The picture flicked to a morose young woman, reporting from a windswept scene, this time based in a city centre: behind the newscaster Kerry recognised the ancient clock tower of Carlisle's town hall. She couldn't make out the words on the ticker tape banner moving across the base of the TV screen, and the audio was too broken to hear clearly. But both were unnecessary. She knew what the organised search signified, and by the reporter's sombre expression it had been unsuccessful.

She glanced down at Swain.

He raised his eyebrows but said nothing.

A tingle flooded through her; dread or anticipation she couldn't decide.

'Is it *him* again?'

'*I haven't a clue.*' He raised his eyebrows, and nodded at the TV. '*What do you think, Kezza?*'

The picture on the screen abruptly froze. A young girl, eyes alive with mischief, smiled at the camera. She resembled Sally enough that a sharp blade drove through Kerry's heart. The titles accompanying the photograph brought bile to her throat.

Hunt For Second Missing Girl Intensifies.

Heavy showers had been a feature all day, and would continue. When she sat at one of the wooden picnic tables outside Euston Station, it was during one of the drier spells, although the occasional drop of rain tapped against her exposed face. She gave up the shelter of the station for the modicum of privacy outside, pulling up the hood of her duffle coat to stave off the damp chill. The weather was poor, but it didn't deter smokers who needed to feed their habits before boarding their trains home, but like Kerry, they chose their own company at other tables. The row of eateries behind her was busy, though fewer people visited the fast food kiosks arranged at the front of the station. Kerry managed to grab a coffee at one of them without queuing, but hadn't removed its lid yet. It sat untouched before her on the table. The wide expanse of paving was greasy underfoot. The ever-present pigeons pecked for crumbs, and the ever-present beggars weaved a well-trodden route between the tables, offering sob stories in exchange for cigarettes and change. Twice already Kerry had sent the same young woman packing, whose tale of having lost her purse and needing money for a ticket home was an obvious lie. Kerry wasn't cold to the young woman's sad predicament; she was simply more concerned by the plight of certain other younger girls.

Earlier, a snap decision saw her hurrying to pack a bag and rush to the station. She didn't book out of her hotel room, she needed somewhere to store her other belongings and her car while she was gone, just locked the door behind her and left without a word, and headed directly for the station. There was a direct train that could have her in Carlisle in around three and a half hours. It was scheduled to leave in another hour, no big delay, and it gave her the opportunity to catch up with messages that had backed up on her phone. Three of them were from Adam, two of them text messages asking her to ring him back, the third a voicemail message: he sounded cowed and said sorry. She was tempted to delete them all, and block his number, but she wasn't a total bitch. She'd purchased the coffee while she thought about what she'd say to him, but when she sat down at the table it was with as little appetite for a confrontation as for the sludgy black coffee.

Swain was nowhere to be seen. Neither was Girl.

She took a deep breath, and called Adam.

The phone rang a half dozen times, and she was relieved. She was about to hang up when he came on the line.

'Hiya. It's only me,' she said, needlessly. It was a phrase she used that Adam and others occasionally poked fun at, one of those northern expressions of greeting that was ingrained in her vocabulary.

'Yeah,' said Adam, and he exhaled a ragged breath. 'Thanks for ringing, Kerry.'

'What do you want?' Her voice was barely above a whisper, and she had her phone under her hood, tight to her ear — the nearest smoker was ten feet away, but still close enough to overhear.

'I, uh, hoped that we could meet to—'

'I can't.'

'Can't...or won't?'

She thought for less than two seconds. 'Can't. I'm not going to be available for a few days, maybe after that we can—'

'Shit. Kerry, look, we need to sort this now, love—'

'You sorted things when you put your oar in with Porter,' she snapped. 'You lost the bloody right to call me love.' A quick glance around showed she'd attracted no untoward attention. She silently counted to ten, calming her breathing.

'I do love you,' he said.

'You hurt me.'

'I was trying to do the right thing. Kerry, you needed help. You couldn't see it, so I—'

'Grassed me up to the chief inspector.'

'No. I reached out. I hoped if you wouldn't listen to me you'd pay more attention to your boss.'

'You expected him to be sympathetic to me?' She laughed, a harsh sound lacking humour. 'You could've had me sacked, Adam!'

'I...I didn't know what to do. I only wanted to help you. I thought that if you were pushed you'd see what I was trying to tell you, and see a doctor or something.'

'I spoke with my psychologist, as you bloody well know, and he reassured me I wasn't having a breakdown.'

It was Adam's turn to laugh scornfully. 'He made that diagnosis based on one telephone call, did he? He has no idea what I was putting up with.'

'Huh! So you were putting up with me?'

'No. Sorry. That's not what I meant. I could see how you were affected; you weren't acting yourself. You were...I don't know. Kerry, you know it yourself...you were acting crazy.'

'I was stressed, under a lot of pressure,' she reminded him, 'and your attitude wasn't helping.'

'Yeah, I know. And I'm sorry. I'm *genuinely* sorry, Kerry. You have to believe me. I was wrong calling Porter like that.'

Kerry held her breath. Thinking.

Drizzle pattered on the table. A pigeon took cover under her bent knees.

'Hopefully now you've solved the case, things will get better,' Adam put forward. 'I was hoping we could meet, talk this through and, well, you know, put it behind us?'

'I haven't solved the case yet.'

'Sorry. I thought that—'

'I'm not talking about the shooting of the Ghedis.'

'Oh.' He knew exactly whose case she meant.

'He hasn't left me, Adam,' she whispered.

'Who? Erick Swain?' She could hear the disappointment in his voice, and it wasn't because he believed a dead gangster was haunting her. 'Jesus, Kerry, I thought with you catching Robson things would have ended there.'

'Aye, well so did I.'

'You're still hallucinating him?'

'Until you accept there's more to my visions than hallucinations, we can't move on, Adam. Can't you understand that?'

'Jesus, yeah, I hear you. But you have to see things from my point of view, Kerry. I don't believe in ghosts and all that rubbish, I just can't.'

'See, that's the problem. It's rubbish, only because you haven't experienced it. How about seeing things from my side for a change?'

'Look, I believe that *you* believe, but...'

'It's still rubbish?'

'Yes. No. I believe you're seeing Swain, but I think there has to be another explanation for it. Something more...logical.'

'Logic doesn't explain the ineffable,' she told him, though he had no grasp of the term – in fairness, she'd never heard it used before Elias Price mentioned it either. 'What I mean is that sometimes you have to trust your instincts, Adam. I can't prove Swain's real, the way I can prove a person's guilt in court. But I can still feel when it's genuine. Swain is visiting me, in fact it's worse. He's here all the time now. And he won't leave until I give him what he wants.'

'But you already arrested that bastard. He's here in Belmarsh. You told me that once you caught Robson, Swain would give you what you wanted and it'd be over.'

'Robson's imprisonment isn't enough for Swain.'

'No, I know what you said before. You told me he wanted him dead.'

Kerry said nothing.

'You really think it's going to take Robson's death before...' he let the suggestion go.

'I'd never do it. You should know me better than that, Adam.'

'I know. I do...but you'll be stuck with Swain until Robson dies? Jesus Christ!'

'Our relationship has changed.'

'You can say that again, I—'

Kerry laughed. This time her voice held a little music. 'I meant mine and Swain's,' she said. 'I've set some boundaries, as Elias Price advised me to, and it's working. Swain doesn't have the same hold over me as before. He does as I say.'

'So he told you what you wanted to hear?'

'He still prefers playing games. He hasn't come clean, but he has suggested I go home.'

His voice raised an octave. 'You're coming home? Good. That's great, I'll come and help you with your stuff if you want?'

'*Home*-home,' she said, 'as in home to Cumbria.'

It was Adam's turn to say nothing.

'It isn't a permanent move,' she told him. 'It's just for a few days. There's something I need to check on, and I can't do it here. Once I get back we can, well, maybe we can talk and...well, if you'd like to we can try again?'

'And will this business with Swain be finished then?'

'I can't promise that,' she admitted.

'Maybe I can make things better.' It was a change from his parting shot the last time they argued, when he claimed he couldn't live his life like that. How he couldn't handle her obsession with the dead.

'I hope so,' she said, and she meant it.

After that, more words became difficult. Kerry felt choked. She made an excuse she had to run, and she ended the call even as he mumbled a reluctant goodbye.

Her coffee was still hot but was as unappetizing as before. She binned it on the way into the station, and checked the huge digital timetable overhead. Her train was at a platform, currently boarding. She joined the rush of humanity as they raced for the best available seats.

Less than five hours later, Kerry stood under the same town hall clock she'd seen on the lunchtime news, toting her overnight bag and a fresh take-out coffee and muffin from a shop behind her. It was early evening, already dark, and the wide expanse of red brick that formed the pedestrianized town centre was empty but for a few club-footed pigeons late to roost. They pecked at imaginary crumbs at the base of a 17th century market cross on a stepped dais about fifty feet away. Aside from a couple of coffee shops, the city centre stores had closed, all the shoppers had gone home, and it was still too early on a Tuesday evening for the nearby pubs and bars to fill up. The scene was achingly familiar, but held little in the way of nostalgia. As a young teen she'd hung out with her friends at the base of the market cross, a hub from which the town could be viewed, and where the girls could eye up the boys. When she was a uniformed constable the city centre formed part of her beat, and she spent many long hours patrolling up and down the main strip, chasing shoplifters during the day and boisterous revellers at night. The incidents she'd dealt with were too numerous to single one out, and certainly none with a twinge of affection.

When moving from country to town, she'd at first been overwhelmed by urban life, and had thought Carlisle a massive metropolis. Coming home from a true metropolis, she saw how small and contained Carlisle actually was. It was a large town really, given city status by virtue of its —admittedly impressive — cathedral. Few people she'd met in London could pinpoint Carlisle on a map, thinking it Welsh, and her accent that of a

Geordie. Like many people from northern Cumbria Kerry was proud of her heritage and fiercely patriotic, or at least she was until disembarking the train about half an hour ago at Carlisle's Citadel Station. She'd felt like a stranger.

Twenty minutes before that, her train had stopped briefly at Penrith station. It was too dark, and her view blocked by the station buildings, to see the crumbling castle beyond. The events that had shaped her life since began that day at the ruins. She averted her face and closed her eyes until she felt the train move on, and the catalyst of her life's quest was behind her. It wasn't an attempt at blocking her memories, but in replaying them – she wanted them untainted by what she might see now if she looked. In her mind she was an eight-year-old tomboy, in ill-fitting wellington boots, drenched under a teaming downpour while her mam bleated in panic at a railway employee. Puttering past, a battered old Land Rover coughed blue diesel smoke, and watched by the ghost of one of his previous victims its bearded driver grinned at Kerry, displaying the yellow tusks of an ogre…or bogeyman?

Shaking that image had proven difficult, and it stayed with her until she arrived at Carlisle and walked to the coffee shop where her mind had gone to the need for sustenance. She sipped her steaming brew under the town hall clock, realising her haste to reach home had thrown stumbling blocks in her way. What should she do now and where the bloody hell should she start? She'd nowhere to stay and no transportation: both needed rectifying. Siobhan lived less than a mile away, on a housing estate in the town's west end. She had no compunction of visiting her mam, let alone staying with her. Ideally, it would be better if she could be gone again from town before her mother heard, unless she had news Siobhan needed to hear.

Being a local, Kerry had never stayed at any hotel in her hometown, but she knew of many. She strolled to the market cross and sat on one of the time worn steps, scrolling through her options on a phone app while she finished her coffee, and ate the moist but almost tasteless muffin. In the end she booked a room at a bed and breakfast a short walk from where she sat, chosen because it was located a few hundred metres from a car rental business. Her stop in Carlisle was only fleeting, and she needed to be mobile again at first order.

She was wakened by a sense of being watched. As she stirred, in unfamiliar surroundings, it took a moment to get her bearings, and she sat up blearily, startling away the shadow looming alongside her bed. It didn't matter that Girl had become a permanent presence throughout her childhood and early teens, she could still be perturbed by the ethereal figure when waking and finding it so close. It made her wonder too, just how near to her Girl got when she was asleep. Did she regularly stand over her, observing her when she was unaware, studying her? Did she ever sit on the bed next to her, or even slip under the sheets, seeking comfort and companionship? During her waking moments she'd caught glimpses of Girl slipping from sight before, but never from this close. Kerry trembled and had no idea why.

She left the bedside lamp off. There was no need for it. The B&B was situated alongside a well-lit main route into town, and there was enough ambient light streaming in through the thin curtains to see by. Kerry kept her head tilted to one side, using her peripheral vision to search for Girl. The darkness in one corner of the room was clotted, and she could make out an amorphous shape in the gloom. Resisting the temptation to view her directly, Kerry settled her vision dead ahead, then allowed it to unfocus. Girl's shape coalesced.

'How does it feel to be home?' Kerry whispered, conscious of the thin walls and other guests sleeping only a few feet away.

Girl's head raised a fraction, and there was something quizzical about her reaction.

'I assume you're originally from Cumbria,' Kerry went on. 'It's where you first showed yourself to me.'

The only response was a slight tilting of Girl's head. Desperately Kerry wanted to look directly at her. But she kept her gaze averted. She sat in the bed, holding the duvet cover over her chest. Nonthreatening. Nonjudgemental. 'It was you who led me back here, wasn't it? Not Swain. You showed yourself immediately after Bilan Ghedi was shot, before Swain died. You came to me then because you knew what was happening again here, and you needed to get my attention because other girls were in danger.'

Girl neither confirmed nor disagreed. She only stood, face draped with straggly hair. Foggy, indistinct, out of focus, there was still something about Girl that struck Kerry. Movement is easiest observed in the periphery, an inherited trait from when early humans were prey animals. Without concentrating on her, Kerry could spot the workings of Girl's fingers as she clutched and released her shapeless dress. It was the nervous fidgeting of a guilty child caught with crumbs on their lips beside an empty biscuit barrel.

'I wish you could talk to me. If only you could speak I might've stopped this from happening now. I might have stopped these girls being taken.'

Shamed, Girl's head dropped.

'I'm not blaming you, Girl. None of this is your fault. Maybe nothing could've been changed to stop that. The main thing is we are here now, and hopefully we're not too late to stop him doing it again.'

Girl's head rose. It was at Kerry's use of the collective word: we. Her clutching hands released her dirty dress. She took a tentative step forward, and Kerry glanced at her. For the briefest instant she could see Girl's smile, and then she froze and was gone.

'Speaking to yourself, Kezza? It's the first sign of going crazy, you know?'

Coughing in scorn, her attention snapped on her unwelcome companion. Erick Swain wasn't averse to being viewed head on. In fact, he demanded attention. He stood at the foot of the bed, his arms crossed, the handcuff dangling. He was translucent, but his internal glow ensured he was picked out against the dim background. He curled up his mouth at one side. Kerry clutched the duvet tighter to her chest.

'You don't have a monopoly on my madness,' she snapped. 'It's the middle of the night, get out of here and scare some stray cats or something.'

He shrugged at the suggestion, then stroked his goatee in contemplation. *'Interesting that you should say that. Certain cats do act as if they're aware of my presence. Not dogs though. They don't know I'm there. Well, I can only speak for Tyke. He had no idea when I went to see him.'*

'You visited your dog? When?'

'After I asked you to make sure he went to a good home. Did finding Robson in Battersea give you the idea or what?'

She wouldn't lie. She'd taken no part in rehousing his Border collie. 'Until Hettie's been to court we can't rehome Tyke,' she said. 'So DS Korba arranged for him to stay at the dogs home in the meantime. He'll be well looked after for now.'

'Good ol' Zorba the Greek. I knew he was a dog man that time he fussed with Tyke in the garden. Next time you see him, tell him thanks from me. I didn't want Tyke going to any of Hettie's lot.'

'Do you know something, Swain. That's possibly the first sign of humanity you've ever shown. It's a shame you had to wait until after you were dead.'

His mouth flickered a smile. He lowered his arms, tucked a thumb in his waistband. Said nothing.

'How do you suggest I tell Danny thanks from you? Don't you think that could be tricky?'

'Korba doesn't judge you. You already told him about seeing me, and he didn't jump to the same conclusion as Adam did.'

'You're right. He didn't think I was going crazy, but that would change if I tried conveying messages from you to him. I value his friendship too much to risk it.'

'Tell him you channelled me through a Ouija board, and I spelled out that he was a dog man and not a pussy like I first thought.'

'You had to go and spoil the moment,' she said with a shake of her head. It was faintly annoying that his words had amused her. 'Any way, you didn't follow me all the way here to talk about your dog.'

'Where else did you expect me to be? I told you, Kezza, you're stuck with me. I'm the jelly in your doughnut, as the Yanks would say.'

'More like the pain in my arse.'

'Tetchy!'

'I'm like that when my sleep gets disturbed. Was there something you wanted, or can I get back to sleep now?'

'I wasn't the one nattering to myself. That was quite a discussion you had going with yourself, girl. Then you said you wished I could talk to you. Remember?'

A jolt went through her. Her conversation had been one-sided, and Swain had taken her reference to Girl as being aimed at her. Proof positive that he and Girl existed on different planes, and he was unaware of her. Not so Girl, she had sensed Swain before he showed.

'I wasn't speaking to you. I was...thinking out loud. How much did you hear anyway?'

'Ah!' He waved away her concern. *'Not much. Just some self-pitying shit. Then about the main thing being we're here now...'* He paused in thought. *'What were you on about when you said it's not too late to for us to stop him doing it again?'*

She didn't correct his misassumption. Let him believe she had referred to him. Maybe it would help loosen his tongue about what mattered if he thought they were a team. 'He's back,' she said. 'The Fell Man. He's taken more little girls.'

His shoulders jerked, nonplussed.

'You don't care that he's doing God-knows-what to more children?'

'All I care about is seeing Robson's corpse. I thought I'd made that clear enough.'

'Oh, you did. And then I thought I saw a spark of humanity in you, when you needed to visit your dog to check he was OK. But I see now that was a blip. We're talking about children, Swain! Little kids, being brutalised by a monster. How can you shrug it off as if it's nothing? You once told me you hated nonces, well why protect this one?'

'Who said I'm protecting him? Fuck the Fell Man. And fuck those little kids. Everybody I ever knew was a kid once and look at how they turned out!'

'You are such a prick,' she snarled. 'Get out of here and leave me alone if you don't want to help.'

He folded his arms again, set his tongue in his bottom lip as he considered. *'You know, maybe I will leave you to it. See how you get on without my help, while I do something for myself for a change...'*

'Yeah. Please do. See how you get on. Let's see who needs who most in this arrangement.'

After a moment, he grunted. *'OK, then. If it means I have to prove a point, I'll tell you this...'*

She stared at him.

'You saw him,' he said.

'What?'

'You saw him. That bloke who looked like Catweazle.' Kerry was too young to get the pop reference. *'The scruffy geezer with the beard down to here,'* he reiterated, while touching his chest.

'You mean the man in the Land Rover, the one that grinned at me after Sally went missing?'

'*Talk about asking the obvious.*' Swain sneered. '*I said once before you were a bit slow on the uptake, Kezza, but you need a bomb up your arse to get you into gear. Yes, I mean the creepy paedo in the Land Rover. But don't you remember...you saw him near Penrith castle, but that wasn't the first time you saw him, was it?*'

Wasn't it?

'*Think about it, Kezza,*' Swain said. '*You've known all along where to find him. You saw him, and he saw you and your sister, and that's where he fixated on Sally. He wasn't at that castle by chance: where do you suppose he followed you from?*'

And he was correct. She did know. Her heart stuttered in her chest, and her throat almost pinched shut. She'd known since she was eight years old where the Fell Man made his lair!

And with her shocking epiphany, Swain flickered out of existence like a doused flame.

Kerry drove west under leaden skies. She passed the immense sandstone edifice that was Carlisle's historic Norman castle, and over the River Caldew, a source of some of the major flooding in Carlisle a few years back when Storm Desmond brought havoc to the region. Continuing west, she bypassed her old neighbourhood, and didn't feel a twinge of regret for missing a visit with her mam. She passed her old secondary school, and experienced a worse sense of loss for it than her mother. The school she attended had been demolished, and a brand spanking, wood-cladded monstrosity built in its place. The school wasn't the only major change she spotted. A northern by-pass to the M6 motorway had opened since last she was home, and a huge roundabout sat astride the boundary of town and country, where she only remembered green fields. Everything looked familiar, but *different*. She felt similarly, because after her sudden recollection that morning, she was a different person too.

The instant she remembered her first encounter with the Fell Man, Erick Swain had blinked out of existence. It was as if she didn't need him anymore and so he *left*. Perhaps remembering was all it took to release his lingering spirit, and he'd gone to wherever he belonged — that was if she still accepted Elias Price's assertion that spirits were real and wandered among the living. Now it was easy to be doubtful again. The more likely explanation was that he'd been a manifestation of her subconscious all along — a coping mechanism as Doctor Ron had assured her — and with her sudden epiphany his usefulness was at an end. In hindsight, Swain hadn't solved the shooting case for her, and she could even convince herself now that it was her own intuition that had led her to the warehouse where Funky and the other fugitives had taken cover. She was a DI with the

Gangs and Organised Crime taskforce; she'd bet that she'd read somewhere in the intelligence they'd gathered on the Nine Elms Crew about the warehouse. So too the Power House, where she'd tracked Jermaine Robson to. It was a known hangout of his and perhaps it was a lucky guess and a large coincidence that he'd chosen to hide at the derelict gym. Even coming home to Cumbria needn't have been through supernatural guidance, but a combination of being at a loose end and viewing the news report concerning the missing girls. At times it might appear he'd led her to decisions and conclusions, but that could easily be explained too: like Swain said, in his colourful fashion, sometimes she took a moment or two to catch on to what her mind had already shown her. What about the disturbances of the air, and the faint electrical discharge she sometimes experienced when he was around? They were psychosomatic, her brain causing physical bodily sensations to the uncanny and illogical nature of his appearances to her; surely anybody would sense a similar skin-crawling response to something menacing that defied explanation.

No, she thought, just stop. Stop pretending!

She had barefaced lied to Elias Price about her gift to communicate with the dead — he could call it a psychic ability, if he chose, but to her it had always been less of a super sense than something intrinsic to her being, as if her brain had been wired up differently. Growing up on a farm, she'd understood the nature of death at an earlier age than most other kids. From the age of four she could associate the sausages at breakfast with the pigs she'd helped feed in their pens, and the roast on Sundays with the lambs last seen gambolling in the fields. It was difficult to miss when her dad went out to the barn to slaughter their next meal. So, at age five, when Grandma Betty had visited her in her bedroom, she could also associate her with the frail old lady she'd last seen sitting in an overheated room in a nearby hospice. She understood that Grandma Betty was there in spirit, while her corporeal form lay devoid of any spark of life in the funeral parlour Siobhan had entrusted her to. After Grandma's visitation she saw other spirits, ghosts, spectres, and could differentiate them from her imaginary friends deliberately conjured to block them out. Yes, from an early age she'd understood the truth of those apparitions, because in each instance every last one of them had wanted something from her, whether it was to impart a message to a loved one on the earthly plane, or to complete some mundane task left undone. Even Grandma Betty had wanted something from her, albeit only the parting gift of the kiss Kerry refused her at the hospice when she'd shied away from Grandma's parchment thin lips and sour smell.

Girl was the anomaly. She wanted something too, but she'd never given a hint what it was. She was the flipside to Eric Swain's bent penny.

Kerry had almost completed a full cycle. From wondrous belief to acceptance, apathy to ignorant bliss, through disbelief. Now she was on the verge of acceptance once more albeit without the fuzzy comfort of wonder or awe. Those were never feelings that Swain had engendered in her. She felt no sense of abandonment after Swain vanished. Good riddance to old rubbish. She didn't need him now, dropping hints alongside racial insults and misogynistic remarks — not to mention unthinkable demands — and it was good to be free of him at last, a genuine relief that left her almost lightheaded.

The epiphany had also left her jittery with anxiety.

Recalling where she'd last seen the Fell Man didn't mean she'd find him there now, decades later. Nor did it mean he'd taken the girls he'd recently snatched back to his historical lair. He could have gone anywhere with them, and she might never find them.

She cursed under her breath. Doubt was not helpful.

Earlier, while waiting for the car rental office to open, she'd wolfed down a full English breakfast. She'd shared the small dining room at the B&B with some other early risers, and though she'd sat alone, she'd eavesdropped their conversations. They spoke in sombre tones of the two missing children, but there were also hints of subdued rage and even indignation in their remarks. Everyone had an opinion when it came to the abduction of children, and rightly so, but often it was misguided. More than once, Kerry heard the parents being blamed. That equated to Siobhan being blamed for the time when Sally was snatched from under her nose, and unfair. Kerry didn't interact with the other guests; instead she sought out a newspaper from the evening before.

The first girl, Hayley McGhee, nine-years-old, had been missing for the best part of ten days — just before Girl had shown herself to Kerry on Wandsworth Road — and Courtney Bell, ten-years-old, for two. The terrible truth was that it was probably too late for Hayley. She suspected her usefulness to the Fell Man had ended prior to him choosing Courtney as his next victim. Was it too late to help Courtney, though? How long did the abductor hold each girl before he tired of her and moved to the next? Years ago, when first he'd been active, his crime spree had spanned less than six months. Including Sally, he was suspected in the abduction of seven girls, which averaged out at one girl every four weeks: if Hayley and Courtney were victims of the same beast, then he'd upped his timescale. The awful likelihood was that the girls didn't survive long before the urge to grab another victim grew too strong to resist. Similar patterns were seen in serial murder cases, where a spree that began slowly escalated towards the end. It was usually when the killer had been consumed by their need to kill that they grew reckless in their over-confidence, and were caught. If the Fell Man was reaching this accelerated state, then who knew how many children were in immediate danger? It might be too late to help Courtney, and sadly most probably for Hayley, but Kerry owed every girl, past, present and future that the Fell Man targeted.

A weather front pushed in from the Solway Firth, funnelled inland by the converging coastlines of Scotland and England. Drizzle smeared the car's windscreen, growing heavier by the minute. She could see nothing of the Lake District; low-lying clouds blanketed even the nearest fells. Huge wind turbines were indistinct giants moving in the murk. They were recent additions to the terrain, another change to the landscape of her youth. The climb grew sheer as she pushed the car up towards Caldbeck. Beyond the village, she followed a single-track road up and onto the moor. The clouds settled around her. Somewhere to her right was Knott, the highest point of an area known locally as the Back O' Skiddaw, and to anyone else as the back of beyond. It was a wild region of barren moorland north of Skiddaw Pike and Blencathra, rarely frequented by the tourists and hill walkers who flooded the more picturesque fells to the south and west.

The road deteriorated the further she progressed, the tarmac pot-holed and crumbling at the verges into deep ruts made by the tyres of tractors and 4x4's. Meeting another vehicle coming the other direction could be problematic, but it appeared she had the fells to herself. She slowed though, because if she drove off the road, the hire car would be mired to the axles in the boggy earth. Coming this way was a bad idea; she should have taken the motorway down to Penrith, and cut across the A66, then turned north again up past Mungrisdale where the roads were better maintained. Both routes converged near the small tarn above which Siobhan had taken the girls on their picnic before going to collect Dad from the train station. Their picnic had been off the beaten path, but to be fair, less than a mile from their family farm near the valley where the Caldew snaked off the fells towards Carlisle.

Back when she was a kid, living on the farm, mobile phone technology was in its infancy, and poorer people like Siobhan and Gary Darke didn't waste money on unnecessary luxuries. Kerry had no idea if her modern smart phone would work up here or if she was in a telecommunications black hole. She slowed, and stopped at a spot where the road widened as it swept around a bend. Thankfully, and surprisingly, her phone had a solid signal. She'd received a number of text messages, but had no time for them now. Comforted that she could call in reinforcements if needed, she slipped the car into gear and it crawled on again, observed by a flock of sturdy sheep that eyed her with an inquisitiveness that bordered on sinister.

On a clear day, the sweeping view from the fells extended eastward to the North Pennines. But as she crested the highest point of the road and began the long descent towards Mungrisdale a sea of mist swallowed the landscape beyond fifty metres. The drizzle intensified, smearing the view even more. Kerry almost missed the turn off onto the higher fell, and had to reverse before making the tight turn. As she ascended the hill, she recalled the last time she'd descended it, and an inane conversation with Sally and Mam about their Christmas wish lists. Mid-way up, she found where her mam had pulled into the field where she'd laid out their picnic blanket. The ancient gateposts, weathered and pitted with algae growth, had toppled and a spill of dry-stone walling had cascaded across the verge. Deep tractor ruts between the collapsed posts were full of muddy water. She parked on the verge below the rock fall, and stepped out onto the gravel track. Her shoes weren't fit for the terrain or the weather, but thank God she'd brought her duffle coat. She fastened the toggles up to her throat and pulled up her hood. Drizzle pattered on her face and exposed hands. She turned her back to the breeze, but it didn't help: the misty rain enveloped her. Shoving her hands in her coat pockets, she bit her bottom lip and accepted her lot.

She could have driven up and around the hill, through the forest to where Brandreth House squatted alongside a pond at the epicentre of a depression between the surrounding peaks. Doing so would announce her presence. Even walking, she could attract attention if she approached from the front of the house. She picked her way over the deep muddy ruts, balancing with one hand on a toppled gatepost, and stepped into the field of yellow couch grass. It had been years since sheep had grazed there, and the scrubby moorland grass and gorse had reclaimed the hillside. Further up, amorphous blotches in the mist, the wind-sculpted trees were knitted denser than she remembered, but then she was taller now than the Kerry who'd scurried among them, playing chase with Sally, decades ago.

And she also remembered another girl who might have stood among them, waving sadly after them as she chased Sally down the hill, and the bearded figure that'd clamped an arm around her and dragged her backwards into the gloom.

She was soaked to the knees by the time she made it under the stunted trees. Her shoes were ruined, and her socks were fit for a bin. The thick woollen duffel coat kept off most of the rain and chill, but her face still felt slick. Periodically she licked and spat moisture from her lips. Stooping, she wound her way between gnarly trunks, but limbs as twisted as goblins' fingers snatched at her hood and tried to wrench it back. Occasionally, she could only progress on hands and knees, until she found spaces where she could crouch under the low canopy. Despite the discomfort, the trees offered cover as she approached Brandreth House, and the mist added to it. Almost, she felt like a disembodied soul traversing a spectral landscape: she was almost invisible.

But the same could be said of an assailant who could creep up on her under the thatch of limbs. Her gaze darted back and forward, expecting the worst, and her earlier anxiety manifested as a distinctive trembling at her core. Her heart thundered. It was an effort to shake the foreboding fear that she was under a predator's scrutiny, but what were the chances that the Fell Man crept around under those trees at any time, except for when pursuing an escapee? She sucked up the fear, used it to fuel her instead, and pressed on.

At the edge of the copse, she squatted, forearms on her knees. The trees ended at the top of a gorse-covered slope dotted with half-buried boulders covered in moss. At the base of the decline was a steep-sided beck, the stream's water brackish as it wended around other boulders dislodged from the hillside millennia ago. More trees crowded the large house in the natural amphitheatre below, most taller and sturdier than those she'd crawled through, having been planted in the distant past when the house was still loved. Other trees had fallen, some tearing up the roots, and made a crosshatch of the woodland. Wild shrubs and bushes colonised the original gardens, and also the yard and outbuildings around the larger structure. Impenetrable bramble patches surrounded the rear of the house, and also cut off approach from the far bank of the stream.

Just beyond the trees there was a hint of an expanse of sluggish water, but the mist made it difficult to tell how far it stretched. Kerry knew that the topography dictated the pond's dimensions, and the shale-covered slope on the far side was less than a hundred metres beyond the house so it was not an endless sea.

All of those extraneous details were distractions. She ignored the surroundings in favour of studying the house. It was better described as a ruin. Twenty-or-so years ago it had been decrepit, now it had been forgotten entirely, abandoned to be reclaimed by nature, dragged down into the boggy earth that surrounded it. The huge slate roof had sunk at the centre, pulled down by sagging walls, and a chimneystack had collapsed years ago, the pile of rubble now scattered across the yard was overgrown with weeds and bramble. Barely a window held a sliver of glass, and a door on the near side was bloated with rot. If not for two details, she would have conceded defeat and accepted her memory was possibly as misguided as her belief in ghosts.

At a crouch she scurried down slope, and to the left, where she'd to push through a patch of discoloured gorse. The beck was only a few feet wide, and the boulders offered stepping-stones, so it wasn't an insurmountable barrier. She crossed tentatively, her shoes struggling to find purchase on the slick moss. When she was across, she went ankle deep in mud that stank of decomposing vegetation. Gagging down her revulsion, Kerry used other rocks and exposed roots as steps to help clamber up the bank between two straggling thickets of bramble. Thorns caught at her jeans, and her coat. But she made it through and onto a path almost as muddy as the edge of the beck. Each footfall sank a few inches, and sucked free. There were faint marks in the mud that might have been tyre tracks, but who knew how old they were? She angled off the path and into waist deep couch grass, hopping from one tussock to the next, as she moved towards the side of the house and its bulging door.

She paused to study one of the details she'd spotted from on the hillside. It was an old Land Rover, well past its mechanical prime more than two decades ago, and now was a hunk of rusty scrap metal. Its tyres had perished, split open, and the heavy vehicle had sunk down to the corroded metal wheel hubs, which had become buried in the encroaching morass. Brambles engulfed the rear of the Land Rover, and the cab and engine compartment spouted coarse grasses and even the limbs of a straggly bush that had put down roots in the void under the passenger seat. Only rusty springs were left of the seats themselves, and the dash was bloated and cracked, leaking puss-coloured foam. The unmistakable stench of rat urine wafted from the partially buried vehicle. Despite the passage of time, and the effects of atrophy, she could still equate the Land Rover with the one that puttered past her after Sally vanished. She could almost picture a face turned to hers from the driving seat, bearded and grinning in sarcastic triumph. Sally had been concealed in the back, and Girl had tried to warn her, but the last Siobhan had wanted to hear about was another of Kerry's imaginary friends when she was frantic to find her other daughter. She turned away from it; it was too easy imagining Sally's terror as she rode in it to whatever horrific fate the Fell Man planned.

The wreck confirmed she'd found the Fell Man's lair, but the second detail told her more. Despite the apparent abandonment of Brandreth House, part of it was still in use. The second detail that brought her off the hill wasn't something she'd spotted but heard. Up on the hillside the drizzle had made it difficult to differentiate but closer to the house, she could distinguish the continuous thrum of a motor from the rain pattering through branches. There was no hint of occupation otherwise, no newer car parked nearby that she could see, no lights visible within, but someone made the crumbling mansion their den.

Crouching alongside the Land Rover Kerry felt for her phone.

But it was too soon to call the police.

She needed evidence that the house was a crime scene first. Even the presence of the Land Rover wasn't absolute proof that the Fell Man had ever used the place; in all likelihood there could be other old cars of a similar make and model to be found abandoned in farmyards all across the fells.

A minute or two more, and she would call the police.

That was all it would take to confirm she'd discovered *his* lair, if she shook off the bloody nerves and took a closer look.

Her motivation for coming to the house had changed. Once she wanted answers, closure, but now if there were any hope at all for saving Hayley or Courtney, she'd take the risk. Yet something held her back, and it was the unholy terror of an eight-year-old girl rather than a detective inspector. The devil of her past was more terrifying than the one she'd allied with recently. Erick Swain had been a kitten by comparison. She groped for her phone, but her hand drew away from it. She slowly extended her fingers to her side, and was relieved when the indistinct figure in her periphery didn't melt away from them.

Girl was there beside her.

Girl reached out insubstantial fingers and touched hers. Her touch was like the flutter of a moth's wings against Kerry's skin, and then Girl withdrew her hand once more. Kerry desperately wanted to look at her, to thank her for the support, but she wasn't allowed. Yet it was enough that Girl had drawn close, and made the brief connection for the first time ever, to get her moving again. She rose quickly, and jogged for the house before she lost her nerve. Girl flitted behind her.

'Is this it?' Kerry whispered under her breath. 'What you've wanted to show me all these years? Oh, God! I wish I'd paid more attention to you back then, and tried harder to get my mother to listen when you showed me who'd taken Sally.'

She got no reply, but didn't require one. Girl wanted her to enter the house, otherwise why accompany her as close as her shadow? When she headed for the rotting door, Girl moved around her and was on her left, and she shook her straggly hair, violently enough for Kerry to catch her meaning and move ahead. She picked a route through thorny tendrils, and stepped over a collapsed wall almost obscured by undergrowth, and into the original front garden. For a moment the drizzle became rain, and it battered down, drumming on her hood. She could hear nothing else, and it wasn't easy to see beyond the length of her probing hands, and Girl was little more than a distorted image at her shoulder.

A window on the ground floor was open to the elements. Jagged teeth of glass clung to crumbling putty in disintegrating frames. Taking a peek inside, Kerry found a room blighted by the elements. The floor, rotted carpet and all, had given way, and the ceiling had collapsed. Huge chunks of plaster had blown from the walls exposing rotting laths like the ribs of a decomposing corpse. Miraculously the flowery pattern on ancient wallpaper could still be made out on some of the fallen plaster. Mould and fungi colonies decorated the corners, and the rags of curtains were black with mildew. The room was a Petri dish seething with cultivated life. She could almost imagine the spores invading her lungs and becoming insidious growths: no way would she enter the house via that room.

It had never been Girl's intention. She bent at the waist, nodding at the main portal at the front of the house. Kerry gritted her teeth. However, she moved for the door. Once the house had been grand, and the main entrance was fitting. It boasted a huge recessed door, with thick sandstone pillars to each side. The steps up to the door were worn, and green with algae, and the door looked as if it hadn't been opened in half a century. A paved path led from door to garden, to a grand gate where a carriage once might have arrived to collect the landowners, but was now caged in by tree limbs and bushes. The paving stones were all warped and cracked and pushed askew by tree roots. It was doubtful that the Fell Man gained entrance to his lair via that route, which was probably why Girl urged her to enter that way.

She reached for the door handle, a large circular brass knob green with verdigris. It moved half an inch to either side, but that was the extent. Kerry didn't hear the latch disengaging, only a faint squeal of rusty metal. She was about to give up on it, but gave the knob a brisk shove. The door moved inward a finger's width. Setting her shoulder to the door, she gripped the handle with both hands and leaned her weight against the wood. The door shifted another few inches. It was unlocked. She could throw her weight against it and force the door wide, but the noise might bring unwanted attention. She planted her feet, and controlling its swing by gripping the handle, she bore her weight against the door again, and it moved another hand's breadth before jamming against something inside. Kerry stepped away, studying the gap, and then took a lingering check around to ensure she hadn't been observed. The rain continued to drum down, but it was the only sound, there wasn't even a hint of the wildlife that must live in the woods and the building blocked the thrumming sound she'd heard earlier.

She was reasonably sure she'd made it this far unobserved, but wasn't confident about going inside. Once within the building she'd be trapped, with nowhere to run.

Why are you thinking of running away?

The thought was hers, not the taunting of Swain she'd grown used to.

You've been waiting to do this for years. Don't turn back now, Kerry.

Girl remained by her side. She was still and silent, but her presence helped Kerry force a little steel into her spine. Everything had led to this moment. If she ran away out of fear…well, how would she ever reconcile with that? Decision made, she pulled back her hood and forced her left shoulder into the gap between the door and the jamb. It was a squeeze, and her duffel coat wrenched around uncomfortably as she shoved forward. The door shifted another few inches, and she forced her head and left arm inside. Grabbing hold of the door handles inside and out, she lifted and pushed at the same time, walking the door open. The process was too noisy, detritus on the floor scraping and the door groaning. She halted to listen for a response. From within she could distinguish the mechanical thrum again, intervening walls and distance muffled it, but that was all. She pushed into what was once a reception vestibule, but was now the receptacle of a fallen ceiling. It was broken chunks of plaster that had jammed the door from opening all the way. The floor wasn't completely blocked though, and a door about two metres away stood open, hanging awry on a broken hinge. She crept forward, and peered into a hallway dimly lit by holes in the roof two floors above. Water flowed freely down the walls, and dripped from numerous places overhead. The place stank of stagnant water, mildew and rats. Kerry wrapped a palm over her mouth and nostrils.

As a copper, she'd had the displeasure of entering many horrible dwellings before, but this ranked up there among the worst of them. Her opinion wasn't swayed when she moved into the hall and the floorboards sagged underfoot. Only a threadbare carpet supported her weight. She kept to the edge of the floor, where the joists were at their strongest, and moved to the foot of a set of stairs. They looked sketchy, some of them already having fallen away, and the bannister leaned outward in places. At a half landing a broken window let in rain, and even crawling vines and brambles from outside. She'd no intention of going up for a closer look. She turned to her right and glanced into the room she'd peered into from outside. Nothing there she wanted to see or touch, so she moved on. And spotted the unusual.

A batch of electrical cables snaked along the floor, some bright orange, others black or white. Every few metres, they'd been cinched together with plastic ties. They were reasonably modern, and untouched by the filth surrounding them. She noted where the cables swept up the wall, and over the bannister of the half landing, continuing up and out of sight on the uppermost floor. The other end continued along the hall and through another door. It led into what was once a kitchen. The room was a wreck like every other she'd seen, but some of the junk and fallen plaster had been moved aside to allow clear passage. Empty bottles littered a counter, alongside fast food cartons and cereal boxes, most of them as scabrous as their surroundings, but some newer. The cables disappeared beneath another stained, but sturdy door in the near right corner of the kitchen. Kerry crept towards the door, listening, and the sound of a motor was now much louder. The door, she assumed, must allow access to a larder or other anti-chamber to the kitchen. She listened. All she could hear was the thrum of the generator.

Somebody had recently brought power to the house again, after it had been off the grid for decades.

She took out her phone. It was enough evidence to call in the local police to conduct a thorough search for the trespasser.

But not enough to bring them running. It could be hours before some weary plod was sent to check things out. Kerry had to give them more.

She tested the door, and this time the handle turned easily. She drew it towards her, and peeked inside. It wasn't a larder: she found stairs going down. The cables were fitted snug to the edge of the stairs, so that they weren't a trip hazard. It was pitch dark below, and she could smell faint diesel fumes. The generator rumbled. And there was another sound that sent a jolt the length of Kerry's spine.

A child emitted a thin scream of pain.

Kerry lurched for the stairs, using the wan blue glow of her phone screen to light her way. She made it down three or four steps before the screen dimmed, and she stumbled, tripped on an uneven plank, and somersaulted into the darkness below.

Kerry woke from blackness into blackness. She had no concept of passing time, so couldn't say if she'd been unconscious for seconds, minutes or for much longer. In fact she couldn't say if she'd lost consciousness at all. She'd fell, tumbling and windmilling down the stairs, to slam with bruising force against an upright joist, that span her sideways and into open space. She had no recollection of the final impact, except she could feel it in every bone now. She wheezed in agony between her clenched teeth. Tried to move. Everything sloshed around her. She was soaked, wet to her ears, and her floundering sent another wave of scummy water over her. She reared up to sit, confused and blinded. The back of her skull throbbed with hot fire.

Moths' wings fluttered across her cheeks, her eyelids, and lastly her bottom lip. Her instinct was to rear away, until she recalled the last time she'd felt a similar sensation. It was Girl, offering her comfort in her time of need. She blinked, searching for her friend, but Girl was a shadow against darkness and her faint ethereal light was dimmed in that deep place.

'I'm...I'm, OK...I think,' Kerry croaked, and hoped she was right. She hadn't tried standing yet, and dreaded that she'd broken something during the tumble down the stairs. If she'd snapped her spine, it was doubtful she'd have been able to sit, but she was no expert. Maybe her legs felt numb because she'd severed the nerves to them! The panic was fleeting, and answered the question for her. She scrambled over on to her knees, and was glad when her legs obeyed the command to stand. She rose up, aching, fighting the pain in her ribs that made it difficult to breathe. Both shoulders were sore, and her left elbow, and judging by the burning sensation in her left hand she'd tried to halt her fall by the strength of her fingers alone and wrenched them back. Her head! She pushed aside her sopping coat hood, touched the hot spot on her skull, and her fingers found matted, soaked hair. But then everything about her was soaked. There was a bump, but no gaping hole with her brain leaking out.

She was ankle deep in water, surrounded by God knew what else.

There was a dim glow.

It was weak light streaming down the stairs from the kitchen above. She limped towards it. Saw where the stairs took a turn as they entered the basement, and formed a landing of sorts, alongside the joist that had spun her out and onto the flooded floor below. There was enough ambient light to spot her phone lying up against the skirting, wedged beneath the electrical cables. She reached for it, hissing in pain when the muscles between her ribs complained. Hit the button to bring it to life.

Its glow lit a tiny halo around her. The screen was cracked, but not broken. Miraculously, even in the bowels of the earth, she still had a signal. A weak one, but it was enough to make an emergency call. Which reminded her.

She spun around, seeking the child who'd screamed in pain. Saw nobody, not even Girl. However she knew her guide hadn't abandoned her. She could sense her nearby, beckoning her to follow. Before she took another step, Kerry brought up the flashlight app on her phone, and extended it at arm's length.

There was no sign of a child. Items of junk, old furniture, a filthy mattress part submerged in the water, and an ancient rusty bucket, but nothing to hint at life. Scummy water had found its way into the basement. It was stagnant, and frothy with contaminants. Whether it was from the boggy water table encroaching on the house, or from rain finding its way inside after the collapse of the chimney and roof, it didn't matter, these days it wasn't the ideal place to bring a prisoner. But somebody had cried out.

'Hello?' she whispered, conscious that her voice might carry further than intended. 'Hello, is there somebody there? Courtney? Hayley?'

The sloshing of the water and the grumble of the generator were her only replies.

She moved forward, taking care where she placed her feet. Tripping again, and losing her only source of light, would be disastrous. Her phone had survived the fall down stairs but wouldn't if dropped in the water. She scanned wider, and spotted where the electrical cables had been suspended well above the water line, strung along a beam near the ceiling. She followed them, and found another set of steps: this time they went up. Only a short distance though, to an anteroom of sorts, or a secondary basement.

Kerry moved to the foot of the stairs, and studied the door blocking her path. It looked as if it had been replaced in recent years, a sturdier metal door with two large bolts on this side. The cables ran through a hole drilled in the jamb. She went up the steps with her breath caught in her throat, shone the light over the bolts. There was no padlock keeping them shut. She worked the lowest one open, eyelids pinching with each squeak. She paused to gather herself. The final bolt was all that stood between her and whoever was on the other side of the door. If the Fell Man was inside, it was all that stopped him from leaping on her. No, he couldn't be in the room because who then must have set the bolts? She reached for the uppermost bolt and slid it open. The door swung towards her on its own weight. She grasped it, her abused fingers aching, and widened the gap.

She leaned in, extending her phone to cast light into the room. The diesel fumes were strongest there, almost thick enough to taste. The sound of the generator was unmistakable now, but it wasn't feeding lights within the room, and it wasn't a prison — or it hadn't been in ages. Once it might have been a coal shed, or some work place for servants or agricultural labourers, but that had been a long time ago before the Brandreths spiralled downwards into ruination. Since then it had been used for something more nefarious. Kerry immediately spotted a number of archaic televisions, and video cassette players, arranged on benches and shelves. Other shelves were stacked high with old Betamax and VHS videocassettes, dusty and cobwebbed, and stacks of mouldering magazines. Some had fallen from a shelf and lay scattered across the floor: pale boobs and rosy bums and more intimate parts on open display...and worse. Most of those images were of girls too young to consent to having been photographed. One thing she was certain of was that those magazines hadn't been purchased through reputable retailers, but swapped on the vilest black market. She didn't need to check any of the titles on the tape boxes to know what kind of films they contained. The room was the den of a particularly sick-minded sex-maniac, whose tastes went beyond the abhorrent.

And yet they were historical artefacts. Not anything that had been viewed in recent times. The TV's and video players were dead. The only concession to mechanical integrity was the generator that thundered away in one corner. It fed power via the cables to a different room, higher up in the crumbling ruin.

So where had the girl's cry originated?

She swept around the light.

Girl stood before one of the shelving racks, her back to Kerry.

Unusually she didn't flee the light, or from Kerry's view. She wanted to be seen. She had her head dipped, as though in prayer. But that was not it. She stood mournfully observing a videotape cassette that lay gathering dust on a counter.

And Kerry knew, and almost shrivelled up inside.

That cry of anguish had been the disembodied voice of Girl leading her to the awful truth. A replay of whatever horrific images had been captured on that tape decades ago, when Girl was horribly abused here in the house before her murder.

'Oh, dear God,' Kerry moaned. If she could she would take Girl in her arms and hug the child with all her might.

She couldn't though, so did the next best thing.

She hit 999 on her phone, identified herself to the control room operator, and requested immediate assistance. Before she finished describing the location of Brandreth House, Girl swept past her, towards another door that Kerry hadn't noticed. She charged after the fleeing spirit, urging the operator to send back up *now!* With the best will in the world, she couldn't expect the police to arrive in minutes. It could take half an hour for responding patrols to make it from the nearest manned station over the moor and find her. It was half an hour too long, but it was what it was.

The door opened into a yard at the far side of the house from where she'd earlier crouched on the hillside. A panel van was parked close to the house. Beyond it, there was a track around the trees and the far side of the pond, a route the van had driven back and forth on many occasions. If she'd carried on driving up the hill past where she'd left her car, it must fork around the hill to the east, allowing access to the house via different roads. The latter, in bygone times, would have been the servants' entrance, the one to the front reserved for the wealthy Brandreths and their feted guests.

Kerry moved towards the van, whispering instructions to the operator, and she took a quick peek inside the back. The windows had been painted black, foiling her. So she opened the doors instead. The storage compartment had been fitted with a futon mattress. Thick quilting covered the walls and ceiling, to deaden sound from within. A steel ring and chains hung from a bracket fixed to the wall that separated the back from the cab. Deep ruts in a thin carpet showed where something heavy had recently been dragged from the back. She informed the operator what she'd found and also gave a brief description of the van, and its number plate.

'I need back up now,' she reiterated, 'and make sure that whoever's coming they know it's about the missing girls.'

She hung up, freeing her hands.

She was about to slip away her phone, but her clothing was saturated, her duffel coat so dense with water that it almost weighed her down. She had no dry place to store her phone safely. She unbuttoned her coat, fought clear of it, and dropped it in a heap at the base of the house wall. As an afterthought she set her phone on a rock alongside it, then rearranged the hood over it to keep off most of the drizzle. All the while, she was aware of Girl urgently beckoning her from under the nearest fir trees. She jogged towards the normally elusive Girl, who waited in place long enough for Kerry to note where she pointed, then darted in that direction. Kerry charged after her, stooping as she ran to avoid the lower boughs. But within seconds she slowed, and moved forward with more caution.

Somewhere ahead a sound repeated: the thwack of steel through dirt.

Each chop of the blade was echoed a moment later by a grunt of exertion. Somebody was at work, and she didn't believe it was an honest day's labour. She crept closer, could hear the sound, but couldn't see its source due to a fallen tree and tangle of brambles that had overwhelmed it. It was still raining, but under the canopy not falling too hard. The pattering droplets covered any sounds she made. Beyond her, Girl stood, and it was perhaps the clearest image Kerry had seen her take. There was more than a hint of pinched lips and a pointing finger. Her stance was that of a viper poised to strike. Her image vibrated with poorly restrained rage.

A thwack of steel in earth sounded once more. But it was different. There was no corresponding grunt of effort. Fallen twigs crunched under heavy boots. Kerry looked for somewhere to hide, but there was nowhere, without throwing herself headlong into the bramble thicket. But she hadn't been discovered yet. Something was dragged across the damp mulch, and a heavy thud followed as it was dropped. Kerry had to look, but first she cast around for a weapon. All there was to hand was a branch about two feet long. She picked it up, tested its weight. Not heavy enough, but better than nothing. She edged around the bramble thicket, craning to see what her senses had already warned her was happening.

A large figure stood no more than three metres away, his broad back to her as he bent to inspect what he'd dumped in the shallow trench he'd dug. It was a man judging by the size, and the breadth of his shoulders, but she couldn't make out much else of him. He wore a heavy rubberised slicker coat, dark green, with the hood up, and the hem swung below his knees. It glistened under the drizzly twilight. His breath was a rasp from deep in his throat. It sounded like a dog growling, until she recognised spiteful laughter. He was a beast, and huge. As he reached for the spade he'd set aside, Kerry glanced at the branch she clutched, and realised how woefully outmatched she was.

Retreat was the better part of valour. And it was the most sensible plan when it came to what was known in police speech as a "dynamic risk assessment". She should back off, retrieve her phone, and observe him from a safe distance until reinforcements could arrive. Except the problem was plans only worked until affected by forces out of anyone's control. Overhead, a rotten branch, burdened with the weight of fresh rain, suddenly gave up its fight with gravity. It clattered down through the canopy, and thumped to earth a mere two feet behind the huge man. Instinct caused him to glance at the source of the sound, just as Kerry took a step back towards cover. She halted mid-step, mouth hanging open, as he swung around to face her, hefting the spade in both hands. She held up her branch; it couldn't help her.

Their gazes met, and held. And both knew what the other was.

His mouth split in a tusky grin, and his deep-set eyes glittered.

That was the only warning Kerry got.

He was so large, and dressed in heavy coat and mud-clotted boots, he should have been cumbersome. But he came at her like a juggernaut, emitting a roar as he swung the spade overhead. Kerry tried to retreat, but her feet refused to move. She screamed in defiance, all the frustration and anger of twenty-plus years energizing her, and she struck at him with the branch, aiming to smash his face to pulp. Unfortunately, it was the branch that shattered into dozens of pieces, and he shrugged off its impact against his shoulder as if it was a fly's bite. He swung the spade down, and she got her left arm under the haft, but his force was elemental. She was battered down, and was sure her left arm was as pulverised as the exploded branch. The steel blade only caught her a glancing blow to the side of her head, but it still felt as if her skull had been laid open. She collapsed, falling away from him and into the bramble patch, where she got hung up and could do nothing but glare up at her would-be murderer. He spun to follow her, hauling the spade up again, but this time with the blade angled down.

She wouldn't plead for her life, but a plea of sorts did screech out. 'What did you do to Sally?'

He paused, blinking down at her.

The name had taken him aback, but it was doubtful he'd recall a victim from all those years ago. Maybe he had expected her to demand to know about Hayley or Courtney...but Sally?

He shrugged. Raised the spade again, and then rammed it down at her exposed throat.

She was dead. Decapitated. The latest victim of the deranged monster she called the Fell Man. All those years had been wasted chasing the beast, hoping for answers, for closure, and she'd failed to learn anything at her last gasp. She would never know who he was, or what had become of her sister, or of any of the other girls snatched, abused and ultimately killed by the evil bastard.

In that instant, that's what should have been.

Two things denied fate.

As it had moments ago to her plan of retreat, nature conspired to thwart his kill. The brambles gave way under Kerry, and she collapsed fully onto her back, so that the spade stabbed through empty air, then bit into the dirt beyond the crown of her head. At the same time, Girl flew at the Fell Man, a fluttering, ragged-winged mass that screeched even as it clawed at his face with sharp nails. She was under his hood, engulfing his face, invading his eyes and mouth. He dropped the spade to swipe her away. He grasped, and crushed, and hurled something away from him. It clattered wetly through branches many feet away.

No. It wasn't Girl, but a crow startled by her from its roost in the thicket, that had collided momentarily with him and fought for freedom when it got snagged under his hood. It didn't matter. His brief fight had taken him metres away, and Kerry was still alive. Her head still rang from the swipe of the spade, and her left arm was all but useless, but the primitive instinct to run or fight flooded through her, and she scrambled, mindless of the thorns digging and scraping into her flesh and clothing as she scuttled deeper under the thicket.

The Fell Man stomped after her, but she kicked backwards with both heels and flung herself under the protection of the mass of barbs. The brambles offered only brief respite. In his heavy rubber coat and boots the thorns were no deterrent, only the creepers and trailers thwarted him from grasping hold of her ankles and dragging her out. He cast around, snatched up the spade and began hacking them aside as he forced a path into the brambles. Kerry rolled to her hands and knees, cringing at the white-hot explosion of agony in her left forearm, and plunged away from him. Under the snarl of creepers was a natural dome, and she huddled there for a moment, gasping for breath, trying to shake lucidity into eyes suddenly grown blurry. Her ears whistled and popped. The Fell Man roared at her, but his voice was muted, and sounded like a rushing flume. She scrambled further out of reach of the scything sweep of the blade.

He abruptly backed away, re-evaluated his attack, and raced around the side of the thicket to cut off escape. Immediately Kerry spun and charged back the way she'd just come, and threw herself through the final mesh of slashed and hacked creepers. She sprang up, and away, snagged by trailing lengths of cut bramble, that rattled and clattered in her wake. She couldn't head towards the house, already the Fell Man had doubled back to cut her off, so she went the other direction, running frantically past where he'd dug the ground. She only took a passing glance, but her heart pinched at the sight of a small figure wrapped in opaque plastic dumped at the bottom of the shallow trench. The sight of his forlorn victim was almost enough to halt her in her tracks, and send her into a do or die fight to avenge her. Except it was a fight she wasn't equipped to win. Injured, her arm definitely broken, she was in no fit state to fight the spade-wielding brute, not physically. She had to outfox him, lead him on a chase until her colleagues could arrive. Yes. Stay ahead of him, lead him in circles, and then back off when coppers equipped with Tasers and batons could take him down.

She ran, and got about twenty paces before a loop of bramble around her right ankle caught on a root. Her foot yanked out from under her, throwing her face down in the undergrowth. Howling in anger, she kicked free of the offending creeper, and battled back to her feet, her left elbow cupped in her right hand. She ducked just in time to avoid a third decapitation attempt, and lurched away, with the Fell Man pounding after her.

Blindly she plunged through slick mud, and then she floundered into deeper water and immediately dove forward to make distance.

History had its way of repeating, but often with a distinct contradiction. This time, instead of Jermaine Robson's flight for freedom coming unstuck, it was her that was suddenly plunged under water and in fear of drowning. The Fell Man was more resolute in his pursuit than she'd been at Battersea Park, following immediately into the pond after his prey. Throwing aside the spade, which was an encumbrance, he'd grabbed her flailing left ankle and jerked her beneath the surface. He bore down on her, forcing her into the thick mud, expelling the oxygen from her lungs. There was little strength to fight back, when every iota of effort was spent on gaining life-saving air. She thrashed the water with both hands; even her broken arm flapped about spasmodically. She kicked, and squirmed, but his arms were thick pillars, inexorably forcing her down.

Bubbles exploded around her face as the last oxygen was pressed from her lungs. Her eyes were wide, but she could see nothing but frothing murk. Her life didn't flash before her. She heard words. *'Yes, push him down. Go on. Do it. Push him down, keep him down, keep him under...drown him, Kerry. Fucking murder him.'* She could weep at the irony. History repeating had a nasty sense of humour.

She was hauled out the water, one of the Fell Man's hands round the nape of her neck, the other bunched in the back of her shirt. He lifted her as if she weighed less than a baby. She gagged, her chest constricting as her lungs almost imploded. She bucked, spasming in his grasp, and she dragged in a breath, which she couldn't immediately expel again. Her lungs rebelled against her. She coughed and dirty water jetted from her nostrils. The next gasp for breath sounded like Swain's keening wail as he'd plunged from the tower block. She was shaken, and the Fell Man jostled her around to peer into her mismatched eyes.

'Who are you?' he snarled.

Kerry spluttered and coughed.

To teach her obedience, he forced her under again, and water invaded her mouth and nostrils.

He jerked her upright, holding her now with only his left fist bunched in her shirt. His other hand slapped her face, and her head snapped around at the blow, and she vomited out more scummy water.

'I asked who you are?' he said. 'Answer me.'

'I'm...I'm a...' another coughing fit assailed her. She felt boneless.

'You're a copper. I know that, you stupid bitch. But *who* are you? Why is this so personal to you?'

'I'm Detective Inspector Darke.' Her words spilled from her in a hoarse flood.

Her name meant nothing to him. He certainly wasn't intimidated by her rank. He looked and acted like a dumb monster, but he was astute enough. 'Why come here alone? Why not just wait for reinforcements?'

'They're coming,' she admitted, hopeful that he'd elect to escape rather than continue down this murderous path.

'No,' he growled, but there was more meaning in his word than regret. 'You came here alone. It means you're an idiot, or you have something personal to prove.'

'You're the Fell Man,' she told him. 'And you took my sister Sally.'

'Did I now?' He thought about it, grunted. 'Well I hope she was more fun to be with than you.'

Abruptly he forced her backwards and, for the third time, Kerry was drowning.

She flopped like a fish in his grasp. Kicked him between his legs, except there was such drag on her foot it lacked power. He was unaffected. He pushed her deeper. Her right hand grabbed and clawed for...*anything*. She found mud and weeds, rotted cloth, thin sticks and something domed and smooth. Her thumb sank into a circular hole, fingers curling over a jagged protrusion. She hoped it was a rock, but it was too light. It didn't matter. It was something...a weapon. With every ounce left in her, she smashed the object directly in the Fell Man's face.

Suddenly she was floating free. She kicked away, and erupted from the pond, spluttering and blinking wildly. Dirty water washed her vision, but in that moment she felt surrounded, insubstantial grey figures encircling her — but not threatening her, they were in a defensive ring. She swiped at her face with her good arm, clearing her vision, but not of the dim motes that floated around her. They were the same shade as the drizzle, but had coalesced to something denser than the mist. Girls. A group of them.

The Fell Man's hood had fallen down. His head was bald, knotty in places with thick veins. Blood poured freely from a deep gash in his forehead. Kerry couldn't see what damage she'd caused to his features because he cupped his face in both hands. Blood dripped between his fingers, and he moaned, deep in his chest. She glanced down at the improvised weapon snatched from the floor of the pond. It was broken, jagged where it had been a smooth dome before. Tanned brown by the peaty water. Bone. Her thumb was still inserted in an eye socket, fingers furled around the nasal cavity. It was a skull. The skull of a human child! Her hand spasmed and the skull sank below the turgid water. In horror, Kerry looked at the shades surrounding her, and knew who they were. Desperately she searched among them for Sally.

'You've blinded me! Aaaah! You've fucking blinded *me!*'

The Fell Man's roar snapped her attention back on him. His left hand was slapped over his left eye. Blood poured from under it, down his chin and under the collar of his rain slicker. Another deep cut parted the skin over the bridge of his nose, also pulsing with blood, and the skin under his right eye gaped like a fish's mouth.

Her tumble down the stairs, followed by her fight with the monster, had taken its toll on her. Bumps, bruises, strains, half-drowned and a broken arm: he'd gotten off lightly by comparison. Whether his blinding was permanent or not, it didn't make much difference to the probable outcome of their battle. He still outmatched her in size and strength, and couldn't care less about the damage he inflicted. He was intent on murder, while she hoped to survive.

She couldn't speak. Her throat convulsed, attempting to expunge filthy pond water from her lungs. Likely there were no words he'd listen to anyway. He lowered his reddened palm, and stared at it with his remaining good eye. There was too much mess to tell if his injured eyeball was still whole, blood everywhere, the eyelids already swelling to the size of her fist. His mouth opened in dismay, and even his large teeth were slimy with blood. His head came up, and he quivered in rage as he stared at her with his one feverish eye. 'I'm gonna rip for your fucking head off!'

He was hip deep in the pond. Kerry's scramble for freedom had taken her closer to shore, but her feet were sunk in the mire, surrounded by the broken bones of murdered children. Fallen trees at the pond's edge blocked escape. To get away she had the choice of trying to swim, or somehow avoiding him, and reaching the place where she'd originally blundered into the pond. Her broken arm made swimming at speed impossible. He could wade after her in seconds and drag her under again. Her gaze darted everywhere, seeking anything to use as a weapon. There were no skulls in easy reach this time. No branches. No...wait!

Kerry lunged to the right.

The Fell Man was after her in an instant. He charged towards her, a frothing wake kicked up behind him: he roared wordlessly as he came.

Suddenly, the wraith-girls flew at him, engulfing him. They swooped and darted like bats, large bats, swirling around him, tearing and clawing, latching onto his coat and head. If he was aware of the assault, the Fell Man gave no sign, but Kerry was paying him little heed at that moment. She kicked and stamped the last few feet, ploughing through sucking mud and grabbed at the handle of the spade he'd dropped. Her left hand was weak, but she cupped the handle, held it a few inches higher on the shaft with her right.

'Keep away from me!' Her bark was surprisingly loud, and sounded nothing like her voice. She jabbed the head of the spade at him.

The Fell Man didn't pause. If anything, he picked up speed as he surged through shallower water, still mobbed but unhindered by the infuriated girls.

'I'm warning you...'

His groping hands were seconds from her.

At that moment Kerry wasn't a detective inspector, she was simply a woman fighting for her life. She swung the spade up, and chopped down with everything she had.

He stumbled to a halt, hands dropping by his sides. His mouth hung open, then canted lower at one side. Kerry didn't release her hold on the spade. Its steel head was embedded in the horrific wound above his too-wide-open mouth: his jawbone was severed, and part of his neck. There was no lucidity in his one good eye, as he sank to his knees in the muck. Only the pressure on the spade handle held him up. Kerry snatched her hands off it. He stumbled forward, but miraculously caught himself on one hand. His other plucked numbly at the spade's shaft. And as though stunned by the violence, all the girls backed off. They stood again in a silent semicircle around the fallen brute.

Insanely, after swallowing all that pond water, Kerry couldn't work any moisture into her mouth. She stood before him, also numbed by what she'd done.

She told Erick Swain there was a line she wouldn't cross, that she was incapable of murder. But she'd never been in a situation like this before. His words echoed mockingly in her brain. *'Tell me that again once I set your hands on the Fell Man.'*

The spade fell loose, disappeared under water.

Fresh blood gouted from the side of the child killer's neck.

He could only touch the wound tremulously, his strength flooding out with each beat of his heart. He tried to press his severed jaw back in line. The agony must have been incredible, but Kerry felt no pity. The girls stood silent and unmoving, mourners around an open grave. They were all looking at her, a silent prompt.

'What did you do to Sally?' Kerry rasped. 'Do you hear me? What did you do to my sister?'

He gurgled something unintelligible.

Kerry moved closer. 'Tell me, you monster. What did you do to Sally?' She glanced briefly at their silent audience. All the girls hung their heads. Sally wasn't among them. 'You killed all these children! But there were others too, weren't there? What did you do with them? *Where is my sister?'*

Her shriek sparked something inside him. He knew he was dying, but killing was in his nature as strongly as his appetite for pre-pubescent girls. He launched at Kerry, intent on taking her with him.

She sucked back her hips, slapped down with her right palm on the back of his neck, and drove him face first into the mud. He floundered, and she too went to her knees, but leaning over his wide back.

'Yes, push him down,' Swain's voice exhorted her. *'Go on. Do it. Push him down, keep him down, keep him under...'* She bore into him, keeping him flat in the muck, feeling him buck and convulse. *'Drown him, Kerry. Fucking* murder him.'

She jerked up, appalled at the lengths she'd almost gone to.

'Stamp on his fucking throat!' Swain's command echoed through her skull like the tolling of a bell, but she stumbled back, staring down at the submerged figure. His blood spread around him, soft bubbles of escaping air popping at the surface. The Fell Man deserved to die, but if he did, how would she ever learn what had happened to Sally? She scrambled to him again, grasped his hood with her good hand, and began dragging him to shore.

He was too heavy; she was too weak. She sank down in the thick muck as her grip gave out. He no longer moved. There would be no answer from him.

She sat gasping, shivering, her brain clogged with fog. She had survived, slain the bogeyman, and saved who knew how many future victims, but she felt wretched. She wept, cradling her broken arm against her abdomen, repeating over and over again, 'I'm so sorry. I'm so sorry...' Her words were for Sally and the other girls who moved in to huddle around her, not for the despicable creature buried face first in the pond slime.

It was minutes before she finally crawled back to dry land. Using a tree limb to help her stand, she turned once to survey the pond. The drizzle had stopped, but the mist still hung over the wide expanse of murky water. Some of the girls had retreated further across the pond, and to right and left. They dissolved into the water, returning to their mortal remains sunken below. Others stood alongside Kerry, but when she looked at them they moved away, seeking their shallow graves among the trees. Dumbly, Kerry staggered after them, noting where each figure melted into the undergrowth, and the ground beneath. In their final moments, Kerry could make out the simplest of details, but none of those mouths that whispered their silent thanks was that of her sister. She continued, following two final figures. One of them paused at the freshly dug grave, and her shoulders hunched as she bent to inspect her corporeal form wrapped in dirty plastic. She glimpsed at Kerry, and her face was vivid for a second, before she smiled sadly too, then almost spilled like water into her temporary grave.

'I'm so sorry,' Kerry said. 'I'm so sorry I didn't make it in time to save you, Hayley.'

Morosely, she averted her gaze from the missing girl's shrouded remains. Only Girl had not returned to a grave. She stood nearby, her hair obscuring her features as usual, but for once she didn't dart to concealment. Her mouth also worked silently, and Kerry was certain she said *thank you*. But for what she didn't know. She hadn't brought closure to Girl, or to her sister: perhaps it was because she'd given final rest to all those other lost girls. She stared at the spirit for guidance, and Girl lifted a finger and pointed towards the crumbling mansion. She darted, but for a few metres only. She paused, then beckoned urgently before streaking away between the trees, and without question, Kerry followed.

She limped along the cracked and distorted path towards the large door she'd entered through earlier. Her duffel coat, and her phone, lay around the corner at the side of the house. To get to them she must either scale a wall shrouded under brambles and stinging nettles, or go all the way around the building and face the thickets back there: she didn't want to retrace her steps through the decrepit building. But Girl was adamant that was where she must go. When Kerry paused, to seek a path to her right, Girl swept back to her, so close that she could make out the blurred image of a face beneath the straggly hair. Girl's fingers plucked at her, moth's wings fluttering on her skin, then jabbed a hand at the door, then upward.

Kerry nodded. As much as she hated to re-enter the Fell Man's lair, she must. She went after Girl who flitted through the gap she'd forced open earlier, and into the reception vestibule, kicking aside some recently dislodged plaster that partly blocked her way. She entered into the twilit hall, the rotting carpet and spongy wood underfoot again, and saw the partly collapsed stairs and sagging bannister of before, and the electrical cables leading to the upper floors. The generator rumbled on, in the basement's anteroom below. Kerry briefly pictured the dank place, those ancient TV's and videocassettes — and more importantly what was recorded on them — and was on the verge of vomiting. She peered at the cables, her brow screwed in understanding.

Girl beckoned her from the half-landing above.

The pain flaring from her broken arm was almost as nauseating as what she dreaded finding above. She wasn't fit to scale the collapsing stairs, but she ascended any way. She kept to the edge of each riser nearest the wall, where hopefully the stairs would retain some support. The entire staircase groaned and creaked underfoot, but she didn't pause. If they fell, she would fall, and there was little to do about it, so finding stable footing above was more important than worrying. At the half-landing she paused to check on Girl. She signalled from the next floor above. Kerry limped up stairs a tad firmer underfoot, and stepped thankfully onto the next landing. Overhead, she could see the sky through the wide rents in the ceiling and roof. It was as grey as ever. Water dripped everywhere. But only until she turned and loped along a corridor to the left. The corridor was dry, and the cables snaked along it at floor level and under a sturdy-looking door at the far end. Girl was a dim shape against it.

Kerry halted. What the hell was beyond that door, and did she really want to see?

Girl dematerialized through the solid door, and made up Kerry's mind. She approached, tentative, and stood a moment, hoping to hear the sirens of her responding colleagues. Instead she heard the faintest of muffled cries, and it came from inside the room before her.

The door wasn't locked. It swung open on oiled hinges, and at first Kerry had no idea what she'd found. There was a wall of blackness directly in front of her. Absurdly, she thought she'd entered some netherworld, the hellish domain of the bogeyman, the *actual* lair of the Fell Man, but she was only partially correct. The blackness wasn't some devilish netherworld, but a massive ream of cloth suspended from the ceiling. When she reached for it, she found a slit in the cloth, and teased it apart, and stepped through the gap into the room beyond. Similar drop cloths had been fixed to conceal the other walls, and they had twofold purpose. The thick drapery would deaden any noise from within the room, and also disguise the location so that it would never be identified by anyone observing what was filmed in there. The electrical cables she'd followed led to a power board, in which was plugged other snaking cables, one of them a LAN to a laptop computer sitting on the floor. There were modern video cameras mounted on tripods, five of them in total, all surrounding a double bed. There was no bedding on the stained mattress, but it wasn't empty.

Girl knelt on the bed, bent over another young girl dressed only in a vest and knickers. The girl was spread-eagled, hands and feet secured by dog collars and leads to shackle rings bolted to the floor boards at the bed's four corners. She was gagged with a length of cloth that was fixed in place with silver duct tape, and her eyes were closed. Girl's fingertips danced gently over the child's face, and as if in response to her touch, the other child's lashes flickered and then snapped open, her gaze immediately fixed on Kerry. Courtney Bell stiffened in shock, and again she made a keening cry, muffled by the gag.

'Courtney…it's OK,' said Kerry, holding out her good hand. 'I'm a police officer, I'm here to help you.'

Courtney writhed on the bed, the leather dog collars nipping into her flesh. Judging by the rawness of her wrists and ankles, she had fought her restraints on previous occasions. Kerry groped to the edge of the bed, and put one knee on it. Girl slipped behind her, but was a present shadow over her shoulder.

'It's OK, Courtney. Stop, you'll hurt yourself. Let me help you.'

Courtney sagged, and fresh tears spilled down cheeks already marked by dried tear tracks. She moaned through her gag again, but this time in desperate hope. For the briefest of instants, Sally's features juxtaposed over Courtney's, and Kerry's heart hitched in her chest, then bloomed with warmth. The child's resemblance to her sister was merely facile, but enough that Kerry's spirit soared. She knew the child *wasn't* Sally, but if she'd to fight the monster all over again, she would die to protect her.

'I promise you,' Kerry whispered as she worked to loosen the collar on Courtney's left wrist. 'You're safe now. Safe. I won't let anyone hurt you, Courtney. I promise you...' She continued soothing the child while she worked next at Courtney's ankles. It was a struggle with only one good hand, but once her feet were loose, Courtney kicked up the bed, and reached to un-cinch her right hand. Once free, Courtney lunged to hug her saviour. Kerry croaked at the agony that exploded from her broken arm, but didn't withdraw: having the girl's small arms wrapped around her was a wonderful feeling. Kerry murmured platitudes, smoothed Courtney's hair back from her face, then gently helped her peel the duct tape away. She spat out the wadded cloth, even as her eyes grew wide.

'He's going to come back,' Courtney wheezed in alarm.

'It's OK,' Kerry assured her. 'He...he can't hurt you anymore.'

'He can. He can. He warned me to keep quiet, because the show was about to begin.' She stared in accusation at the nearest video camera. Kerry followed her prompt and saw a steady red light on its front. Every camera she glanced at bore a steady red light. They were all recording...all of their images being relayed live to a despicable audience!

She was tempted to kick them all over, and grind the video cameras to broken components beneath her heels, but the camera array and computer was evidence of the Fell Man's awful enterprise. Instead, she wrapped her good arm around Courtney and dragged her off the bed, swearing savagely at however many sick-minded bastards sat at the other ends of the live broadcast. Cradling Courtney against her chest, she rushed for the gap in the drop cloth, and the door beyond. Each step brought a flash of pain through her injured arm, but she ignored it. She only wanted Courtney out of that terrible place.

Fog billowed along the corridor towards them.

They both coughed at the noxious stink carried with it, and a qualm of fear speared Kerry. It wasn't fog...it was smoke! Yellow reflections writhed on the walls at the head of the staircase.

Kerry was stunned at the absurdity. How could a house so sodden burn? How had a fire ever started where the fuel was damp wood and musty cloth? One thing she was certain of, an electrical short wasn't to blame, because the cameras were recording and there was power to the laptop too. She could also hear, or maybe feel, the rumble of the distant generator.

Forget how the bloody fire started; find a way out!

'We can't go that way, Courtney,' she said, steering the child back the direction they'd just come. 'We have to find another way.'

'There's no way out!' Courtney yelped, and dug in her heels as Kerry tried to urge her towards the room they'd fled from.

'There has to be a window...something.'

'No. They're nailed shut. Boarded up. I know. I tried to get out before.'

'Shit!'

Peering back at the staircase, Kerry wondered if there was any hope of making it down. Already flames were leaping towards the hole in the roof, drawn by an updraft. The wet beams overhead sizzled, steam adding to the smoke. Escape in that direction was impossible.

'Another room then...' They had passed doors in the corridor. Some of them hanging off their hinges: Kerry recalled the windows all being smashed when viewed from outside. The room adapted as the Fell Man's film studio could have been boarded up, but not the others.

There had to be a room the monster used when he wasn't torturing his victims. 'This way!'

Abruptly Girl was before her, both hands up to halt them. She swept around Kerry, gesticulating at a corner to the left of the room where Courtney had been held. Kerry hadn't noticed the second corridor when following Girl into the room earlier, and had been too busy rushing to get Courtney out when exiting.

It was a short corridor, barely ten feet long, and it accessed a second staircase in much better condition than the one currently blazing. Back when servants cared for the Brandreths, they would have used the unobtrusive set to gain access to the quarters on the second floor. They were apparently the stairs the Fell Man had employed when coming and going from his torture room. All the wreckage had been cleared from the steps.

'Down there.' Smoke rolled towards them. 'Down, down, down,' Kerry repeated, pressing Courtney before her. At first the girl was fearful of meeting the Fell Man on his way back but the choking smoke and sparks curled over them, and she clattered down the stairs on bare feet. Kerry hobbled after her, unsteady, cringing every step in pain. They exited into another corridor, where they passed a series of small, derelict rooms, but paid them no notice. Weak daylight marked the edges of an outer door at the far end. 'Go, go, go.'

The door was held shut only by a simple latch. Courtney snapped it open and shoved open the door, and both of them almost fell out into the weed-choked rear yard. Bramble thickets reared overhead, but a route had been hacked clear alongside the back of the house. They stumbled along it together, Kerry again cradling Courtney against her, this time as much to help hold her up as support the child. They staggered out onto the track alongside the house, and Kerry spotted her duffel coat and phone where she had dumped them.

No sign of the panel van.

How? The Fell Man was dead. He couldn't have survived the wound to his neck, or being left submerged in muddy water in the pond. How could he have returned to escape in the van or…shit!…set the fire that would obliterate the evidence of his crimes? Flames fed by accelerants were racing through the building from the basement's anteroom, where the taped evidence of Girl's abuse was being destroyed, and they would destroy the chamber where Courtney had been held as well. *How could a dead man have set that fire?*

As a child, Kerry believed the Fell Man was a supernatural creature, as an adult, and detective, she'd come to realise he was a monster, but of the human variety. Now she wasn't as certain any more.

She snatched up her phone and stabbed 999, hollering into it while leading Courtney to safety around the far side of the pond. Behind them the burning house roared furiously as joists collapsed and walls tumbled down. At a safe distance, they stopped to wait for the responding emergency services, and they peered back at what was now a conflagration. They shouldn't be difficult to locate now, because the plume of black smoke rising from the burning ruins was stark against the looming fells. Girl stood between them and the fire, unmoving for a change even though directly ahead of Kerry. She remained insubstantial, but her stance could be easily defined. She watched the fire consume the horrid place of her death with her head tilted back in satisfaction. Then she turned around and peered at Kerry from under her straggly hair, and her mouth made a tight grimace before she offered a brief nod. She dematerialized, but her leaving wasn't the same as when the other girl's showed Kerry their lonely resting places. Girl wasn't finished with her yet.

Neither was Kerry finished with the Fell Man.

AFTER...

Kerry spent the next three nights recuperating in a private room at the Cumberland Infirmary. From her elevated window she had a commanding view over the Victorian canal basin, and the River Eden, as well as the northern ramparts of Carlisle Castle, but she rarely had time to enjoy the vista. When she wasn't answering questions from CID, doctors and nurses tended to her, or she slept. She'd suffered a litany of injuries, some more serious than others. Bumps, bruises, scratches and ligament strains. Two of the fingers on her left hand needed resetting after their dislocation when she fell into the basement, and the subsequent smash of the spade to her forearm required surgery to repair both the radius and ulna bones. Stitches to her scalp where the spade had glanced off her skull. More worrisome for her doctors was the concussion she'd suffered after her tumble down the stairs, and — initially — the threat of secondary drowning after inhaling so much pond water. After the latter was ruled out, she was on infection alert, and also at the risk of contracting pneumonia. She was pumped full of antibiotics to stave them off and was kept under observation.

She felt like crap and looked much worse. Her face was swollen out of shape, and she'd swear somebody had used a rasp on her tongue and throat. It even hurt to blink. Her eye colouration had given one junior doctor pause for thought, until she assured him her heterochromia was a birth defect. It was only after she caught a glimpse in a mirror that she realised her amber eye was also completely bloodshot: she avoided mirrors after that. Not that she cared too much about herself. She asked about Courtney Bell, who was safe and back in the loving care of her family. She wept for Hayley McGhee and all the other children she'd been unable to save: being hailed a heroine meant little when so many children had been raped and murdered for the pleasure of a pay-per-view audience. And she asked about the Fell Man.

Carl Brandreth — scion of the original landowners — was dead. The police had discovered his corpse face down in the mire where she'd left him; he'd bled to death from the neck wound. Brandreth wasn't *the* Fell Man; he was *a* Fell Man. In her heart Kerry had known he wasn't the only culprit, even as she fought to the death with him. She only had to recall what she'd witnessed as a child — the Fell Man must have had a companion, because how could he have dragged a girl back to the house and followed them to Penrith in the Land Rover at the same time? The hulking Carl Brandreth was not the bearded monster that snatched Sally from the grounds of the castle. He was not the brain behind the abductions, but a dumb brute happy to supply his crumbling home as a remote location where the children could be held and to do the dirty, clean-up work afterwards. And obviously, it was the other bearded man that'd set the house ablaze to cover up the evidence of their crimes, leaving behind Brandreth as his scapegoat, and then made off in the panel van while Kerry and Courtney perished in the flames. The van hadn't been found, and as yet there was no clue to the bearded Fell Man's identity. Investigators were sifting through the burnt wreckage of the house on the fells, and there was a major operation underway to exhume the graves — on land and in water — of the victims. The general consensus was that the Fell Man was legion: the tools of a vile paedophile ring whose reach stretched as widely as the Dark Web did, where untraceable Bitcoins were swapped to enjoy the most vile form of entertainment. In its original sense, *fell* meant wicked or evil, and it was true, fell men and women were numerous. Cut off one head and another sprang up like the mythical hydra. If she could, she'd fight them all with the same determination as she had Carl Brandreth, but if she had to she'd make do with hunting and finding only one: the bearded man. He had killed Sally and he had killed Girl.

Siobhan Darke paid a visit. She was in her late fifties, but looked ten years older: her once vivid red hair was now predominantly white, but tinted yellow at the temples from smoking too many hand-rolled cigarettes, and her complexion blotchy rather than freckled. Kerry had hoped to avoid her mam, but now the woman was there, she experienced a burst of affection, and it worked like one of those wondrous placebos Doctor Ron once mentioned to her. Siobhan told her she loved her baby girl, and they held each other for a time, before Siobhan then made an excuse to leave…and asked if Kerry could 'see her right with a few quid to help pay her rent'. Kerry gave her the contents of her purse — recovered along with her handbag from the hire car she'd abandoned on the fells — in full knowledge that her mam's rent was paid directly to the housing association through her benefits. Siobhan wouldn't make it past the convenience store opposite the infirmary without buying alcohol, but Kerry didn't begrudge her a conciliatory drink. Sally's remains were still missing, and closure was denied to their mother too. Gary Darke, her dad, never showed face, but then that wasn't unexpected.

Danny Korba was desperate to visit her, but had to make do with a brief telephone call, as it was impossible for him to travel up from London when he was carrying both his and Kerry's workload. Kerry soothed his conscience, assuring him she needed him to stay put, and make sure the replacement DI didn't get his feet under the table in GaOC — that was if she ever made it back, a point she didn't raise with him. Besides, she told him, she was a mess and she didn't want him seeing her with a face like a panda. His retort was unexpected: 'Why not? You have to look at mine day in and day out, and I think I get the better end of the deal. You're an incredibly good-looking woman, Kerry, and I'll never tire of seeing you.' It hurt to smile, but also felt good. As she had for her mother, she experienced a genuine pang of affection for her best friend, and a longing to see him too, and had to hang up quickly before she began weeping.

During her second night in hospital, the first after her surgery to fix her shattered forearm, she dreamed vividly of Erick Swain. He still wore the tie-dyed shirt and scruffy jeans, and his silver earring, but he'd lost the rigid cuff from his wrist. In her dream, Kerry was in the same hospital bed, her arm in a cast and an antibiotic drip fed intravenously through a cannula on her right wrist. He sneered at her from where he lounged in a visitor's chair alongside her bed.

'If you're still set on rent-a-ghosting in and out of my life like this,' she said, 'the least you can do is be helpful. I still don't know who the real Fell Man is or what he did with Sally. You promised to tell me...'

'I told you to go home,' he said. *'It got you to where you needed to be.'*

'That was on me. It was my decision to come back.'

'I nudged you into making the decision. Poked loose your childhood memories. I'd say I've paid my dues.'

She exhaled through her nostrils. 'I see you've lost your handcuff. Does that mean you aren't shackled to me anymore?'

He didn't reply, only sneered.

'So why are you here? If you've nothing to tell me and nothing to hold you here anymore, why show up at all?'

'To luxuriate in your agony,' he replied, but his sneer warmed a little. *'No. I might just have mellowed in death. I came to thank you.'*

'For what? Clearing you of murdering the Ghedis doesn't make you any less of a scumbag. We both know what you are, Swain. A killer.'

He raised his eyebrows. *'So what does that make you?'*

By definition Kerry *was* a killer. 'There's a difference,' she said. 'I only killed Brandreth to survive.'

'And I only killed who I did to survive,' he countered. *'The situation might've been different, but dead's dead. If I hadn't taken them out, they'd have done the same to me.'*

She shook her head. Even in her dream her skull pulsated with the effort. 'You killed out of greed. For control. For the thrill of it.'

'When you went to that old dump of a house, you wanted something. You were greedy for it, or you'd have taken other coppers with you. You wanted to control the situation to your liking. And, tell the truth, Kezza, when you slapped Brandreth in the skull with that spade, you got a little tingle down in your lady parts, didn't you?'

Her tongue felt like damp cotton wool. 'You might have mellowed, but you're as vulgar as ever.'

'Yep. There's no changing a leopard's spots.'

'Actually, there is. You said you came here to thank me. I didn't expect that from you.'

'I'm not a total wanker. I paid my dues, but I also give credit where it's due, Kezza. I came to thank you for setting the ball rolling with Robson.' He winked grandiosely.

'What do you mean?'

He snorted. Then leaned forward. *'Ask Adam.'*

'Ask him *what*?'

'Don't act naïve, Kezza. Cell doors don't get left unlocked all by themselves.' He winked once more, flicked her a salute of gratitude and was gone.

She woke, and wondered if she'd even been asleep because there was no difference between the two. Feeling sick to the stomach, she groped for the telephone next to her bed to ring Adam.

'Kerry? You're awake. It's the middle of the night. Doesn't matter. How are you, love?' By the sound of his slur, he'd woken from sleep too.

'What did you do, Adam?'

'Uh, what? I've booked a train for tomorrow. I'm going to come up and collect you.'

'What happened with Jermaine Robson?'

'Oh, right. Him.'

'He died, didn't he?' She didn't need confirmation, because Robson's death was the only thing that could have released Erick Swain from the shackle that held him here. Despite the evidence to the contrary, she'd tried to convince herself his latest visitation was a dream, but had to accept she was wrong. She would also lay a bet on Robson's time of death: it would coincide with when Swain dropped out of existence sometime after he spoke with her the other morning in the B&B, the reason he'd been absent the entire time she'd been at Brandreth House.

'Yes.' Adam didn't expound at first. He was being guarded. After all, his fiancée was a detective inspector…correction, his ex-fiancée.

'What happened?'

'Uh, well, nobody knows how for sure. Somehow his cell door came unlocked, and a couple of Swain's boys got in with him. They had shivs.'

'*Somehow* a cell door is left unlocked in a high security wing?'

'It was a mechanical failure, not human error. It happens. Besides, you told me that you'd never be free of Swain until Robson died. You should be relieved things have been taken out of your hands.' He audibly swallowed. 'Last time we spoke, I offered to make things better, and you said you hoped so. Remember?'

Kerry closed her eyes and groaned.

'He has gone,' said Adam. 'Swain. He's gone for good now?'

'I…yes, I think he's gone.'

'Good. Yes, that's good. Kerry…I didn't believe he was real before, but now…well, let's just say he got what he asked for, so won't trouble you any more. He isn't in *our* way anymore. Look,' Adam went on, 'I'm getting the first train up in the morning. I'll be with you before noon.'

'Don't.'

'I've already got your stuff from the hotel and brought back your car to the house. Once I get you home, everything will be all right. You said we could try again…'

'No, Adam. No. We can't.' She hung up.

He got the message loud and clear. Adam didn't arrive on the morning train, but DCI Charles Porter did. It was inevitable, she supposed. She was only surprised he hadn't arrived accompanied by Superintendent Graeme Harker, or another of his professional standards investigators. Her part in the killing of Carl Brandreth would have to be fully reviewed by Cumbria Constabulary, and the Met. She'd be the subject of an investigation by the Independent Police Complaints Commission too, and not forgetting the DPS. She was the focus of another media storm, and wherever there was a camera Porter didn't like to miss a photo opportunity. She cringed when she heard him identifying himself to the security guard outside her door.

But when he entered her private room, he was more sanguine than the last time she'd seen him. He was dressed in casual clothing, and was the less imposing because of it. He smiled when he saw her awake, adjusted his spectacles and approached almost bashfully.

'Hello, sir,' she said.

'We're away from the office now, please…call me Charles.'

'So you haven't come to arrest me?'

He blinked in surprise. 'I came as a concerned friend.'

'Friends usually bring grapes and Lucozade.'

Again he blinked, and Kerry smiled. 'I'm only joking, sir.'

'Charles,' he reiterated.

She didn't feel comfortable calling him by his given name. She indicated the chair alongside her bed. 'Please...sit down.'

He sat. Awkwardly. His viewpoint was lower than hers, not a position he chose to take whenever they'd spoken before. 'So...?'

'So.' Kerry's lips tightened.

'I was going to ask how you're feeling, but, well, I can see for myself.'

'It looks worse than it is.'

'Ever the martyr, aren't you, Kerry?'

'Joan of Arc has nothing on me.' As soon as she made the quip, she grimaced. Recalling how Adam had used the saint as a metaphor for her behaviour, and reminding her that Joan was burned at the stake. 'Actually, I'm not going to lie. I feel bloody awful.'

'Not surprisingly.' He chuckled politely. 'It was quite an ordeal you went through.'

'Aye, you can say that again. Who'd have thought a little nostalgia trip would've turned into such a nightmare?'

He studied her swollen face, and her eyes in particular. For once he didn't appear perturbed by her mismatched colouring. But then her paler eye was much darker than normal with pooled blood. 'You and I both know it was nothing of the sort. Even our colleagues here don't buy your story about visiting your childhood haunts, and stumbling across the abducted girl. But to be honest, Kerry, nobody cares. You saved a child and stopped a monster. That's what matters most.' He stared between his knees, twining his fingers together. 'I don't care where your information came from, none of it anymore. Sandy, uh, Superintendent Tinsley reminded me that it's the result that matters, and, well, I have to concur. You're one hell of a detective, Kerry, and I'm sorry it's taken me so long to admit it. I want you to know you'll be welcomed back to GaOC when you're ready.'

'So you're denying my request for transfer again?' she asked.

'The transfer to Homicide and Major Crime we talked about? I'd rather not lose you to them, Kerry.'

'I've already withdrawn that transfer request. I'm talking about the nationwide taskforce being formed to investigate the Fell Man case. I want to be part of it, sir. I want to help dismantle the paedophile snuff ring the bastard supplies to. I want to catch *him.*'

'It's a National Crime Agency case now, Kerry. Their cyber crime teams are on it, and it's already apparent that the offenders are spread worldwide. You're a talented officer, and yes, you were instrumental in saving Courtney Bell and stopping Carl Brandreth, not to mention uncovering the remains of his previous victims…but this isn't a case you can help further with.'

'But I have a clear link to him…the original Fell Man.'

'I'm sorry, Kerry, and sympathise with you. But a transfer's not something I can grant, and it's not something I'm sure I would if I was able. Besides, don't you think it's best to keep the Fell Man case at arm's length, before it consumes you again?'

She breathed out. Arguing the toss with him then wouldn't be helpful. She was disappointed, but while she still had access to the formidable investigative resources of the Met, she'd take it…and nothing would stop her conducting an unofficial investigation if it came to it. Besides, she wouldn't be consumed again: she was already consumed by the need to discover who the bearded Fell Man was, and bring him and those he worked on behalf of to justice. She was still consumed by the need to find Sally, and also to bring eternal rest to Girl. 'I'll be back at work as soon as I'm given the all clear,' she promised, and for emphasis hitched her broken arm in its sling. 'But speaking of keeping things at arm's length, well, Danny might have to carry on steering the ship a little longer.'

He chuckled at her weak joke, before realising she was staring at a point behind his right shoulder. He struggled to avoid looking for whom she aimed a victorious smile and nod at, and instead flapped a hand at an annoying moth that kept beating its wings on the back of his neck.

Thanks

I'm indebted to Luigi Bonomi, Alison Bonomi, William Massey, Mike Craven, Tony Forder and Karen Ratcliffe for their guidance and feedback. Without their input this book would be a very different read, and poorer for it.